PATH TO THE NIGHT MOUNTAINS

Book II in the Coalition/Orthodoxy Universe

J. E. Bruce

BooksForABuck.com
2015

I0598403

Copyright 2015 by J.E. Bruce, all rights reserved. No portion of this work may be copied or duplicated without express written permission from the publisher.

Cover images copyright Jason E. Jenkins and Douglas Scortegagna under Creative Commons License. Cover design by Rob Preece.

This is a work of fiction. Any resemblance to real persons or locations is strictly coincidental.

In memory of Red and Matilda,
and my parents, Aileen and Gene.

I and the public know
What all schoolchildren learn;
Those to whom evil is done
Do evil in return.
~*W.H. Auden*

Chapter 1

Aboard Huui'teh, *eleven years ago.*
Currently in orbit above the disputed planet of Cotopaxi.
Four minutes before drop.

THIS IS INSANE! an inner voice screamed over the undulating howl warning of imminent hull breach.

YOU'RE A'TUU'SHAHN! another snarled, harsh and hollow, accompanied by the thumping echo of running feet pummeling along the smoke-filled corridor's deck plates, everyone still able converging on the *Huui'teh*'s main flicker stage at a dead run.

Khusaaq glanced around, suddenly fearful his private, warring thoughts had been, in his desperation, yelled out loud, that his mounting panic had been exposed to all.

Within all the clamor of the rush to abandon the dying ship, even if he had likely no one would have heard him, even Gaalan Nahru'tzhri, who stood beside him, her face serene despite the organized chaos that surrounded them, the choking haze and the noticeably failing ruby glow of the emergency back-ups. Hers was the face of a true hero, smeared with a combination of blood and soot as it was, freshly disfigured by shrapnel, a face, a mind calmly anticipating, even welcoming a glorious, worthy martyrdom at any moment—the way all A'tuu'shahn aspired to die.

He wasn't quite so ready. This was only his second tour, and one lesson he'd taken from his first was that he wasn't cut from the same cloth as Gaalan, or—he was beginning to seriously suspect—most other A'tuu'shahn'i. He was, in a word, *terrified*—roil-in-the-gut, wobble-in-the-knees and mouth-dry-as-sand terrified.

He'd never understood why Gaalan had appeared oblivious to such a glaring flaw in his personality—Ja'andai had certainly seen it as he saw all of his failings. Where Ja'andai was the perpetually frustrated taskmaster, whose chronic disappointment had, more often than not, taken a violent form, Gaalan was his champion, always finding examples to praise and reasons to encourage. She'd always seen him, always treated him as the perfect copy of Ja'andai he was supposed to be—yet another immaculate martyr to yet another cause not worth fighting and dying for. Ja'andai's life and career had been meteoric in all senses of the word: intense, brilliant—and fleeting. Khusaaq had always suspected—feared—his would be equally brief, if not so dazzling and noteworthy, but he never imagined it would be quite *this* short-lived.

And a world *without* Gaalan? That was utterly unthinkable.

"Ta'ahn," he began as the last of those headed for the flicker bay darted by, each laden down with as much survival equipment and weaponry as he or she could carry, hoping his raised, smoke- and fright-husky voice didn't crack, didn't fail him, didn't expose him or the true depth of his desperation, "I beg you, there's nothing to be gained by remaining, we need you to command us—"

"You and I have our own paths, Ruh'ta'aq," she replied with the same maddeningly cheerful composure as her expression, albeit her voice raised to be overheard. "I've lived my entire life for this moment, anticipated the ultimate freedom, to experience... *everything.*"

The ultimate freedom—an A'tuu'shahn euphemism for death—the only acceptable escape from their lifestyle as the known galaxy's mercenaries of choice. But Gaalan had never struck him as someone quite so eager to die. Willing, yes. But excited? And she was; he saw the intense gleam of anticipation in her smoke-reddened eyes as she again met his frightened stare. But she'd changed, subtly, since accepting this contract, her moods had darkened and her tongue had sharpened, even towards him, her acknowledged protégé.

She placed her hand on his armored shoulder. "Someone needs to remain aboard, to keep the Matarii distracted for as long possible—which in truth won't be all that long. With luck, they'll attempt to board, take the ship as a prize, finally get their hands on our technology—with a large number of troops I'd imagine as they've already proven themselves to be extremely reckless—and only I can synchronize the destruct codes on our dead and dying for the maximum effect. The colonists are counting on you—I'm counting on you."

Of course you are! Everyone's counting on me! He swallowed convulsively then managed tightly, "May the Elkanasu guide and guard you, Gaalan Nahru'tzhri."

"And you as well, Khusaaq Ruh'ta'aq," she replied, her steady voice barely audible over the muffled concussions and ominous groaning of a ship in its death throes. "Now go— *hurry!*"

He donned and secured his helmet but as he turned to leave, to follow the others, no more accepting his fate than he'd been moments before despite the awful finality of it all, she grabbed him once more and spun him around to face her and he felt an intense surge of relief: *She's changed her mind!*

She pressed her bloodied face against his blast visor. "Do me and Ja'andai proud, Ruh'ta'aq." Then she was gone, swallowed up by an especially thick, black and acrid cloud that had belched from the airlock leading to the ruined bridge— towards the eternal and welcoming embrace of the Elkanasu, her actions guaranteeing she'd take their dead, the fatally injured with her.

He stared after her, momentarily tempted to follow, then, with a rattling intake of breath, he instead turned and ran as fast as he could down the passageway in the opposite direction, leaping over or dodging debris, the free-floating flotsam of the dying ship, feet pounding in cadence with his heart and...

....skidded to a stop in the center of the staging bay. The bulk of the surviving crew had already flicked to the planet, only a handful awaited his arrival—there was just enough power left in the failing mechanism. They stood closely packed, nervously checking their equipment or praying with unusually intense piety—or both—clearly fighting the same panic coursing through his veins. They were depending on him, too. *Do me and Ja'andai proud, Ruh'ta'aq...*

Khusaaq placed himself among the others, tapped the chin plate of his helmet and said in a dry, strained voice that didn't sound at all like his own: "Ready, Nahru'tzrhi." He unholstered his pistol then glanced around to make sure the others had their maser rifles held at the ready.

The flick-down site was a collapsed cistern complex on the outskirts of the Rimmer colony of Cotopaxi, and while the survivors who'd already flicked down had done so safely and going by their terse communiqués hadn't run into any resistance from the colonists—hadn't, in fact, run into any colonists, *period*, as A'tuu'shahn'i they'd all been schooled in the knowledge that it never paid to be overconfident as to the warmth of welcome to one's arrival—an unexpected one doubly so.

"Hunker down everyone," Gaalan's unruffled voice crackled harshly from his earpiece, *"you're flicking into really tight quarters."*

Khusaaq had no sooner dropped to a crouch, the rest following and forming a tight, outward facing circle, when he felt familiar tug of the flicker effect start to wash over him. It suddenly and briefly wavered as it sucked the remaining lifeblood from the dying ship, then grabbed hold with a jolt so violent it came close to knocking everyone off balance. He clenched his teeth and held his breath as the brightly-lit staging bay abruptly receded in a series of smaller and smaller images, his universe collapsing in so many ways—and then came a blinding flash, a massive, eerily silent explosion that bloomed within the confines of his helmet, viciously shaking his brain, rattling his teeth and dazzling his eyes, followed by the stomach twisting sensation of falling...

...and abruptly, the awareness of something solid under his feet. He reflexively tensed, but instead of the expected killing shock of impact, he realized he was still holding his crouch.

He cautiously reached down, startled and at the same time greatly relieved when his gauntleted fingers touched firm, albeit broken ground.

Still blind, unable to make out the readouts on his blast visor much less his surroundings, he pressed the palm of his armored hand against the shattered flooring, then he cautiously ran his hand further afield, bumping into another booted foot which immediately reacted by flinching sideways, followed by a startled oath. Only then did he become aware, over the near continuous muffled *booms* of distant explosions, of the chorus of panicky breathing—his own, overlaid with that of the others—and he eased himself down onto his knees, waiting for his eyes, still dazzled by the explosion, to recover.

His breathing slowed and he heard movement, tentative scrapes of campaign boots on pulverized plastacrete, followed by soft grunts as those around him also dropped to their knees or eased themselves into a seated position now that the surge of panic was subsiding. "Anyone injured?"

He counted the unsteady denials—nine in all, so none, amazingly, had been lost. "Stay exactly where you are until you're fully recov—"

BOOM!

The particularly loud report rolled down the length of the cistern, startling everyone and raining down bits of ceiling in its wake; it was a truly eerie patter in the all-consuming darkness, and sounding like approaching footfalls to nerves already on edge.

He waited a moment then added, "Can anyone see anything?"

More denials from the oppressive dark.

Then, as comprehension set in, someone close by— *Telipinu?*—cursed softly. Another— *Tanaali?*—muffled a sob. Yet another began reciting the Elkanaghalli prayer for the dead—this voice he was positive about it: *Saar'kali.*

"Shut up!" he snapped, his panicked rebuke aimed at Saar'kali, but the effect was immediate: utter silence. Even the labored breathing stopped.

He was relieved no one could see him trembling, could see tears rolling down his own scarified and tattooed cheeks. He tried blinking them away, blinking away the lingering blindness, shaking his head to clear the dizziness from the force of the explosion his visor had been unable to react to, frozen as it was, as he was, as they all had been, within the flicker effect when the their training corvette, and their beloved commander, were blown to bits.

Slowly, painfully slowly he began to make out dim shapes, light and dark... then dusty-blue sunbeams streaming down through a curved and cracked ceiling... and shadowy, faintly glimmering forms all around him. Forms that, like him, cautiously shifting position, slowly turning this way and that, taking in what they could see of their cramped and ruined surroundings as they all came to the same startling conclusion: they'd just survived a catastrophe judged unsurvivable.

Telipinu, who'd been kneeling beside him, abruptly staggered to his feet, dusted himself off then offered Khusaaq his armored hands, which Khusaaq gratefully accepted and Telipinu jerked him to a wobbly-legged stand.

Khusaaq took a deep breath and tried as best as he could to collect his wits as he looked around. Those who'd flicked down earlier had emerged from the deeper, darker recesses of the cistern and quickly gathered around them, urgently, quietly asking about *Huui'teh*, about Gaalan. They found not a shred of solace in the hushed and stammering answers they received.

It was anyone's guess if their distress calls, the colony's distress calls had managed to pierce the Matarii's jamming, if anyone was mounting a rescue or counterattack, be it Rimmer or A'tuu'shahn'i. The only certainty was that he was now in command of a grand total of forty two A'tuu'shahn'i, all younger and even less experienced than himself, all but two others—Qharubi and Telipinu—on their first tour and on what was supposed to be little more than a training exercise, now with orders to protect an isolated Rimmer colony at all costs... against the full wrath of the Matarii Star Empire.

Chapter 2

Abandoned Coalition outpost, Rasal Ghul Seven.
Five days ago.

Qar'qaah ever-so-slowly lifted his head from the bony cradle of his arm, drawn out of an exhausted half-sleep by the annoyingly harsh, rhythmic blat of a perimeter alarm. He peered with sunken, gritty eyes at what lay beyond the nearby open doorway: the painfully bright glare of yet another scorching-hot, strength-sapping and dusty Rasal Ghul afternoon.

The others, huddled next to him in the only semi-safe shelter remaining, the long-derelict outpost's plastacrete emergency bunker, raised their heads to stare muzzily around them.

Qar'qaah motioned to the others to stay where they were, then he managed, after several false and wincing starts, to lurch to his feet as he muttered angrily to himself for having set the alarms on far too high a sensitivity in the first place. He'd been meaning to change the adjustments after several earlier warnings had been triggered by nothing more sinister than an especially strong gust of dust-laden wind, but each time he thought about it, he'd found the task of walking—stumbling and staggering to be more accurate—to the perimeter control station, in the process leaving the protection of the base's failing diffusion screen just too daunting, just too risky that this time he might not make it back.

The diffusion screen itself required constant maintenance, its ancient generator sputtering to a stop at irregular intervals and for no apparent reason except age, but at least that only required a short walk around the bunker to the generator shed in the blinding sunlight, the freezing darkness of night or in the midst of a sandstorm, followed by maybe a few minutes, maybe an hour, maybe an entire day of intricate, knuckle-bloodying work to get it rattling and coughing back to life, each time fighting the worry that maybe that would be the time he wouldn't be able to get it started again, and of course all done without even the miniscule protection from the killing radiation offered by the bunker's laminated plastacrete dome.

It was a job only he did—only he left the bunker to work on any of the base's crumbling equipment, only he risked the exposure. The others had protested, Endooki even going so far as to suggest they take turns, but he was adamant and they, albeit unhappily, acquiesced. He was, after all, their commanding officer and it was his responsibility to keep them safe, just as it was his responsibility to hold the base until Khusaaq returned. Those had been Khusaaq's orders after all and this time he was determined to live up to those orders, not to mention Khusaaq's always unreasonably high expectations.

Only Khusaaq and the others hadn't returned when expected, even taking into account rough seas and untrustworthy Blatto boat crew. Days of mounting apprehension, of desperately scanning what he could see of the surrounding ocean for any sign of the appropriated Blatto boat returning from a trip that should have taken no more than four days, had stretched into a week. And then another week, and another... There was no mistake, no losing count of time. He'd carefully scratched a tick mark on the outer wall of the bunker, where none of the others might see it, recording each passing day. Eighteen days in all since he'd seen Khusaaq and the others off, twelve since a tatter-winged Blatto arrived, only to make the devastating claim that the returning boat had sunk in a storm with all aboard presumed lost.

He'd thought about stopping his recording, briefly pondering the point of continuing. If the Blatto had been truthful, then there really was no purpose other than keeping a macabre record of just how long it took for him and the others to succumb. Then he reminded himself that if he stopped, it meant he'd truly given up all hope, that he'd accepted his fate and the fate of his men as a forgone conclusion, and that simply wasn't what an A'tuu'shahn was supposed to do. A'tuu'shahn'i were engineered to survive, or so he'd been told so many times he'd lost count. A'tuu'shahn'i didn't give up. A'tuu'shahn'i were supposed to die as they lived: fighting. It was an intoxicating image, especially to the young, the impressionable.

He'd found himself taken in by it, to die a courageous death, always battling a worthy foe. He'd never considered the messy edges of reality, where death wasn't clean, wasn't heroic, where one was marooned and left to the mercies of a binary's pitiless radiation—a slow, agonizing and very shambolic death.

He wobble-stepped closer to the open doorway, using the wall for support, then grabbed the doorframe and shielding his eyes as best he could from the glare, scanned the visible horizon, looking for what might have possibly tripped the alarm. There was a breeze—there was *always* a breeze, a hot, bone-dry breeze despite the island base being surrounded by a vast but slowly evaporating ocean—but it was not so strong to pick up and carry enough of the fine dust to trigger the motion sensors. *Perhaps a Blatto?*

Despite the less than warm welcome he and his four companions had given the one claiming to be a survivor of the sinking of the boat, other Blatto had been spotted along the perimeter of the outpost, digging holes, for what purpose he could only speculate, and while they did take flight at the first hint of danger, they always returned, on foot or on wing—hence the decision to increase sensitivity of the motion and pressure sensors in the first place.

Perhaps they're testing us, toying with us. Trying to determine if we're still alive. That had been Laihiri's voiced theory the first time the alarm was tripped in the midst of a powerful nighttime dust storm, leaving them with jangled nerves, unable, unwilling to sleep until the following day, when dust-driven wind again triggered the alarms. Exhausted, more than ready to believe they'd found their culprit, something no more menacing than the wind, they'd shared a meager meal from their dwindling food stocks then slept away the rest of the day.

A week had passed with no more strong wind-storms—and no false alarms, validating their belief. Nevertheless, the pointless panic the alarms had caused needed attending—the sensors needed to be adjusted, again, only this time to a slightly lower threshold. He just hadn't gotten around to it, and now, another likely false alarm, one that burned up precious calories in heart-pumping fright, in unnecessary movement during the worst heat of the day, calories all needed simply to survive. He mentally kicked himself again. *I'll do it now, today—no excuses. And while I'm at it, I might as well check the diffusion generator and the filters on the water purifier.* He nodded to himself, cementing his plan, then, hearing the scrape of movement, glanced over his shoulder.

Endooki, despite being signaled to remain where he was, now joined Qar'qaah at the doorway, silently lending his eyes to the visual search. After several minutes and seeing nothing, the two looked at each other. Endooki shrugged, shoulder bones visibly sliding under salt-rimed and badly blistered skin. Besides dust and the Blatto, nothing moved beyond the perimeter. The ceaseless wind had long ago scoured the landscape clean of any vegetation that might have survived the suns' radiation; it had also removed any hiding places, having reduced any outcrop or hillock to little more than low, softly rounded hummocks while filling any depression with dust so fine that a deep pool of it could swallow the unwary whole.

There'd been a good reason the Coalition had placed this clandestine satellite base where they had: on an isolated island, one of a dozen or so that made up an otherwise unremarkable and utterly barren archipelago far from the closest mainland— the last place anyone with any sense would bother to look, believing that the island, just like Rasal Ghul Four, home of the Coalition's primary research station, was just too hostile to support anything worthwhile, least of all a secret outpost. At one time the small satellite base had been guarded by elaborate sensory camouflage where, if by some marvel it was discovered, no one could approach from land, sea or air without being detected in plenty of time for the base's staff to mount a defense.

Most of the abandoned outpost had fallen to ruin in previous hundred years, its sophisticated sensory disguise and impressive defensive weaponry cannibalized by the Blatto for uses unknown since they appeared to employ only the most basic of technologies. What was left was beyond even Qar'qaah's abilities to repair or repurpose. Only the perimeter monitors and the absolute basics needed for survival—the diffusion screen, food synthesizer and water purifiers—had remained in a fixable state, a matter of luck due to their placement within the base, and silent testimony to the tenacity of the original inhabitants, who, Qar'qaah judged, had managed to last for some time after losing contact and therefore resupply, from the parent research station.

It was obvious by what he'd found when he set about getting the diffusion screen up and running again that none of the surviving base staff had much engineering expertise and when critical components finally broke down due to simple lack of maintenance, none knew how to fix it. There was still a supply of the basic chemical compounds needed to synthesize food, still sealed after almost a century, although he and the others limited their consumption of it, just enough calories to keep them alive once they'd run out of their own emergency food packs as one never knew what the radiation might have done to the chemicals on a molecular level, and the outpost was surrounded by an ocean after all, the purifiers able to turn the viscous brine into potable water, so it wasn't hunger or thirst that killed the original inhabitants. In the time since, the wind had scattered their remains, or maybe the Blatto had collected the corpses along with bits and pieces of equipment. All he knew was that aside from a scant few personal effects—a name badge, an expensive stylus, an earring—no sign of the original occupants remained.

Endooki, his bony knees knocking from the strain of standing, turned to shuffle back to their sleeping spot, close enough to the doorway to avoid the dangerously stagnant air of the deeper corridors, but not so close as to be fully exposed to the grit-laden wind. Qar'qaah hesitated, tempted to follow, but the matter of adjusting the sensors remained. If he returned to his sleeping spot, even for a brief rest, he wasn't sure he'd find the energy, much less the interest to get up again.

Just the thought of making the short trip was daunting and he found his earlier resolve immediately start to crumble, despite the continuing blat of the alarm. His hips and knees ached, the furnace-like afternoon heat burned down his throat with each intake of breath and his eyes, already dry, were now risking an even more painful dusting of grit as a small dust devil began to spin lazily nearby.

Maybe this evening... when it's cooler. He nodded to himself. *Yes, this evening—definitely this evening.* With that, he absently hit the kill switch, silencing the alarm which continued to flash its warning, but just he started to turn, to follow Endooki, he caught out of the tail of his eye the briefest flicker of white.

His heart skipped a beat and his wheezing breath caught in his throat. *Could it be?*

He leaned forward, as far as his throbbing knees would allow and fixed his full attention on where his eyes had caught the faint glimmer within the quivering air and was immediately rewarded by spotting another flash of white. This one he was sure of... well, almost. Rasal Ghul's mismatched suns had a nasty habit of playing tricks with the light, but rarely did those tricks take on the appearance of something white, quite the contrary—and white was the color of an A'tuu'shahn duty uniform under such conditions, where high visibility, to avoid unfortunate mistakes in identity, and reflectivity of the suns' harshest rays were paramount. And the flicker appeared to be getting closer—or larger, he couldn't tell which with the very air itself refusing to cooperate.

He took an incautious step beyond the doorway, swaying slightly as he let go of the supporting doorframe, in the process drawing the attention of Endooki, who'd only just resumed his seat, along with that of Laihiri, Raudah and Nihaal. All staggered to their feet, curious, suddenly wary as to what had such a grip on Qar'qaah's attention, strong enough to pull him out into the open, into the merciless sunshine.

As Qar'qaah squinted at the tantalizing, fluttering speck of white, he allowed himself a small glimmer of hope that it wasn't some mirage, some trick of the light—or simply a hallucination brought on by little food and worsening radiation poisoning, that Khusaaq and Matoosh and the others hadn't drowned as the Blatto claimed, a shattering assertion that had cost the hapless creature its life. Qar'qaah had refused to believe it, couldn't use his A'tuu'shahn synesthete's abilities to tell if it was lying, as Blatto, they'd quickly discovered, were one of only a few alien species—all of them insectoids—who had no perceptible aura whose change in hue would warn of deception, and out of frustration he'd strangled it with his bare hands when the creature refused to recant its story. While intensely satisfying at the time, his actions had put everyone on edge as they waited for the presumed retaliation, hence him increasing the sensors' sensitivity levels to their maximum.

And now... hope that he *had* been right, that the Blatto *had* lied, or, at the very least, had, along with its fellows, abandoned the boat at the first sign of trouble and didn't look back. That the weeks of waiting, constantly propping up the others' dwindling hopes for rescue while struggling with his own mounting despair, of cobbling together fixes that would keep the generators running just a little longer no matter how exhausted he was, how sick they all were... that it might all have been worth it.

Laihiri and Raudah came abreast of him, breathing hard, and a moment later, Endooki and Nihaal joined them, the five standing shoulder to bony shoulder, using each other for support against the gentle buffeting of the breeze. Then they saw what he'd seen, and as they watched, the flickering white speck abruptly separated into two, and a moment later, five... and then eight distinct figures, still too far away to see clearly through the eeling air.

"They've... they've c-c-come back!" Nihaal managed to stammer. Heads bobbed in stunned response, blistered lips drew back in tired, intensely relieved smiles.

Qar'qaah took an unsteady step away from the others, then another. He wanted to cry, would've, if his eyes weren't so dry, and he really wanted to run, knew if he tried he'd fall flat on his face within a few paces, yet the draw was suddenly almost overwhelming to greet the officer as befitted Qar'qaah's position of being in charge of the outpost in his absence, at its periphery. He cautiously increased his speed to an awkward, joint-jolting lope, the others immediately following at the same incautious, clumsy speed.

As more white-clad figures precipitated out of the heat-shimmer, Qar'qaah came to an equally sudden, equally ungainly stop. His companions mirrored his actions, and again gathered around him, everyone wheezing loudly, coughing sporadically and shaking from the exertion, despite only covering a short distance. Qar'qaah wasn't sure, with the approaching figures shifting and flickering, but he thought he could now count *sixteen* separate white forms.

A cold chill ran down his spine. *Something's not right—Khusaaq only took eleven others with him...* He risked a sidelong glance at the others, managed a hoarse, "Get—get back to the bunker—*quick.*"

The others turned to him, hesitant, their hopeful, breathless smiles instantly evaporating.

"Go!" he rasped.

"And you, Kon'ta'aq?" Nihaal asked, starting to back-step.

"I'll join you shortly, now do as I say—*go!*"

The others started to lope as fast as they dared, towards to the bunker.

Qar'qaah gave the approaching white shimmers one last glance, but just as he turned to follow his companions he caught a dazzling flash out of the corner of his eye. An instant later the beam swept past Qar'qaah, barely missing his right shoulder only to strike Laihiri square in the back and the soldier crumpled.

Nihaal, Endooki and Raudah staggered to a stop, believing Laihiri had simply tripped and fallen and started for him.

"RUN!" Qar'qaah screamed, but not quite quickly enough. Another shocker beam streaked past, hitting Raudah in the belly. He was thrown backwards only to land spread eagle and inert on the ground not far from Laihiri.

Qar'qaah dropped to a crouch, then onto all fours and tried to reach Laihiri as Endooki and Nihaal scrambled for Raudah, each grabbing an arm. They tried to drag Raudah but another shocker beam sliced through the dusty air and struck Nihaal and he too fell, face first, onto the hard-pack.

"DON'T MOVE!" a voice boomed in trade use Standard, the command seemingly coming from every direction.

Qar'qaah glanced wide-eyed at Endooki; A'tuu'shahn'i
never surrendered—that was another truism hammered into one
and all since birth—but none were wearing armor, only trousers
and under tunics from their duty uniforms and while they were
armed, they were totally exposed, absolutely no cover but the
crumbled bodies of their companions and now only two
against... he had no idea. In the brief seconds he'd been
distracted, more grubby white figures had appeared as if
condensing out of the breeze-blown dust.

He squinted into the glare and quickly counted twenty-one
separate figures and they were in the process of spreading out.
He fought the temptation to glance around, to see if more were
approaching from behind. It didn't matter. Then his burning
eyes caught another telltale flash—only this wasn't weapons
fire, it was sunlight on something shiny; it briefly dazzled his
eyes. That was the cincher: Rimmers, wearing Rimmer battle
armor.

"STAND UP!" the encircling voice boomed again. "KEEP
YOUR HANDS WHERE WE CAN SEE THEM!"

"Kon'ta'aq?" Endooki whispered, having drawn the same
grim conclusion, *"what are your orders?"*

"A'tuu'shahn'i don't surrender," he replied, to which
Endooki dipped his head. Then Qar'qaah slowly gathered his
legs under him, and somehow managed to get to his feet,
wobbling and staggering as he did so, with Endooki following
his lead, just as unsteady, watching him closely, awaiting his
final order.

"STAY EXACTLY WHERE YOU ARE AND RAISE
YOUR HANDS ABOVE YOUR HEADS—*DO IT!*"

Qar'qaah hesitated, his hand hovering near his holstered
pistol; beside him Endooki, about to lose his precarious balance,
widened his stance ever so slightly.

In response a shocker beam struck Endooki from behind and
he fell, sprawling across Raudah.

Qar'qaah risked a quick glance at him then fixed his now
utterly enraged stare on the approaching Rimmers. *"You
bloodless cowards!"* he hissed, then glanced around him,
realizing he had a choice to make, and make quickly. He could

vaporize the bodies of his troops—his friends, thus denying the Rimmers corpses to dissect, to identify. But they'd still have a body—*his*. He couldn't vaporize them and himself—not before the Rimmers would unleash their weapons on him. Or he could take out as many Rimmers as possible before they in turn struck him down. The choice was obvious.

He whipped out his pistol and screaming obscenities began shooting. Four Rimmers fell before a shocker beam brushed him, sending joints of agony through him. He toppled, somehow managed to squeeze off three more shots, two of which hit their targets, then as he desperately tried to get back to his feet, he was tackled from behind, knocking the wind out of him and his pistol from his hand.

He screamed, tried to shove his attacker off of him, tried to reach his pistol, but three more Rimmers joined in. He was just too weak, too ill to fight them off and suddenly he found himself pinned, face down, a Rimmer painfully grasping each of his limbs and holding them outstretched, with a fifth kneeling on his back. He could barely breathe, he couldn't move.

Then a shadow fell over him and he managed to turn his head, just enough, and through the tangle of hair, he peered up at yet another Rimmer. In fact he was now totally surrounded, a solid wall of white Rimmer armor, and all had their shocker rifles pointed at him. The Rimmer who stood over him pushed up his mirrored visor, exposing his face along with an expression of pure hate. Then he smiled coldly, said, "Calm down you stupid yowie. We're here to recue you."

Chapter 3

Coalition colony of Cotopaxi, eleven years ago.
Midday. Fourteen days into the Matarii siege.

"Fool." Telipinu's whispered observation—aimed at the human as the man walked with tenuous bravado towards the nearest Matarii firing platform—was said without malice, without disgust, without any inflection whatsoever. Just the succinct labeling of someone about to die, about to become yet another pointless sacrifice to the Cotopaxians' tightly-clutched belief that the Matarii would, if given a chance, *listen* to reason, despite all the evidence one could possible ask for to the contrary strewn out before them. The claim was invariably followed by the colonists' oft-voiced complaint that in fact it was their A'tuu'shahn defenders who were too suspicious, too eager to fight to even consider a peaceful resolution. Some, granted a minority but a very vocal minority, had even gone so far as to suggest that it was the A'tuu'shahn'i who'd provoked the Matarii by making planetfall in the first place, escalating an already tense standoff—all based on a truly unfortunate misunderstanding, per the colonists—into what was now entering the fourteenth day of a hellish siege.

Some of the colonists had been grateful, if fearful, of A'tuu'shahn'i in their midst, pinning their hopes, their very survival on the mercenaries' protection—not that they had any other options. But the forty-three A'tuu'shahn'i who'd made planetfall hadn't been anywhere near enough to provide the colony and its scattered outliers with any viable, long-term defense, and that number, in the awful days that had followed their unplanned landing had dwindled considerably, hence the growing movement among the surviving colonists to find another, peaceful, alternative.

Khusaaq had not once tried to stop the Rimmers from their foolishness—it was their colony after all, he was only an alien mercenary, a fact one particular settler, a farmer by the name of Petr Kelso had a very annoying habit of pointing out at every opportunity, employing a litany of epithets humans used when referring to A'tuu'shahn'i to salt his lengthy harangues: yowie, staafük, tupilak, shaper, yōkai, merc, black dog. Such appellations were usually whispered with sneering bravado, followed by a darting-eyed undercurrent of dread, as if fearful the remarks might be overheard by the aforementioned yowie, who might, reasonably, take offense at such obvious slurs. But not in Kelso's case; he had absolutely no doubt yowies were present and he spat the monikers out, smugly taunting Khusaaq, safe in the knowledge that despite all else, A'tuu'shahn'i wouldn't knowingly harm someone they were being paid to protect, using words like weapons. But his slurs failed to elicit the desired response, any more than Rimmer weapons could pierce A'tuu'shahn armor. Not that that made it any less exasperating to Khusaaq or his troops, piled as it was on top of tempers worn thin and nerves rubbed raw.

Khusaaq could reason with the colony's latest de facto leaders, yes; he could spell out all viable options, yes—essentially parroting Gaalan's advice, advice that for him had fallen on new, yet equally doggedly deaf ears. He'd listened politely to their demands and calmly rebuffed their accusations no matter how truly inflammatory, just as Gaalan had done—he was now the face of the Orthodoxy after all, even if the colonists never saw his face, or the faces of his troops for that matter. He and his soldiers were little more than calculatingly fleeting shimmers in the pale azure sunlight, eeling ripples in the starlit dark, the glint of movement caught in of the tail of the eye—in other words, the manifestation of all the ugly, monstrous epithets. But did he or his troops ever physically stop any one of the colonists from committing what in essence was nothing more than suicide? No.

It's all so hopeless, Khusaaq thought as he watched the human stumble and stagger over a wasteland of clotted earth—earth that just days before had been lush farmland. Now it was a desolate, smoldering and monochromatic killing field, created by the Matarii as a constant reminder of what was to befall the rest of the colony, and now held by A'tuu'shahn'i snipers grimly determined to stop them. *We can't—we know that, the colonists are beginning to realize that, but at least we'll take a few Matarii with us.* He peered skyward. *We'll make you proud, Gaalan, damned if we won't.*

He made note of the fact that the morning, which had dawned cloudless if smoke-hazy, was now overcast, with a conspicuous thickening darkness to the north that trailed, from cloud to ground in long, billowing veils. His long-range helmet sensors confirmed his suspicions. *Rain.* And it was slowly headed their way. He'd never actually seen rain or witnessed a storm from the perspective of a planet's surface and for a moment he allowed himself to marvel at it, in its gathering power—still hours away from reaching them—of the clouds churning slowly higher and higher, of the diaphanous black curtains of rain falling across the horizon.

Rain would have been a welcome prospect a few weeks ago for the agricultural settlement, but not now. Rain would only heap more physical misery on those holed-up in the fissure-riddled and largely unfinished escarpment complex or any still trapped alive but unreachable in the rubble of the colony proper.

With a sigh, Khusaaq dropped his slitted gaze back to the human just as the colonist stopped and glanced back the way he'd just come—perhaps to remind himself of what was at stake, perhaps to say one last farewell—and as the Rimmer did so, Khusaaq caught a glimpse of the human's haggard, grubby and beard-stubbled face. *Lennox?* He peered at the man; even without his visor's confirmation, he was absolutely sure. The Rimmer was indeed Lennox, the fledgling settlement's quartermaster and now the sole surviving colonial administrator. Lennox had a wife and three children, the youngest of which had been fascinated by the eerie, disembodied shimmer of Khusaaq's ghillie armor. He and his troops could have made themselves entirely invisible beyond just a very slight distortion, visible only when they moved, their armor was certainly capable of that and more, but he'd ordered that all adjust their ghillie armor's camouflage so that close up their presence was just barely discernable to the colonists, but not so obvious the Matarii, using long range scopes could get a bead on them.

He'd assumed this would have a calming effect on the colonists—knowing their protectors were close at hand, but it hadn't exactly worked out as he'd anticipated. The little girl had tottered towards him, even tried to touch him, much to the horror of her mother, the horror of all the colonists present at that very first meeting after he and his troops had made their unplanned planetfall, before her father snatched her away, the child bawling in her frustration. The eldest of Lennox's children was a bright and obliging yellow-haired boy and at fourteen, actually older than his youngest troops—not that the colonists knew that. Khusaaq could only imagine how they'd react if they knew they were being defended by raw troops on their first training mission, barely more than children themselves. The middle child, another boy, had kept himself hidden behind his mother, only peering around her when he thought Khusaaq's attention lay elsewhere—but how can you be sure a glimmer isn't staring back at you? Khusaaq was, and was tempted to use the human expression, *"Boo!"* just to see the boy's reaction, see the startled reactions of the rest of the colonists who were still rattled by his close encounter with the little girl. He refrained, telling himself it was a childish urge and at fifteen, he was far too grown up for such behavior.

I wonder who put Lennox up to this? Or maybe it was his idea? Lennox had, after all, been one of the most resolute—at first—that the colony, with A'tuu'shahn help of course, could fend off any Matarii attempts at eliminating the settlement, that it was rightfully theirs—

As if such legal niceties meant a whit to the Matarii...

Lennox had given eloquent speeches that had bolstered the colonists' flagging morale—had even roused the morale of some of Khusaaq's more impressionable soldiers. And when Khusaaq had last spoken with Lennox, only the evening before, the Rimmer was still talking of rescue, of Coalition and Orthodoxy reinforcements—masses of them—arriving any moment and what would happen to the Matarii when that happened? Lennox had been almost gleeful at the prospects. Khusaaq's heightened senses hadn't detected any hidden agendas, any deceit in the man—at least no more than what was typical of a Rimmer. Certainly nothing to suggest this.

When did that all change? How did I miss it? Perhaps this human understood all along what the outcome would be and had finally succumbed to the near-insatiable desire just to get it—or at least get his own death—over with.

Khusaaq knew that feeling, damned if he didn't. Knowing at any moment he could be blown to bits, or worse see his troops or colonists die horribly, of hour upon tedious, tense hour, and hours stretching into days just waiting for that to happen, of second- and third-guessing every decision, every order, jumping at any unexpected sound, barely able to eat, much less sleep— unless he accessed the sleepers available via his armor and under the circumstances he was loath to do that.

He'd come to know all too well that tipping point when the unrelenting, visceral dread of being killed or making a mistake that got someone else killed suddenly gave way to the overwhelming craving just to get it over with. His armor had chemicals on hand to combat those feelings too, but the resulting effect was to dull the senses, if ever-so-slightly—and he couldn't, wouldn't risk that, not where a split second of indecision could mean the difference between life and death, and not just for him but for everyone. Besides, no A'tuu'shahn worth his or her family glyph would admit to even contemplating, much less actually using tranks. They had been infused into their armor to ease the anxiety of the dying, not to settle the nerves of the living.

Instead he and his soldiers had been running on very little food—severely rationing themselves from the very start, not knowing when or if reinforcements would arrive—and even less rest, their bodies fueled instead by a now dwindling mixture of adrenaline and their armor's supply of stims. In a matter of a few days both would run out, and when that happened... he knew the fate that awaited all of them—a particularly grisly one too for any of the colony's leaders who'd rebuffed the Matarii's initial demands—like Lennox—and even worse for any A'tuu'shahn'i luckless enough to be captured, assuming the

Matarii knew how to disarm A'tuu'shahn armor before the wearer, or the armor itself, detonated it.

Martyrdom. Suicide. There'd always been a fine but *very* distinct line between the two in Khusaaq's mind, in the minds of all A'tuu'shahn'i without the highly-charged emotional values placed on each by other species, especially humans—but now the labels were interchangeable, very, *very* intoxicating and as close as a bright red, recessed button on his helmet's chin plate, accessible only by the tip of the tongue.

This man, this James Lennox, wasn't the first to take this gambit—five others had tried over the previous seven days— two in one day alone—all had failed spectacularly in their single-minded pursuit of getting the Matarii to listen to reason, to revisit the Matarii's earlier demands now that the Matarii had the colonists exactly where they wanted them, and in the process had proven to the Rimmers that they had the will and the materiel to back up their threats.

Lennox likely wouldn't be the last to make this fool's errand. It might take ten or twelve more such martyrs to finally rid the colonists of the last of those who truly knew what was coming and didn't want to be around when it came, even if it meant leaving their families to pay that price, guising their utter desperation as a public display of courage. To die a hero in the eyes of their fellow colonists, their families.

How incredibly noble...

Khusaaq suddenly hated Lennox, hated the others who'd acted on that desire, for deciding enough was enough. He couldn't. He was A'tuu'shahn; he was supposed to be immune to such things, despite worrying the tip of his tongue raw over the past few days, not toying with the recessed button, but rather against his own teeth. He felt every death as if it was his own, relived each, over and over, the images, the sounds and smells seared into his memory, a constant, background chorus stridently demanding its due, while hating with every fiber of his being those who had made good their permanent escape into silent oblivion.

And now it was Lennox's turn.

Fool.

Khusaaq glanced sidelong at Telipinu and acknowledged the soldier's whispered remark with a slight shrug, feigning indifference. It was all he dared risk in their tight and precarious aerie overlooking the devastated plain that stretched out in front of them, past the Matarii's immense and impressive emplacements, past the aliens' massive armored crawlers and mobile firing platforms all arrayed facing the escarpment, a plain that stretched all the way to distant, smoke-blurred and now storm-dark horizon. It had indeed been an ideal site for an agrarian settlement: an abundance of flat, arable land, a year-round supply of surface and underground water, temperate climate—too ideal to go uncontested.

Beside him Telipinu inhaled, then exhaled slowly and shook his helmeted head.

It was no secret that Telipinu reviled all Rimmers. He'd relegated the odd assortment of aliens who made up the Coalition to little better than greedy, sniveling cowards—but cowards with enough wealth to buy what they didn't have the stomach to fight and die for. Rimmers were no better than Loopers or the Gorm. These were the strongly held and often voiced opinions of his superior officers to be sure, and with no proof, no life-experience to the contrary, ones Telipinu had eagerly embraced.

The Cotopaxians—humans all—hadn't won Telipinu over, but a few individuals among those he'd had prolonged contact with had at least given him pause for thought. The group he'd been assigned to guard was comprised mostly of women with their children, along with a few elderly. Most of his charges hadn't succumbed to mindless panic as Telipinu had expected during the Matarii's initial softening up of the colony—a day-long pummeling from the safety of their orbiting destroyers, the Matarii's idea of a gentle knock—the settlers had in fact done as he'd patiently, or in a few cases not so patiently directed.

And the first night, as he and his hundred-plus charges hunkered down in the damp and stifling darkness of one of the multitude of cisterns that formed a sprawling underground warren—temporary refuge at best—many, appreciative that their ghostly guardian had kept them all safe and thinking the worst was over, or close to it, had willingly offered to share their meager supply of food and water with him. They'd done so even though they had no idea if he and his fellow A'tuu'shahn'i were true biologicals or were, as was widely rumored, organic machines.

Telipinu had no doubt the offers were genuine, not just a gesture, and those acts of selflessness had given him reason to at least reconsider his harsh views—but only on a Rimmer-by-Rimmer basis. Only a few weeks before Telipinu would have laughed derisively at Lennox's feeble gesture and made some ugly crack about now many Rimmers did it take to parley with the Matarii—the answer? As many as the Matarii can kill with the weapons they had on hand, plus one, or so the joke went. But now? Just a softly worded, *"Fool."*

And Lennox was.

Khusaaq had tried—Gaalan had tried—to convince the colonists that the Matarii couldn't be bargained with, that the initial Matarii demands were not an opening for political dialogue, but a pretext to attack. Anyone who knew anything about the Matarii knew they didn't take prisoners. They didn't negotiate. Matarii just *took*. And they were about to overtake the colony he and his soldiers had tried so desperately to protect for the past thirteen days, with everyone, including his young troops, hoping against hope for rescue, for reinforcements to arrive in time. What he hadn't told any of them was that if reinforcements had been dispatched, even taking into account the time it would've taken to gather the needed forces, the vanguard still should have arrived by now.

To deprive anyone, Rimmer or A'tuu'shahn, of that last, infinitesimal sliver of hope was just too cruel.... Besides, he'd caught himself glancing skywards on more than one occasion, his fatigued attention drawn to a faint flash of light detected by his visor, evidence, he had desperately wished, that the Matarii were now occupied elsewhere. But in each case, the flare turned out to be nothing more than a trick of low-angled sunlight, the glint off one of the Matarii's aerial recon units, or, more often than not, another incoming salvo piercing the upper atmosphere.

What his troops did know, what all A'tuu'shahn'i knew was that the Matarii were notorious for playing with their victims, making a macabre game out of the inevitable, using the enemy, civilian and soldier alike, as target practice—as long as there was little or no risk to the Matarii themselves.

The Matarii were living up to their reputation and then some, which to Khusaaq meant only one thing: the aliens knew they had little to fear from the timely arrival of Coalition or Orthodoxy reinforcements.

And Rimmers call us *monsters...*

Nothing was left of the once heavily populated nucleus of the sprawling agricultural colony—the first day of orbital pounding, followed by the nighttime planetfall of a sizable strike force and then another full day of street-by-street fighting had left its residential quarters, precious seed silos and immense outlying greenhouses heaps of smoking prefabs while the settlement's only hospital—clearly marked—had been singled out for particular attention. Reducing the upper floors to rubble on the first day wasn't enough. Now all that was left of the three-story structure was a deep, smooth-as-glass-walled crater. The power station had shared a similar fate.

More than half of the colonists had died in the first day's onslaught, most dying still believing the Matarii wouldn't dare attack a Coalition colony—wouldn't obliterate a hospital where so many had gone seeking refuge. He'd lost six soldiers trying to convince the last holdouts otherwise. He'd lost eleven more on the second day—seven killed outright, the rest missing but presumed deeply buried in the debris along with countless colonists who'd refused to leave what shelter they'd found—the now infamous cisterns. Once the Matarii had discovered the underground system's existence, they'd systematically blown it up. It was impossible to tell if any of the muffled blasts that rocked the colony that night where the result of A'tuu'shahn armor exploding, either at the direction of the wearer, trapped and dying, or by the armor itself, sensing its occupant was dead, or the Matarii ground troops finishing the job they'd started by dropping charges down any gaping hole they happened across.

Three more of his troops had suffered such severe injuries in street fighting they'd volunteered to remain behind to await the advancing Matarii then detonate their armor for maximum effect. Their selfless actions had taken out two fully manned troop movers and at least six mobile firing platforms—two hundred and fifty enemy, possibly more—but the Matarii had more troops, more war engines, lots, *lots* more and now with an even greater and *personal* desire to make an example of the recalcitrant settlement and its A'tuu'shahn'i defenders.

This was the colony's last stronghold: the administration complex built into the side of a massive escarpment with a panoramic view of the surrounding table lands. What had been intended as a symbol of the fledgling colony's permanency was going to be its deathtrap.

The Matarii were spoiled for choice as to exactly what to do to bring the matter to an end: make a full-on assault, sit back and starve the colonists out—a time consuming task and Matarii were not known for their patience with other species, sentient or not—or bring the entire escarpment down on them in one massive rail gun barrage.

Option one risked the loss of too many Matarii; option two might take weeks, even months—more than enough time for the Coalition or Orthodoxy to come to investigate a promising colony suddenly gone silent. Option three was quick, with minimal risk to the Matarii themselves, but a lot of time and effort had been put into the close to completed complex already, a complex that could be easily converted to Matarii needs—far less costly and time-consuming than starting from scratch, and if the Matarii planned on holding the planet against any counter-claimers, they'd need a large, and largely sensor-proof compound such as this for stockpiling materiel and housing troops.

If the Matarii did in fact decide on option three, there was absolutely nothing Khusaaq and his handful of soldiers could do to stop them, so he removed that possibility from his calculations, which left option one or two and those, even under the best of circumstances only prolonged the inevitable.

He'd warned the colonists that the complex was the worst place to hole-up, that they'd be better off making their way in small, A'tuu'shahn-led groups to the rugged, heavily forested and cave-riddled mountains behind the escarpment where they could spread out and fight a guerilla war until reinforcements did arrive, where the sensors of the Matarii destroyers couldn't penetrate the heavy bio-mass and rock with any accuracy. But in the colonists, in their panic, had ignored him and bolted for their stronghold, their symbol of permanence, taking what they could of their lives... for the most part useless material goods which only slowed them down. Not having the troops to stop them, he and his soldiers were forced to follow, scooping up those who'd fallen or carrying those who'd been wounded, all the while firing at the pursuing Matarii, leaving everyone exposed.

They'd lost another two hundred and eighteen colonists during that disorganized and panicked flight across open, exploded ground. There just weren't enough A'tuu'shahn'i to defend them all, or to help most. Many had to be left behind—far too many, still alive, screaming for help or cursing the wraithlike forms of A'tuu'shahn'i who ran past, already heavily burdened with children and the injured clutched in their arms or flung over shoulders and appearing to fly over the smoking debris while making easy targets for the Matarii. Their A'tuu'shahn rescuers wore armor; the colonists only their clothing.

He was now down to twenty-three, including himself. Twenty-three, to defend slightly fewer than fifteen hundred, over half of whom had suffered injuries, some minor, most not, against... he had no idea. He didn't even want to think about it.

That second night, as he sat watch in the shattered remains of an access culvert, he could see movement out on the plain, heard faint pleadings for help, and saw living firebrands stumbling mindlessly among the still fiery rubble. He and his troops, at his order, had carefully picked them off—his idea of being humane, but in the eyes of many of the colonists who realized what was happening and demanding they stop, this action made his troops, his orders—*him*—no better, no different than the pitiless Matarii.

Had they just listened...

He shrugged again then turned back to the matter at hand. This new aerie, one Saar'kali and Tah'sidi had happened across days before while mining one of the numerous entrances to the complex was much higher and less exposed than the access culvert of the second night. It was a ventilation blast-hole left over from the original construction, and did boast an impressive, albeit utterly demoralizing view: everywhere he looked, he saw firing platforms and troop crawlers, and among the assorted war engines, just beyond the range of A'tuu'shahn hand weapons, individual Matarii were darting here and there, taking up positions or scouring the still smoldering debris looking for anything of value that had somehow survived the past thirteen days of near-continual bombardment, their pristine, silvery armor glinting in the smoke-smudged sunlight.

He turned back to the object of Telipinu's wearily pragmatic aside and with fatalism born of recent experience, watched as Lennox continued his slow, deliberate walk towards the nearest platform. *Fools, the lot, and we're all going to die defending them—which, I suppose, makes us even bigger fools.*

Khusaaq had learned in his dealings with the human that Lennox was an Earther, born on the very home world of his own species—even the same continent—and had found himself fascinated when Lennox spoke briefly of the parallels between this world and Earth, eagerly hoping the man would elaborate. Instead, Lennox had gone on to say that he'd brought his young family to this planet, hoping to start over, to create a new life without, as Lennox had put it cryptically, "All the baggage."

When Khusaaq had gently pressed him for more information, Lennox had awkwardly demurred, clearly thinking Khusaaq's interests in Earth were of a professional, not personal nature. Rather than push the issue and arouse even more unease among the already fearful colonists, Khusaaq had reluctantly let the matter drop, letting Lennox take the conversation where he wanted.

Lennox and his fellow settlers had believed everything the Coalition had fed them about Cotopaxi: that it was a rare jewel of a planet with a wide temperate zone, rich in arable land and rare minerals, everything a newly established colony would need in order to be fully self-sufficient within five generations, ten at most, everything he and his fellow settlers could ever want, there for the taking... after paying a hefty homesteading fee of course. And that was all true. Khusaaq had found himself spellbound by Cotopaxi's sheer beauty, its free running rivers, endless forests, fire-belching volcanoes and glittering, cloud-dotted oceans and most captivating of all, huge, snaking chains of snow-capped mountains.

He'd never seen such a pristine world, even from orbit; he'd never walked on living soil, never breathed air that hadn't been artificially generated, purified and sterilized. He'd imagined Earth—*his* Earth, the wild and very ancient Earth of his long distant ancestors looked much like Cotopaxi. He'd become so entranced with the idea of experiencing what his remote ancestors had experienced, if only fleetingly, that two nights before and while briefly alone, he'd gone against his own orders and had removed his helmet, making himself visible to any Rimmers who might be nearby, as well as detectable to Matarii sensors had they been trained on his exact location—risks he was willing to take, knowing he'd never get another chance— then he stared upwards at the twinkling night sky as he savored the heady and very alien, yet somehow hauntingly familiar smell of a living, breathing and essentially untouched planet. Of *hearing* the chill green wind as it gusted down from the snowy highlands behind the escarpment and teeming with a thousand separate scents, *feeling* it brush against his skin—of seeing, with his own naked eyes, the far distant and snowy peaks that glistened like jewels in the starlight, so evocative of the Elkanaghalli image of paradise, the *Night Mountains*—those ancient strongholds that had once protected his far distant ancestors from the encroachment of "the others"—and the twisting path one's life took to reach them, to finally become one with the Elkanasu, to return... *home.*

He'd never imagined the like, never believed he'd actually see a real-life version of such a deeply held and very sacred symbol and was, in a word, utterly enthralled. And the irony that he was now protecting those very same "others", and would in fact lay down his life protecting them wasn't lost on him.

For the colonists, for the Matarii, Cotopaxi was a world worth fighting and dying for. But as an A'tuu'shahn, his association with this fragile utopia had been meant to be transitory at best—viewed only from the cold detachment of space, studied only through instruments, never touched, never smelled, never tasted... and never, *ever* desired.

But now he was here, things had changed. In those few precious helmetless moments, *he'd* changed. He wanted what the colonists had wanted—perhaps even what the Matarii wanted—a new life, a chance to be something other than a faceless and feared mercenary who paid for others' dreams with his blood, his life or the lives of his friends, sent where ever and whenever the Q'shaathrah had use for him without ever questioning his fate.

The experience had left him even more embittered, even more afraid and most of all deeply disturbed by the strange thoughts that raced around in his mind, thoughts that had no source, no home: thoughts that refused to be stilled.

He was different than other A'tuu'shahn'i. He'd known that for a long time—Ja'andai had known it too, tried to break him of his peculiar feelings, his maddening desire to question everything, the more taboo the better, and when that didn't work, forced him to hide his feelings, his insatiable curiosity, to bury them deeply. That hadn't worked either, despite Ja'andai's regular and increasingly severe beatings, despite his own anguished and unanswered pleas to the Elkanasu to make him like everyone else, able to completely shut out the hideous racket of war, to selectively remember just as other A'tuu'shahn'i could, to cast aside the ugly, the agonizing, the terrifying, and remember only the heroic. To fully accept what was—to embrace it without question.

He saw no glory in killing, no profit, no gratification in wresting away a prize from one undeserving alien only to hand it to another, with the strong possibility of being paid to wrest it back in the very near future. But with his excruciatingly accurate retentive memory, he saw and felt everything, *remembered* everything as if it had just happened. And Cotopaxi, in its intoxicatingly primeval state and with its own Night Mountains, called to him as no one else ever had, nothing else ever could.

He found himself again gazing at the far distant peaks, their dazzling, snowy heights just discernible through the smoke haze and the storm-darkening skies. They called to him, beckoning, welcoming, and he wondered if he could make it—if his soldiers and any colonists who wanted to accompany them could reach their protection, reach the arms of the awaiting Elkanasu—

No. He exhaled forcefully in hopes of ridding himself of such foolish thoughts. *Those* were not *his* Night Mountains. There were no awaiting Elkanasu among the crags to defend them against the Matarii and the horrible and yes, totally meaningless deaths that awaited them. These mountains were Cotopaxian, they belonged to others. Not to him. *Never* to him. His first command, his only command would end here within sight of those intoxicating snow-covered peaks.

He risked a deeply troubled stare upwards. Cotopaxi's brilliant, blue-white sun was at zenith, its disc visible through the smear of smoke and ominously thickening cloud layer. Without intending to, he again briefly let his mind wander, and it turned to thoughts of what sunlight felt like on bare skin. Like water, or wind? Or something altogether different?

I wish I'd never taken my helmet off...

"What are you thinking?"

Khusaaq jerked his eyes off the threatening sky and dropped them to Telipinu. The soldier was staring at him intently. He could just see Telipinu's eyes glittering behind the blast visor, made more transparent for ease of keeping an eye on the Matarii—or so they'd told each other. In truth their body armor, after prolonged wear and if relying strictly on sensors, began to take on a decidedly claustrophobic feel even to the most habituated, the wearer totally reliant on the armor's array of very accurate and reliable sensors rather than his or her own equally acute senses of smell, taste, hearing and touch. Even Gaalan, veteran of countless and prolonged battles, had confessed to such. There was no way to simply crack the helmet's seal, ever-so-slightly—the designers had made sure of that, to eliminate the temptation. The miniscule but telltale amount of heat or moisture along with exhaled organics and molecules of carbon dioxide, were more than enough to home in on. So the helmet was either fully locked on or fully off.

Lightening the filters on the blast visor helped, Gaalan had said, if just a little, giving the wearer a truer sense of the world around him or her. And so Khusaaq had passed her technique along to the others, but only for very brief moments when no colonists were nearby and just long enough to tamp down the sensation of being slowly suffocated to a more tolerable— controllable—level.

He wet his lips, said, "If that tight beam got through."

Telipinu—who knew him the best of anyone, was in fact the closest to him despite being a lowly Barkaat within the rigid caste system—wasn't fooled, not at all. Nevertheless he played along: "If it had, they'd have sent reinforcements by now." He took a deep, ragged breath as he again fixed his eyes on the now distant, dwindling speck that was Lennox. "We're on our own, Ruh'ta'aq."

"Likely so."

For several minutes neither spoke, both watching Lennox, then Khusaaq asked, "And you?"

Telipinu flicked him a sidelong glance and dropped his voice to a conspiratorial whisper, despite them speaking on a private channel: *"What's it like?"*

"Like?"

"You know," he tapped the side of his helmet with an armored finger.

So, I wasn't alone as I'd assumed. And likely this would be the young trooper's one and only chance. Khusaaq could hardly deny Telipinu any more than he'd been able to deny himself. "See for yourself."

Telipinu hesitated as if suddenly regretting asking, depending upon Khusaaq to say no, then he slowly, cautiously, released the locks and slipped off his helmet, and after another pause, took a tentative breath of the smoky air. He coughed, coughed again, muffling the explosive noise as best he could in his gauntleted hands, then he squinted sidelong at Khusaaq. "You might have warned me."

"I honestly didn't think that was necessary."

Telipinu chewed on that then replied, "I've smelled better— *lots* better." He touched his face as a gust of warm, sooty breeze spun past, ruffling his sweat-sticky hair and he smiled broadly at the marvel of it, at the utterly strange feel of it. He reached out, armor-clad fingers spread wide, and made a quick grab, as if fully expecting to catch the wind. He opened his hand, peered down at it and laughed softly then with a sidelong, almost embarrassed glance at Khusaaq, he quickly donned his helmet. He wriggled around in their cramped hideaway to get marginally more comfortable on the rubble and muttered, "I'm really hungry and thirsty—I'm tired of sucking on tube rations and drinking my own piss, even if it's been filtered and sterilized ten times over."

"Me too."

"It still *tastes* like piss," he griped softly, as if he'd expected Khusaaq to disagree and since he already had his protest ready, had gone ahead and used it, "and body-hot piss too..."

This time Khusaaq only grunted his full agreement.

"...leaves me to wonder if the designers ever tasted their work," he finished sourly. For several minutes he studied the Matarii placements before he again looked at Khusaaq. "Think they'll attack today, ta'ahn?"

It was a question Khusaaq had been asked every day, every hour... almost every minute since making planetfall and he'd gotten quite good a prevarication when it came to the colonists, and their leaders, none of whom really wanted the truth and all openly embraced what he suspected they suspected was anything *but* the truth. But to another A'tuu'shahn? To Telipinu? Always the truth.

"If I were them I would—I'd image they're getting rather bored with their game."

"Wishful thinking?" Telipinu grinned then, instantly sobering, said, "I want this over with—this waiting to be killed is killing me."

"Yeah...."

"I wish the Rimmers had listened to you, Ruh'ta'aq."

Khusaaq eyed him, then chuckling softly, returned his gaze to the retreating back of Lennox, now visible only with the use of his helmet's sensors. He keyed up the magnification before asking, "When? Any time specifically?"

Telipinu hesitated, drawing Khusaaq's now curious gaze.

"When you suggested we make a run for the mountains." He heaved a loud and heavy sigh. "Fresh water—really cold I'd wager, fresh air—none of this..." he waved his hand around as best he could in their cramped aerie, "smoke and shit and hot piss-water." He paused again then added, "I bet we could have made it. I bet we could survive until someone comes looking—and they will, eventually..."

"Eventually, perhaps."

"...this colony is too valuable to just go silent without someone wondering why."

"I'd think so. Then again, maybe the Coalition isn't willing to go to war over it."

"And the Orthodoxy?"

"It's not their war." *Their—not our.* Khusaaq thought about that, and realized it was oh-so true. *It's* our *battle, but not* their *war. They aren't going to risk getting entangled with the Matarii over a single ship and its crew. They'll just file for compensation for the losses, the Coalition will pay up, awards will be bestowed posthumously, and that will be that.*

As if thinking the same thoughts and coming to the same despairing conclusion, Telipinu went quiet and stayed quiet for several minutes, then said softly, "Is it too late?"

Khusaaq glanced sidelong at him. "Too late...?"

Telipinu motioned to the mountains, to everything they represented and Khusaaq suddenly wished he hadn't given Telipinu permission to remove his helmet, hadn't given him permission to briefly experience the real Cotopaxi, to... *hope*. "We might make it, but I doubt any colonists would, assuming we could convince them to even try—"

"Then let's not," Telipinu grumbled, eyeing the distant Lennox.

"—and Gaalan Nahru'tzhri's last order was to protect the colony at all costs."

He turned to face Khusaaq. "But the colony's destroyed, Ruh'ta'aq."

"Really?" he growled a little more fiercely than he'd intended, Telipinu's remark hitting a particular soft spot. "I hadn't noticed."

Telipinu hastily backtracked: "I... I didn't mean that the way it sounded, Ruh'ta'aq, truly. What I meant was, the colony is gone, which means all contractual agreements to protect the colony went with it."

Khusaaq eyed him. Telipinu, always a stickler for details— just like Qharubi, who was almost obsessive about the finer points—had, again just like Qharubi, actually read the contract; he hadn't—he'd barely given it a glance. At the time, a quick skim of the major points seemed all it was due. Who was he to question the minutiae? "Gaalan Nahru'tzhri—"

"With all due respect, Ruh'ta'aq," Telipinu interrupted, "Nahru'tzhri would not expect, nor, I believe, want us to die for a lost cause. And this is about as lost as lost can be."

Now it was Khusaaq's turn to chew on something, but before he could ponder the issue further, Telipinu motioned towards Lennox; the man had reached a barren patch of relatively flat ground.

Telipinu began to count, slowly, softly, *"One... two... three—"*

Lennox abruptly halted, stopping Telipinu in his accompanying dirge, and carefully withdrew something from under his tattered jacket. For a moment neither Khusaaq nor Telipinu could quite make out what the Rimmer held in his outstretched hand, then a gust of wind thinned the smoke and they saw what it was: a filthy white rag tied to a stick—a universal signal not of cease-fire or parley, but of surrender.

"That piece of duplicitous Rimmer filth...!" Telipinu snarled then glanced sidelong and wide-eyed at Khusaaq as his armored hands balled into impotent fists. *"He's sold us out! He's sold everyone out!"*

"Indeed." Khusaaq wondered if this was Lennox's idea, or one foisted on him as the colony's last surviving bureaucrat by the others in nominal charge—nothing more than a ragtag bunch of self-serving, self-appointed loud-mouths—a decision the Rimmers had simply "forgotten" to mention to their A'tuu'shahn defenders. Under other circumstances Khusaaq would have been furious at such a monumental betrayal. Under different conditions, conditions that only affected the colonists and left him and his soldiers out of the equation entirely, he might have even chuckled at the utter absurdity of the human's actions, the vain stupidity and yes, the sad futility of surrendering to the Matarii. "But not for long."

Lennox raised the stick, gave the flag a tentative wave.

Telipinu eagerly, now almost maliciously resumed his count without losing a beat, hoping the Matarii would do what he could not, at least not without a direct order. *"Four... five... six..."*

They didn't disappoint. Those in the firing platform took notice and blew Lennox and his dirty white flag to bits.

Chapter 4

Aboard ship, three hours ago.

"*Kon'ta'aq...?*"

Qar'qaah fixed his muddled thoughts on the whispered voice, a familiar, frightened voice.

"Kon'ta'aq... wake up, please." The request was followed by a gentle shake of his wrist.

He forced open one eye, then the other and the blurry face that hovered over him slowly came into focus. He used his tongue to pry apart his gummy, blistered lips, swallowed to moisten his throat then managed a very croaky, "En... dooki...?"

The familiar face broke into a very relieved smile.

"But... but you're dead."

The smile vanished as quickly had it had appeared, replaced by an indignant scowl. "Am not."

"But... I saw you, saw the others..." he glanced around him at the sound of shuffling feet, bracing himself, not sure what to expect. The worried faces of the other three, Nihaal, Raudah and Laihiri weren't at the top of his list. In fact they weren't even on the list of possibles. And all looking very much alive, if desperately ill? All were naked, their horribly emaciated bodies shocking even to him. And all were shackled, wrist and ankle, with just enough slack to allow them to walk, to keep their balance.

Only then did he realize he too was shackled—but legs only. He tried to get his elbows under him; Laihiri helped with an assisting arm and Qar'qaah, once upright, looked around him again, this time taking in not only his companions, but their surroundings: a small, featureless and brightly lit room, five bunks, makeshift toilet facilities in one corner and a closed hatch, its lock-light glowing an activated red. "Where are we?"

Nihaal replied, "We were on a Rimmer ship—"

"They said they'd been sent by Khusaaq Sha'ashahn, to rescue us," Raudah interrupted, then snorted, "Not that we believed them. They shot us! Sha'ashahn would never have allowed that."

"No... he wouldn't have." Qar'qaah again looked around him, then his gaze jerked back to Nihaal. "You said we *were* on a Rimmer ship—you mean we aren't any longer?"

It was Endooki who answered, "We were transferred a short time ago. The Rimmers had kept you drugged—"

"You mean they *overdosed* him," Laihiri grumbled, then looked back at Qar'qaah and placed a skeletal hand on Qar'qaah's equally skeletal shoulder. "We thought we were going to lose you, Kon'ta'aq, but as soon as we were transferred, the doctor here gave you a counteractant, said you'd come around shortly... and you did."

Qar'qaah nodded as he eased his legs off the thin pallet he'd been lying on. "Any idea whose ship we're on?"

The four shook their heads in unison then Endooki replied, "They kept us hooded during the transfer, told us by intercom we could remove the hoods once we were locked in here. What we heard and smelled when we came aboard, I'd say at the ship's crewed by least one Looper, a Thalamian and maybe a human. Their doctor, at least she was claiming to be a doctor, is Matarii. We *saw* her, and along with two other Matarii who came with her, kept their weapons on us as she examined you."

"At least she gave us something that actually helped with the pain," Nihaal muttered, rubbing his sunken belly. By their gloomy expressions, Endooki, Laihiri and Raudah were unwilling to give the alien doctor even that much.

Qar'qaah couldn't help it; he swallowed convulsively as the only possible explanation to their present predicament came to mind: *"Slavers."*

Again, the four responded in unison, this time with very unhappy nods.

He looked at each of them in turn, asking, "But... why would the Rimmers who took us prisoner tell you Sha'ashahn had ordered our rescue... then hand us over to slavers?"

"I think they hoped by saying so, we'd cooperate, wouldn't give them any trouble, until they could make the hand-over,"

Raudah replied. "You know Rimmers—anything to avoid risking their own skin."

"They kept warning us to behave," Laihiri said and glanced at the others, who nodded their incensed agreement, "withheld food and water, refused to give us anything when we didn't do precisely as they ordered, no matter how insignificant—"

"Did they hit you?" Qar'qaah asked, noticing the fresh bruises, the still oozing scrapes all of them bore.

"They roughed us up a bit—nothing serious," Endooki said with a slight twitch of his shoulders. "Just trying to prove they were bigger and badder."

That elicited a loud, derisive snort from Raudah. "Prove they're nothing more than cowards you mean." He held up his manacled hands. "They were too scared to take these off, make it more of a fair fight. One even punched Laihiri in the stomach—while he was hooded and all because he didn't move fast enough!"

"And they kept you drugged," Nihaal added, "said you, as our commanding officer, would be the first to suffer the consequences if we 'tried anything stupid'."

"Consequences?"

"An open airlock was mentioned a few times," Laihiri muttered.

"But how'd Rimmers know where to look for us in the first place?" Qar'qaah asked, raking a tangled lock of filthy hair out of his eyes.

"Because we have friends in high places," a voice said, startling them. They all turned to find a Matarii standing in the now open hatchway, grinning at their collective surprise, and behind her stood another Matarii and a Looper. All were pointing blasters. "And now that you're awake, Kon'ta'aq, my captain has some questions she'd like to ask you." She motioned to Qar'qaah with her blaster. "Now, be a good Akka'a and come along."

Aboard Baidarka, *present day.*

"Is this some sort of joke?" Commander Robert Aquila growled as he fixed his bleary-eyed glare on a very agitated and uncharacteristically disheveled Amalfitano and equally distressed Tasende, the two seated across from him at the *Baidarka*'s conference table. "Because if it is, I'm not in the mood!"

Zarijan Izraad, the *Baidarka*'s Intelligence Officer, who was seated beside Aquila, gave her own gritty eyes a rub. Ten minutes before she, like Aquila, had been rousted out of a sound, not to mention well-deserved sleep by a frantic page from Amalfitano, and she turned her own annoyed stare on the twin objects of Aquila's wrath.

"Robert, this was no joke, believe me!" Amalfitano replied.

"Now let me get this straight." Aquila braced his elbows on the table. "You two went bar-hopping on Tuli—"

"Not bar-hopping!" Amalfitano protested. "Just one damned bar—well, okay, for complete disclosure, a strip-club," he flicked Izraad a sidelong, apologetic glance, "but just *one*, and one highly recommended to me by none other than Councilor Pakanga himself!"

Aquila squinted at him. "And once at this strip-club Councilor Pakanga highly recommended, a Thalamian, suddenly and without any known provocation, tried to kill you?"

"Yes! Exactly!" Amalfitano nodded vigorously as he glanced at the still very rattled-looking Tasende.

"And you're absolutely *sure* it was a Thalamian?"

"Of course! Who else looks like a bright blue flatworm with rows of pink eyes and six limbs?" He flapped his arms about for emphasis.

"Not to mention a tentacle hairdo," Tasende added in a slightly tremulous voice as he wiggled his chubby fingers in front of him, then as Aquila's irate gave fell on him, he immediately began picking nonexistent lint off his rumpled clothing.

Aquila pursed his lips, tapped his finger on the table top. Point made, he shifted his glare back to Amalfitano. "And you two managed to escape its clutches and certain death by throwing the Tulian version of a Long Island ice tea in its eyes."

Amalfitano started to reply then, sat back and stared long and hard at him. "You think I've made this all up, don't you? You think I deliberately made this all up—*don't you?*" he asked, his voice suddenly brittle, laced with anger and betrayal. "Do you think Xosé made it up too? That this is all some sort of elaborate prank—"

"Not like you haven't pulled my leg before, so no, I wouldn't put it past—"

"So that's what you think?" he hissed, lurching to his feet. *"We're almost murdered and you think it's all some big joke?"*

Aquila glared up at him and replied with equal heat, "Sit down, Doctor. *Sit!* I intend on getting to the bottom of this, here and now!"

Amalfitano hesitated then abruptly sat down, his shoulders slumping. He took a deep, ragged breath, exhaled then met Aquila's sincerely annoyed gaze. "Robert, I *swear*, it happened just like we told you."

"Maybe it was all an innocent mistake—you two were, I have no doubt, quite inebriated at the time."

"Well, sir," Tasende began, his voice still edged with a noticeable quaver, "I, uh... well, I don't consider a Matarran blaster pointed at my face particularly innocent."

"It was *my* face," Amalfitano corrected tetchily, glancing sidelong at his companion, "not *yours*, Xosé, but I agree wholeheartedly with your sentiment."

"Besides," Tasende continued, undaunted this time, "what's a Thalamian doing in a strip-club? They're asexual, and it's not like it could imbibe—if it tried, its insides would turn to mush." He looked hopefully at Izraad—the expert on all things alien— for support.

She only stared back, unblinking and clearly unsympathetic, having been the target of his and Amalfitano's idea of a practical joke on more than one occasion herself.

"If you don't believe us," Amalfitano said, trying another tack and in a slightly more mollifying tone as he leaned back in his chair and crossed his arms, "how 'bout contacting the local police? I'm sure they have a report of the incident—there were certainly a helluva lot of witnesses."

Aquila stared at the man, a look of total incredulity on his sleep-scruffy face. He couldn't help it: he burst into laughter, adding, "You honestly think patrons of some seedy strip club are going to *voluntarily* step forward? If Pakanga recommended it, it's likely a hotspot for other high-profile types who go there knowing they'll be guaranteed anonymity—and if that's the case, you think they'd want to risk getting their names publicly linked with the place?"

"Well, not when you put it that way, no, but—"

"I must say, you have more faith in people than I do!"

Amalfitano fixed him with an icy stare. "Okay, so you don't believe me—*us*. Fine. Is that all*?* 'Cuz I'd like to go to my quarters and have a drink... an uninterrupted one at that. Personally, I think my nerves need some settling."

"Personally," Aquila replied coldly, "I think you two have had more than enough to drink already—"

"Commander Aquila...?" the relief com-op's voice unexpectedly boomed from the desktop speaker, startling them.

Aquila hit the speaker toggle with slightly more force than needed, snapped, "Aquila here."

"Sir, I've got Lieutenant Matho of Sector HQ on closed channel three."

Matho? What the hell could she want at this hour? Aquila's bloodshot eyes cut to Izraad, but she only shrugged, equally baffled. "One moment, Burnham." He turned to Amalfitano and Tasende. "We'll have finish this discussion later, gentlemen— and until I can get to the bottom of this, you're both to remain within the Kanaloa Medical Complex at all times."

"Meaning we're confined to the hospital?" Tasende asked plaintively.

"And the *Baidarka* of course," Aquila said.

"No more shore leave?" Amalfitano replied, incredulous, as his eyes darted to Izraad, then back to Aquila.

"I think that would be prudent, yes."

Tasende made a soft gurgling sound and sagged, dejectedly, into his chair.

"So, that's *it?*" Amalfitano replied testily.

"I'll make some quiet, back door inquiries," Aquila answered, then held up his hand at Amalfitano's blinking, open-mouthed astonishment. "I have no intention of creating a diplomatic incident that could get shore leave revoked for the rest of the crew. And I seriously doubt, Crewman Tasende..."

Tasende reluctantly looked up from his intense study of his lap.

"...that you'd want any more such... *incidents* placed on your record, so just this once, I'm going to keep this between us—but *only* this once, understood?"

Tasende nodded keenly. "Yessir, thank you sir."

"Dismissed," Aquila said and motioned irritably to the doorway.

Amalfitano rose, visibly seething. *"Thanks,* Commander. Thanks for believing me. You don't know how much your trust in me means to me. Goodnight!" He spun on his heel and stalked out of the *Baidarka*'s conference room.

Tasende mumbled his own goodnights, heaved himself out of his chair and hurried unhappily after his chief.

Aquila shook his head as he stared after them. Amalfitano and Tasende were well-known pranksters—they'd hoodwinked him more times than he could recall—all in good fun—they'd even managed to pull Vildur's leg once or twice, and when alcohol was involved... well, all bets on the scope of a prank went out the proverbial airlock. But this one, even he had to admit, took top honors, with both men playing their parts to the hilt, even scuffing up their civvies to look more the part. *So... maybe it wasn't a prank—maybe they'd gotten themselves involved in a bar fight... not like that hasn't happened before, too. Maybe they wanted to hide the fact, spare Tasende more trouble... I dunno. They've both had too much to drink, that's for certain, but claim they were almost murdered?*

He shook his head again and then rubbing his temples with both hands, let out a long, exasperated sigh. Feeling that wasn't quite enough to fully express his feelings, he dropped his head onto the conference room table top, his forehead impacting with a soft *thump,* then he sat there, immobile, arms limply hanging at his sides. "I'm getting too old—"

"Sir?" Izraad prompted, "Lieutenant Matho is waiting?"

He sat bolt upright and hurriedly thumbed the activator. "All right, Burnham—patch her through." He combed his hair out of his eyes then smoothed it down with both hands.

"Please enter your personal code, sir."

He did so; there was a pause, then Burnham, said, *"Go ahead, sir."*

"Commander?" Matho's disembodied voice asked.

"Yes, Lieutenant?"

"Commander, I apologize for waking you at this hour—"

"I was already awake, Lieutenant. And I have Lieutenant Izraad here with me."

"So much the better. Admiral Keon asked that you and the Lieutenant be informed that we have a potentially explosive situation on our hands."

His eyes slid to Izraad. "Situation?"

"Involving the Briseis—*a little over seven Standard hours ago she handed over the five Hahtooshans she'd rescued from Rasal Ghul to an Orthodoxy ship."*

"But... what Orthodoxy ship?"

"Exactly the point, Commander. The plan was, as you are aware, for the Briseis *to retrieve the Hahtooshans marooned on Rasal Ghul Seven—which they did, successfully I might add, despite the Hahtooshans refusing to surrender and instead firing on our people, critically wounding five marines and regrettably killing one..."*

Aquila risked another sidelong, this time rolling-eyed glance at Izraad. Despite Khusaaq providing very precise instructions on how to go about safely recovering the five, no one involved in planning the rescue had any illusions about it going smoothly, but a Coalition death? Critical injuries? He exhaled, rubbed his pounding forehead. What had been hoped to be a cornerstone in the fledgling alliance suddenly looked more like a coffin nail.

"...then deliver them to Tuli, where they were to be repatriated with Khusaaq Sha'ashahn and receive medical care aboard the Faridour *before their final disposition was determined."*

"Yes," Aquila acknowledged impatiently, "so what happened?"

"A Hahtooshan ship, the Huui'teh, *made contact with the* Briseis, *and its captain, Mizahn Nahru'tzrhi informed the* Briseis' *captain that they had been ordered to make rendezvous in order to get the soldiers into Hahtooshan care as soon as possible."*

Aquila braced himself, knowing he was not going to like the answer to his next question. "And...?"

"The Hahtooshans have no vessel called the Huui'teh, *Commander, and no Nahru'tzrhi by the name of Mizahn—"*

Aquila almost said, *"Shit!"* before he remembered to whom he was speaking and swallowed it whole.

"—the instant the Briseis *escaped the interference sphere of Rasal Ghul, she contacted HQ, but—"*

"But by then our mysterious *Huui'teh* was long gone."

"Yes, even a tracer was unable to get a fix. Once it had the Hahtooshans aboard, it immediately turned back to Rasal Ghul, presumably to use the system's interference as a blind to make good its escape."

"And cover its tracks." He blew out his cheeks, resumed his vigorous, one-handed forehead massage. "So, now what?"

"The admiral asks that you personally assure Khusaaq Sha'ashahn and Narbrooi Hahtra'tzrhi that this unexpected turn of events is in no way to be interpreted as the Coalition reneging on its agreement. We've dispatched the destroyer Eryx *and frigate* Matyszak *to Rasal Ghul, and along with the* Briseis, *they will attempt to track down the* Huui'teh. *The Hahtooshans, too, have sent two warships, which should arrive at the system in four days."*

"By then the trail will be as cold as space, Lieutenant." *And whoever grabbed the soldiers will be across the border and into Looper territory, or into The Barrens,* he added to himself.

"I understand that, Commander. Rest assured, the Briseis'
captain was horrified when he learned he'd been duped."

Aquila bit back a reflexive snort. *Oh, I bet he was—I bet he*
was so damned eager to get rid of his passengers if he could've,
he would've have dropped them down a black hole. He knew
the *Briseis*'s captain personally, briefly served with Martin
Pelenor, knew his reputation—and more importantly, his
political allegiances, which weren't that far off from Behardien
and her cronies. He hadn't been happy when he found out what
ship—or, more importantly, which captain—had been tasked
with rescuing those marooned on the planet, but, as he'd tried to
convince himself at the time, the *Briseis* was the closest, and
time was of the essence.

And then for Pelenor to lose a crewmember, a marine, killed
by the very people he'd been dispatched to rescue, to have five
others critically wounded doing something all would have
found beyond odious, if not downright inexplicable, to say the
least... It left Aquila to wonder what had gone so terribly
awry—Khusaaq's instructions had seemed straightforward
enough—and he found himself tempted to ask, but he quickly
reminded himself that Matho might not know what went wrong,
might not tell him even if she did. Instead he said, "Sha'ashahn
may not accept my assurances, Lieutenant, and neither may
Narbrooi Hahtra'tzrhi."

"The admiral has the utmost confidence in your diplomatic
abilities, and that of Lieutenant Izraad, to convince Sha'ashahn
and Hahtra'tzrhi of our sincerity and our desire to locate the
abducted Hahtooshans."

Gee, thanks. He scowled at the speaker grille. "We'll do our
best, Lieutenant."

"Excellent. Matho out."

Aquila exhaled then gave Izraad a sidelong look. "Any
brilliant suggestions on how we go about this—without risking
Narbrooi or Khusaaq strangling us with their bare hands?"

"I suggest we contact Narbrooi first. No doubt he's already
been informed by his own government and is patiently, or, more
likely, not so patiently awaiting our... explanation—"

"Not Khusaaq?"

"Narbrooi, unlike Khusaaq, has so far shown remarkable openness, and Khusaaq has a very personal connection with these abducted soldiers—Narbrooi does not. Perhaps Narbrooi will indeed accept that this was not some sinister plot on the part of the Coalition—"

"Wanna bet?" Aquila interrupted sourly. "'Cuz I'm not sure I accept it *wasn't.*"

"I doubt Khusaaq will accept it either, and reasonably so. It does seem far too coincidental, and clearly the crew of this mysterious *Huui'teh* knew to orchestrate their rendezvous while still within Rasal Ghul's interference sphere so as to make it impossible for the *Briseis* to confirm the 'change in plans' or trace their course—"

"And the matter of the rescue itself was supposedly a tightly held secret—just to reduce the risk of someone attempting something like this," Aquila replied.

"Clearly Intelligence hasn't rooted out all of Senator Behardien's co-conspirators."

"Or maybe some in Intelligence didn't feel the need to rush things?" Aquila asked. "And what about the rescue itself? Khusaaq strongly believed if Pelenor followed his instructions to the letter, it could be done with minimal risk to everyone involved—but one marine killed, five others critically wounded?"

"And I noticed she didn't mention the condition of the rescued Hahtooshans—maybe our people weren't the only ones to suffer."

"Yeah," Aquila replied with little enthusiasm.

Izraad continued, "Plus there's still the matter of William's mysterious blaster-toting Thalamian. Perhaps the two events are linked?"

He eyed her.

"Something did happen, that I can tell you. He and Crewman Tasende were not only visibly shaken up, but their thoughts were scattered, fearful—"

"But they've fooled us—*you*—before. And they'd both clearly had a few too many, far too many in fact." He waved his hand in front of his face as if to waft away the lingering reek of alcohol.

"True."

"So it's possible they saw what they thought was a blaster," he continued, "and in their inebriated state, panicked—"

"But..."

"But...?" Aquila asked reluctantly.

"What better way to throw the proverbial monkey wrench into this alliance than to assassinate two people critical to the creation of Hahtooshan-specific vaccines?"

"Or kill a marine who's come to rescue you—proving to everyone Hahtooshans can't be trusted, don't even understand our way of thinking and don't want to, that they are in fact the cold-blooded thugs everyone thinks they are."

Izraad only shrugged.

Aquila chewed on his lip for a moment then asked, "But an assassination attempt on Tuli? With Hahtooshan troopers patrolling everywhere?"

"Not everywhere—that would be physically impossible, even with the resources available to Narbrooi, and even if possible, I doubt they were patrolling strip-clubs. Besides, if they were, they might have been a bit distracted—I doubt most would have never seen such goings on in their lives. I strongly suspect they're all, one might say, a wee bit innocent in that department. Distracted enough they might not have noticed a pistol-packing Thalamian."

Aquila eyed her skeptically, her feeble attempt at humor falling flat, as he rubbed the back of his neck, then taking a deep, steadying breath, muttered, "Here goes," he thumbed the com-unit's activator. "Burnham, contact the *Faridour*. I need to speak with Narbrooi Hahtra'tzrhi immediately."

Chapter 5

Inside the administrative complex of the Cotopaxi colony, eleven years ago.
Nightfall of the fourteenth day of the Matarii siege.

"Either you come with us or you die. It's as simple as that."

The sixteen Rimmers, nine men and seven women—the surviving Cotopaxians' self-appointed representatives—stared at what appeared to be little more than faintly glimmering columns of air within the narrow confines of the passageway in disbelief rapidly turning to horror mixed with impotent rage. The Rimmers themselves were, as usual, surrounded by a shared nimbus of gray with the requisite flashes of yellow and not for the first time Khusaaq found himself wondering if all humans were born liars or it was a habit they acquired later.

He'd also noted that Petr Kelso was not among this group, and was briefly hopeful this meant a more adult conversation, but by the looks he was garnering, clearly Kelso's unexplained absence wasn't going to change the timbre of the meeting.

"I think you've upset our hosts, ta'ahn," Qharubi said to Khusaaq over their private channel. "Perhaps you—"

"What the hell do you mean, go with *you* or *we* die?" one older man, tall, gaunt and balding, snarled as he took an impolitic step closer—a Kelso wannabe, or, more likely, his replacement. Unnoticed by the human, Qharubi did the same, his hand coming to rest on his maser pistol as he placed himself slightly ahead and to the left of Khusaaq.

Khusaaq was unmoved, physically or emotionally, as he glanced at his visor's readouts as they scrolled across his visual field, noted the man's aura was far more active than the others, with brief bursts of brilliant yellow. *Viehl, Sergy, chief surveyor.*

If it had been Viehl's intention to intimidate or impress it didn't work, at least on Khusaaq, who, over the previous weeks, had become inured to Rimmers' empty, but seemingly obligatory posturing, part and parcel of their collective obnoxiousness. He knew this human wouldn't dare step anywhere near close enough to pose any sort of real threat, as if a Rimmer civilian—or soldier for that matter—could pose a genuine threat to a fully armored A'tuu'shahn. And in truth, the colonists present had no idea just how many A'tuu'shahn'i were standing in front of them in the sporadically lit corridor—one, or all of them? In this case there were only two. The rest were busy elsewhere, hurriedly preparing for their impending departure.

There was a universal, unspoken rule among aliens when dealing with A'tuu'shahn'i: never get closer than a respectful three meters from any visible distortion. Perhaps in this case it was the odd, liquid-like and faintly pulsing yet utterly silent shimmer of their ghillie armor—a calculated, yet sublimely understated act that carried a maximum impact of visual intimidation—that kept the other colonists at what was collectively perceived as a safe, polite distance—six or so meters in this case; perhaps it was the reasonable worry of accidentally bumping into one of the feared mercenaries, maybe even stepping on his or her proverbial toes—assuming A'tuu'shahn'i had toes, proverbial or otherwise. Khusaaq seriously doubted if aliens wasted any time wondering about such trivialities, suspecting instead that the only time Rimmers thought about A'tuu'shahn'i was when they needed muscle— far cheaper than their own precious hides of course—to accomplish their latest intrigue.

"Hear the Hahtooshan out, Sergy," a stout, red-cheeked, red-haired woman grumbled as she sharply elbowed her way to the front of the small, grim-faced crowd to stand close, but not too close to Viehl.

Delbruch, Lisa, his visor promptly notified him. *Horticulturalist, senior grade.*

"Why?" Viehl said, turning briefly to Delbruch as his finger stabbed in Khusaaq's general direction. "They're the reason we're in this unholy predicament!"

"Then the sooner my soldiers and I leave, the better," Khusaaq said. *"Yes?"* It seemed a perfectly reasonable solution, and his voice reflected it. Unruffled, rational, the antithesis of Viehl's, which was verging on panicked fury.

"But... but you *can't!*" another Rimmer spluttered.

Khusaaq gave the constantly scrolling feed on his visor plate a glance as it instantly highlighted one bit of data: *Musal, Falla... farmer.* "Oh, yes we can, Mister Musal—"

Musal opened his mouth then snapped it shut, suddenly and clearly taken aback, deeply frightened in fact that a merc, of all creatures, knew his name. He took a step back, then another, hurriedly melting back into the crowd; Qharubi noticed and chuckled softly.

"—and we will, as I said, in now slightly less than one Standard hour—fifty three Standard minutes to be precise." As if to emphasis his point, Khusaaq's multitude of sensors picked up a distant, rolling, *'boom'*, an instant before everyone heard it, the corridor, the entire complex acting like an echo chamber, and the Rimmers glanced nervously around them, clearly thinking the worst while ribbons of fine dust wafted down from cracks in the unfinished ceiling.

But this was no Matarii bombardment. The thunderstorm was almost upon them, the first bands of wind-driven rain were already falling on the plain, on the ruined colony and on the Matarii emplacements. It would be only a matter of minutes now before it reached the escarpment; within an hour, the storm itself would be directly overhead, bringing with it a goodly amount of intense electrical activity. He didn't need his armor's intricate web of sensors to detect the precipitous drop in pressure with the associated and equally rapid build-up of static energy. The planet's thick atmosphere was turning itself into a gigantic capacitor; it made his skin tingle, caused the glimmer of his ghillie armor to quiver, if ever so slightly. "We've placed motion or pressure detecting mines at all of the entrances, along with an assortment of booby-traps and other unpleasant surprises that will collapse the passageways, so I urge that you not attempt to leave using—"

"That won't stop the Matarrans!" Viehl snarled.

"You're right—it won't. Slow them down, perhaps. Annoy them greatly, most definitely. But no, if they decide to advance on this complex, and I believe that's exactly what they plan to do, nothing will stop them. This is why we need to leave, *now*, while we still have a chance—"

"You were *paid* to protect us, you goddamned yowie, or have you forgotten?"

"We were contracted to protect the colony," Khusaaq replied evenly, employing Telipinu's infallible logic. "The colony, even you, *Mister Viehl*, have to admit, no longer exists." He'd hoped Viehl would react as Musal had to being named, but was mistaken; Viehl was too angry, too scared at the grim prospects to notice.

"And whose fault is that?"

"Not mine, certainly, or my troops—in following my commander's final orders, we've given our all to protect you—"

"Yeah, right! Viehl snorted. "And exactly how many of my fellow colonists have died since you agreed—and were paid in full in advance I might add—to 'protect' us?"

Khusaaq pointedly ignored Qharubi's incensed, albeit whispered profanity-laced threat to add one more colonist to that list. He pursed his lips, took a deep breath before replying evenly, "I strongly suggest you take *that* matter up with the Matarii—"

"But if you leave the Matarrans will slaughter us!" Delbruch interrupted, her eyes darting between Viehl and the glycerin-like combined shimmer that was Khusaaq and Qharubi.

"You have weapons—your complex's arsenal is well stocked," Khusaaq answered, "surprisingly well for a colony of this size. I strongly suggest you use them—"

"Most of us have never used a weapon!" another protested—*Wu, Johan,* Khusaaq's visor dutifully obliged, *botanist*—"We're farmers, scientists! We didn't come here to fight a war!"

"That *is* a most regrettable oversight, Mister Wu, but it does not change the fact that we leave in forty seven Standard minutes in order to take full advantage of the storm. Now, if there's nothing else?" He waited, giving the colonists a chance to get in a last word, but when no one spoke—most clearly too stunned to think of anything worthwhile or mind-changing to say—he added, "Those who wish to accompany us are to meet us at the intersection of corridor ten-west and nineteen-north." Then, on a private channel, he murmured to Qharubi, "Let's go," and started to walk back the way they'd come. As he did so, he overheard Viehl whisper to Wu, *"Fucking merc cowards—we never should have paid in advance,"* clearly thinking Khusaaq was well out of earshot, to which Wu murmured his hearty agreement.

Khusaaq stopped, turned back and took in the motley group of Rimmers who stood clustered together under the harsh, spotlight glow of one of the corridor's widely spaced and sputtering overheads.

One by one, the colonists noticed his continued presence, sensed his silent, unhappy scrutiny and tried to look guiltless— even Wu made a decent effort to look suitably blameless.

"I didn't say we were just going to run and hide, Mister Viehl. Quite the contrary. I intend on making things extremely unpleasant for the Matarii, and as costly as possible—*for them.* Those who choose to accompany us must expect such—there will be absolutely no accommodation for those who cannot keep up."

"You're suggesting we leave our children, our parents, our wounded behind!" Viehl fired back.

"I made no such suggestion. I merely stated the grueling nature of the undertaking I am proposing. *You,* Mister Viehl, are most welcome to remain here. In fact I strongly urge you do so. And one more thing—we A'tuu'shahn'i have an *exceptional* sense of hearing. Next time, you'd be wise to make sure you are in fact alone before you start casting aspersions—assuming for you there will be a *next* time." With that Khusaaq pivoted smartly on his heel and started down the corridor, intent on putting as much space between himself and the truly tiresome Viehl.

Qharubi remained where he was, one armored hand pressed flat against the glass-smooth wall of the passageway. It was a long abandoned, debris-filled construction corridor, but one that was the quickest route between newest and most exposed western wing, where his troops had positioned themselves to take advantage of the excellent view of the surrounding plain, and the oldest, southern-most wing of the massive complex, the deepest into escarpment and safest, where the colonists had taken refuge.

On their way to the meeting with the Rimmers, Khusaaq and Qharubi had placed explosives at strategic spots along the entire length of the corridor, all rigged to detonate remotely, once they and however many Rimmers decided to accompany them were well away from the complex.

"Ta'ahn..."

Khusaaq, still chewing over his interaction with Viehl, assumed Qharubi was placing one last mine and would catch up, but warned by the ominous tone of Qharubi's voice, he stopped, turned to him.

"I'm reading faint traces of an energy pattern used to bore these walls."

"And...?" he replied irritably. Viehl had left him with a throbbing headache and a sour stomach. He was in no mood for a report on the techniques used to build the complex.

Qharubi turned to him. "This isn't Rimmer work, ta'ahn."

Khusaaq, his physical woes instantly forgotten, fixed his own visor's sensors on the wall, then the ceiling. As he absorbed the information, the very distinct, telltale traces still held within the living rock, his throat muscles tightened in response. *"Matarii...."*

"Indeed, Ruh'ta'aq."

He jerked his eyes to Qharubi. "They were here first—this is *their* planet, *their* complex!"

"It would appear so, Ruh'ta'aq, and certainly explains why they've refrained from bringing it down on our heads."

Khusaaq took a deep, rattling breath, then glanced murderously back at the settlers, who still stood a little way away, whispering heatedly to each other. *Duplicitous Rimmer filth indeed.* It was well known that the planet fell within the buffer zone between space claimed by the Matarii Star Empire and the Coalition, but the Coalition had satisfactorily explained this to the Q'shaathrah, or so Gaalan had assured him, saying that they'd laid claim to it shortly before the war broke out, and because of that felt they were within their rights to colonize it—partial reparation for all the colonies destroyed by the Matarii. And Gaalan, eager for a 'unique' training exercise, as she put it, had seized upon the contract.

He took another, even deeper breath, settled his rage—or tried too, but in truth this was a betrayal beyond even Lennox's secretive but pointless attempt at surrender, beyond anything he could have envisioned—managed to settle his voice, then he strode back to them, Qharubi on his heels. "Mister Viehl."

The Rimmers flinched as one, their heads swiveling sharply towards the sound of Khusaaq's disembodied, rapidly approaching voice.

"I have a question," Khusaaq continued as he came to a stop, but much closer to the Rimmers than before; the colonists could sense it, could see his and Qharubi's armor's eerie, distortion swell before their eyes and all instinctively back-stepped, some more than others and not just because of their unexpected nearness. "And I warn you, I expect a completely honest, *forthright* answer. I know the truth so it will go *very* badly for you if you think you can continue to lie."

"Lie?" Viehl tried to laugh, but it came out as a very nervous, high-pitched titter, even to him, so he replaced it with what was clearly supposed to be a very offended scowl; his aura, on the other hand, became little more than a dazzling waterfall of sparkling yellow. "About what?"

"Cotopaxi. It was first claimed by Matarii, correct? Not Coalition as my Orthodoxy was led to believe, which makes *your* settlement illegal."

"What? NO!"

"Then please, if you will, explain to me why these very walls bear the unique signature of Matarii boring equipment—*not* Coalition."

Several of the Rimmers, including Delbruch, Wu and Musal—but not Viehl, Khusaaq noted—gasped in startled unison, *"What?"*

"Either your Coalition has lied to you, or you and they have lied to *us*—a very serious blunder regardless. This complex, or, at the very least this part of this complex, by happenstance, the oldest part, was built by Matarii *for* Matarii—"

"That's not true!" Viehl fired back.

"—and by the degradation of the residual energy trace, I'd place the age of construction approximately forty nine Standard years ago, well *before* the outbreak of what your Coalition refers to as the *First* Matarii War. And your colony was established... *when?"* He waited; Viehl only stared back with nervous, darting eyes, his flushed face now freckled with beads of sweat, the flashing of yellow that surrounded him increasing in intensity.

"Since you appear utterly ignorant of your colony's own, and rather brief history, Mister Viehl, I will enlighten you: your colony was established approximately twenty-two Standard *months* ago, with nothing of Coalition construction being older than that." He glanced sidelong at Delbruch. "Is that correct, Miss Delbruch?"

She only nodded, a quick and unsteady nod as she fixed Viehl with a very angry, accusing glare as if hoping by doing so, she would redirect Khusaaq's attention back to the man. Others too were staring at Viehl. Most still in open-mouthed shock, others in growing ire as the full impact, the awful ramifications of the accusation hit them.

Khusaaq continued, his voice, despite his earlier efforts, now taking on a decidedly menacing edge. "I am unaware of the Matarii ever putting this much work, in fact, any work into something they planned on handing over to others. Quite the contrary. The Matarii have a well-known habit, one might even go so far as to call it a pathological obsession, of destroying anything they fear has even the most infinitesimal risk of falling into alien hands. So I find it deeply curious that they would leave behind anything as useful as this complex, and to the Coalition, which even today they consider their primary adversary? That is simply beyond plausibility."

He paused; his visor's scanners had registered a massive jump in Viehl's heart rate, blood pressure and breathing while he'd been speaking—not that he needed that data to confirm what he already knew. While the human could lie—*was* lying—

his aura could not. The rest of the Rimmers were extremely afraid, clearly flustered, but their reactions, their auras told him they were just as stunned, just horrified by the discovery as he and Qharubi had been. But not Viehl. Viehl had known all along.

He'd lost twenty of his own defending Viehl, had lost his ship, his beloved commanding officer and over half her crew defending these colonists, some of whom, he now had no doubt *knew*, just as Viehl *knew*.

Khusaaq felt a shiver of mounting blood-lust run down his spine and felt his own armor respond, causing the surrounding liquid shimmer to quiver violently, this time visibly to all.

Beside him Qharubi growled a very succinct and obscene précis of Viehl and his ilk as he eagerly fingered the trigger of his pistol, but he knew better than to actually shoot the Rimmer, despite the almost overwhelming urge—*that* was Khusaaq's prerogative and Khusaaq's alone.

Khusaaq slipped his own pistol from its holster, carefully adjusted the beam width and destructive power, all without the Rimmers being aware as he continued calmly, "My ship was destroyed, Mister Viehl, protecting you; most of her crew were killed." He took a step closer. "Of those of us who managed to flick to the planet, almost half have died protecting you, defending a settlement that had no right to be here." Another step. "So I give you one last chance. Tell. Me. The. Truth."

Viehl turned wildly to his fellows. *"You believe what this fucking merc is telling us? It's using this as an excuse to abandon us!"*

"Tell the Hahtooshan the *truth*, Sergy!" Musal yelped, his terrified eyes darting between Viehl and the distortion that now filled the narrow corridor. "Or you're gonna get us all killed!" Others, hearing their own worst fears in Musal's warning, began cautiously backing away from Viehl.

Viehl noticed, turned desperately back to Khusaaq. *"I am telling the truth! I don't know what the hell you're talking about!"*

Khusaaq took one last step closer. "Wrong answer, Mister Viehl."

To the colonists it appeared as if a pinpoint of light, like an exploding star, had unexpectedly appeared within the now rapidly eeling air, only to leap out and engulf Viehl in an eerily and utterly silent, eye-dazzling flash then vanish just as abruptly. One instant he was there, the next he wasn't, and without even an unpleasant whiff to mark his passing.

After a momentarily delayed response, the Rimmers heaved back as one. Some staggered into the corridor's unforgiving walls, others tripped over their own suddenly leaden feet to land hard and sprawl across the debris-strewn floor, all dumbfounded, too shocked to scream, to run, those on the floor too scared to even get back to their feet, all instantly reminded in the most immediate and truly shocking way of who and what their guardians really were: *yowies*.

Khusaaq really couldn't blame them for their stunned paralysis—in fact he was counting on it. "Any of you who were truly unaware that your colony was blatantly unlawful under the rules governing the right of first settlement of a newly discovered planetary body, section one, subsection one-A of the Accord of Ulises of which your Coalition *is* first signatory," he said, his calm, metallic voice now without a hint of anger, "are still welcome to join us and take your chances, if that's your choice. Any who knew... I strongly suggest you remain here, to explain, and yes, to *fall on the mercy* of the rightful owners of this planet because you will receive *no* mercy from us. Tell those who choose to accompany us that they now have forty Standard minutes to meet us at the appointed location and to bring only what *they* can carry and is necessary for their survival, absolutely nothing more."

When the colonists remained frozen in place, he added, "We will not wait a moment longer." And when that failed to work, he said in a louder, commanding bellow, *"SHOO!"*

Like a conjurer's trick, the spell holding them in place broke. Those still on the floor staggered to their feet and, as one, the Rimmers bolted haphazardly away, down the narrow, smooth-walled corridor.

Chapter 6

District council chamber, Alhajoth, planet Tuli.
Dawn, planetary time. Present day.

Izraad, Aquila and Teague stopped to allow the rather officious Tulian aide to open a pair of massive, polished wood doors with a flourish, then, at the aide's open hand-sweeping gesture, they entered the luxuriously appointed council room.

As Aquila glanced around him, Izraad caught his immediate reaction, that this was a far cry from the venue of his first meeting with the Tulians. That had taken place in the provincial city of Girsu, in the surprisingly unassuming and rather bucolic chambers of the Tulian High Council, a setting deliberately evocative and richly adorned with relics of the Tulians' cultural roots.

This council chamber on the other hand served the district of Jidgantjara, for which Alhajoth was not only the capital but also the planet's primary space port, and the room reflected it. It was cosmopolitan, sleek and, aside from the huge, floor-to-ceiling window that dominated one side, utterly unadorned. It could have easily been mistaken for a boardroom anywhere in the Coalition, as calculatingly ubiquitous as the High Council chambers in Girsu had been aesthetically unique.

"President Seitakap, Councilor Pakanga *and* Narbrooi Hahtra'tzrhi will be with you momentarily," the aide said then silently withdrew.

"That doesn't bode well," Teague muttered under his breath, aware the room might be—and likely was bugged.

Before Aquila could even nod his agreement, the doors opened again and in strode the three grim-faced men.

A little more than three hours had passed since Narbrooi had surprised Aquila and Izraad by cutting off Aquila's attempt at assuring him the disastrous rescue and subsequent abductions was in no way reflective of the Coalition's sincerity. Instead the Hahtooshan admiral had insisted that the Tulians also be fully apprised of the situation, to hear the Coalition's account in full as he heard it and to that end had arranged the early morning meeting, face-to-face and on Tuli.

"Please, be seated." Seitakap motioned to the chairs that ringed the table.

Izraad slipped onto one of the high-backed chairs, next to Aquila, and, as it happened, directly across the table from the chair Narrooi selected an instant later, with Teague seating himself to her left. To Narrooi's right sat Seitakap, with Pakanga on his left. Positioned in front of each was a small viewer.

As Seitakap spoke quietly to the aide, and everyone pretended not to notice, Izraad, instead of staring at nothing in particular like everyone else, took advantage of the brief distraction to study the mercenary who now sat across from her—a man possessing an aura so vastly different from Khusaaq's, a man fully at ease with himself, his position *and* his reputation.

Over the previous weeks she'd become habituated enough with Hahtooshan tattoos to see through the distracting mask to the face—*to the person*—beneath. Narrooi, clearly, had been strikingly handsome in his youth—before his brutal profession had prematurely aged and etched its own telltale inscriptions on his angular and ritually scarified face.

Here and there she could see a time-healed scar, and the left side of his face, from throat to forehead was pockmarked with the reminders of a long ago explosion that had riddled his entire left side with shrapnel. All could have easily been erased with some judicious cosmetic surgery—the fact that they hadn't spoke as eloquently about who and what he was as his iconic clan glyph tattoos—or, she quickly amended, perhaps the Elkanaghalli had religious proscriptions against such, just as they had against bone and organ replacements. Khusaaq too bore a large number of old, disfiguring scars on his legs, arms, back and torso.

Narrooi had a crooked nose, high forehead and cheekbones and deep-set eyes—the disturbingly pale gray-blue eyes of a Hahtooshan made even more startling by his coffee-brown complexion that in turn was overlaid by inky black, incredibly intricate tattoos and equally complex, matching scarification.

The aide abruptly hurried off, closing the double doors behind him, and as Seitakap cleared his throat, signaling the start of the meeting, Narbrooi fixed his gaze on Aquila, suddenly pinpoint, unwavering—the chillingly serene gaze of a cold-blooded killer, no softening of that aspect, certainly no apologies. Narbrooi was the embodiment of what it was to be a Hahtooshan: a carefully contained, tightly controlled and highly explosive mix of supreme arrogance, absolute determination and an unrivaled ability to wreak havoc. He was a commanding presence with an exceedingly dangerous edge.

At Seitakap's nod, Narbrooi began without preamble: "My soldiers have located the Thalamian who attempted to assassinate Doctor Amalfitano and Crewman Tasende."

"What?" Aquila gasped.

Izraad too couldn't help but raise her brows in surprise, having relegated the matter of the Thalamian to a far lesser importance; she still wasn't entirely convinced it wasn't part of yet another drunken prank gone awry. Teague just looked utterly baffled, and turned his questioning stare on Aquila.

"You mean you were unaware of this incident?" Narbrooi replied.

"Well... no," Aquila began, still off balance. "I mean yes, Doctor Amalfitano reported it to me—to us," he nodded to Izraad, "But—"

"You did not believe him?" Narbrooi asked, a slightly ominous undertone to his voice as he leaned back in his chair and crossed his arms. "I would think such a report would be taken very seriously, especially an attempt on two people so critical to one of our concurrent crises."

"It's not that I didn't believe him, Hahtra'tzrhi, but you must understand, he and Crewman Tasende are well known practical jokers—"

Narbrooi's eyes narrowed to slits. "I fail to see any humor in such a matter."

"Neither do I, I'm just saying I wasn't entirely convinced this wasn't their idea of a prank. Nevertheless, I confined them to the Kanaloa Medical Complex and the *Baidarka* of course, until I could get to the bottom of the matter, said I would start making inquiries, but before I could, I was contacted by HQ—"

"And the abduction of our soldiers became paramount," Narbrooi finished for him, and to Izraad he didn't sound particularly pleased with Aquila's decision, not that the man had much choice in the matter.

"Doctor Amalfitano and Crewman Tasende were shaken up but unharmed, Hahtra'tzrhi," Aquila said almost defensively, "and safe back aboard *Baidarka*. I had every intention of following up on it—"

"It never occurred to you that the two incidents might be linked?" Narbrooi replied.

"Yes, it did," Aquila replied as he again glanced at Izraad, Narbrooi's gaze following. "Again, I felt the matter of the abductions took priority."

"While I appreciate your concern for the abducted, Commander, far more lives are at risk if vaccines are not developed and developed quickly. Any delay, such as say, the deaths of the two primary researchers, could, and most likely would, result in the deaths of thousands, even more if it caused either side to rethink this alliance."

"I fully understand that, Hahtra'tzrhi," Aquila replied irritably.

"Good," he said, point made.

"Hahtra'tzrhi," Izraad began, "may I ask how you knew about the attempt on Amalfitano and Tasende?"

It was Pakanga who answered: "I informed him, Lieutenant. The owner of the establishment your doctor and crewman were visiting and where this truly unfortunate incident took place is a close friend. He personally greets all patrons of his establishment, and was so pleased they'd taken me up on my recommendation he'd given them the best seats in the house. When the attempt took place, well, as you can imagine, everyone panicked—a blaster discharging in a respectable club? Nothing like that had ever happened before, and he suspected who the intended targets were and immediately notified me. I in turn notified Hahtra'tzrhi."

"But *not* me, even though the targets are members of my crew?" Aquila asked, finding reason to be angry after being put on the defensive by Narbrooi's pointed questions.

"I asked him not to," Narbrooi said before Pakanga could even open his mouth to reply.

"May I ask why?" Aquila measured his tone as he crossed his own arms.

"I felt it would be the prudent thing to do, to prevent the Thalamian's accomplices from realizing their confederate had been captured and making good their escape."

Aquila's expression went from indignant to genuinely confused. He glanced at Teague, then Izraad, then turned back to Narbrooi. "I... I don't understand—"

"Then permit me to fully explain," Narbrooi replied and at Aquila's uncertain nod, continued, "Within ten minutes of being notified by Councilor Pakanga of the incident, which had occurred slightly less than five minutes before, my troops located the Thalamian."

"That was fast," Aquila said. "Are you sure you have the right Thalamian?"

Narbrooi smiled, a cold smile. "When my troops are put on a task, Commander, it never takes long. And yes, there's absolutely *no* doubt they apprehended the right Thalamian."

"So they apprehended this Thalamian," Aquila said, clearly trying to ignore the underlying menace in Narbrooi's voice.

"And it admitted to being hired to murder Doctor Amalfitano and Crewman Tasende," Narbrooi replied.

"Hired?" Aquila asked. "By whom?"

"By a radial colonial faction, which goes by the name of... the Raumalle Revengers?"

"*Mladić...*" Aquila whispered.

"Indeed," Narbrooi replied a slight dip of his head. "Your late Captain Mladić's name did crop up several times during the interrogation—as did Senator..."

"Behardien?" Aquila finished for him,

"Yes." Narbrooi smiled, a slow, drawing back of the lips, before continuing, "Along with the names of two other

Rimmers who were actively involved in the plot: one Jonathan Urbat—"

"Urbat?" Izraad's eyes widened.

"Ah," he said, clearly pleased by her response. "I see you've heard of him, Lieutenant."

"Yes, he was one of Mladić's henchmen, was aboard the *Walafar* as far as the crew roster was concerned. Intelligence reasonably believed he'd been aboard and killed—"

"Regrettably not," Narbrooi interrupted. "A human accompanied the Thalamian to the nightclub and acted as lookout. This human was, according to the Thalamian, none other than this Jonathan Urbat."

"And the other?" Aquila asked with audible apprehension, sensing bad news, really, *really* bad news.

"Ensign Tace Pardix."

"What?" Aquila gasped. "But... but he's—"

"Chief navigator aboard your vessel?"

Aquila managed a stunned nod.

"He's also a member of this extremist group—a 'bona fide, slavering, crazy-assed, xenophobic zealot', according to the Thalamian." Narbrooi paused and, cocking his head to one side, added, "Wasn't Doctor Amalfitano's entire family killed during the Battle of Raumalle?"

Izraad squinted at him. *You damn well know they were.* "Hahtra'tzrhi, if you're suggesting Doctor Amalfitano is in any way connected with this group, let me assure you—"

"I'm not... *suggesting* anything, Lieutenant," he interrupted, his pale eyes sparkling maliciously. "A'tuu'shahn'i rarely 'suggest'. We find little use for such time-wasting niceties." Point made, he continued, "Doctor Amalfitano's motives are *beyond* reproach. I was only mentioning an interesting... coincidence."

Like hell you were.

Narbrooi replied to her unspoken response with an impervious grin, then: "According to the Thalamian, it was Ensign Pardix who notified the Thalamian and Urbat exactly where to find Doctor Amalfitano and Crewman Tasende—you see, the good doctor actually invited your navigator to accompany them to Councilor Pakanga's friend's establishment. Ensign Pardix, realizing this was just the situation he and his coconspirators had been waiting for, said he'd catch up with them as soon as he got off duty and asked where they'd be. The Thalamian said it had no trouble at all finding them, all thanks to the doctor's most excellent directions."

Izraad couldn't help but shake her head.

"Hahtra'tzrhi," Aquila began, "with all due respect, the Thalamian is mistaken. Ensign Pardix is a highly valued and trusted member of my command crew, he—"

"You Rimmers have an expression, 'a picture is worth a thousand words'?" Narbrooi withdrew a small data disc from a hidden pocket behind his bandoleer and handed it to Pakanga, who unhappily slipped it into a nearby viewer's slot and tapped the activator. Narbrooi smiled at the three Coalition officers, then settled back in his chair and turned his full attention on the interrogation vid as it began to play across the viewers.

Seitakap shifted uneasily, not wanting to watch, but also not wanting to offend his Hahtooshan guest; the aged Pakanga clearly didn't care how Narbrooi might take his reaction and kept his pinched gaze fixed on the far wall, not that that muffled the appalling sounds of the interrogation from his ears.

Narbrooi had viewed the vid several times, had, in fact, been present during the interrogation of the Thalamian and politely ignored the Tulians' less than appreciative response to A'tuu'shahn techniques at extracting information from unwilling prisoners.

Out of the corner of her eye, Izraad caught Aquila's wince and Teague's distressed stare. She remained superficially unfazed by what she was watching and hearing, keenly aware that Narbrooi was favoring her with a covert, appraising look of his own, clearly waiting for some sign of squeamishness on her part. Instead she met his stare.

He dropped his gaze to his hands and she sensed his startled thoughts: *Definitely not one to underestimate.* She almost grinned, pleased at *his* unexpected discomfort. *Damned right I'm not.*

He abruptly rose, briefly drawing everyone's uneasy gaze, gave his medallion-encrusted bandoleer an annoyed tug, then strode over to the large, floor to ceiling window that gave the lofty conference room an unparalleled view of the island citadel of Alhajoth. Beyond, the bloated orange disc of Tangaloa was riding low in the early morning sky and a thick, coppery fog still blanketed the lower city.

The rich ocher light washed over his copper-colored duty uniform, turning it a disturbingly blood-red shade—the hauberk's constantly morphing texture flickering like the embers of hell—and Izraad, well aware of the ghillie suit's chameleon-like qualities, wondered if it was a deliberate act of visual intimidation on his part, or just lucky happenstance. Finding herself intensely intrigued by the man himself and curious as to what beyond the window had drawn his undivided attention, she left the vid images to the others and followed his gaze. She could always request a transcript... later. She had no doubt HQ had already received one.

As Narbrooi's pale eyes took in Alhajoth's tall, whorled spires and the interconnecting delicate latticework of suspension bridges, she eavesdropped on his surprisingly unguarded thoughts to find that part of his mind was calculating targeting vectors.

Then she realized what he was really doing: he was trying to solidify the problem at hand, get his mind around it so he could then blast it and all the lingering doubts, the thorny questions about this very uncomfortable alliance to hell.

You've spent too much time in space, my friend, too much time fighting—not all problems are so easily or spectacularly solved.

As if sensing *her* thoughts, he took a deep breath, exhaled slowly then coaxed his mind into seeing the city's spectacular skyline for the visual marvel that it was, festooned with all manner of architectural witches' hats.

Using his distraction to her advantage, Izraad studied him through the lens of his very sketchy Intelligence bio, gathered not through Coalition assets because when it came to Hahtooshans there were none, but through even more sketchy exchanges with far distant alien contacts. Narbrooi, she'd learned, was barely forty, yet had already attained the rank of Hahtra'tzrhi—Fleet Admiral—an astounding accomplishment even among Hahtooshans, and evidence enough of his ruthlessness, matched only by his brilliance and unshakable self-confidence.

He brought with him a record of one military triumph after another against far-flung alien star systems whose fates were of absolutely no concern of the Coalition. As far as Intelligence could determine, he had never fought for—or, more importantly, *against*—the Coalition, and therefore he'd aroused little interest and only among those who'd spent their closeted lives gleaning what little they could about Hahtooshans, pinning their "expert" reputations on what was little better than gossip based on disparate, often very dodgy and heavily biased sources.

Yet behind the façade of entrenched arrogance, Izraad detected something rueful about the mercenary officer and that prompted loose a memory of something Aquila had said, shortly after their first prolonged interaction with the *Faridour*'s laconic captain, during their welcoming dinner to Tuli: "Somewhere in the back of that mind of his, there's gotta be a pretty complete autopsy."

She nodded to herself. *Definitely 'a man of twists and turns', a sociopath befitting a Greek tragedy or Homeric poem.*

Before she could ponder the man, or matter further, the vid ended and the screens darkened.

Aquila and Teague shifted in their chairs, then, like Izraad, turned their full attention on Narbrooi, any doubts as to Pardix's complicity, or the efficiency of Hahtooshan interrogation techniques having completely evaporated. It had taken them less than three minutes to extract from the surprisingly truculent and defiant Thalamian exactly what they wanted and with shockingly precise detail, and Izraad made a mental note to never, ever find herself in a similar position.

Narbrooi, his pale eyes still fixed on the kaleidoscopic view, hands clasped behind his back with thumbs encircling his thick, metal-studded plait, began speaking quietly, almost as if he was speaking to himself, in the process causing the others to lean forward in their chairs so as to not miss what he said: "The Thalamian was clearly nothing more than a hired thug—picked, I strongly believe, because few would suspect a Thalamian of being a paid assassin and reasonably so, although its appearance did cause some consternation in the saloon—a Thalamian in a bar?

"And your friend, Councilor Pakanga, with his habit of personally greeting all patrons, was able to provide a very accurate description to my troops, which aided tremendously in its quick apprehension. Doctor Amalfitano's actions also greatly aided us locating it so quickly..."

"Doctor Amalfitano actions?" Izraad asked. "What—"

"He didn't inform you that he threw his beverage in its eyes?"

Izraad couldn't help it; despite the gravity of the matter, she chuckled. "Yes, he did. But—"

"According to an employee who was a witness to the attempted assassination, when the doctor noticed the Thalamian was pointing a blaster at him, he threw the contents of his glass at it, which, I gather, was an exceedingly potent mixture of alcohol. The temporarily blinded Thalamian, now in agony, reacted by squeezing the trigger—fortunately, it missed the doctor and Crewman Tasende, in fact no one was hit, but the result was complete panic among the saloon's patrons. How the Thalamian managed to escape from the establishment is a matter of conjecture, possibly it was just carried along in the rush of people fleeing, but it didn't get far. My troops found it in an alley nearby, huddled between two garbage bins and moaning, and knew they had the right Thalamian when they smelled alcohol on it."

"That would certainly make for an unshakable positive ID," Izraad agreed, envisioning the Thalamian, thinking its miseries, while extremely painful, were limited to alcohol-scalded eyes, only to find itself surrounded by a Hahtooshan security detail and realizing with dead certainty that things were about to get a hell of a lot worse.

Narbrooi continued, "I doubt those who paid for its services ever considered the assassination taking place in a saloon, but it was a golden opportunity—both Doctor Amalfitano and Crewman Tasende and without a security escort and in a darkened bar where the Thalamian could, presumably, slip in unnoticed?—one they couldn't pass up, no matter the risk to the Thalamian itself, something I greatly doubt was of much concern to its employers. It's very likely they planned on eliminating it once it had done what it had been paid to do— fortunately we got to it first. Fortunate for us, that is, not the Thalamian.

"I have no doubt it told us what little it knew... before it regrettably expired." He released the hold he had on his plait and shook his head in feigned regret, the motion spilling down the length of his metal-clad braid, the pride and trademark of all Elkanaghallis, which in his case fell to the cuffs of his knee-high campaign boots. *"Such delicate creatures..."* He paused then added in a slightly louder, harder voice, "Regrettably, we've yet to apprehend its human accomplices and until we do, Doctor Amalfitano and Crewman Tasende remain a target."

At Izraad's sidelong stare, Aquila pulled his tac-pac from his pocket. *"Baidarka, this is Aquila."*

Stoker's familiar voice replied, "Baidarka *here—"*

"Mister Stoker, locate Ensign Pardix."

"Yessir. " There was a pause, long enough for Aquila to start to fidget anew, before Stoker's disembodied voice replied, *"Ensign Pardix is not aboard, sir. According to the flick-down log, he switched shore leaves with Crewman Mara and flicked down to the planet six and a half Standard hours ago. "*

Izraad met Narbrooi's pointed, over-the-shoulder stare.

"Shortly *after* we captured the Thalamian," Narbrooi confirmed an instant before Stoker continued, *"And sir, I can't explain it, but he clearly jumped the gun a bit, flicking down fifteen minutes before the allotted shore leave began. "*

Oh, I can explain it. Damned straight I can. Aloud Aquila asked, "What were his flick-down coordinates?"

There was another brief pause before Stoker replied, *"A public flicker chamber in a northern suburb of Alhajoth, sir, not far from Sharra... um—"*

"Sharran-Su'a," Pakanga finished for him. "Alhajoth's space port."

"Ah... yessir," came Stoker's uncertain reply.

"I need to speak with him, immediately, Ensign."

"That'll be a problem, sir. I'm looking at the shore leave logs and Ensign Pardix didn't take a tac-pac with him. "

Aquila and Izraad exchanged glances—the seemingly innocent oversight, on top of the unauthorized shore leave departure, lending credence to the man's complicity—as Aquila asked, "How long was this shore leave rotation?"

"The standard eight hours, sir—"

"Notify Security to detain Ensign Pardix the moment he flicks aboard. Aquila out." He slipped the tac-pac into his pocket and met Narbrooi's annoyingly smug, 'I told you so' stare.

"Now you understand my precautions, including not notifying you—"

"You thought I would have tipped off Ensign Pardix?" Aquila replied, indignant.

"Not intentionally, no, Commander, but, as you just admitted a few moments ago, he is, or, should I say *was* a trusted member of your command crew. Besides, I felt I was providing you with... what do they call it? Plausible deniability? Yes..." He nodded. "...plausible deniability if the situation turned against us, or if something... *untoward* happened to your ensign." He paused, but Aquila looked far from mollified. So with an indifferent shrug he continued, "I've forwarded the interrogation vid to your Headquarters, and have given Admiral Keon my personal assurance that once we apprehend Ensign Pardix and Mister Urbat—and it's only a matter of time before we do—they will be handed over, eventually."

"Alive," Aquila replied coldly.

Narbrooi smiled sweetly. "Of course, Commander."

Pakanga cleared his throat then said, "As long as Doctor Amalfitano and Crewman Tasende remain within the Kanaloa Medical Complex, or aboard the *Baidarka*, as you've now ordered, Commander, they should be safe—"

"Should?" Narbrooi interrupted as he looked sharply first at Pakanga and then Aquila. "Commander, can you personally guarantee that no other members of your crew share Ensign Pardix's extremist views?"

Aquila shook his head. "No, I can't, Hahtra'tzrhi—in fact I'm sure a goodly number do. I just never thought any would take them this far. Doctor Amalfitano and Crewman Tasende are well-liked, highly respected members of my crew."

"So, undoubtedly, is your Ensign Pardix."

Aquila had no quick answer to that.

Narbrooi turned back to the window, blew out his cheeks as he gave the sparkling city one last look, then he stalked back to the table. "I would prefer they be housed and work aboard *Faridour*, where I *know* they'd be completely secure, but…" he waved off the protest that had formed on Seitakap's lips as he resumed his seat, then continued, "I presume both the doctor and Crewman Tasende would be more at ease, and therefore more productive, working here on Tuli and sleeping in their own quarters aboard your vessel, than aboard mine—*but* they will be under *my* protection, at *all* times."

Aquila reluctantly nodded, not happy with what he might be agreeing to, even less happy that he really had no choice in the matter.

"I am also given to understand that your ship has sustained a fair amount of damage, damage caused by our vessels and the Matarii?"

Aquila nodded again and even more reluctantly, not sure where Narbrooi was headed with this unexpected line of questioning.

"I offer you the use of my space dock, which is currently in orbit, along with its repair crews—all free of charge, call it a demonstration of continued good will on our part, despite recent, extremely unfortunate events. I think you'll find my crews every bit as skilled and efficient as those at Mirfak, likely far more so. I've already cleared this with Admiral Keon, who was most delighted, if genuinely taken aback by the offer—I think he expected me to be so angry at the news of the botched rescue and the subsequent abductions that I'd retaliate by blowing your vessel out of the sky..." He grinned, a genuinely pleased, if smirking grin at Aquila's startled blink. "...but fortunately I'm not prone to such displays of... what do you Rimmers call it, 'pique'? Yes." He nodded. "Pique. I'm sure you will want to verify this before you permit us to effect repairs, yes?"

"Yes... but thank you," Aquila replied unsteadily, then narrowing his gaze, asked, "But... may I ask what you meant by *botched* rescue?"

"The admiral did not tell you?"

"I didn't speak directly with him, but rather his aide—"

"Lieutenant Matho," Narbrooi interrupted with a curled lip. "A very self-important woman is your Lieutenant Matho, who, I sense, is not particularly fond of A'tuu'shahn'i in general..."

Izraad could almost read Aquila's thoughts: *You don't know the half of it.*

"...and me in particular," Narbrooi added.

You can make a safe bet on that, Izraad added to herself.

"Lieutenant Matho made it clear to me and to Lieutenant Izraad that the rescue didn't go to plan," Aquila answered, "that a marine was killed, five others critically wounded—"

"They were extremely fortunate they didn't suffer more casualties," Narbrooi grumbled, then eyed Aquila. "The rescue party completely disregarded Khusaaq Sha'ashahn's instructions, despite Admiral Keon's assurances to me, *personally* and to Sha'ashahn as well that they would follow them exactly.

"Instead they encircled and surprised the five, then started shooting. The A'tuu'shahn'i, reasonably believing they were under attack, fired back. Your peoples' weapons, luckily, were only set on heavy stun. Our maser pistols have no such setting, as I'm sure you are aware, and the marooned party returned fire with every intention to shoot to kill. As I informed Admiral Keon, I am not about to offer up an apology or compensation for the death or the injuries incurred—the fault rests with the rescue party's commanding officer. It is he who owes me an apology, owes Sha'ashahn and the Orthodoxy an apology, not that I expect it will be forthcoming."

"I honestly didn't know, Hahtra'tzrhi," Aquila said, exhaled, muttered, *"Dammit,"* and shook his head. "And I really am sorry—"

"Thank you, Commander. I believe *your* sincerity."

But not Keon's is what you mean, Izraad thought.

"Do you have any idea the condition of the Hahtooshans?" Aquila asked. "I mean before they were regrettably turned over to the people claiming to be Hahtooshans? Lieutenant Matho didn't say."

"All, per the captain of the *Briseis,* were recovered alive, suffering from advanced radiation poisoning, but their medical staff had not had a chance to fully examine them, much less start treatment, despite them being aboard for almost two days, giving their own injured priority, when the *Huui'teh* appeared and demanded they be turned over."

Aquila exhaled, rubbed his forehead. *"Dammit."*

"You should be aware, Commander," Narbrooi added, "that I have lodged an official complaint against the captain of the *Briseis,* demanding he be turned over to us for suitable punishment, or, barring that, to be court marshaled for gross dereliction of duty under your Coalition Expeditionary Forces uniform code of conduct, title five, and knowingly negligent behavior under article three-B."

Aquila raised his brows.

"According to his own report that was given to us," Narbrooi continued, "a heavily *redacted* account I might add, Captain Pelenor intentionally disobeyed orders, felt following Sha'ashahn's instructions would take too much time, and with the Rasal Ghul binary undergoing a very active phase, this would put his ship and crew at undue risk—and since their safekeeping is his primary responsibility, he took it upon himself to retrieve our people in a way he saw fit, thinking he knew, as he stated, 'how best to handle a bunch of half-dead yowies,' with no concern for their welfare, or, as it unfortunately turned out, the welfare of his own crew."

"I fully understand."

"I have also demanded uncensored copies of all reports associated with this matter, including those of the *Briseis'* second in command and her medical officer be turned over, as I believe such will prove that both were complicit in the charge of gross dereliction of duty as the second in command led the landing party and the medical officer deliberately withheld medical care.

"I have no illusions about the chances of the captain or the documents being handed over, or, if history is any guide, my grievances coming to anything substantive within your Coalition, but…" he shrugged, "…you never know, and it will certainly put this Captain Pelenor, not to mention his two officers on notice they now have genuine, personal reasons for fearing A'tuu'shahn'i and with us now allies, he and they are at far greater risk of… *accidentally* running into one of us."

Izraad couldn't help it; an image immediately came to mind of the luckless Thalamian.

"As for *Huui'teh…*" Narbrooi propped his elbows on the table and steepled his armored hands, then pressed his metal-clad fingers against his lips, his unblinking, steely-eyed gaze never wavering from Aquila's.

After a moment of mutual scrutiny, he leaned back in his chair, crossed his arms and continued, "Your intelligence service is correct—there is, currently, no vessel in our fleet by that name. The vessel is in fact, and based on sensor readings from the *Briseis*, none other than the *Palraiyuk*—the survey ship I mentioned to you that went missing a little over a Standard year ago?"

Aquila nodded. "While mapping a planetary system in the Dubhe arm. So, missing no longer."

"Exactly. However there *was*, at one time, an A'tuu'shahn ship named *Huui'teh*. Perhaps you remember, if not its name, then the events that spelled its doom—it was the Orthodoxy vessel dispatched to protect your illegal colony of Cotopaxi and subsequently destroyed by the Matarii when its commanding officer refused to abandon the Rimmer... *squatters."*

Cotopaxi. The name lingered like a very bad taste in everyone's mouths. The ill-fated settlement refused to die, despite the best efforts of the Matarran Star Empire. It no longer existed—hadn't existed for well over a decade, the seedling colony and its once fertile host planet had been left a radioactive desert—but it steadfastly refused to be relegated to a historical footnote.

And by Narbrooi's unexpectedly bitter, wholly unguarded reaction that hit Izraad like a fist to the stomach, it clearly haunted his life as it haunted Khusaaq's—now Cotopaxi's sole survivor. And with Matarrans again saber-rattling along the border with Coalition space, the ghosts of Cotopaxi had returned full force, demanding their long overdue revenge.

Narbrooi took a deep breath then whispered, *"They made a wasteland and called it peace..."*

"Tacitus," Teague said, almost reflexively and speaking for the first time. The man prided himself on his vast knowledge of ancient historians and philosophers and found it impossible not to miss a chance at demonstrating that familiarity—*but to a Hahtooshan admiral?* Izraad thought to herself with a wry, private smile.

Narbrooi flicked him an arched, sidelong look, as if he really hadn't expected to be overheard—or, Izraad corrected, didn't expect anyone to acknowledge it, briefly forgetting he wasn't among his own officers who would have likely known better. Then to Teague's obvious relief, Narbrooi replied with a slight, acknowledging nod. "I find a deep and strangely abiding camaraderie in the words of your ancient historians, Lieutenant, as well as your ancient philosophers and generals. I have devoted a good deal of my life studying them, analyzing their writings, their tactics. They saw their world much as we see ours—where very complicated truths have been winnowed it down to their purest essence, devoid of all the..." he waved his hand about, "the superficial and superfluous *sensitivities."*

"Not all problems are black and white," Izraad replied, drawing Narbrooi's gaze.

"I've yet to come across one that, once fully... *dissected*, isn't, Lieutenant," he answered irritably, then turned his full attention back on Aquila and continued in an ominous voice, "Whoever did this clearly knows A'tuu'shahn history and understands our psyches—Cotopaxi and its aftermath remain a festering wound to us, Commander. Many within the Orthodoxy had hoped that this alliance between your Coalition and the Orthodoxy would be a step towards an eventual healing. Whoever did this knew *exactly* what they were doing."

"Indeed," Aquila replied simply.

Narbrooi again studied him with his piercing eyes—again just long enough to make Aquila visibly uncomfortable—the admiral's expression an uneasy pact between unadulterated menace and unfathomable melancholy. "One must learn to... *embrace* one's enemies, Commander, or so the Uzun'i tell us in their most ancient and revered text, the *Maak-Ahaggar*, because enemies can change *if* you don't undercut their sense of possibility.

"In my experience embraced enemies are far more likely to take the opportunity to slip a knife between your ribs than impress with their whole-hearted willingness to change, but..." he shrugged. "I am always open to the chance, as miniscule as it may be, that I am wrong when judging another's motives.

"I would therefore be the last to suggest that our alliance was welcomed with open arms by all A'tuu'shahn'i," Narbrooi continued. "Far from it—many would have far preferred an armistice over an alliance—even I have my grave doubts as to the merits, the sustainability of this... *pact* between our two peoples, and this was not at all helped by the attempted assassination of your doctor and crewman, the chosen method of the rescue or the unfortunate hand-over of our people, but in truth we A'tuu'shahn'i are weary of playing a supporting role in human history, and far be it for *us* to trump *your* sense of possibility." He lightly touched the grip of his ritual dagger then fixed his gaze, his full attention on the jewel-toned panorama beyond the floor-to-ceiling windows.

Aquila, Izraad and Teague glanced at each other, unsure if this meant the meeting was over, but then Narbrooi started speaking again:

"We find ourselves in a truly unique time and situation—where the vanquished and long-forgotten have a chance at a voice equal to the victors when it comes to writing what up until to now has been a *very* one-sided account of our shared history, and while we A'tuu'shahn'i would have far preferred to choose the time and place to reveal our true identity rather than have it forced upon us, since it is now out in the open we've decided that it is not in our continued best interest to be little more than a curious footnote, relegated to the shadows, marginalized and effectively silenced like our distant ancestors..." He exhaled forcefully, shook his head while everyone waited uneasily for him to finish.

It didn't help Izraad's unease that Narbrooi also left unsaid *exactly* what role he and the Orthodoxy wanted to play.

"Let me assure you, Commander," he added, "that we do not tolerate vigilantism, or sedition for that matter. It's... bad for *business*, which suggests this act was not one committed by A'tuu'shahn'i." He smiled coldly as he caught the slight tightening of the corners of Aquila's mouth. "Tarqk Nahru'tzhri was known for his... shall we say... *unorthodox* command style, but the wholly reckless actions he took, and which you were, regrettably, forced to deal with were entirely due to the effects of the virus, as you well know. We are not by nature a lawless society, Commander, quite the contrary. So do not judge all A'tuu'shahn'i by his example—or for that matter, by Khusaaq Sha'ashahn's, who is, by any standard," he paused, then added with audible disgust, "*an aberration.*"

Aquila squinted at him. "Pity."

Narbrooi arched a brow. "For your Coalition, or for my Orthodoxy? Despite the Q'shaathrah's judgment to accept Sha'ashahn's explanation for his actions concerning the virus, with many religious scholars even going so far as to suggest this is the *paas'nah* expressing itself in the purest form..."

Izraad and Aquila briefly exchanged quizzical glances before Narbrooi continued,

"...to many he's a traitor nevertheless, not just to the Orthodoxy, but also, and perhaps even more importantly, to memory of those who were lost at Cotopaxi—*the true heroes of Cotopaxi,*" he said with startling fierceness and again rose abruptly, this time clearly signaling that the hastily convened meeting was over.

The others quickly followed suit as Narbrooi continued in the same tone: "Warn your crew to be extremely cautious while on shore leave, Commander. While I believe the doctor and Crewman Tasende were the singular targets, there is always the risk of others being taken to be used as hostages." He again fingered his ritual dagger as his eyes cut to Izraad, then he fixed his stare on Aquila. "At the Tulian High Council's *request*, I'm sending an additional fifteen thousand troops to the surface, and will provide added protection to the Kanaloa Medical Complex and its surrounds, as well as for your doctor and crewman. But this is a very large planet and we cannot be everywhere." He turned to Seitakap. "If you will excuse me, Mister President?"

The Tulian president barely had time to nod before Narbrooi strode from the conference room.

Chapter 7

Doctor Amalfitano's private quarters aboard the Baidarka.
0830, ship time. Present day.

"Will...?"

Amalfitano opened one gritty eye a crack and slowly turned it towards the familiar voice.

Aquila stood in the doorway of the darkened cabin, his unmistakable stocky frame silhouetted against the glare of the outer office lights. Behind him stood Teague and Izraad.

"Will, we need to talk to you."

"Whatever you have to say can wait," he grumbled then rolled onto his side, away from the door, the painful brightness of the overheads *and* Aquila and drew his blanket over his head.

"No, it can't."

Cazzo! He tossed the blanket aside, eased himself onto his back and smacked the over-bed light switch with his fist then squinted up at his unexpected and unwanted company as the three officers filed into his small cabin. By their expressions, they were clearly surprised to find he'd slept in his civvies.

He sat up, dropped his feet to the floor, then running his hands through his disheveled gray hair, said, "Okay, what's so damned important it can't wait?"

"You might want to stay where you are," Izraad said, placing her hand on his shoulder.

Amalfitano scowled up at her and twitched off her hold.

"Will," Aquila said, "remember your Thalamian?"

He fixed Aquila with an icy, albeit red-tinged glare. "If you woke me up just to tell me you didn't like my 'joke', you can damned well leave. I got your message loud and clear."

Aquila sighed, "Will..."

"What?" he growled as he began punching his sleep-flattened pillow back into a slightly more fluffy state.

"Will, what I'm trying to tell you is that we located your Thalamian."

"What...?"

"We—well, actually Narbrooi's troops—found your Thalamian."

"What?"

"William," Izraad said, drawing his stunned stare, "the Thalamian you saw really existed—"

"But it's not *really* a Thalamian, right?" he asked, sensing that the other shoe was about to drop, that perhaps this was Aquila's way of getting him back for the prank he thought the doctor had pulled on him.

"Oh, it was a Thalamian all right,' Aquila answered. "Hahtooshans are *very* thorough in making sure of things like that."

"Oookay," he replied slowly, sensing Aquila was holding something back—something critical. "So, the Hahtooshans locate 'my' Thalamian, in a bar, presumably, and find out it really is a Thalamian, but they also find out it has a perfect reason for being there, right? Just like it had a perfect reason for being in that strip club. And this Thalamian denies trying to kill me and Xosé, *right?"* He lurched to his feet.

"Sit down, Will," Aquila said, his smile vanishing.

He continued to stand, glaring balefully down at the shorter Aquila.

"That's an order, Doctor."

Amalfitano huffed, but at Izraad's pointed cough, resumed his seat.

"Will you *please* just listen?"

He continued to glare up at Aquila as he crossed his arms.

"Will, the Thalamian really was a Thalamian—"

"You already told me that," he snapped peevishly.

"And I thought you were going to hear me out."

"Okay, okay. So sorry I interrupted you, Commander. Please *do* go on."

"Will, the Thalamian didn't have a 'perfect' reason to be in that strip club, in fact it didn't even have a good reason to be there—in fact it shouldn't have been on Tuli, period."

Still too involved in his anger, Amalfitano did not instantly grasp the significance of what Aquila had just said. Then he blinked, and looked back at him, all traces of his anger gone. "What did you just say?"

"The Thalamian had no authorization papers, no transit permits, not even a Thalamian passport. *Nothing.*"

Amalfitano blinked again.

"What the commander's trying to tell you, Doctor," Teague said, deadpan, "is that the Thalamian was an illegal alien."

He stared up at Teague for a moment in open-mouthed disbelief. Suddenly he began to chuckle then laugh. "You know... Edwin... you... you missed... your calling," he spluttered. "You... you should... have been... someone's straight man." He looked up at Aquila, then back at Teague. "Oh, wait... I guess you already are," he added, then surrendered to another spasm of laughter as Teague narrowed his blue eyes, suspecting that Amalfitano was laughing at him, rather than at what he'd said.

Finally realizing that no one else was laughing, in fact quite the contrary, he wiped his eyes and cleared his throat. "You know, you really got me, Robert. A great set-up and an even better follow through. And I never thought Edwin could carry off a punch line like that. Shows there's hope for you yet, Edwin."

"*Will...*"

"Robert, I have to hand it to you. You managed to pull me in with that joke, hook, line and stinker—oh, sorry, Edwin, I really meant *sinker*."

"*...we're not joking,*" Aquila replied quietly.

"What? What do you mean *not* joking? Come on, enough! You got me, but I'll tell you right now, I think you were using an unfair tactic. Yeah," he nodded, "using Edwin was definitely unfair."

"William," Izraad began, "Robert's not joking, Edwin's not joking. And the Thalamian definitely *wasn't* joking. It was a hired assassin, sent to kill you and Tasende."

Amalfitano's smile froze on his lips then evaporated completely. He looked up at Aquila, then Teague and finally Izraad. "But... but *why?* I mean why us? You couldn't meet two more lovable people than Xosé and me."

"Aside from your 'lovable' personalities," Izraad replied, "you're also the lead researchers on human viral threats to Hahtooshans."

"And someone wanted to murder us for that?"

Izraad crossed her arms. "You find that surprising?"

"Uh, well, no, but on Tuli? I—"

"Only you two have *exclusive* access to *and* the unconditional assistance of the Hahtooshans," she interrupted. "If the Thalamian had succeeded in murdering you, whoever hired it would've killed two birds with one stone, so to speak, by not only slowing research on Hahtooshan-specific vaccines, but sowing serious misgivings about this whole Coalition-Orthodoxy alliance—on both sides."

He fixed his startled gaze on his knees. *"Minchione…"*

"William," Izraad continued as she sat beside him, "by your unusual, yet very effective diversion, you managed to save your lives." She forced a smile as she took one of his hands in hers and gave it a comforting squeeze.

"Diversion…?"

"You don't remember throwing your drink in its eyes?"

"Oh." Amalfitano blinked. "That diversion."

"That's how the Hahtooshans made a positive ID," she added. "A Thalamian who reeked of alcohol? Plus, they found it not far from the bar, nursing its blinded eyes."

He looked up at Aquila. "But now the Hahtooshans have the Thalamian—"

"Had."

"Had…? You… *you mean they let it go?"*

"Not exactly."

"Exactly what?"

"It… well, it didn't respond well to questioning."

Amalfitano scowled at him, then suddenly his eyes widened. "You mean—"

"Yes."

"Oh."

"But it had two human accomplices and so far the Hahtooshans have yet to locate—"

"Human accomplices…?"

"One was one of Mladić's people," Izraad replied, "who unfortunately for you was on Tuli, and not aboard the *Walafar* when she was destroyed."

Amalfitano felt a cold knot form in his belly. "And the other?"

"Tace," Izraad replied softly.

Amalfitano turned back to Aquila, swallowed convulsively then repeated unsteadily, "Tace... *Pardix...?"*

Aquila nodded.

"But... *no,"* he shook his head vehemently. "I don't believe it!"

"I didn't either, at first," Aquila replied. "Despite the Thalamian directly implicating him, but as of fifteen, or, should I say *thirty* minutes ago, our *almost* always punctual Ensign Pardix is officially AWOL."

Amalfitano looked away and shook his head in disbelief. It had only been a few weeks since the Matarran ambush, an ambush that had left the navigator with life-threatening injuries. Had it not been for Drakin's quick thinking and his own surgical skills, the ensign would have bled to death. *"Tace... of all people—"* He jerked his head up. "We—meaning Xosé and me—passed him in the corridor as we were on our way to the flicker chamber. I... I invited him to join us!" Amalfitano bit his lip then added huskily, "He said he'd switch shore leave rotations and catch us up... *gods*—I left precise directions as to where to find us!"

Aquila nodded then said, "He switched rotation all right, as soon as he heard his Thalamian friend had been grabbed by the Hahtooshans—and bugged out fifteen minutes early to boot. Turns out, our Ensign Pardix is a member of a radical colonial group called the Raumalle Revengers."

Amalfitano's eyes widened. "Raumalle..."

"Revengers. Ironic, yes?"

He fixed his stunned gaze on his hands and managed, "I've heard of them of course, but I never—"

"Problem is," Izraad interrupted, "like Ensign Pardix, at least half the crew harbor personal grudges against the Hahtooshans."

Amalfitano nodded. Ensign Lesedi's feelings were well-known; and then there was Delatorre, Tanser, and—he realized the list went on... and on. He snorted softly and shook his head, then looked up at Aquila. "A coupla weeks ago I was at the top of the list of those wanting all Hahtooshans dead for what they did at Raumalle. Now, I'm at the top of someone's else's list for trying to *save* the very same Hahtooshans from bio-genocide." He shook his head again, exhaled slowly. *Cacchio.* "Now what?"

"Now we—and the Hahtooshans—keep you and Crewman Tasende under lock and key."

Amalfitano's preoccupied stare turned into a worried squint. "And what do you mean by that?"

Aquila motioned to the outer office. "See for yourself—well past high time you were up and at'em any way."

Amalfitano slowly got to his feet. He gave his sleep-rumpled and scuffed-up civvies a yank here, a tug there, ran his fingers through his disheveled hair, and then, with a shake of his head, walked out of his cabin, into the office—and with a startled flinch, stopped dead in his tracks.

Not two meters away stood six fully armored Hahtooshan troopers. He turned his startled gaze on Aquila. "You've... you've g-g-got to be joking!"

"Nope. And I seriously doubt if Narbrooi is, either."

Amalfitano looked back at the heavily armed soldiers as his age-old, reflexive fear of Hahtooshans returned with a vengeance.

Khusaaq was one Hahtooshan he'd come to think of as a close friend, and yes, despite the short time he had known him, the son he'd never had. Even the perpetually churlish Matoosh had earned his admiration for his dogged determination to walk again, if nothing else. But these troopers looked to be downright hostile, not to mention very uneasy. He couldn't help but notice two of them fingered their holstered maser pistols as they eyed Izraad and her Intelligence grays.

Except for helmets, all wore full battle kit, which included a mind-boggling array of other, even more menacing looking weaponry not to mention the armor's constantly morphing texture. Helmets instead were secured to their weapons belts, ready for quick retrieval. But since they were not fully encapsulated, at least he was spared the disquietingly glycerin distortion everyone associated with the mercenaries.

Lined up as they were, at rigid attention, they bore an uncanny resemblance to a firing squad. Amalfitano swallowed convulsively, then stammered, "But... but h-h-how are we supposed t-t-to work?" He had a fleeting image of accidentally backing into one of the twitchy troopers in the lab and igniting the very galactic war he was so desperately trying to avert. "They'll g-g-get in the way—"

"They're all combat medics, William," Izraad added with a sidelong look at the grim-faced soldiers who stood, shoulder to ghillie-armored shoulder, in Amalfitano's cramped office. "Narbrooi selected each of them personally, and you did agree to working closely with his medical staff—"

"And I have been!"

"By com-net," she replied. "The situation has changed—dramatically."

"Then have Delatorre assign some of his men!"

"Narbrooi insisted you be guarded by his people," Aquila said. "Under the current circumstances, as much as I hate to say this, I have to agree."

"No!" Amalfitano shook his head with as much offended temerity as he could muster with six yowies within easy grabbing distance. "This is overkill!"

"Be careful what you wish for," Izraad said under her breath, but just loud enough for him to overhear and shoot her an appalled look.

"Too bad," Aquila replied. With that, he turned on his heel and walked out of the office. Teague smiled thinly, then wasted no time in following him, clearly eager to place as much ground between himself and the obviously disgruntled mercenaries as possible.

Amalfitano stared after the two then looked fiercely at Izraad. She replied with a casual shrug and an innocent smile. He scowled at her, and with a shake of his head, turned to his unwanted bodyguards. He cleared his throat, ran his fingers through his hair. Tried to settle his nerves. *Bodyguards... my bodyguards. Good gods...*

The six stared back; their heavily, and almost identically tattooed faces now completely unreadable, and two, he suddenly realized, were women. Why that should have surprised him—the chief medical officer of the *Faridour* not to mention the flagship's second in command were women after all—but it did. Perhaps because neither looked like the ferine Suhjai, or the elegant but foreboding Tu'indai for that matter. These two were as tall and every bit as muscular as their male counterparts.

"Okay," he began with false bravado, "let's get one thing straight. You stay the hell out of my way, got it?"

"Of course, Doctor," one, the furthest to Amalfitano's left, replied in perfect trade-use Standard. "Unless, of course, your life or the life of Crewman Tasende is threatened, then *you* must do exactly as *we* say."

He gave the soldier's rank insignia a quick glance, then squinted at him and realized the mercenary looked vaguely, strangely familiar. "What's your name, uh… *Raz'ta'aq?*"

The Hahtooshan sergeant responded with typical Hahtooshan suspicion: "Why do you want to know?"

"You'd prefer I call you 'hey you'?" Out of the corner of his eye, Amalfitano noticed the quick exchange of uneasy glances among the other Hahtooshans and sensed he'd said something wrong—very wrong.

As if to confirm his suspicions, the burly medic growled, "That *would* be strongly inadvisable—"

"You're clearly in charge."

The Hahtooshan stared back at him, gray eyes narrowing to slits. *"Yes."*

Amalfitano exhaled forcefully, added, "Look, Raz'ta'aq, I don't like this any more than you do. But none of us have a choice, right?"

The soldier glanced at his fellows then conceded, "No."

Amalfitano rubbed his hands together, hoping he looked more confident than he felt. "All right, now we're getting somewhere." He looked briefly at Izraad before again fixing his even gaze on the Hahtooshan sergeant. "I'm William Amalfitano. You may call me Will, or William, whichever you prefer."

"No."

"No?"

"We will address you as Doctor."

"If *you* insist, fine. But *I* insist on knowing your name."

"Raz'ta'aq is sufficient."

"Which means, he," he pointed irritably to the soldier standing next to the sergeant and after a glance at his rank insignia, said, "is kon'ta'aq number one, then she's..." he pointed to the next in line, "kon'ta'aq number two... and so forth?"

"As you wish," the sergeant replied.

"I don't *wish*. I can't work with numbers. I want *names*—starting with yours." Amalfitano squinted at him, but when it became clear the Hahtooshan was perfectly willing to wait him out, he added, "Shall I ask Hahtra'tzrhi?" He started to reach for the desk-mounted com-unit's activator. "I'm sure it's at the tip of his tongue."

"Murh'sooli," the soldier growled, stopping Amalfitano's finger a hair's breadth from making contact with the toggle.

"See? How hard was that?"

What followed was silence. Not a happy silence. Not at all.

"Okay, ah… Murh'sooli, since we're stuck with each other, how about we make the best of the situation?"

Murh'sooli replied with the barest trace of a nod.

"Then let's get to work—planetside. Time's a wasting, as they say."

The troopers looked at each other, then back at Amalfitano.

"We had a late night, so Tasende's likely in need of a wake-up call." He motioned to the door while trying not to grin at the image of the man being rousted out of bed by the soldiers. Then again, he'd come to learn that Hahtooshans were, as a society, obsessively fastidious, so their reaction to the pathologist's notoriously less-than-pristine living conditions might, he realized with a private smile, *might* be even more entertaining. "His cabin's that way. Third door on your left after you leave sickbay. Green frame, cabin thirty-two E. It's clearly marked—can't miss it."

All but one of the other soldiers took the hint. Murh'sooli and an equally sullen-faced companion hesitated. "After you, doctor," Murh'sooli said and gestured to the doorway with an armored hand.

Amalfitano squinted at Izraad. "You *will* pay for this, you realize that."

"At least this way you'll be around to collect." She wiggled her eyebrows suggestively, to which he squinted in reply. "Sure you don't want to change first?" She glanced down at his clothing.

"Why the hell should I?" With that, he stalked after the troopers as Murh'sooli and the other soldier silently fell in behind him.

"Like I'm going to be assassinated in my own goddamned sickbay," Amalfitano grumbled. Yet in spite of his outward frustration and anger—and his deeply-held fear of Hahtooshans—he found himself strangely and secretly relieved. The incident in the strip club had shaken him. And added to that was the knowledge that people were *really* were out to kill him—and one of them was a well-respected crewmember.

But to entrust my life to a bunch of cheesed off Hahtooshans? He licked his lips. *I could use a stiff drink.*

Speaking of— He glanced back at the formidable Murh'sooli and wondered if the sergeant's orders could be tweaked just enough to include barhopping escort duty. The soldiers' company would certainly guarantee an uninterrupted evening, not to mention the best seat in the house, with or without the establishment owner's blessing. And none of the troopers, he realized, were sporting Elkanaghalli daggers or a long plait, which meant that they *weren't* Elkanaghalli and might actually appreciate the experience.

Not sure if the omission of Elkanaghallis had been intentional on Narbrooi's part, or just lucky happenstance, he decided to take advantage of the situation at the first opportunity. *Yes,* he smiled to himself, *this might not be so terrible after—*

A loud, *extremely* startled yelp stopped him in his tracks. Unprepared, Murh'sooli almost collided with him.

"Ah, I see they found Xosé's cabin." He looked back at the sergeant and grinned.

Chapter 8

Intersection of corridor ten-west and nineteen-north, administrative complex, Cotopaxi colony, eleven years ago. One hour after planetary nightfall.

"This is everyone?" Khusaaq asked, arms akimbo as he surveyed the unkempt and haggard-faced crowd of Rimmers standing nervously before him—one hundred and ninety three in total, about a quarter of them children of varying ages, the rest evenly divided between men and women. Some were quite elderly and didn't look up to the rigors of what lay ahead.

In truth none of them did—most had visible injuries and each, based on the bio-vitals his scanners fed to him, were every bit as exhausted as his troops. He'd also noted from the moment the colonists arrived at the appointed spot at the appointed time that while Delbruch was among them, Wu and three others who'd been witness to Viehl's summary execution were not.

He was mildly surprised that those present had followed his orders to the letter this time and were carrying only the absolute necessities: food, water and blankets. All of the adults, along with a few of the older children, were also equipped with weapons. The children hefted spears and the like, clearly recently and hurriedly fashioned out of materials found within the complex itself. The adults all carried shockers or heavy-duty shocker rifles and everyone, including the otherwise unarmed youngest children, was carrying at least two extra power packs. Matarii armor was immune to shocker fire at a distance, but up-close and if the fire was sustained, the alien within was vulnerable to being cooked alive—a lesson the colonists had learned by observation and clearly taken to heart. *Not so A'tuu'shahn armor,* Khusaaq thought with a grim smile.

The complex had contained a well-stocked arsenal—perhaps not such a surprise if the Coalition was well aware from the get-go that the Matarii had prior claim on the planet and reasonably assumed they might try to get it back, they just hadn't anticipated the Matarii taking it this far. Under

Telipinu's critical eye, Khusaaq's troops had raided it well before the Rimmers had, taking everything they could carry, which was quite a lot. Like his efforts and the efforts of his troops at mining and booby-trapping, what he, his soldiers and the colonists had at their disposal would do little to slow the Matarii once they decided to attack. That said, having weapons gave everyone some sense of control, reason to hope that some of their number might come out the other end of this prolonged nightmare alive.

Those remaining behind would have ample weapons to choose from, but whatever defense they mounted would have little effect against determined Matarii. At least *their* fate was no longer any of his concern.

"Yes," Delbruch replied as her eyes cautiously searched the faint shimmer no more than a few meters away, hoping perhaps to catch a silhouette, a shadow, to know exactly where he was—*what* he was. "The rest are too frightened to leave."

"Frightened of us, you mean. Or should I say too frightened of *me.*"

She hesitated then biting her lip, nodded.

He felt deep satisfaction at executing Viehl, a fact that continued to surprise him. He'd killed before, countless times, close-up using a utility knife or even his hands to assure a quick, quiet and undetected dispatch, or his pistol when complete stealth was not of supreme importance and speed was; he'd killed at a distance from orbit using any number of the staggering array of energy weapons at his disposal; he'd killed scores of Matarii over the past few days and he'd personally put more than a few severely injured colonists out of their misery—a purely compassionate act even if the settlers vehemently disagreed—but he'd never, *ever* killed in a fit of supreme rage before.

He'd never killed an unarmed and therefore essentially helpless, albeit in Viehl's case richly-deserving, foe. In fact he'd had more than a few heated and largely one-sided arguments with Ja'andai—in truth he couldn't recall any time their interactions hadn't started or ended with an argument—over the morals of doing so, with him evoking the fundamental tenant of the Elkanasu to never harm those who pose no harm, no matter their underlying motivations. Ja'andai had considered his revulsion to what was at times—at least according to Ja'andai—a matter of necessity a source of great annoyance and supreme disappointment. While Ja'andai was deeply pious, a true and revered pillar among other equally pious Elkanaghalli'i, he shared what to Khusaaq had always seemed to be the extremely paradoxical view held by other, equally devout Elkanaghalli'i and embraced by A'tuu'shahn'i as a whole: they were mercenaries and mercenaries *killed.* They killed without guilt, without hesitation and without question if the job demanded it, it was as brutally simple as that. Ja'andai's always at the ready explanation for this? If one looked hard enough—assuming one chose to look at all—no victim was truly harmless. If you waited long enough, they'd always prove your worst fears true and better to be safe than dead yourself.

In respect to Viehl, that much was true.

Are you proud of me, now, Ja'andai?

Gaalan had repeatedly assured him that he'd eventually overcome this... personal failing, this unnatural reluctance at promptly dispatching any non-A'tuu'shahn who got in the way of the mission, the contract. He just needed more first-hand experience dealing with infuriatingly obstinate and always deceitful aliens to learn the value of what she referred to as "highly selective purges" on the overall success of an assignment. "Kill a few, save a lot," was her motto. And it had served her well. It had served the Orthodoxy well. As to what the Elkanasu thought of this... he couldn't say. Every time he'd begged them to answer him, pleaded for the same soul-satiating enlightenment seemingly bequeathed to all other A'tuu'shahn'i, that some aliens simply deserved to die, his entreaties had gone unanswered.

Looking back, he realized that perhaps that was answer enough: even the Elkanasu could be hypocrites—if the ultimate reward was high enough. And now he'd joined those ranks, had finally overcome his revulsion at the concept—at least on a case by case basis. Despite his lingering satisfaction, despite his belief that Viehl had earned his fate, that he'd given him several opportunities to tell the truth and the human had persisted in his lies, lies that had cost everyone so dearly, Khusaaq still couldn't shake the sense that he'd somehow lost forever something very precious when he pulled the trigger.

He'd suspected his summary dispatch of Viehl might cause many of the humans to revisit their chances with the Matarii. Or perhaps most of those remaining behind knew about the true nature of the colony and had taken his threat seriously. It didn't matter now. This was a far more manageable number of colonists for his few troops to deal with, yet sizeable enough that if some did survive what lay ahead, they'd serve as living proof that while unable to hold the colony itself, he'd done his absolute best to fulfill Gaalan's final order by saving as many colonists as possible, even after the ugly truth behind it had been uncovered.

He gave the group another quick, appraising sweep with his scanner-augmented eyes, eager to get started, to escape from the increasingly claustrophobic and now blatantly deceiving complex and out into the vast and rugged hinterlands. To fresh air, fresh water....

Perhaps we might make it to the Night Mountains after all, some of us at least—

"I'm sorry," Delbruch continued, drawing his minds-eye off those enticing and very distant peaks. "I tried to convince them, make them see your point of view, to appreciate the magnitude of the lie. I didn't know, truly. None of us here…" she motioned around to the others, "…knew."

"Very well," he said, dismissing the topic. It, like the colonists who had chosen to remain behind, was no longer relevant. He lifted his gaze, said in a louder voice: "Form into groups of ten or so—no more than fifteen if at all possible."

The Rimmers promptly began sorting themselves out, families sticking together, individuals like Delbruch forming bands of their own.

"Ta'ahn…"

Khusaaq looked to his left. Saar'kali and the four sent with him had returned and with time to spare.

"…all locks' alarms are disabled, ta'ahn."

"Any problems?" he asked, noting all five were breathing hard as if they'd run most of the way.

Saar'kali replied, "There... there was some... some fresh rockfall in all but... but two of the corridors but we... we shifted it." He paused between ragged breaths to call up the visual feed from his visor for the others to see, overlaying the images with a grid of the western wing of the complex. "Corridors fourteen-west, eighteen-west and fifteen-north have... have all sustained damage since we first located them—"

"Clearly the aerial bombardment is beginning to destabilize the entire wing," Khusaaq murmured, taking in the raw data that flowed across his visor. It had been obvious from the start that the western annex had never been finished, and the maze of ventilation tunnels and access corridors had yet to be reinforced—Telipinu had even put forth that the annex had been deliberately abandoned simply because of the brittle nature of the surrounding host rock. This made the wing's unmapped passageways ideal, if dicey, escape routes, ones that only the most determined—or desperate—would risk.

"Indeed, ta'ahn," Saar'kali replied. "One more direct hit will probably collapse a goodly portion of it."

Khusaaq couldn't help but smile. Finally, events appeared to be going their way. "Then the sooner we get going, the better, yes?"

"Yes, ta'ahn," Saar'kali said as he accepted a heavy backpack full of mines from Qharubi, part of an unexpected cache of explosives they'd happened across in a hidden, blast-proof locker in the arsenal, more hard evidence that some among the colonists or their Coalition backers had anticipated serious trouble—just not of this scope.

Khusaaq turned back to the Rimmers who had been oblivious to his and Saar'kali's private conversation and was pleased, not to mention greatly relieved that the humans were obeying his orders and so quickly—

Perhaps they're just as eager to leave as we are, he thought as Ichkeul joined him, arms full to overflowing with more appropriated Rimmer weaponry—puny in comparison to their own, but they were in no position to nitpick—then without being asked, the soldier began stuffing what he held into the shielded rucksack Khusaaq carried on his back, Ichkeul standing close enough their armors' combined distortion concealed the transfer. While Khusaaq's armor easily adapted to the extra and very substantial weight—he was now carrying, in armor, weapons and supplies, triple his own body weight as were the others—he briefly wondered if Telipinu had left anything in the arsenal for the remaining colonists. He shrugged, settling both the now bulging pack and his qualms about leaving so many behind. *They had their chance....*

Satisfied the pack was balanced, he turned his attention back to the Rimmers and found himself staring at eighteen tightly-packed groups.

He tapped his chin on his visor's tac-net, opening a public channel. "I will assign one of my soldiers to be the guide for each group. Stick close—once outside, we will not stop no matter what. Understood?"

One human, a boy Khusaaq immediately recognized as Lennox's eldest son, stepped cautiously forward, out of the protective, one-armed embrace of a gaunt-faced woman who clutched a far younger child to her hip—Lennox's wife and little girl, the same little girl who'd so desperately wanted to touch him. Lennox's middle child was nowhere to be seen and he didn't waste any time wondering what had happened to him. The haunted look in his mother's bruised eyes was eloquent enough.

"*Surha,*" the boy began respectfully, using the universal form of address when the object of that address was of an unknown gender or was genderless, "how are we to closely follow you outside, where it's pitch dark, when we can barely detect your presence here, where there's some light?"

Other Rimmers glanced anxiously at each other, clearly fearful, having just learned that the merc in charge was not one to annoy without great risk.

It had been a conundrum Khusaaq had pondered as well, had put forth to his troops to offer up suggestions. Saar'kali had surprised him by being the first to come up with a simple yet most ingenious solution.

"Peter, correct?" Khusaaq asked a second after his visor supplied him with the data.

The boy visibly paled, but answered without audible tremor, "Yes, surha."

Since it had been Saar'kali's idea, it had seemed only fitting he have the honor of demonstrating it to the Rimmers. So, at Khusaaq's signal, and murmured, "Ha'tat, if you will?" the young trooper stepped forward, loops of thick rope held in his outstretched arms. While his gauntleted hands were invisible to the Rimmers, the rope was not.

Saar'kali stopped in front of the Rimmers. "The leader of each group will hold onto one end of each length of rope," he began, his voice, Khusaaq noted, carefully modulated by his blast visor to sound far older than his thirteen years. "The soldier assigned to your group will hold the other. The rest will follow that Rimmer. Understood?"

Several of the humans, including the younger Lennox, smiled with intense relief.

"By the look of 'em, I bet they were thinking we were all going to hold hands," Telipinu grumbled over their private channel and Khusaaq struggled not to chuckle out loud. Khusaaq himself was still on an open channel; had he done so, everyone would have heard him.

As several Rimmers eagerly stepped forward to receive the loops of rope, Khusaaq continued, "Groups will separate once outside. It's far too risky to stay together, far too easy for the Matarii sensors to spot such a large heat signature, even with all of the electrical activity in the atmosphere. Small, widely separated groups have a greater chance of making it to the relative safety of the mountains. My troops know where we are to regroup—stay with them, do *exactly* as they tell you. If they tell you to stop and rest, to get some food and water into you, do so. If they tell you to hide as best you can, do so—and don't come out of hiding until they tell you. If they tell you to keep moving no matter what, do so. And stay *together*. I cannot stress that enough: we will not risk waiting on anyone, or searching for anyone who becomes separated.

"The leader of each group is solely responsible for keeping hold of the rope, of keeping those with him or her together. If something happens to that leader, *you* as a group must immediately replace that person. My soldiers will be far too busy watching for any Matarii pursuit, guarding against any ambushes, searching for safe passages to assist you. And once we leave the complex, no one can turn back. Some of my troops are assigned to follow, to lay mines and set booby-traps. Do you understand?" He watched heads nod, heard murmurs of acknowledgment. "Any who feel they cannot follow these basic but critical rules, say so now, and withdraw. Once we move, my soldiers and I will not tolerate any discussion, any disagreement. My goal is to get as many of you as I can to safety. Anyone who interferes with that will be dealt with in the most expeditious means." He glanced around, giving any doubters one last chance to make their feelings known by stepping out of their groups and leaving the same way they'd come.

When no one took him up on his offer, he continued, "Excellent. My soldiers will be communicating in Standard and on open channels except when they are providing positional or tactical information. So, for the most part what they hear you will be able to hear. I doubt the Matarii will be able to pick up on our short range tac-nets and pinpoint their sources, but I'd prefer not to test that theory, so speak to your guides only when absolutely necessary—and keep any talking between you to an absolute minimum."

He paused, said, "Trust us and we'll get through this, all right?" That was greeted with more nods, more replies of agreement but most held a hint of uncertainty. With that, he began assigning soldiers to groups, starting with Ichkeul, who picked up the free end of the rope Peter Lennox clutched in both hands—a gentle tug was all the boy needed to play the coil out, to give each a little distance, then Ichkeul said to his charges, "My name is Ichkeul—you can call me that, or you can call me by my rank, which is Raz'ta'aq—"

"Just don't call Raz'ta'aq hey you," Qharubi said. The other soldiers laughed, leaving the Rimmers to stare at each other in utter bewilderment, clearly unsure if the odd barking sound they were hearing *was* laughter or something else. It wasn't like they'd heard A'tuu'shahn'i laugh before.

"Hey you," Khusaaq said, feeling it politic to include the Rimmers in their joke, "sounds very much like an A'tuu'shahn'i obscenity: *ha'ahyuut,* which loosely translates as 'fucking bastard'."

A moment of utter, deafening silence followed, A'tuu'shahn'i eagerly waiting to see how the Rimmers would react and Rimmers not sure they should laugh. One woman belatedly clapped her hands over her small child's ears. Then a boy giggled, a sudden, uncontrollable burst of nervous tittering. Another teenager joined him, chuckling softly. Then several others—adults this time—began to laugh. More joined in, soon almost everyone was either laughing or grinning, although to Khusaaq it all seemed a bit forced. Even Lennox's wife managed a brief, tired smile as she fixed her gaze on the shifting distortion at the end of the rope opposite that held by her surviving son.

"Time to go," Khusaaq said and motioned to his troops, who, at the head of each group, readied themselves, readied their charges, calming them with quick introductions, which, Khusaaq noted, were now going both ways—not that his troops needed the colonists to identify themselves, their visors had already done so. But it was a gesture on the part of the Rimmers, and one his soldiers responded to with encouraging remarks.

Ichkeul took point, and at Khusaaq's nod started off, his charges following him down the corridor at first at a cautious walk, but then quickly upped their pace to a hurried trot as a distant rumble shook loose some fine dust from the ceiling. The other groups followed, at irregularly timed intervals, spaced haphazardly enough apart Khusaaq could only hope they didn't trigger the Matarii sensors. *Only one way to find out.*

He remained behind, along with Qharubi, Saar'kali, Telipinu and Tanaali, the youngest among his surviving troops. In fact she was the youngest of those who had managed to flick down to the planet. That she was still alive was in itself the strongest recommendation as to her fitness to accompany him rather than lead a group of Rimmers. She'd performed far beyond his expectations, far beyond what Gaalan had ever expected from what she'd dubbed and therefore doomed as, 'an Am'rataan from a lower-caste house of absolutely no consequence and therefore with no prospects,' in one of her less charitable moods, moods that had become more frequent during their ill-fated mission of guarding the colony.

Clearly Tanaali was determined to prove Gaalan—or anyone else who prejudged her—wrong. To add to her liabilities, she was also a good head and shoulders shorter and barely two thirds the weight of any of the others—diminutive even by female Am'rataan standards—perhaps another goading factor in her single-minded drive to make something of herself. Her small size made her ideal for squeezing into gaps in the rockfall to place mines deeply enough any pursing Matarii's sensors couldn't detect and Matarii hands couldn't defuse, but not so deep the mines' sensors couldn't detect any pursuing Matarii.

Khusaaq and his small, heavily armed group watched as, one by one, groups of Rimmers hurried down the corridor.

Instead of taking the obvious route to the nearest entrance, Ichkeul and the others led their groups on a circuitous route through the deserted wing, the other A'tuu'shahn'i following Ichkeul, but only up to a point. Soon groups diverged, taking different routes where corridors intersected. There were a total of five egresses—three corridors and two large ventilation ducts—that gave access to the rugged hinterlands, all long abandoned and best of all, as far as Khusaaq could determine, no longer even appearing on the official plan of the complex.

Telipinu had come across two of the outlets while doing recon shortly after the colonists' mass exit to the complex. A thorough search had turned up three more—some in greater disrepair than others, but all still passable—vital information Khusaaq had kept from the colonists, having learned never to trust them not to bolt at the worst time and in the worst possible direction.

Each passageway's exterior airlock had been carefully disabled only a short time before by Saar'kali and his team and in a way that didn't set off any alarms. As far as anyone—be they colonist or Matarii—who might be monitoring the complex's many portals were concerned, all were still sealed—assuming these particular and long-forgotten openings to the wild world beyond were even being watched.

Finally, the last group of colonists disappeared around the corner: signal to those remaining to be on their way as well.

With a simple, "Go," from Khusaaq, all but Qharubi, who was in the process of placing a limpet mine in an inconspicuous hollow, started down the corridor.

Qharubi tapped in a series of commands on the mine, activating it then, with a curt nod to Khusaaq, the two hurried after the others without once looking back.

Chapter 9

Kanaloa Medical Complex, Alhajoth, Tuli.
Noon, planetary time. Present day.

"**Y**ou three, wait *here*." Amalfitano pointed to the polished floor. "Understood?"

Murh'sooli crossed his arms and replied, "Our orders are *very* clear, Doctor. We're not to let *you* out of *our* sight."

"I won't *be* out of *your* sight. I'll be right over there." He gestured to the nearby doorway. "I just want you out of Sha'ashahn's sight until I've a chance to explain why I'm here with battle-armored body guards. Got it?"

Murh'sooli gave the doorway a sidelong and very dubious glance.

"Besides, everyone here," Amalfitano motioned around him, to the bustling corridor deep within the vast Kanaloa Medical Compound, "has been vetted by the Tulian High Council…"

Murh'sooli looked suitably unimpressed.

"…*and* by Narbrooi Hahtra'tzrhi. So, *no* bad guys…" He managed a quick, nonchalant nod and a murmured, "Good morning," to a passing doctor, as if having a heavily armed Hahtooshan escort was the latest fashion accessory.

The woman responded with a curt nod of her own as she picked up her step and hurried by.

"So," Amalfitano continued, "absolutely *no* shooting, *understood?*"

Murh'sooli eyed an approaching lab tech and the small trolley full of ominous looking equipment he was pushing.

The tech, catching the mercenary's pointed and decidedly uncompromising stare, abruptly turned around and started pushing the trolley back the way he'd just come, and at double-time no less.

"Understood, Doctor," Murh'sooli replied with a hint of a smile as his eyes followed the rapidly retreating tech.

"Good," Amalfitano replied uneasily as he walked over to the open door. Beyond, somewhere within the stacks of

Hahtooshan-supplied consoles and composite was his quarry—Khusaaq's now familiar voice was clearly audible as the unseen Hahtooshan kept up a running diatribe of frustrated curses—but before Amalfitano could enter, a very familiar voice said, "I'd wait a minute if I were you."

He turned and seeing Corsali approaching, grinned. "Sirin! Funny meeting you here."

"I was about to say the same thing—I didn't see you in the lab this morning, is everything okay?"

"Late night last night. Decided to spoil myself and sleep in."

She arched a brow, clearly not taken in—his uncharacteristically rumpled appearance and in civvies no less—not helping his credibility in the slightest. "Did you forget to set your alarm?"

He grinned. It seemed as good an excuse as any. "Guilty as charged."

"So what, pray tell, explains *them?*" She jerked her thumb at the three soldiers.

"Making new friends in my oodles of spare time?"

It was no secret that security had been suddenly and substantially beefed up in and around the planet's main hospital complex just outside of Alhajoth—a very reasonable condition on the part of the Hahtooshans and one that was wholly embraced by the Tulians, who were still recovering from the shock of Tarqk's unprovoked attack.

As the epicenter of research on Hahtooshan-specific therapies, the hospital had always been a logical target for anyone wanting to slow, if not stop that research. But Tulian cultural sensitivities required that the added safety measures be as unobtrusive as possible and largely performed by the Tulians themselves—something Izraad had told him had not gone down well with Narbrooi, per Seitakap. The Hahtooshan admiral had felt a show of brute force was in order to deter anyone hoping to nip the fledgling alliance in the bud.

To give the laconic Hahtooshan admiral credit, at first he'd grudgingly acceded to the Tulian High Council's mandate by ordering his troops to remain camouflaged behind their chameleon-like ghillie armor at all times while planetside, which not only satisfied Tulian customs, but in many ways proved to be an even greater deterrent. Everyone knew Hahtooshans were about, they just didn't know where. But quickly evolving events had overtaken that carefully maintained façade of normalcy—and came carried on very visible and very ominous-looking campaign boots.

Amalfitano was painfully aware that his arrival, accompanied by three *visible*, fully-armored Hahtooshans, was not only a breach of Tulian propriety but a startling reminder to everyone who crossed their path that Tuli, by publicly aligning with the Orthodoxy, had shed all claims of neutrality when it came to the increasingly volatile machinations of the Rim's hegemonies. The Tulians hadn't gone looking for trouble; trouble had come to them and in buckets and nothing would ever be the same. Clearly the Tulians were starting to come to grips with the harsh reality that Hahtooshan troops patrolling their vital infrastructure—visible or not—were only the beginning.

He blew out his cheeks and gave his bodyguards another sidelong scowl as if the three personified all the evil that Tarqk had unleashed when he'd targeted the hapless planet. Before Amalfitano's thoughts continued down that spiral, an especially loud and angry epithet drew his dark gaze back into the large room the Tulians had set aside as the location for their planet's first of many planned com-nets.

He shook his head, dreading being the bearer of such bad news, and turned to the woman who stood beside him. Sirin stared into the room, drawn to a string of Hahtou curses, her bright blue eyes searching for the location of the one-sided harangue.

Sensing his gaze, she looked up. "It's best not to walk in unannounced when he's this worked up—wait 'til he settles down—shouldn't take long." She pointed to a sign on the door, a hand-lettered warning, KEEP OUT.

"Oh. Well... since we're both here," he began, "and it looks like we have a few minutes, it gives us a chance to talk." And that was true; he, Sirin, Khusaaq and Tasende were dealing with grueling schedules, with Sirin shuttling between Khusaaq,

Tasende and himself, between the lab aboard the *Baidarka* and those within the sprawling Kanaloa Medical Complex—the planet's primary research hospital—along with assisting in Matoosh's therapy. Under those conditions, she rarely had time to wave hello or goodbye before dashing off, carrying an armload of report flimsies or dumping another load on his desk. He knew if something unexpected, something untoward came up, she'd find the time to tell him—or Izraad—and he'd felt the best course of action was to let Khusaaq and Sirin sort things out for themselves *by* themselves, with as little outside interference as possible. But that always-presumed luxury was gone, replaced by a new, very real urgency. "How's he doing? How are you both doing?"

She eyed him, clearly sensing this wasn't just a social visit or an overdue house call. "Overall... I'd say better than—" She was cut off by a loud report of something hitting the far wall, causing Amalfitano to flinch reflexively, followed by another snarled Hahtou obscenity.

Sirin appeared oblivious—or, Amalfitano amended, *inured* to the exasperated havoc playing out in such close proximity as she continued, "As I was saying, better than expected—"

Something else hit a wall with a muffled *thump* and he realized her timely warning had not just been empty words.

"In fact I was just coming to collect him for lunch like I do every day," she continued. "Otherwise he does have a tendency to skip meals if I'm not there to insist he stop and eat."

At Amalfitano's arched look, she added, "It's not deliberate—he just gets so absorbed in what he's doing, he completely loses track of time—going by Matoosh, this isn't a new habit. He's always been this way. Why don't you join us? We can grab something at the cafeteria, then go sit outside and you can ask him how he's doing."

"That's why I'm here. His bio-band can tell me a lot, and a face-to-face can tell me a lot more and one is long overdue, but as you are well aware, he'd not always forthcoming. So I'd really appreciate, while we have a few minutes alone, your input and insights—anything you've noticed, anything you found odd or unexpected, no matter how seemingly insignificant, or, for that matter, anything you've found happily unanticipated."

She pursed her lips then said, "Nothing major, or I would have told you, but, well, for starters, his right leg's still really bothering him, in fact I'd say it's a little worse..."

Amalfitano couldn't help but shake his head, not for the first time mentally kicking himself for not replacing the femur when he'd had Khusaaq in surgery, while he could rightfully claim he was blissfully ignorant of Elkanaghalli prohibitions on such matters and Khusaaq wasn't in any position to have a say; the far more extensive bone replacements hadn't caused spiritual fallout for Matoosh after all, at least none he'd heard about and Matoosh had proven, time and time again that he was not one to keep even minor grievances bottled up—

"...especially after a long day, which all of his days are, not that he'll admit it of course."

"Is he taking those painkillers and muscle relaxers I prescribed?"

"Honestly? No."

Amalfitano exhaled, shook his head.

"I wanted to tell you, but he asked that I not. He said you had too much to deal with as it was, that he didn't need them but you'd worry anyway. I think part of it is that subconsciously he expects his clothing to take care of it, to feed him the proper dosing so as not to affect his critical thinking, and when it doesn't—"

"The *Faridour*'s CMO hasn't suggested he have his uniform recharged or whatever they call it? I'll talk to her about it—it likely slipped her mind with everything else going on, or—"

"He didn't ask."

He raised both brows.

"He's not trying to tough it out," she added a little defensively, "I think he's just not used to, well... thinking about it, as strange as that seems and if that makes sense, so he just pushes it aside, accepts it as part and parcel of his day. And it's not just him. Matoosh is the same way, although his therapist did tell me he does take what you prescribed him, but only so he can finish his daily therapy regimen—and sleep at night so he can get up and do it again."

"I'll talk to him. He's not helping anyone, least of all himself, by this. Anything else?"

"He's developed a fine tremor in his hands—it comes and goes. He says it's just that he's tired, that it's happened before, but it seems to be getting... well, not worse, but more often? Then again, he's pushing himself really hard."

Amalfitano filed that information away as possibly very worrisome, but said aloud, "That's a common physical manifestation of stress and not enough sleep, and maybe needing to eat. You said he needs to be reminded."

She nodded, seemingly satisfied. "It does seem to be most obvious when he hasn't eaten in several hours."

"Anything else?"

"He has nightmares... every night—"

"About the mind-stripping?"

She shrugged. "Lieutenant Izraad warned me he'd relive it in his sleep, that it was a perfectly normal response, so I didn't want to worry you. But now I'm not sure it is about the stripping. He keeps mumbling something—"

"Something?"

"*Monnh'hayrhan.*"

"Mon... hah... ran?"

"Yeah. Over and over, *monnh'hayrhan.* I've asked him about it, but he always brushes it off, says it doesn't mean anything—Matoosh says the same thing, but he's just a little too quick in saying that, like maybe Khusaaq had a word with him, literally. I even went so far as to ask Lieutenant Izraad about it, along with telling her about the nightmares—"

"She never mentioned anything to me," he grumbled.

"Maybe she didn't want to worry you either. Anyway, we talked, I asked if she had any suggestions that might help and also if she could find out what it means—"

"And?"

"As far as the nightmares, she said she could offer up desensitization therapy, but we both agreed he wouldn't agree to that even if there was a specialist here on Tuli who performed it, which there isn't, so she said the next best thing would be for me to get him to talk about it, but we're all putting in such long hours, and he's so exhausted when he comes home, we're all so exhausted... well, truthfully, it just hasn't happened—and maybe I'm just a little afraid what he might say," she admitted.

"As far as what *monnh'hayrhan* means," she continued, "the lieutenant came up dry—said there wasn't anything that sounded remotely like it in any of the Hahtou lexicons Intelligence has on file—she even did a complete search of all linguistic files, just in case it isn't in fact Hahtou—there were a few hits, but they were so far afield, such a stretch that she felt they could be discounted. She said that it still might be Hahtou, but an archaic word or name or term that's no longer in use."

"Or maybe you're reading too much into it, maybe it is just a nonsense word."

She shook her head, "No, it's not. It means something to him—it means a *lot*. I was even tempted to ask Narbrooi—"

Amalfitano arched a concerned brow.

"—but I didn't, and I *won't*," she added, sensing his disapproval. "If Khusaaq doesn't want me to know, then he doesn't want me to know."

"Exactly." He draped his arm around her shoulder, added, "He'll open up to you, Sirin. You just need to give him time."

"Yeah." She replied then forcing a smile added, "All in all, I guess he's adjusting better than I could've hoped, maybe... *too* well? I mean he comes home every night, we... well, you know," she flashed him a rather embarrassed smile, then added, "I mean, everything is fine in that department, and he even seems to enjoy walks along the beach, not that we get much of a chance to do that. I know it's all so overwhelming, sensory-wise for him, but he *is* trying, he really is."

"Zarijan and I told you that the first coupla weeks would likely go better than expected—it's to be, well, expected. This is all so new for him, he hasn't had a chance to take stock, to fully come to terms, so he's modeling his behavior on the expectations of those around him."

Sirin's gaze briefly returned to the chamber, to the unseen Hahtooshan within. "But he will, fully come to terms I mean, eventually—you're sure."

"Yes," he gave her shoulder a reassuring squeeze, hoping he sounded more certain than he felt.

"I just wish he'd be a little easier on himself and take his time—"

THWACK.

She briefly eyed the doorway as they both overheard what was clearly a Hahtou obscenity, then continued, "I keep telling him there's no rush, that his service agreement is open ended, but he goes at it like everything was supposed to be finished yesterday and, well... you can hear the result. He gets supremely frustrated, he utterly exhausts himself—and it's all so unnecessary. And..." she shook her head, sighed.

"And what?"

"I guess I'm afraid of what will happen when he does complete the work to his and the Tulians' satisfaction."

"You mean what will he do next? According to Seitakap he'll be spoiled for choice for work. Every province, every town is clamoring for its own com net—"

"You're assuming he's going to want to stay here."

Amalfitano shifted uneasily from foot to foot. If he'd been apprehensive about how Khusaaq was going to react to the news, he was now doubly so but he kept his voice calm, while reasonably concerned. "And you aren't? Where would he go? To be blunt, it's not like he can return to the Orthodoxy—he knows that. And I think it's safe to say that Coalition worlds are off limits, at least for the foreseeable future. Non-aligned worlds would be dicey at best."

"I dunno," she shrugged. "Sometimes I feel like he's been caged, that he wouldn't stay if he had a choice—"

"Sirin... he loves you. If he really wanted to leave, he would, Narbrooi and this contract be damned. He stays *because* of you, but he's also grappling with a radically different life while maintaining a grueling work load and all without fully recovering from the mind-strip and his physical injuries. You and I will be there to help when he starts to have adjustment anxiety, and he will—likely sooner rather than later and don't think when he does that you've done something wrong, or he's having second thoughts. He's a soldier, been a soldier his entire life, knows nothing else and has spent most of that life on one ship or another. Now he's on a planet, working, for all intents and purposes as a civilian, at least for the foreseeable future. Experiencing anxiety with such a colossal transition is to be expected, and it's perfectly *normal*. Just be there for him, let him progress at his own speed. Don't try to rush things, okay?"

She replied softly, "Yeah."

"And as tempting as it is, as well-intentioned as it might be, avoid doing things that he would reasonably consider a breach of trust, even a minor one—"

"Like asking Narbrooi to answer questions Khusaaq won't."

"Yeah." Amalfitano hesitated before asking, "Is there something else?"

She shrugged. "I dunno. Maybe it's just me. Maybe I'm having some adjustment anxiety of my own."

"Again, it's completely normal and to be expected—from both of you. You're newly-weds who've been thrown into the very epicenter of this ungodly mess the Coalition has gotten itself into, without any warning, any prep, not even a quickie honeymoon to settle the usual case of nerves—"

She chuckled at that.

"—I'm having severe anxiety and I'm only dealing with a bunch of uncooperative bugs!" He grinned then sobering, said, "You know you can talk, anytime, to me, to Lieutenant Izraad or Doctor Fleming. Drakin if you'd prefer. We're all here for the two of you."

"I know—I mean *we* know. But thank you. And trust me, when the worst of this is over, we *are* taking that honeymoon, and it won't be a quickie, either."

"Good!" He gave her shoulder a squeeze then said, "Now, how's Matoosh's therapy progressing?"

She smiled at his not so subtle change of subject. "If you can call swimming in a tropical lagoon therapy."

"Sounds idyllic—" He couldn't help but flinch again as something hit the wall perilously close to the open doorway, followed by an equally loud curse.

"Would be... except for Matoosh," Sirin continued, unperturbed by the unbridled mayhem going on so close by. "But it is working, I shouldn't suggest otherwise—his therapists are amazing. He's now fully able to walk on his own, even run for short distances, albeit with the back and leg braces, and he can easily outdistance me or his therapists when it comes to swimming. His upper body strength is astonishing. So is his 'fuck you, I'll do what I want' attitude. But... all in all, he really isn't a bad sort, he's just suffering from the Hahtooshan version of adolescent angst."

Amalfitano replied with a dubious grunt and a sidelong glance at the dour Murh'sooli and the young sergeant's even younger, even more sullen-faced companions. "Yeah, getting kinda familiar with the type myself." His only satisfaction, such as it was, was that the three Hahtooshans seemed just as jumpy as he each time Khusaaq unleashed his exasperation by hurling something at a hapless wall with what sounded like killing force.

Sirin followed his gaze, studied the three Hahtooshans for a moment then, her curiosity seemingly satisfied, turned back to him. "Matoosh's actually come a long way. He's even been tutoring me in Hahtou when we have a few minutes together, and I've come to find he has quite a wicked sense of humor— mostly at my expense, mind you, but still..." She then added with a trace of mischief, "Maybe tomorrow you could join us for one of his therapy sessions? See for yourself just how far your other patient has come in such an amazingly short period of time?"

Amalfitano sighed, a decidedly aching sigh. Up until his near-fatal foray into the sleazier side of Alhajoth, he'd found himself on more than one occasion fantasizing about spending a week with Izraad on some deserted beach, just the two of them, but it had remained just that, a fantasy. Neither had found any free time—almost every waking hour had been booked solid, he with his research and her with all the political complexities that came with any newly-formed alliance, this one doubly so. Given his druthers—his work versus hers—he'd stick with his bugs. Granted, they might mutate and probably would, given the chance and the fully predictable incentives, but otherwise they delivered precisely what they promised, unlike the politicians Izraad was forced to deal with.

Then came the attempted assassination and any hope of spending time alone with Izraad on a secluded desert isle went out the nearest airlock. His idea of a romantic getaway did not, in any way possible, include an armored escort whose orders included not letting him out of its collective sight and where an unexpected gasp or groan might cause his bodyguards to think the worst and react accordingly.

Before he could reply to Sirin's dubiously motivated invitation with a decidedly wistful, "I wish,"—Matoosh and his teenage angst notwithstanding—Khusaaq suddenly wriggled out from under a nearby console, wearing the ubiquitous Hahtooshan sleeveless under-tunic, trousers and knee-high campaign boots.

He lurched to his feet and turned to grab a tool; happening to notice who was standing just outside the doorway, he hurriedly dusted himself off and started towards him. "Doctor!"

Amalfitano watched his approach with a critical eye. Narbrooi and Aquila had agreed to let him see Khusaaq first, talk to him, feel him out before Aquila and Izraad apprised him of the attempted assassinations.

Outwardly, aside from a noticeable limp, Khusaaq looked to be healthy; he'd even put back on a little of the weight he'd lost. Something else about his outward appearance had subtly changed but Amalfitano quickly brushed that aside—it was what he couldn't see that worried him. Without consciously being aware of it, Sirin had painted a very concerning portrait, a mosaic of someone who, deep down, was barely keeping the superficial appearance together. He gave himself a hard, mental kick. *I should have come sooner and damned the workload... maybe I was afraid too...*

Khusaaq wiped his fingers on his dun-colored trousers then held out his tattooed hand in a very non-Hahtooshan gesture of greeting. Amalfitano sensed Sirin had been schooling her Hahtooshan charges in Coalition etiquette. "Sir."

Amalfitano firmly grasped his proffered hand, then instinctively pulled Khusaaq tight against him, gave him a fatherly bear hug and murmured, *"Nahran."* To his immense relief, Khusaaq accepted the hug, as well as the endearment, 'son,' without the typical Hahtooshan resistance to being touched, not to mention public displays of affection.

But no sooner had Amalfitano started to smile when he felt Khusaaq's entire body stiffen.

He immediately let go, stammered, "I—I'm sorry, I was just so happy to see you..." his voice trailed off as he realized Khusaaq was looking past him, eyes narrowed to suspicious slits, nostrils flaring.

"Jatat-sseh...?"

As Khusaaq angrily stepped around him and into the corridor, Amalfitano silently cursed himself. Khusaaq wouldn't need to *see* the soldiers to be warned to their presence—he'd smell them. Of course the ever helpful Murh'sooli hadn't thought to remind him of this capability—and he made a mental note to have a chat with the laconic sergeant about such lapses, later.

"What is this?" Khusaaq asked again, this time in Standard, his eyes never wavering from the other Hahtooshans.

"They're my bodyguards—"

"Bodyguards...?" Khusaaq briefly met Amalfitano's stare before again fixing his suspicious squint on the three. "To protect you from me?"

"Of course not!" Amalfitano laughed—until he realized Khusaaq was deadly serious. "Narbrooi just wants to make sure no one interferes with my work..."

Khusaaq arched a wary brow.

"...so, everywhere *I* go, *they* go—same with Xosé. Pain in the ass if you ask me, but..." he shrugged, feigning nonchalance, "...as you know, there's simply no arguing with Narbrooi." He left unsaid his sudden realization that he and Tasende weren't the only ones with bodyguards. Khusaaq, being a prime target after all likely had them from the get-go, but his would be fully encapsulated in their armor at all times, if nothing more than to be protected from tool projectiles—and invisible to human eyes.

"Oh. Of course." Khusaaq replied dubiously. He slowly pulled his narrowed, chary stare off Murh'sooli and the others and turned his full attention on Amalfitano.

Amalfitano, in turn, stepped back and looked him up and down, then met his gaze squarely. "You're looking well."

Khusaaq nodded as he gave Sirin a quick, acknowledging glance. "She's taking very good care of me."

"It shows." Amalfitano gave him a light pat on the belly. "I would've come to see you sooner, but—"

"We all have a lot of work to do. And Sirin, I know, has been giving you regular updates."

Amalfitano nodded, "Yes," then looked around, adding, "And speaking of work, Seitakap tells me you're way ahead of schedule on this hub?"

Khusaaq's lips suddenly parted in a boyish grin, the guards and his suspicions—like Sirin's, that this wasn't just a friendly, spur-of-the-moment visit—temporarily set aside. "Come, *husahn,* let me show you!"

Before Amalfitano could fully grasp, could savor the fact that Khusaaq had just called him 'father,' Khusaaq wrapped his arm around his shoulder. *"Come!"*

Together they walked back into the room and over to the main console, Sirin following.

Twenty minutes later, Amalfitano, having been given a tour of the com-net, accompanied by an exhaustive explanation only another engineer could truly understand, much less appreciate, nodded. "I'm impressed."

Khusaaq gave him a sidelong look and grinned broadly, genuinely pleased by the compliment.

"Think you could take a break?"

"Now?" Khusaaq glanced at the console and the tools strewn across its surface. "But I just—"

"Lunch," Sirin interrupted, pointing to the console's chronometer. "You need to eat, and Doctor Amalfitano wants to join us."

"Oh." He looked around at the scattering of tools, clearly torn, then turned back to Amalfitano as the doctor said, "And we need to talk, son."

Chapter 10

Khusaaq and Sirin's bungalow, Tuli.
0134, planetary time. Present day.

Sirin rolled over to face the bedroom doorway as she overheard the faint but distinct beep of the front door lock, followed by the hiss of the door sliding open. She smiled in intense relief when she overheard Matoosh's whispered grumble and Khusaaq's softly worded response as the two entered their shared abode. A moment later, she caught a glimpse of Matoosh as he shuffled by on his way to his own room; the young Hahtooshan's grimmer than usual expression did not bode well.

Her smile faded, but she clung to the fact that Khusaaq *had* come back to her. *That's all that matters.*

She watched in silence as he walked into the darkened bedroom, quickly and quietly undressed, then padded over to the bed and carefully eased himself down onto its edge.

He stared into the darkness, then, after a moment, dropped his head into his hands and let out a soft, weary sigh and his shoulders slumped.

"Khusaaq...?"

He lifted his head and looked down at her, his eyes glittering in the faint starlight. "I didn't mean to awaken you."

"Wasn't asleep."

"I didn't mean to worry you, either."

She stroked his bare back. "Dinner's made, I just need to heat it—"

"Matoosh ate at the hospital."

"And you?"

"Not hungry."

There was no point in pushing the issue this time, so instead she said, "Then why don't you lie down?"

"Not sleepy, either."

"Neither am I," she murmured as she gave his arm a tug and at her urging, he sprawled beside her. "You haven't slept more than a few hours at a time in days—you're exhausted, you need to get a solid night's sleep—and now this happens."

"Yes... *this.*"

She draped her arm across his stomach and pillowed her head on his chest. Listening to the thudding of his heart, feeling the slow, even rise and fall of his chest as he breathed, she tried to ignore the taut muscles of his shoulders or what she knew he was thinking. *You were just starting to trust us, starting to believe in us. Now this.* "Want to talk about it?"

"Not really, you wouldn't—"

"Don't you dare give me crap about me not understanding." She gave him a thump in the kidney with her fist—not hard, but just enough. "How can I understand if you don't talk to me?"

He exhaled, his eyes fluttered closed. "It's... extremely complicated—"

"You always say that. Give me a chance. I truly want to understand—I want to help."

"I know you do. I... I just can't talk about it right now. Later?"

"Promise?"

"Promise."

She knew he wouldn't take advantage of the pain killers Amalfitano had given him to help him sleep. But there were other ways....

She lifted her head and caressed his jaw, his lips; he kissed her fingers then rolled onto his side and jerked her against him.

Watching his face, his eyes, she ran her hand down his back and finally over his "spirit lock"—the tight knot of tattoos at the base of the spine that all Hahtooshans bore and believed linked body and soul together—and smiled at his sharp intake of breath.

She'd quickly learned that these particular tattoos' underlying electro-receptors were good for something Amalfitano and Cyllo had never considered—or, at least had not publicly voiced. Tracing out the intricate patterns that flowed across his lower back not only stimulated the dense web of receptors, but the man. *Perhaps that explains why*

Hahtooshans balk at being touched, she mused as she felt his body respond. *Although you don't seem to mind it at all.*

"*I love you,*" she whispered in his ear as she began to caress him.

"And I you, *toq-bhir*, never, *ever* doubt that." He kissed her again, this time on the lips.

After a moment of her fondling, and now fully aroused, he gently pushed her onto her back and eased himself on top of her. Feeling his naked body against hers, feeling his weight pressing down on her as he eagerly nuzzled her throat, she felt all the fears of the day start to melt away.

Chapter 11

Hinterlands of Cotopaxi, eleven years ago.
Just before dawn, fifteenth day of the Matarii siege.

"All charges set," a breathless Ichkeul reported as he and Saar'kali wearily clambered the last dozen meters up the cone of loose and sharply-angled scree to where Khusaaq, Telipinu and Qharubi were waiting, the three crouched under a rocky ledge which provided some shelter from the pelting rain and gusting wind. For the two making the climb—their third in as many hours—there was no protection from the buffeting gale or the slick, tricky footing, made worse by the darkness and fatigue.

Khusaaq replied with a softly worded and equally weary, *"Excellent,"* as he scanned the sky visible from their precarious hiding spot. The storm was continuing to rage, hurling bolts of lightning which crackled and skittered through the charged air.

While they'd managed to elude the Matarii's aerial recon units in the lower, heavily wooded foothills as the storm, with its unpredictable squall lines dashing scores of the small devices into trees or exposed rock before their handlers had accepted the futility and recalled the what remained back to their base, Matarii scouts on foot had been far more persistent, surprisingly so, and had succeeded in tracking them as far as the mouth of the gorge.

Khusaaq's elaborate precautions—avoiding providing the colonists, those who'd remained behind and even those who'd accompanied them, with any sense as to where he and the others were really headed, mining and booby-trapping all of the complex's egresses along with strategic points along all possible escape routes, of keeping the groups separated for as long as possible, creating a myriad of false trails which were also mined, using the ferocious nighttime storm as cover—had all gone for naught. All he'd done is given himself, his soldiers and the Rimmers a few more hours.

Once it became obvious that the Matarii were on their scent, he'd ordered the widely scattered parties to regroup before the violent weather fully engulfed the deeply furrowed hinterlands—their only chance now was to find a spot where the Matarii's numerical superiority on the ground would count for nothing while still using the storm to keep orbital sensors at bay. He needed a natural choke point, and in the rugged foothills, which were riddled with crumbly-walled canyons and sheer-sided ravines, he was spoiled for choice.

He decided upon this particular gorge because it offered the best overlooks and the most difficult terrain to traverse—according to Qharubi and Saar'kali, who'd gone ahead to plumb its rain-drenched depths. Now he, Qharubi and Telipinu were hunkered down on a long, relatively flat, ribbon-like outcrop, just below the zigzagging ravine's dangerously spalled and treeless rim, where a single misstep on the loose, rain-slick footing could send one tumbling to one's death, their only allies the storm, the darkness and the treacherous, craggy gorge itself. He'd thought about sending the Rimmers and their A'tuu'shahn escorts on, into the steeply rising peaks while he and a handful of his troops remained to keep the dogging Matarii occupied for as long as possible, but in truth his soldiers were simply too exhausted to continue, the colonists, in keeping up with the forced pace of their guides, even more so. They'd come close to losing a number of the Rimmers on the climb up the unstable talus cone to reach the outcrop, his soldiers using the last of their own reserves to carry those who couldn't make it on their own, helping others with a steadying if invisible hand which no colonist refused, and at times a well-intentioned, well-placed prodding shove which no Rimmer dared to protest.

So now the colonists, along with all but the four with him, were holed up in a deep fissure further along the outcrop, safe from anything save a direct hit, a near impossible angle for the Matarii far down in the gorge or their gunners from orbit.

Khusaaq dropped to his armored belly, wriggled over to the outcrop's crumbly edge, as close as was safe and wrapping his fingers tightly around the rock lip, peered into the gaping, rain-pelted dark that was the deep ravine.

His helmet's scanners quickly picked out four widely separated groups of Matarii—an unexpectedly large number of reinforcements drawn in by their scouts' reports of detecting their quarry's coalescing trails at the mouth of the gorge—and who now cautiously picked their way along the floor of the densely wooded and perilous chasm, skirting the near bank of the defile's dangerously rain-swollen river, all unerringly closing in on the only way up to their aerie, the scree cone. With its wide base and narrow top, only a few Matarii at a time could climb to the outcrop, making them and any who followed easy targets—assuming they got past the imbedded mines which if detonated, either by a well-placed step or by remote, would collapse the cone, unleashing an avalanche of razor sharp rock and boulders roaring down on those below. Flicking troops directly onto the rim was a non-starter—the Matarii might be eager, even reckless, but they weren't stupid. Between the storm, which would play havoc with sensors, and the treacherous footing, what few survived such a maneuver could be easily picked off.

He exhaled forcefully and shook his head. The Matarii had made far better time than he'd anticipated, the truly terrible conditions scarcely slowing them down. Their surprisingly quick progress had left Saar'kali and Ichkeul barely enough time to set the remaining mines, adding to what the two had already placed at the base of the scree cone on earlier trips, and those he, Telipinu and Qharubi had strategically positioned along the rim, nearer the mouth of the ravine where the weathered rock face was at its weakest. He just needed to be patient, wait until the majority of the Matarii were bottled up within the gorge, within the killing zone, then detonate all the mines at once, bringing that part of the ravine down on their silver-skinned heads—assuming the storm, the ancient gorge, the unproven Rimmer mines that he and his troops had rigged to explode remotely and the Matarii all willingly cooperated with his plan. Timing had to be perfect, far too many things could go wrong... and so far fortune had not kept them constant company.

As a hard-breathing Ichkeul and Saar'kali crested the lip and scrambled over to their cramped aerie, Khusaaq acknowledged each with a curt nod. Then he looked past them, in the general direction of the fissure, where the Rimmers and his remaining troops were holed-up. The narrow split in the rock was well-hidden behind a curtain of hanging vegetation and an impressive, if temporary waterfall that sluiced off the summit. For the thousandth time, he wondered if he shouldn't have forced everyone to continue, to run if need be and leave behind those who couldn't, to keep moving while they still had a little lead time. It had, after all, been a split-second decision to make their stand here, fearing nothing even marginally better might present itself, knowing everyone was close to utterly done in, using the depths of the fissure in one last desperate gambit that the Matarii's sensors couldn't penetrate both the electrical storm and the surrounding rock and they'd move on in their search, assuming their quarry had done the same.

But it was now clear the Matarii knew where they were—maybe not precisely, but close enough. All that remained was to make the aliens' determination as costly for them as possible—a little over two hundred A'tuu'shahn and Rimmer lives in trade for fifteen hundred Matarii, possibly more?

"We'd already be dead had we remained in the complex," Telipinu said, as if reading his bleak thoughts.

Khusaaq even more cautiously wriggled back from the rain slippery edge. Once tucked back against the overhang, wedged between Telipinu and a large boulder and out of the worst of the rain, he snapped, *"And this is preferable?"*

The helmeted heads of the three seated nearby, silent participants to the conversation, swiveled towards them.

"You gave us a chance, ta'ahn," Telipinu continued, placing his gauntleted hand on Khusaaq's armored shoulder, "which is more than we had back there—"

"I should have left the Rimmers," Khusaaq growled, scowling fiercely at nothing in particular, "they only slowed us down. *We* could have made it." He picked up a small rock, then using what strength his exhausted, armor-augmented arms could muster, hurled it far out over the rain-drenched ravine, secretly envisioning it braining a luckless Matarii far below.

"Made it *where*, ta'ahn?" Telipinu asked. "To the Night Mountains?"

Khusaaq started to nod—and then it hit him: the Matarii had them just where they wanted them, meaning well away from the complex the aliens so badly wanted to reclaim and with as little damage as possible—he doubted the remaining Rimmers had put up much of a fight, if they'd fought at all—and he'd *led* them here, he'd led them *all* here, A'tuu'shahn, Rimmer *and* Matarii, to this isolated gorge where the Matarii could finish them off, all because of his foolish, his *blind* desire to reach some mythical refuge.

"They don't exist, ta'ahn," Telipinu continued softly as he released his hold on Khusaaq's shoulder, "you know that—"

"Telipinu," Qharubi warned in a low, ominous growl.

Khusaaq glanced sharply at Telipinu, unwilling—unable— to concede that point. The Night Mountains and all they represented was a symbol too deeply engrained into his psyche, too much a part of who and what he was, too much of what it was to be Elkanaghalli, too integral to the Elkanasu mythos...

While Telipinu couldn't see Khusaaq's hostile glare, or the equally ferocious, outraged stares of Qharubi and Saar'kali behind their blast visors, he could sense it: as a secular Barkaat, Telipinu knew he was treading on very dangerous ground, especially with Elkanaghalli'i, and even more so with Elkanaghalli'i of Khusaaq and Qharubi's storied and extremely pious lineages. But Telipinu was also Khusaaq's closest friend, perhaps in large part because he *wasn't* Elkanaghalli and so wasn't constrained by outmoded and rigid beliefs, and not for the first time felt little hesitancy in speaking his mind even on matters that cut right to the bone.

"...certainly not here on Cotopaxi. It was a nice dream though... while it lasted." Greeted by a collective and very stony silence—even Ichkeul, a secular Quu'dahn, knew better than to say anything—Telipinu, feigning obliviousness, scooted over to the edge and very slowly scanned the entire length of the gorge visible with his visor's sensors. "Does seem rather odd they've sent so many, doesn't it?—now that they know where we are, why not just withdraw and blast the gorge and us into the stratosphere? That's what I'd do..." He nodded and wriggled back under the protection of the overhang, into the still unhappy company of his fellows. "Definitely what I'd do."

Khusaaq dismissed his observation as nothing more than pathetic attempt at distraction—Telipinu knew he'd overreached himself this time—as he continued to glower at him, seething at his audacity, and yes, deeply stung by the bitter truth of his words: *There are no Night Mountains, no refuge, no... hope. Not* here, *certainly not.*

He looked around him again, at the crumbling outcrop, the spalled rock and precariously perched boulders that were their blind as if their surroundings were all somehow willing, yes, *eager* participants in the delusion, the deception, then his slitted gaze darted to the hidden cleft in which the Rimmers, along with most of his troops, had taken shelter—a chance to grab something to eat, to drink, if any had any desire with their bellies cramping in fear... and most, he suspected, just wanting it to be over.

And I brought you all here—you trusted me, trusted I'd lead you to safety.

His only solace, such as it was, was that his illustrious family, who'd pinned such hopes on him after Ja'andai's untimely death, would never know what had really happened on this ancient and weathered mountainside and would now turn their expectations onto his unfortunate Doh'ha, who was barely more than an infant. *I pity you.*

His last command—his *only* command—a complete and utter failure... a brutal fact that would mercifully die with him and those who'd regrettably placed their faith in him. The Elkanasu would know, but they kept their secrets, revealing all only to those they deemed worthy enough to join them, a possibility, he was sure, that was no longer attainable for him. His family would be compensated for its loss, diplomatically chosen words would be spoken by the Q'shaathrah, honoring his few and less than stellar accomplishments, his name would be registered in the Abhijit'tischinjgra book of records, just below that of Ja'andai's, along with a notation of his birth and death, his highest rank, and that would be that. His life, the lives of the others, snuffed out... and for what? *Nothing. Absolutely nothing.*

He exhaled forcefully, hoping to purge his lungs, his mind of the wasted anger, the futile bitterness and peered up at the sky, now a churning mix of sharp, assailing rain, brief, intense flares of cloud-to-cloud lightning... and here and there, a scudding gap that provided the briefest glimpse of a twinkling, tranquil starry night far, far above.

Home...

Just the thought sent an agonizing pang through him—so far away and yet seemingly close enough to touch. He dropped his pinched gaze, looked around him again, at the rain-drenched rim just as another, particularly brilliant flash of lightning briefly illuminated the entire gorge and the ancient, weather-beaten and balding crags that surrounded it—

I'm... here. The revelation struck him with enough force to bring tears to his eyes: the Night Mountains weren't some impossibly remote landmark, some ragged, snow-capped line that edged the perpetually distant horizon, an unreachable goal, like the stars glimmering so peacefully above the raging storm, tantalizingly close yet always just out of reach for those who weren't worthy enough to gain their protection. *We made it!*

Their arrival on this particular site had been no accident, no desperate act, no poorly-considered decision. Qharubi had readily admitted that he and Saar'kali had purely by accident stumbled across this particular gorge mouth on their way back from their sortie, after giving up hope of finding anything that would provide even the most basic of defenses, and a quick foray of its depths had proven it was by far and away the best choice—far better than they could have wished for. So, the Elkanasu had guided them *here*, to this very spot—he was sure of it now—they *had* heeded his increasingly despairing pleas. He clapped a mental hand over the instant, petty thought, *About time!* before it became fully formed, where the Elkanasu might overhear it.

Suddenly all of the anger, the fear and near crippling self-doubt simply... slipped away. In their place he felt a sense of peace he'd never felt before, of being in the near-presence of the Elkanasu. He looked around him again, taking in his surroundings—the torrential rain that sheeted down the rock face forming curtain waterfalls, the wind-feathered water plunging into the darkness, the bare, glistening and lightning-illuminated rock of the rim itself, the lurking, shadowy presence of the higher mountains beyond—as if seeing them for the first time while he savored their wild beauty and the heady sensation of finally being where he belonged—where he was truly meant to be: the Night Mountains were all around him.

He didn't need to know the Elkanasu's ultimate end game—why they'd picked this particular gorge, this specific outcrop over another. All that mattered was that his directed actions had served some greater purpose and in doing so he'd be rewarded—and he'd brought the others with him, A'tuu'shahn *and* Rimmer. The Elkanasu had encouraged him to bring them—had refused to let his conscience leave the Rimmers behind, which meant they'd be welcomed too. He caught a stray, almost giggling thought about what Ja'andai and Gaalan would think of him bringing Rimmers into the embrace of the Elkanasu, but then he squelched it. If things went as planned, he'd find out soon enough. Besides, it was not up to them to decide who was worthy and who wasn't, any more than it was for him. That was for the Elkanasu and the Elkanasu alone and if they felt these particular Rimmers were worthy, then so be it.

He tilted his head back, and closing his eyes, listened as the rain hammered in an almost mind-numbing cadence against his helmet and blast visor. *Yes...*

The uneasy whispers of those around him finally wormed their way into his consciousness, reluctantly drawing his attention back to the matter at hand—even Saar'kali, who despite being an Elkanaghalli was usually not one to pick up on subtleties, had sensed something profound had just happened to his commanding officer.

He reached out, lightly touched Khusaaq's forearm. *"Ruh'ta'aq...?"*

Khusaaq took a deep breath, glanced sidelong at Saar'kali, acknowledging his concern, then turned to Telipinu and murmured, "You're wrong, my friend. We're here—we made it."

Telipinu began warily, "Here? But... I don't—"

"The Elkanasu—they've brought us here, to this very spot."

That garnered astonished gasps from everyone, followed by quickly muttered and long overdue prayers from Qharubi and Saar'kali as helmets swiveled on metal-collared necks, everyone looking around, clearly hoping to see, to feel what Khusaaq had seen, to experience that which had left him so absolutely certain of his claim—and certain he was, the tone of his voice left no room for any doubt, which meant all would soon join the Elkanasu, a fate most A'tuu'shahn'i, even most Elkanaghalli'i believed was beyond their reach—if they believed at all.

Telipinu, Saar'kali and Ichkeul turned to Qharubi—a Rasharawan'tischinjgra, a family almost as old as Khusaaq's and every bit as pious—for some sort of corroboration for Khusaaq's stunning announcement, but he was as staggered as they were and replied with a slight twitch of his armored shoulders, unwilling to risk the ire of the Elkanasu—or Khusaaq's—for his own uncertainty.

Khusaaq, responding to an urge he could not ignore, a desperate yearning that appeared suddenly and fully formed in his mind, carefully, if clumsily eased himself free of his now empty backpack with shoulders that ached and overused muscles that had stiffened and then, after another pause, fully accepting the risks, fully aware of the message he was sending to the others, removed his helmet. He placed it beside him then again turned his gaunt, haggard face skyward, closed his eyes against the revitalizing sting of the icy rain, the bracing wind, and as his nostrils sucked in the potent, charged scents, he began to laugh, a soft laugh at first, but it quickly filled his chest, his soul, shaking his entire body.

Qharubi followed his lead and cautiously removed his helmet, then one by one the other three did the same and as they felt rain for the first time, felt the wind, and smelled and saw with their own eyes the powerful storm that swirled around them, they too began to laugh in sheer joy and pure, almost childlike amazement, the near sensory overload of sounds, smells, the highly-charged air, the rain and wind—

BOOM!

The especially loud report startled them into darting-eyed silence. Another, equally loud boom followed, and a third. Then a dazzling bolt struck the treeless rim a little distance behind them, sending razor-sharp shards of rock spinning in every direction.

"INCOMING!" Qharubi yelped, grabbing his hastily discarded helmet. And it was: no lightning this time. Everyone scrambled for what cover they could find along the narrow outcrop.

No sooner had Khusaaq wedged himself, along with Qharubi and Telipinu, into a space between the outcrop and a massive boulder that was barely large enough for one, much less three A'tuu'shahn'i in full armor when another salvo struck close to where they'd been seated only a scant few moments before, exploding the rock face.

Qharubi cursed furiously between startled and sopping heaves of breath.

Telipinu cleared his throat then turned to Khusaaq and wiping his soaking wet hair out of his eyes said matter-of-factly: "Perhaps it was a mistake to remove our helmets."

"You think?" Qharubi growled and immediately donned his, his violently shaking hands fumbling with the catches.

Telipinu shrugged, or tried to in their cramped hide-out, then he too put on his helmet. He waited for Khusaaq to do the same then turning to Qharubi said, "It was worth it though, wasn't it?"

Qharubi exhaled forcefully, then conceded irritably: "I didn't say it wasn't. I just have a thing about having the shit scared out of me especially right before I'm to present myself to the Elkanasu."

Telipinu replied, "I'm sure it won't be a first for the Elkanasu..."

Qharubi grunted his unhappy agreement.

"...and they do say what doesn't kill you will certainly try again," Telipinu added as he peered upwards as if trying to spot the guilty party.

"Yeah, they do say that," Qharubi growled. "And Matarii are persistent, if nothing else."

"Fortunately for us they're so offhand in their targeting," Telipinu said helpfully. "You can bet if A'tuu'shahn'i gunners had gotten a momentary bead on us, they wouldn't have missed."

Khusaaq, realizing the Ichkeul and Saar'kali were nowhere to be seen, peered around the boulder. "Saar'kali, Ichkeul... report!"

"Saar'kali here, ta'ahn."

Khusaaq breathed a sigh of relief, then repeated, "Ichkeul... rep—"

"Ta'ahn..." Saar'kali interrupted, *"Ichkeul... he's been hit. I can't tell how badly—my helmet's sensors were fried with that last barrage."*

"Same's true for mine," Khusaaq replied; he didn't need to ask the others. Qharubi's angry muttering as he banged the flat of his gauntleted hand against the side of his helmet was answer enough. "Are you safe where you are, Ha'tat? Are you injured?"

"Got thrown against the overhang—but I'm safe, ta'ahn," Saar'kali replied, *"But Ichkeul—"*

"Stay where you—" Khusaaq was cut off by another strike, this one a little further away, close to the underlying fissure. It was followed almost immediately by another, this one even closer to the fissure that left the rock sizzling.

To Khusaaq this was clearly more a matter of chance rather than something far more worrisome: the Matarii were simply firing at random, likely out of mounting frustration, hoping to flush their prey out of hiding. As if to prove his hunch, the Matarii began strafing the entire rim of the gorge, zigzagging back and forth between one side and the other and he had to wonder what the Matarii troops bottled up in the ravine thought of this reckless tactic on the part of the crews in orbit: one minor targeting miscalculation and the gunners would wreak havoc on their own and he could only hope they were in fact as sloppy as Telipinu maintained.

So far none of the barrages had struck below the rim, which suggested the gunners were a little more skilled than Telipinu gave them credit, and it was now their side of the gorge's turn for a strafing: a skittering strike very close by sent the three into tight tucks behind the boulder, all the while hoping the pounding wouldn't shift the boulder, pinning, or worse, crushing them. There was nothing Khusaaq could do for those sheltering deep inside the fissure—to try to reach them, exposed on the slippery and loose scree and under the heavy bombardment, even without the Matarii actually spotting them, would be little less than suicide. His troops knew their jobs: protect the Rimmers in their care no matter what. Right now his full attention was on those with him, particularly Ichkeul.

He eased himself loose of Qharubi and Telipinu, and cautiously peered around the boulder, but without the augmentation of sensors, his visored eyes were of little use in spotting the soldiers. Ichkeul and Saar'kali were as invisible to him as cloaked A'tuu'shahn'i were to aliens and to go searching would be as rash as trying to reach the cleft.

He sagged back against Telipinu and muttered a curse.

"Ta... ta'ahn?"

Khusaaq jerked his head up. *"Ichkeul?"*

"Ye... yes, ta'ahn."

"How badly are you injured?"

"Can't tell—sensors out, but I... I think... pretty bad. Hard... hard to breathe. Can't feel my legs..." His voice trailed off into a low, agonized groan, followed by several panting breaths.

"Saar'kali," Khusaaq said, "look around you—find a nearby landmark so we can find you."

There was a pause, punctuated by several rattling gasps from Ichkeul then Saar'kali said, *"We're just below—"*

Another fusillade hammered the rim behind them, sending sizable chunks of rock whirling high into the air, only to clatter and splinter around them, a near-lethal hail for anyone not wearing full armor.

Khusaaq, Telipinu and Qharubi again squeezed together, protecting themselves as best they could with armored arms and legs and with the boulder and outcrop on either side.

Instead of stopping, the salvo continued, increasing in intensity and now coming from several directions. The very rock beneath them shook, loosening more of the spall and sending it shifting sideways, towards the edge of the outcrop.

Khusaaq hunkered down, squeezed his eyes shut and swallowed convulsively. *Maybe I was wrong about—*

The barrage abruptly ceased, leaving the mountaintop around them steaming and sizzling and in some spots actually glowing a deep, angry red. He waited a moment, and when the withering fire failed to resume, he said, "Stay here, no matter what—"

"Where you going?" Qharubi growled, grabbing his arm just as he started to rise from his crouch.

"To help Ichkeul and Saar'kali while the Matarii are reacquiring their targets. Get them to the fissure—"

"Not alone you can't," Telipinu said, grabbing his other arm, the two effectively holding him in place.

"I need you two to remain here, detonate the mines as planned—"

"I honestly don't think there's any need to delay doing just that," Telipinu replied. "In fact the longer we wait, the greater the chance we won't get the chance."

Qharubi added, "Let's blow the gorge, *now!* I'd imagine most of those Matarii columns are just below us—give their troops a little taste of what their ships have been handing out so freely—and white out their targeting sensors long enough to reach Ichkeul and Saar'kali—get everyone to the fissure."

Telipinu nodded enthusiastically, helmet bobbing madly.

"Saar'kali—you heard?" Khusaaq asked.

"Yes, ta'ahn—and for what it's worth, I fully agree—"

"So... so do I," a weak-voiced Ichkeul interrupted. "Blow it to the far side of Pu'taak's Rift, ta'ahn."

Khusaaq almost smiled as he opened a channel to those in the cleft. "We're detonating the mines—tell everyone to hunker down—have the Rimmers cover their heads as best they can, there's bound to be some rockfall, everyone stay well away from the fissure opening—we'll be joining you shortly. Got injured with us."

"Understood, ta'ahn," a voice he immediately recognized as that of Tanaali replied. "We await you."

"Saar'kali, you got a fix for us?" he continued.

"Yes, ta'ahn, we're just a little to the north of the overhang, the one with the sharp angle to it... there are three medium-sized boulders directly below it..."

Khusaaq lightened his visor and squinted into the rain, which had begun to slacken, as had the wind; the storm, which had been such an ally was now unraveling—worse, he could see a thin, watery band of light on the horizon. Dawn was approaching.

"...we're behind a fallen slab—"

"Got it!" Khusaaq replied as he spotted the overhand and boulders and just below it, a faint, but telltale glimmer—an indistinct mix of orange and white with the occasional flash of worrisome purple. He marked their location in his mind then turned as best he could to Qharubi and behind him, Telipinu. "On my mark, detonate then run—we grab the others then head for the fissure—"

"May the Elkanasu guide and guard us," Telipinu whispered.

"They've already made good on the first part," Qharubi replied, "I cannot see them reneging on the second."

Khusaaq clapped his hand on Qharubi's shoulder, then, "Ichkeul?"

"Yes... ta'ahn?"

"We're coming for you. Saar'kali, do what you can to shield yourself and Ichkeul—it's bound to be one big explosion."

"The bigger the better," Saar'kali replied, "and teach those silver-skins not to tangle with A'tuu'shahn'i!" Then: "We're ready anytime you are, ta'ahn."

Khusaaq carefully eased himself out from between the boulders, Telipinu and Qharubi following, all keeping to a crouch, looking around, glancing skyward, hoping for some warning of the next salvo while also keeping a wary eye on where they put their booted feet.

"Now!" Khusaaq snarled.

Qharubi and Telipinu activated the firing sequences then they all ran pell-mell along the ledge.

The gorge was suddenly and violently rocked by a fresh series of massive explosions, this time from below and cascading all the way to its mouth. The very ground under their feet suddenly seemed to lift, then slam back down. They didn't slow, they didn't stop, despite the mountaintop shuddering and huge sections of the spalled rim suddenly giving way and sliding into the rain-filled darkness. They kept running, leaping over loose and shifting patches of scree, dodging boulders already precariously unbalanced and now rolling towards the black maw of the ravine.

They reached the fallen slab without serious mishap and hunkered down, using their own armored bodies to shelter Ichkeul as the gorge continued to convulse with more, and, to everyone's surprise, increasingly powerful explosions.

"I... I THINK WE MAY HAVE OVERDONE IT JUST A BIT!" Qharubi managed to yell over the echoing cacophony that even with their helmets left them nearly deaf.

Khusaaq didn't even have time to nod his hearty, utterly unnerved agreement before he suddenly found himself airborne and tumbling violently high above the gorge, buoyed by a rapid series of massive shock waves that welled up from the hellish maelstrom which only moments before had been the dark, rain-drenched ravine. He tried to tuck himself into a ball as his armor was pelted with rock, to protect his visored face, but he couldn't keep control of his limbs, which flailed about wildly, seemingly boneless. Just when he thought it couldn't get worse, of course it did. He abruptly stopped going up, and started coming back down even faster, with the now-shattered rock of the rim approaching a truly sickening rate.

An instant later his world of dazzling explosions and concussive forces that loosened teeth and addled the brain abruptly... winked out.

Chapter 12

The bungalow, Tuli.
Dawn, planetary time. Present day.

Sirin opened her eyes. The faint purplish-pink light of a Tulian sunrise filled the room. She stretched languidly, and smiling, looked over her shoulder.

Her smile froze on her lips; Khusaaq was not asleep beside her. She rose from the bed, grabbed her negligee and slipping it on, hurried down the corridor to Matoosh's bedroom.

The door was ajar. She knocked, whispered, *"Matoosh?"* and peered into the room.

His bed too was empty, the covers lying in a tangled mound on the floor as if hastily thrown aside—and most telling of all, his uniform, which had been neatly folded on top of a small chest since he'd come to stay with them, was missing, as were his campaign boots and braces. *Gods!*

She ran back down the corridor, to the front door and looked at the glowing time lock. The last time the door had been opened was oh-one thirty-four, when Khusaaq and Matoosh had returned from the hospital, so they hadn't left to finish up some work. She turned around, desperately looking for some clue, some explanation as to where they could have gone—and noticed that the lanai's door, the only unalarmed door in the bungalow, was open. She knew she'd closed and locked it the night before, before going to bed.

Perhaps... perhaps they went for a swim! Yes! Clinging onto that, she dashed out onto the lanai, down the steps and onto the path that led to the hospital compound's private lagoon. As she raced down the tree-lined trail, her heart hammering in her chest, she searched what she could see of the beach, and then the breeze-ruffled waters of the lagoon.

To her growing anxiety, she saw no one, but no sooner had she stepped onto the beach's cool sand when she overheard guttural voices. A hundred meters or so down the crescent shaped beach she saw three figures standing not far from the water's gently shifting, phosphorescent edge.

Realizing it was indeed Matoosh and Khusaaq, and feeling an intense sense of relief, she started towards them. As she approached, it suddenly dawned on her that the third man was *not* Matoosh's physical therapist. It was, in fact, none other than Narbrooi, and dressed, uncharacteristically, in just under tunic and trousers. Khusaaq wore only trousers and boots. Matoosh was in full kit, and carried what looked like the rest of Khusaaq's duty uniform draped over one arm.

It was also clear that Khusaaq was arguing with Narbrooi by the fiery tone of their voices and animated gestures.

Sirin stopped, unsure if she should interrupt or leave them to sort out their disagreement. The decision to leave or stay was made for her as Matoosh spotted her. The heated conversation immediately ceased and Khusaaq and Narbrooi turned to stare at her.

Khusaaq muttered something to his companions and started towards her at a limping lope; Matoosh and Narbrooi remained where they were.

"Is everything all right?" she asked as he approached.

One glimpse of Khusaaq's expression warned her that everything was definitely *not* all right.

Instead of replying, he drew her against him and kissed her on the top of her head. *"I love you, toq-bhir,"* he murmured. "I love you more than life itself. Never, *ever* doubt that."

She roughly pushed herself out of his embrace and looking up, searched his intense gray eyes. What she saw confirmed her worst fears. "You're going after them, aren't you?"

"Yes."

"But... you have no idea where they are!"

"Our tracking abilities are far more advanced than your Coalition's, Sirin. We have a *very* good idea where they are, or, should I say, where their abductors are taking them. It's my intention to be there, waiting for them, when they arrive."

"But... but your men... they may already be dead—"

"Then I will avenge them," he replied softly.

"And what about me?"

He wiped a lock of hair from her eyes with a hand that shook; the fine tremor in his hand was back and very noticeable. "I *will* come back, Sirin." His fingers lightly caressed her jaw, her lips.

She jerked her head aside, out of reach. "Will you?"

"You doubt my word?"

"It might not be up to you—you're planning on going after people who want you dead!"

"I know."

"They didn't use the name *Huui'teh* by accident, didn't grab your men just as a lark—they knew how you'd react—"

"By taking the bait?"

"In a word, yes."

"Then I will do as they wish and take the bait, but—" he placed a silencing, if shaky finger against her lips, "—*without* springing the trap."

She fixed her suddenly watery gaze on the choppy lagoon as hot tears rolled down her cheeks.

He used the same finger to wipe them away. "I must do this, Sirin."

"But... how?" she whispered, refusing to look at him.

"Hahtra'tzrhi has agreed to supply me with a ship and a crew, and Matoosh is one of the best foldboat pilots in the fleet."

She suddenly wrapped her arms around him and pressed her wet cheek against his bare chest; he stroked her hair. For a moment neither spoke.

Finally she asked, "When?"

"Soon."

"How soon?" When he didn't answer immediately, but instead glanced back at his companions, she followed his gaze and suddenly realized that they weren't just watching them. They were *waiting* for Khusaaq. She looked up at him.

"Within the hour."

She blinked in stunned disbelief, but her shock quickly turned to anger, and to an overwhelming sense of betrayal. "And you planned on leaving without telling me? You... *you goddamned bastard!"*

"Actually, that was Hahtra'tzrhi's one condition for supplying me with a ship. I was in the process of explaining to him that this was totally unacceptable when you unexpectedly appeared."

"But... *but what about your service agreement?*" she snarled, knowing she was grasping at straws. "You *promised* the Tulians—"

"Last night and with Matoosh's help, I managed to get the com-net up and running—it's not as encompassing as planned, but it is now functional and will certainly serve as the Tulians requested, so I have lived up to the spirit, if not the letter of the contract, and if the Tulians demand more, and they very well might, Hahtra'tzrhi has given me his word that he will supply them with the technicians required to complete the task to their exact requirements."

"Fine time for him to be so goddamned generous," she growled, flicking the Hahtooshan admiral a sidelong, hateful glance.

"Indeed, but it is his way, at least with me." He took her hands in his, drawing her gaze back to him. She tried to pull free but he easily kept his hold and drew her tightly against him.

Held in his warm embrace, she felt the rage, the hurt, slowly drain away, taking with them what had been an almost overwhelming sense of contentment. *"I should've known it was too good to last,"* she whispered as she pressed her face against his chest. *"I should've known..."*

He caressed her breeze-blown hair, again kissed her on the top of her head then replied, "I am who and what I am, Sirin— I've never hidden that from you. And those men are my responsibility. I was forced to leave them behind once, I cannot turn my back on them a second time, I... I cannot abandon them—"

"So you abandon me instead!"

"I'm not abandoning you—you know that."

"Then take me with you!"

"No."

"But—"

"I said *no*. This is an A'tuu'shahn matter—"

"Meaning you don't trust me."

"Meaning I want you to remain safe—I *need* to know you are safe in order to do what I must do. Do you understand?"

She fixed her watery gaze on the lagoon, on the dazzling sunrise, and after a moment, nodded reluctantly.

"Now, I must ask one more thing of you, *toq-bhir*."

She wiped her eyes, cleared her throat and looked up at him. "What?"

He glanced sidelong first at Narbrooi, then at Matoosh. "You mustn't tell anyone. There's a chance your Coalition would try to stop me, or leak the information, as someone did with the rescue, and I would prefer to take those responsible for this by complete surprise."

"But... but someone's bound to notice you aren't at work, and what about Matoosh? One of you taking time off, maybe, but both—"

"Tell them we're aboard *Faridour*—it isn't exactly a lie, as we will be, shortly. Suggest it has something to do with the abduction, that Matoosh and I were recalled to discuss the situation. I doubt anyone will question you, and if they do, refer them to Hahtra'tzrhi—I seriously doubt anyone would *dare* question him. All I ask is twenty-four hours." He again looked over his shoulder at his waiting companions then turned back at her. "Forty-eight would be even better." He smiled his most disarming smile, the same guileless smile that had drawn her to him in the first place. "Is it agreed?"

She hesitated before replying softly, *"Of course."*

He slipped his hand into his trouser pocket, then grasped her hand, pressed something small and hard into it, and carefully folded her fingers around it. "I want this back upon my return."

She looked questioningly up at him, then, at his tight smile, dropped her gaze and unfurled her fingers to find his Coalition Battle Commendation in the palm of her hand.

"I must go now, toq-bhir, before Hahtra'tzrhi changes his mind." He kissed her again, lightly touched her lips with his fingers, then turned and loped back down the beach, towards Matoosh and Narbrooi.

As Sirin watched him, watched as he rejoined the others, she realized with a sinking heart than he never once looked back.

Chapter 13

Aboard the A'tuu'shahn foldboat, Jirah.
Present day.

Matoosh chuckled softly as he took possession of the foldboat's pilot's seat then, grinning, looked up at Khusaaq. "Anytime you're ready, Sha'ashahn."

Khusaaq nodded, leaned over Matoosh's shoulder and thumbed the com-button on the pilot's console. *"Faridour,* we're ready for departure."

"Acknowledged," replied the bay tech.

An instant later, he felt more than heard the release of the grapples that held the foldboat in its berth in the belly of the massive destroyer.

"Jirah*, you are free of the bay. May the Elkanasu guard and guide you, Sha'ashahn,"* the unseen tech added before cutting the connection.

Khusaaq lightly grasped Matoosh's armored shoulder. "Go."

Matoosh didn't have to be asked twice. The small vessel vibrated to life then slowly pivoted away from the planet.

"Best speed, Ruh'ta'aq," Khusaaq murmured. As he stared at the computer-generated image of *Faridour*, and below it, the disc that was Tuli, he felt intense surge of relief wash over him. He glanced down at his hands to find that they'd stopped trembling. Over the past days the tremor had gotten so bad at times he could barely use the tools he needed for the task of setting up the com net, was, in fact, constantly dropping them— or hurling them aside in frustration when he found he couldn't hold them steady.

The tension had been building from the moment he'd made official planetfall as Tuli's new communications expert—and had come to a crescendo upon hearing of the kidnappings and the attempt on Amalfitano's life. At first he'd just chalked it up to the jitters he always felt in starting a new contract, of feeling the anxious gaze of the Q'shaathrah on him, the collective worry that this time he'd realize their worst fears about him. That he'd fail so spectacularly nothing could save him—that the lie that had been his life would finally be exposed.

And when that finally did happen, when he risked and lost all to stop Tarqk, only to discover that the Elkanasu had been guiding his actions all along, it was all rather... anticlimactic, despite the personal consequences, as deep and wide-ranging as they were.

For a short time—a matter of hours—he thought he was finally rid of the chronic fears, the protracted but gathering sense of impending dread. The worst *had* happened... or had it? When the nightmares returned that first night on the planet, when the tremor returned, he quickly realized these weren't caused by the apprehensions that had always dogged him, apprehensions he thought he'd finally shaken.

It was the planet itself.

Cotopaxi had been a young world as habitable planets went, primeval and wild, with a hot, blue-white sun pin-point in its sky, whereas Tuli was ancient, a lovingly cultivated garden bathed in the warm, orangey-glow of its age-bloated star. He'd told himself countless times that those very basic differences would make all the difference, but they hadn't, and in truth he'd known that from the instant he'd first flicked down to the planet in his desperate attempt to escape. The strong, earthy smells, the chorus of sounds, the vibrant colors, the lingering touch of a breeze, the pungent tastes... everything had conspired against him, the ghosts that had pursued him his entire life tripping him up at every opportunity. Ghosts he'd desperately tried to evade by avoiding contracts that required planetfall. He'd been largely successful at that stratagem... until he found himself and those under his command marooned on Rasal Ghul Seven, ironically, a veritable corpse of a world.

Tuli was anything but. It was a sensory overload of life... just as Cotopaxi had been and with that realization came another: he couldn't stay, he *had* to leave, even though he knew he couldn't—there was simply no place to go and no way to get there even if there was. Narbrooi would see to that because not only was Khusaaq's reputation riding on his successful completion of this assignment, so was Narbrooi's, despite the officer doing everything he could to make the task that much harder—sabotaging him at every opportunity while stopping just short of sabotaging the mission.

What had begun as a tremor in his hands and the occasional muscle-twitching unease in his shoulders and back had grown over the subsequent days to a near obsession—the desire, the panic worsening by the hour, the minute, refusing to leave him alone even in sleep, in fact sleep made it worse, made the recurrent nightmares that had paid him sporadic visits him since Cotopaxi so much more vivid, so much more real and now every night—the smells, the sounds, the tastes of a living planet were everywhere, inescapable, a constant goad to his syntheste's already overly diligent subconscious.

It was all he could do to hide his mounting unease from others, from Sirin most of all, knowing no one could possibly understand that if he didn't leave, Tuli would suffer the same fate as Cotopaxi. He didn't know how, he didn't know why, he just knew with cold certainty that if he remained, he'd destroy another boisterously alive planet, only this time, a planet with a large population, a planet with Sirin and Amalfitano—the closest he'd ever had to a loving family. And if his worst fears were realized, he'd again be a hostage to the yawning uncertainty as to whether the culpability for his actions were his and his alone or if he was still little more than the unwitting pawn of the Elkanasu. Either way, he'd left to deal with the ramifications, the overwhelming guilt alone.

When he'd been confronted with the news of the attempted murder of Amalfitano and Tasende, and then the kidnappings of his men, his first reaction was shock, then horror, followed immediately by rage, all washing over him in full view of Sirin, Amalfitano, Aquila and, most importantly Izraad. She'd visibly winced and flinched in cadence with his rapid, utterly unguarded cascade of reactions. But what her chempathic abilities didn't sense, what no one else saw, because he bottled up the response as quickly as he felt it surfacing, hiding it behind the deluge of other, *expected* emotions was relief— hideous, overwhelming and utterly self-serving *relief*.

Escape from the near-suffocating fears for the planet, escape from history repeating itself—as utterly irrational as he knew his fears to be—was at hand. Narbrooi could hardly refuse his request—not even the Q'shaathrah would dare to question his motives for requesting a leave from his contract in order to mount a rescue of his closest kin—his Doh'ha.

And now here he was, aboard a ship—an A'tuu'shahn ship—speeding away from Tuli with orders from Narbrooi himself to track down his missing men and to deal with their kidnappers any way he saw fit. It was almost too good to be true... only one aching matter remained: Sirin.

Leaving her behind was the obvious, the smart choice, or so he'd assured himself. With him gone, Tuli would be safe—she would be safe. Had he brought her along, there would be no such guarantees. He squeezed his eyes shut. *Toq-bhir... I did this as much for you as I did it for me, for my men.*

Matoosh, oblivious to Khusaaq's roiling thoughts, toggled a switch. *Jirah* leapt forward, towards the outer planets and the beckoning vastness of interstellar space, where he, like all A'tuu'shahn'i, felt the most at home. After all, it had been their home, their only home, for tens of thousands of years.

Khusaaq exhaled, in the process shedding the last of his anxiety then turned and looked around him. Narbrooi had been good to his word, supplying him with a skilled, five-man crew, four of whom were currently seated at their own bridge consoles. The fifth, a medic, was perched on the edge of a jump seat at the rear of the small chamber, but as Khusaaq's gaze fell in him, he rose smartly and dipped his head.

"With your permission, Sha'ashahn, I'd like to re-familiarize myself with the sickbay."

"Of course." Khusaaq nodded then turned back to the pilot's console. He smiled as he watched Matoosh effortlessly maneuver the foldboat through the minefield of Tangaloa-Tuli's unusually dense Oort cloud. It was like old times. He almost expected to find Qharubi seated in the navigator's seat, grinning from ear to ear as he tried to plot a course Matoosh could not possibly follow.

Instead, that station was occupied by one of Narbrooi's hand-picked crew, and going by the complex combination of glyphs and scars that swirled and cut their way across his handsome, youthful face, he was Kri'taaka—a secular offshoot of the Elkanaghalli, but with the genetically enhanced ability to 'see' other dimensions, making Kri'taaka'i superior and much sought after navigators. And of course a faint but ever-present, writhing cyan luminescence surrounded all Kri'taaka'i along with their distinctive, slightly sweet, cool cobalt blue smell, just as he, an Elkanaghalli, was perpetually enveloped in the sight and sharp scent of pure, warm white, as befitted the first caste, the most beloved of the Elkanasu.

The navigator, sensing Khusaaq's appraising gaze, looked up. "Ta'ahn...?"

Khusaaq reluctantly drew himself out of the soothing familiarity, the soul-deep sense of contentment at being surrounded by the A'tuu'shahn world as only A'tuu'shahn'i could experience it, where sights, sounds, even words had their own colors, their own distinct flavors, a deeply comforting and familiar realm of richly intricate patterns, tastes and textures, unlike the washed out world of humans, perpetually bathed in a monochromatic, cloying and faint shadowy gray. Even the ship burned with its own slithering light, filling his mind with its unique, complex and ultimately calming spoor. He cleared his throat, asked, "What's your name, Kon'ta'aq?"

"Shu'hah, Sha'ashahn."

Khusaaq jerked his chin towards Matoosh. "You have the honor of navigating for one of the finest pilots in the fleet, Shu'hah Kon'ta'aq."

Shu'hah glanced at Matoosh then looked back at Khusaaq. "I know, ta'ahn."

Khusaaq turned next to the huge soldier who was manning the engineering console, surrounded by a shadowy, icy aurora of flickering and shifting violet blue—the sight and slightly acrid smell of the shade instantly evoking the equally cold, forbidding nature of the Quu'dahn caste itself. "And you, Ruh'ta'aq?"

The burly engineer replied in a deep rumble, "Tejat, ta'ahn."

Khusaaq shifted his gaze to the Elkanaghalli seated beside Tejat, at the tactical console, and you, Ruh'ta'aq?"

"Toubeh, ta'ahn," she replied as she dipped her head and touched the grip of her ritual dagger with her left hand.

Khusaaq nodded, pleased that Narbrooi had seen fit to select an Elkanaghalli—perhaps the better to keep an eye on him— then he fixed his hard stare on the last crewman, the weapons officer, veiled in the distinct, hot metallic taste of crimson... a Khighalli.

"And you, Kon'ta'aq?"

"Rukoobi, ta'ahn," the gunner replied, just as the medic reappeared in the hatchway.

Khusaaq turned, took in the newest arrival's cool astringent shade of pale gold with matching Dakkeesh tattoos, and raised his brows in query. "Yes?"

"All is in order, ta'ahn," the medic replied.

"And your name, Kon'ta'aq?"

"Jaa'qwah, Sha'ashahn."

Khusaaq again looked at each in turn, then crossing his arms said, "You've all been briefed on our mission."

The five nodded in eager unison, with Matoosh looking on.

"You do understand that your only compensation will be from the Orthodoxy."

There was a murmur of acknowledgement then Rukoobi spoke up: "Sha'ashahn, we all volunteered." He looked around at his crewmates and at their smiling, prodding stares, added, "When we heard that you were personally leading the rescue, we asked to be part of it. Truth be told, the entire crew of the *Faridour* volunteered, all hoping to participate, to be commanded by you. We were the ones most fortunate enough to have been selected."

Khusaaq, taken aback, glanced at Matoosh only to find the soldier grinning up at him. He tipped his head and said, "I am honored," hesitated, then continued, "We have our work cut out for us. Our first priority is the safe retrieval of our people. I then want to make examples of those responsible so no one else will even toy with the idea of repeating their... *blunder.*" As he spoke, his ghillie uniform abruptly changed from the copper of shipboard attire to the rich, iridescent black of battledress.

He could feel his skin, his tattoos—the very fabric of his being—becoming one with the uniform in preparation for what lay ahead. He looked around him again to find his words had had the same effect on his crew—and the ship. The pale cerulean patterns that had been languidly eeling across the floor, the ceiling and walls began writhing in earnest as their hue became a more intense azure, the cool, crisp scent of the ship more potent; the effect made his heart, his lungs pump faster.

He was home and the hunt was on.

"And our destination, Sha'ashahn?" Shu'hah asked, his fingers hovering above his console.

"Poonda Five." Khusaaq turned to the overhead tactical.

Shu'hah nodded to Matoosh. "Course laid in, Ruh'ta'aq."

"Maximum fold," Khusaaq murmured, then lightly grasping the back of Matoosh's chair, allowed himself a small smile. He was still amazed that Narbrooi had been so generous, not only with a diverse and veteran crew, but with the ship. Built for speed and stealth, rather than awe-inspiring armament, *Jirah* was capable of fold twelve.

"Maximum fold," Matoosh repeated; an instant later the small vessel neatly folded space around it, leaving behind only a series of rapidly fading spectral doppelgängers.

Chapter 14

Amalfitano's office, hospital complex on the outskirts of Alhajoth, Tuli.
1848, planetary time. Present day.

Amalfitano lifted his gaze from the stack of flimsies and scowled at Murh'sooli.

The fully armored soldier stood rigidly beside Amalfitano's desk, gauntleted hands clasped behind his back, narrowed eyes fixed intently on the nearby door as if expecting a massive assault at any moment. He'd been standing in the exact same position, with the exact same forbidding expression on his heavily tattooed face, for the entire afternoon while the other two assigned to Amalfitano were busy in the virology lab right next door, putting their medical know-how to the best possible use, the three alternating rotation every eight hours, like clockwork until Amalfitano called it a day and all four flicked back up to the *Baidarka*, where the rotation continued, only there he always had two guards present, one close by and visible, the other also near at hand but fully camouflaged while the third caught some well-earned sleep.

Murh'sooli, as was his habit, was his afternoon-evening and always visible guard. Amalfitano had joked with Izraad that it was because the medic wasn't a morning person. In truth the Hahtooshan's acerbic mood never changed. And Izraad had commented that his choice of shifts had absolutely nothing to do with the fact that this particular shift meant that he ate dinner with Amalfitano and Izraad—never obtrusive, just there in the background—and the dinner trays always included some confection or other sweet treat for dessert which Izraad always begged off and which she always offered the medic. Murh'sooli always grudgingly accepted it as if it was a supreme sacrifice on his part to wolf down yet another generous slice of pecan pie or chocolate fudge cake, never once handing it off to his invisible companion.

Amalfitano gave the sergeant another sidelong appraisal. *Keep that up and you're gonna need to let out your armor a size or two.* Aside from the occasional throat clearing or facial twitch, the burly medic might have easily been mistaken for a rather pretentious—and decidedly kitschy—statue.

Through Izraad, Amalfitano had learned that the tattoos and scarification all Hahtooshans bore was more than just an idiosyncratic brand of kinship, each caste having its own style, from the minimalist decoration of the Am'rataan'i, as befitted the youngest of the nine castes, to the extremely ornate of the Elkanaghalli'i, the oldest. The adornment was also a record of personal achievement.

This man, this medic, was Dakkeesh, as were all those assigned as bodyguards for him and Tasende, or so Izraad had said, and reasonably so she'd added, as the caste specialized in the medical arts. While not all Hahtooshan medicos were Dakkeesh—a prime example being Suhjai—all Dakkeesh were doctors, medics or medical researchers. And this particular Dakkeesh bore several ugly, puckering scars on his face and throat—all relatively new, Amalfitano judged—not to mention the constant, niggling feel of familiarity.

"I know you from somewhere."

Amalfitano's out of the blue observation briefly drew the medic's stony, gray-eyed gaze and a grumbled, "Yes... ta'ahn."

To Amalfitano's ear, the Hahtooshan's version of "sir" was clearly an afterthought—a *very* reluctant afterthought.

"Where?"

"Here."

Amalfitano eyed him. "Of course *here*, but you looked familiar the instant I met you aboard the *Baidarka.*"

Murh'sooli shifted his substantial weight from one campaign booted foot to the other, a clear signal that he felt equally uncomfortable with the topic, but Amalfitano persisted—he hated mysteries, hated when pieces failed to fall into place. And Murh'sooli was definitely a puzzle, a massive, maddening and not particularly attractive puzzle to boot.

"I *asked* a question, Raz'ta'aq. I *expect* a straight answer."

The sergeant drew himself up to his very impressive height, crossed his thick, armored arms, then fixed Amalfitano with an annoyed stare and replied with an equally annoyed, "Why is this important?"

"Because I say so."

Murh'sooli chewed on that for a moment then replied, "In the jungle—"

"You were that medic!" Amalfitano interrupted with sudden recollection. "The one who treated Khusaaq!" He grinned and slapped the table with his hands, causing the medic to flinch. *"Of course!"*

Murh'sooli collected himself, responded with an indifferent shrug and resumed his previous parade rest stance, gauntleted hands again clasped behind his ghillie-armored back, narrowed eyes fixed on the door.

Amalfitano, satisfied, resumed his study of a report. *Of course…*

Several minutes passed in total silence then he overheard the medic again shift his weight.

"Would you *please* sit down?"

Murh'sooli flicked him a quick, sidelong glare. "No… ta'ahn."

"Then do your guarding over there." He motioned to the far corner of his cramped hospital complex office. "I can't concentrate with you hovering over me."

Murh'sooli's deep-set eyes darted to the spot, then back to Amalfitano. "No."

Amalfitano leaned back in his chair and threw up his hands in exasperation. "What is it with you goddamned Hahtooshans? Do you take lessons in being insufferable, or is it an inborn talent?"

"Both," Murh'sooli replied straight-faced, startling Amalfitano into a reflexive snort.

He looked up at his unwanted companion and shook his head in grudging admiration. He hadn't seen that one coming. "Didn't think Hahtooshans had a sense of humor."

"Who says we do?"

"But you…" Amalfitano began then shook his head. "Never mind. My mistake."

"Indeed, ta'ahn."

Amalfitano started to open his mouth, but was cut off by a knock at the door. "Come."

Out of the corner of his eye, he saw Murh'sooli straighten up as one hand came to rest on the grip of his holstered pistol. *As if an assassin is going to politely knock…*

The door slipped open and Sirin stepped in, a fresh stack of reports in her hands.

Amalfitano knew that the news of the kidnappings and his own botched assassination had hit Khusaaq hard. While Khusaaq's abrupt leave-taking for consultations aboard the *Faridour* was perfectly understandable, even expected, he sensed there was far more going on than Sirin was letting on. Not that whatever that was had in any way hampered her effectiveness in getting the deluge of reports categorized, and in record time. In fact from the moment she arrived at his office that morning—an hour earlier than normal—she had attacked the problem with, even for her, a singular intensity—a classic case of unintended consequences. Or—as he saw what she held in her hands—a case of no good deed going unpunished.

He couldn't help it: he groaned and slumped back into the chair; Murh'sooli, if it was possible, just looked even more annoyed.

She glanced first at Amalfitano, then up at the imposing and decidedly peeved Murh'sooli. "Ah, did I interrupt something?"

"No," the two snapped in unison, then glared at each other.

"Ooookay," she replied, dubious as she placed the thick stack of flimsies on the desk. "Well, it's almost nineteen hundred—"

"Nineteen hundred?" Amalfitano gasped with genuine shock. The last time he'd checked, it was barely past noon.

"Yes, and Lieutenant Izraad wanted to know if you're going to flick back to the *Baidarka* anytime soon? Said she's getting rather peckish and will go ahead with dinner if you plan on staying much longer."

That drew a decidedly aggrieved sigh from Murh'sooli.

Amalfitano dropped his gaze to the updated culture reports and gave his suddenly weary eyes a vigorous knuckle-rub.

"These can wait until morning." Sirin patted the stack. "Xosé said to tell you that the lab's all cleaned up and the bugs locked away—he and his guards flicked up a little while ago, and if you don't mind me saying so, sir, you look like you need to quit for the night too." Her eyes slid up to his grim-faced bodyguard and clearly wanted to add, "You, too," but wisely didn't.

"Yeah," Amalfitano sighed and heaved himself out of his chair. "Why not." He started for the door then stopped and looked back at her. "Coming?"

"I have a few more reports to compile and distribute."

"Don't stay too long—you've been at it longer than we have."

"Won't, promise—got a good book waiting for me."

"Sure you don't want to spend tonight aboard *Baidarka?"*

"There's a chance Khusaaq'll be flicking back down later tonight. Meanwhile, I'll be fine. Now *shoo."* She motioned to the door.

"How 'bout if Murh'sooli here walks you to your bungalow—maybe even stays, just to make sure—"

"Thanks," she replied before Murh'sooli could protest, "But Narbrooi's already assigned me a bodyguard in light of everything." She jerked her chin to the open doorway. Beyond, next to Amalfitano's other two restive guards, stood a third soldier, whose facial tattoos, he couldn't help but notice, were decidedly less elaborate than the three medics. What the guard lacked in facial ornamentation, he more than made up for in sheer brawn: he was at least a head taller than the other Hahtooshans, and looked to outweigh the stocky Murh'sooli by a good twenty kilos. "Silly, if you ask me with all the extra security already in place, but he insisted and he's not exactly someone you can say no to."

Amalfitano managed a weary chuckle as he rubbed the back of his neck. "Tell me about it. But... all right. See you in the morning—you coming straight here or are you back to the regular routine of helping with Matoosh's morning swim first?"

"I haven't heard yet," she answered distractedly, her back to him as she straightened up a precariously untidy stack of flimsies on his desk before they cascaded to the floor.

"All right, we'll see you when we see you," he replied and with a sidelong glare at Murh'sooli and a grumbled, "Well, what the hell are you waiting for?" strode out of the office.

Chapter 15

Aboard Jirah.
Five hours into High Watch. Present day.

Khusaaq stopped at the open hatchway of the small galley, crossed his arms and, bracing his shoulder against the oval hatch, smiled as his nostrils picked up on the familiar, rich oily black and almost cloyingly sweet scent of barra—a mild stimulant favored by A'tuu'shahn crews.

Jaa'qwah, his broad back to the hatchway, was quietly arguing with himself as he tried to put the finishing touches on what was clearly supposed to be a midday meal. The bowls of food he'd already placed on the small table, while having a savory aroma every bit as enticing as the barra, looked positively revolting.

"I didn't know you doubled as a cook."

Jaa'qwah glanced over his shoulder, and, seeing who it was, came to rigid attention, almost spilling the contents of the bowl he was holding. "Ta'ahn!"

"At ease," Khusaaq murmured as he stepped into the galley.

"Yes, ta'ahn." Jaa'qwah smiled briefly as he looked around him. "I thought I'd prepare something hot and a little more filling than the protein wafers." He placed the bowl on the table, then shrugged, "I really won't have much to do until we retrieve our men, or we run into resistance."

"I will need my duty uniform rejuved—Matoosh as well."

"Of course, ta'ahn. Come to sickbay at your convenience— and I'll remind Ruh'ta'aq to do the same."

"Good." He'd had plenty of opportunity to have his uniform rejuved on the *Faridour*, and had the time, if barely, to undergo the complete physical the ship's medical officers had requested—and had found reasons to avoid both, fearful Narbrooi would use any excuse to declare him unfit to lead the mission. "And..." he lowered his voice, *"I have a problem with my leg."* He couldn't help but rub his right thigh, a behavior that had become more a nervous tic of late. *"I don't think it's healing properly."*

Jaa'qwah nodded and to Khusaaq's relief didn't ask why he hadn't sought care on *Faridour*. "Then may I suggest you come to sickbay immediately after we eat?"

"Yes, I'll do that." Khusaaq looked at the food before him. *Now would be even better.*

Jaa'qwah, aware of his less than favorable response added: "I don't think I have the synthesizers configured properly..."

Khusaaq struggled not to laugh out loud. *Now why would you think that?*

"...with so little notice, techs had time only to make the most basic adjustments before we left, assuming, and rightfully so, that with Tejat aboard, he could finish up. But so far he's been extremely busy..." he flicked Khusaaq an oblique look. "It *is* perfectly edible and very nutritious, ta'ahn."

Khusaaq gave the offerings another quick glance. They reminded him of his first introduction to Amalfitano's favorite dish—that too had looked and *smelled* positively unappetizing and its odd, rubbery texture not to mention being told that one of its main ingredients was a type of fungus—albeit a synthetic fungus—hadn't helped. But it *had* in fact tasted far better than it looked, so perhaps there was hope for these offerings too. He smiled at the young medic. "I'm sure it is."

Once *Jirah* was beyond the last of Tangaloa's planets, and, more importantly, beyond the long-range sensors of any ships orbiting Tuli, Khusaaq had retreated to the communications console on the bridge and familiarized himself with the dossiers of each of his crew. Narbrooi had indeed picked the best of the best, a fact that both surprised and pleased him immensely. He pulled down a chair and slipped onto it. "You are of the sixth house of Dakkeesh."

Jaa'qwah nodded as he placed a bowl and a mug in front of him. "Yes, ta'ahn."

"Your record is exemplary."

The medic grinned as he ladled some of his culinary efforts into the bowl. "Thank you, ta'ahn."

Khusaaq stared down at the lumpy brown pool and tried not to make a face. *It looks like shit...* "You do realize that to most A'tuu'shahn'i I'm a traitor."

Jaa'qwah, in the process of filling Khusaaq's mug from the decanter of frothy yellow barra, stopped and gave him a sidelong look. "Ta'ahn, you are the Hero of Cotopaxi and—"

"Was the Hero of Cotopaxi," he replied with a reflexive twitch of the shoulders.

The medic placed the decanter on the table. "Ta'ahn... may I speak freely?"

He motioned to another chair. "Always, Kon'ta'aq."

Jaa'qwah eased himself down onto it then stared at his muscular, tattooed hands for a moment, clearly ordering his thoughts.

Finally he met Khusaaq's questioning stare. "Ta'ahn, our limited gene pool was already dwindling to a precarious level, with more and more dangerous mutations cropping up with each generation. While not common knowledge, the Battle of Nyaat Cluster was the tipping point, with so many lineages lost..."

Khusaaq nodded; the Battle of Nyaat had taken place at the same time as Cotopaxi while at the opposite end of the Orion spur, and the truly staggering and unprecedented losses the Orthodoxy had suffered in that doomed campaign had catapulted him into the role of hero at a time when his fellow A'tuu'shahn'i, whose deeply held belief in their collective invincibility had been shaken to its core, were in desperate need of *living* heroes. Nyaat had been billed as a grand campaign like no other in recent memory, with plenty of opportunities for advancement and acclaim. Every A'tuu'shahn worth his or her family glyph was clamoring to take part.

Gaalan had boasted to all who would listen that she'd be one of the first to be offered her pick of assignments, of ship and crew; it was a chance of a lifetime, and for her a chance, likely her last chance, to refurbish and revitalize her flagging career. Instead she discovered that her more recent scandals continued to outweigh her storied military past, that the need for qualified officers did not mean all was forgiven. Instead she was handed the task of protecting a Rimmer colony, a deliberately demeaning task deemed so inconsequential that she was provided only with an aging koursan and an inexperienced crew—the Orthodoxy had need of its best ships, its most experienced crews elsewhere, or so she'd been told.

It had been a very bitter pill for her to swallow, despite her claims that this *was* a contract worthy of her time and experience, a chance to train up a new generation to her exacting requirements, and one, he'd long suspected, that had led to her decision to sacrifice herself at Cotopaxi. To die a hero, all past mistakes expunged, all rumors quelled, a standing in death her own family, much less the Q'shaathrah couldn't possibly deny her, or so she'd thought. But she'd misjudged the true depth of their grudges, couldn't have possibly anticipated the unqualified catastrophe that was Nyaat. So, they'd replaced her with him, recognizing, lauding his actions while blatantly ignoring hers—

"... a loss from which we as a species will never recover."

Khusaaq jerked his eyes, his mind back to Jaa'qwah as the medic continued,

"We must have a massive infusion of new genes in order to remain viable as a species—and there is the now well-known fact that we have no resistance to even the most common of communicable human diseases. We're again standing on a knife's edge—one accident, one more setback and we will plunge into oblivion, this time permanently." He paused, shook his head, then again met Khusaaq's hooded stare. "You did what you did to save us from not just from our enemies, ta'ahn, but also from ourselves and from our own prideful arrogance. Dakkeesh *know* this—we've repeatedly warned the Q'shaathrah but our words have always fallen on deaf ears..."

Khusaaq couldn't help but think of Ouda'yai, the *Makhaira*'s senior medical officer, and his futile efforts at convincing Tarqk of the dangers of the viruses they'd recovered from Rasal Ghul. Ouda'yai's warnings had fallen on deaf ears as well, and he'd paid for his dogged persistence with his life— of course, eventually so had Tarqk, along with the *Makhaira*'s crew.

"...you, and you alone, through your bold actions and because of who you are, forced them to see what they have refused to accept for so long. You *are* a hero, ta'ahn, not just for Cotopaxi and the dozen other campaigns in which you greatly distinguished yourself, but for what you've done to save all of us." Jaa'qwah flashed him a smile then dropped his gaze at his hands, embarrassed at his effusiveness.

Khusaaq started to reply as he always had, giving all the credit to the Elkanasu or to others, while almost greedily seizing the blame for himself. He'd paid a very heavy price for his impulsive humility, humility even he knew bordered on the pathologic and often served no purpose other than to garner suspicion and resentment. Before he could open his mouth to demur, Jaa'qwah continued.

"Rukoobi wasn't exaggerating—the entire crew of *Faridour* volunteered when we heard of your mission. Truthfully, ta'ahn—the *entire* crew, save Hahtra'tzrhi of course."

Khusaaq ran his fingertip around the lip of his steaming mug, tried and failed not to respond with a pleased, albeit startled smile. "That must have set well with Narbrooi."

Jaa'qwah replied cautiously, "Hahtra'tzrhi is a most... *intense* man, ta'ahn—"

"You mean he's a hidebound, sanctimonious Elkanaghalli."

Jaa'qwah swallowed convulsively. *"Ah—"*

"Just as I was," Khusaaq added with a soft chuckle. He flicked the medic a glance, grinned broadly then took a deep gulp from his mug and savored the strong sweet taste, warmth and comforting aroma of the barra, then clutching the mug in both hands, looked back at the young Dakkeesh. "Tell me about the others."

"I know Toubeh Ruh'ta'aq only by reputation, ta'ahn," Jaa'qwah replied, his words clearly measured, watchful, unsure if Khusaaq had fully taken him into his confidence, or was just assessing him, his loyalties and his possible motives. "She only recently transferred aboard *Faridour*, but the bridge crew speak very highly of her." He motioned to the decanter, and at Khusaaq's nod, poured himself a mug of barra, took a sip, swallowed then continued, "Shu'hah Kon'ta'aq is an excellent navigator—one of Hahtra'tzrhi's favorites as he's very steady, not easily provoked or rattled—I think he's more than up to Matoosh's challenge, if I may be so bold to say. Tejat Ruh'ta'aq is in line to become chief engineer of *Faridour*. He keeps to himself—as with most Quu'dahn'i he prefers machines to flesh and blood—"

"And Rukoobi Kon'ta'aq?" Khusaaq interrupted, his own prejudices tainting his voice.

"He can be a bit of a hothead, ta'ahn, I won't claim otherwise—overconfident, willful, in other words, a typical Khighalli," he added with a wry smile. "But when it comes to weapons, he really is as good as he thinks he is—according to Shu'hah perhaps even better." He leaned close and added in a conspiratorial whisper, *"I believe Hahtra'tzrhi is privately hoping you can settle him down a bit."*

Khusaaq snorted. "I'll do my best." He let the piping hot barra pool in his mouth, savoring its familiar taste. As he did so, he realized how much he had missed… *this*, being aboard an A'tuu'shahn ship, surrounded by an A'tuu'shahn crew—and he smiled.

Late one night when he and Sirin had been curled up together on the lanai of their bungalow, he'd mentioned the intense feeling of missing all of the common, background familiarities, the intricate mixture of sights, smells, tastes and textures that were so much a part of what it was to be A'tuu'shahn. She'd told him he was experiencing the A'tuu'shahn equivalent of a security blanket—a synestheste's security blanket.

He hadn't really understood what she meant until now. Here those deep-rooted familiarities were omnipresent to the point of being overlooked; on Tuli their complete absence, replaced by an utterly alien cacophony, was painfully evident, jarring and left him chilled to the bone.

He jerked his thoughts off Sirin, off Tuli—back to the present and in the process noticed that Jaa'qwah was staring at something behind him. He hastily swallowed his mouthful and glanced over his shoulder.

Toubeh stood in the open hatch.

She acknowledged his startled stare with a slight nod and, "I did not mean to intrude, ta'ahn."

"Please, join us." Khusaaq gestured for her to take a seat. "Jaa'qwah was just about to call everyone for midday meal."

Toubeh slipped onto another chair, one directly across from Khusaaq and poured herself a mug of the barra as Jaa'qwah rose and paged the others. She brought the mug to her lips and took a cautious sip as she studied him over its rim.

Aware of her covert scrutiny, Khusaaq took a gulp from his own mug. He swallowed, wiped his mouth with the back of his hand and said, "I make you *very* uncomfortable."

Toubeh placed her mug on the table and replied, "I would be lying if I said no, ta'ahn."

"Then why volunteer?"

"You... *intrigue* me, ta'ahn."

"Indeed? Why?"

"You carry the paas'nah, among other things."

"You know about that."

"Of course. It's common knowledge—didn't you know?"

"That I carry it?" He couldn't help his flippant response, chalking it up to being around humans far too much.

She blinked, not sure if he was joking or serious. "No, I... I meant that it's common knowledge, ta'ahn. I've never met, never even heard of someone who carries the recessive gene, but you... you carry the dominant gene. I was raised to believe it had been completely eliminated from the Elkanaghalli line with the death of Sin'oaah."

The suicide of Sin'oaah you mean—and in front of the assembled Q'shaathrah no less. "Clearly not," he shrugged, feeling that was the safest response, but in truth he hadn't even thought to wonder who knew. Narbrooi did, the Q'shaathrah did of course, but he'd never considered it being widely known. In fact he'd banked on it not being common knowledge. That it wasn't explained a lot and he found himself perversely humored by this as he suddenly saw a lifetime of awkward conversations or the muted reactions of superior officers in a whole new light. A living, breathing conduit to the Elkanasu was, after all, not someone you wanted to risk upsetting. Tarqk had been the exception: the officer had gone out of his way to taunt him, probing to see if the rumors were true.

She leaned towards him, glanced at the seemingly preoccupied Jaa'qwah, then whispered, *"And the Elkanasu— they spoke to you, on Cotopaxi."*

He shook his head then answered in a normal voice, seeing no need to hide their conversation from a non-Elkanaghalli. "The Elkanasu guided me on Cotopaxi—or, I thought they did at the time..."

That did draw Jaa'qwah's eye.

"...now I know they did."

"How?" Toubeh asked, like Jaa'qwah taking the hint and dropping any pretense at privacy.

"They told me."

Her brows shot up; so did Jaa'qwah's. "They... *told* you?" She glanced up at the medic who now stood beside her, a forgotten bowl in his hands.

"Yes." Khusaaq brought his mug to his lips and said, "We had quite a lengthy talk." Then he took a sip.

"Talk?" she repeated, almost but not quite incredulous and at the same time, hopeful. "You mean they talked to you... and you—"

"Talked back?" He smiled at the double meaning; he had, after all, been rather insolent at the time. "Indeed I did."

"And yet—"

"I'm not dead?"

She visibly tried to collect herself as a thousand questions instantly formed on her tongue, making her lips twitch.

He fully understood her response. The Elkanasu simply didn't sit down with an A'tuu'shahn, even an Elkanaghalli, and have a friendly chat over a cup of barra. It was common belief among A'tuu'shahn'i and a closely held conviction for Elkanaghalli'i that the only time you heard the Elkanasu was when they'd come to collect you, and that was completely contingent on you being worthy—a criterion which always seemed to be on the move, always just out of reach. Even someone who carried the paas'nah was a passive, albeit direct go-between.

To have someone who was alive and breathing and seemingly healthy suggest that he'd not only heard the Elkanasu, but had talked to them and they'd talked back was, in a word, stunning. And unlike some among the Q'shaathrah, even some among his own clan, Toubeh didn't look like she was considering the logical alternative: that he wasn't entirely sane.

He took a deep gulp of the barra, swallowed, then added, "It was a very revealing conversation."

"In... in what way?" she asked after a moment of deciding which question to ask, and a prompting glance from Jaa'qwah, who was equally curious but knew his place as a secular Dakkeesh.

"I'd be willing to discuss what we talked about in detail, to both of you," he gave Jaa'qwah a nod, "to the entire crew in fact," he replied, absently rubbing his aching thigh. "Perhaps later?"

She noticed and while clearly disappointed, replied, "Of course, Sha'ashahn. Any time of your choosing—"

An explosion of laughter from the corridor drew his attention and Toubeh's and startled Jaa'qwah, who, after his brief lapse had gone back to trying to look invisible in the cramped galley. A moment later Matoosh, Shu'hah and Rukoobi appeared in the hatchway. In their brief time together, the three had clearly bonded.

Matoosh grinned at Khusaaq as they each grabbed a mug then quickly seated themselves at the circular table meant for four and jostled for room. "Shu'hah was just telling me that Mihr-Suhjai also volunteered for the mission." He filled his mug with barra, then shook his head as he quickly filled Rukoobi's and Shu'hah's. "Sadly, she was deemed medically unfit. Pity that."

Khusaaq chuckled then leaning back and taking a more measured sip from his mug watched in rapt silence as Rukoobi hungrily scooped up a lumpy spoonful of Jaa'qwah's attempt at food and shoveled it into his awaiting mouth.

The gunner chewed thoughtfully for a moment, then looked up at the expectant Jaa'qwah with slitted eyes as he visibly forced himself to swallow.

Khusaaq couldn't help himself. He burst into laughter.

Chapter 16

Khusaaq and Sirin's shared bungalow, Tuli.
2155, planetary time. Present day.

Sirin eagerly parted company with her standoffish guard at the front door, intensely relieved that he hadn't demanded on doing his guarding inside the small cottage. He was clearly just as relieved when she hadn't insisted he come inside. There was simply no need. The Tulians had their own security patrolling the hospital grounds including its residential sector and there were plenty of Hahtooshan troopers about as well, invisible in their ghillie armor; the guard's presence was nothing more than a perfunctory gesture on Narbrooi's part, one which was received as it was given. More maddening: the soldier himself was decidedly aggravated with his assignment, and the short walk from the hospital complex had been made in record time and, after one very awkward attempt on her part to engage him in small talk, in complete and, for her, strained silence as she did her best to keep up with his long strides since he seemed utterly unwilling to accommodate her shorter ones.

Once the door had closed, and locked—at the guard's gruff insistence—she leaned against it and sighed heavily as she looked around her, suddenly struck with the reality she'd so successfully hidden from everyone all day: Khusaaq was gone, very possibly forever. What just the day before had been the physical underpinning of her new life was now nothing but a silent, and very empty house.

With a shake of her head, realizing she wasn't the least bit hungry, or tired for that matter despite the very long day and the *very* invigorating walk home, she changed out of her uniform and into Khusaaq's favorite negligee then grabbed her data reader from the dining table. With a defiant glance at the locked front door, and the unseen guard beyond, she opened the lanai door, stepped outside and curled up in a chair just as she did most evenings, maintaining the ruse that Khusaaq would be arriving any moment even though it was only for her own benefit.

But instead of studying the reader, preparing for the next day's daunting workload, she found herself searching the dazzling, star-filled sky as the cool evening breeze ruffled her hair. "Come back to—"

The soft chime of the doorbell startled her and she glanced over her shoulder, surprised and, she realized, greatly annoyed at the intrusion.

She briefly toyed with the idea of ignoring it then, realizing that the twitchy guard might assume the worst and react accordingly—possibly even raising the alarm with Tulian security, drawing even more unwanted attention, she reluctantly rose and wiping her eyes, walked over to the door and pressed the com-unit. "Who is it?"

"Who da ya tink?" came a familiar hissing lisp.

"I know her," Sirin said for the guard's benefit, then sighed, not the least bit in the mood for company, even if that company was Drakin and thumbed the release.

The door slipped open, but instead of being greeted with the smiling face of her closest friend, she was confronted with the unsmiling face of the Hahtooshan guard.

His gaze fell and his eyes widened, and she suddenly realized her negligee was untied. She quickly wrapped it tight around her.

"Hi dere," Drakin said, grinning as she slipped past the burly soldier, whose eyes were now firmly fixed on the toes of his campaign boots.

Sirin couldn't help but smile and motioned for her to enter. As the door slipped closed, the guard reassuming his menacing, parade rest stance just outside, she asked, "Not that I don't appreciate the visit, but what are you doing here?"

"I tought you could uz sssome company."

"They're only going to be gone overnight," Sirin lied.

"I know, but… well, okay, zo I needed an excussse."

"Excuse?"

"To get off ssship. Diz whole ting wit Pardix—everyone'z a tad jumpy." She forced a toothy smile.

"Yeah."

"Had dinner yet?"

"No, not really hungry, actually." That, at least, was true.

"Too bad. Take out." Drakin held up a large sack then motioned with a scaly shoulder to the door. "By da way, whoz da cutie?"

"Cutie…? Oh, you mean *him.*" Sirin made a face and feigned a shiver. "Gift from Narbrooi."

"Really? Tink if I asssk him nisssely, he'd give me one, too?"

Sirin laughed. "That's not what I meant. He's my bodyguard—you know, with this whole thing of Pardix and such. But trust me, if I could, I'd happily give him to you."

"Oh." Drakin, her attention still fixed on the guard outside, continued, "Maybe he'd like to join uz? Dere's plenty and he lookz like he haz a hearty appetite." She wiggled her brow ridges.

"I doubt it—joining us I mean; I can't speak for his appetite."

"Pity. He lookz like he could be *very* entertaining."

Sirin had to physically shake her head to rid her mind of the images that remark conjured up.

Drakin shuffled over to the small dining table and set her offering on it. She then began to pull boxes out of the sack. "I hope you like fried fissssh."

"Ah... yeah, sure." Sirin no sooner accepted a box from Drakin when the doorbell chimed again.

"Expecting ssssomeone?"

"Ah, no, as a matter of fact."

"Maybe our friend wanted anudder free peek?"

Sirin scowled at her.

Drakin looked suitably contrite before adding, "Or maybe he sssmelled da food, iz a tad peckisssh and wanz to join uz?"

"Yeah. Maybe." Sirin pulled her thin robe around her, then walked back to the door and without thinking, pressed the release. The door slipped open.

Standing just outside was her guard. She placed her hands on her hips and said tetchily, "Yes?"

He toppled forward and she jumped back as he fell heavily and face first onto the floor at her feet. She pulled her horrified stare off him only to realize that Pardix was standing behind him.

"Back!" he whispered, motioning angrily with the soldier's maser pistol.

Sirin did as she was told only to find herself backing into Drakin just as another man, a total stranger, slipped around Pardix and stepped over the inert body of the guard, a shocker in his hands. Both wore Tulian security uniforms.

He pointed the shocker at Sirin and Drakin. Nodding to Pardix, he said, "I've got'em covered."

Pardix shoved his weapon into his waistband then grabbed the guard by his belt and grunting and swearing under his breath, barely managed to drag him across the threshold and into the bungalow. He then hit the door release and it snapped shut. He thumbed the lock, following up by thumbing each of the access ways, doors, windows, closing and locking them in place as well. Satisfied, he nodded to his companion. "All secure."

"Wat da hell?" Drakin, recovered from her initial shock, fixed her beady gaze on the stranger. "And who da hell are you?"

"Jonathan Urbat." He smiled as he met Sirin's startled stare.

"What do you want?" she asked.

"We want your merc lover, Blondie."

"He's not here," she replied defiantly.

"Not here, huh?"

"That's what I said, but if you don't believe me search the place—go on."

As Urbat looked around him, Drakin slowly knelt down beside the guard and felt for a pulse. Sirin, her attention drawn to what Drakin was doing, noticed what the nurse had noticed: a tiny, seemingly innocuous hole between the Hahtooshan's armored shoulder blades which was oozing blood—

"Fucker's not dead." Pardix grinned as he gave the soldier a vicious kick to the flank.

The Hahtooshan, to everyone's surprise, made a feeble grab for his missing maser pistol. This time Pardix stomped on the guard's gauntleted hand then he kicked him in the head.

"STOP IT!" Sirin grabbed Pardix's arm and tried to pull him away as he kicked him again.

The renegade navigator roughly jerked himself free of her grip, then with a sidelong grin at her, knelt and, pressing the soldier's own pistol against his now profusely bleeding temple, in the process drawing the guard's glazed stare, said, "Make any more stupid moves, you fuckin' yowie and I'll happily blow you to kingdom come—"

"Remember the *plan*, Tace," Urbat warned.

"Fine," Pardix grumbled then straightening up, looked at Drakin. "Find something to tie him up with—*DO IT!"*

Drakin squinted fiercely at him. Realizing the futility of arguing, she looked around. The only close and obvious choice was the tie of Sirin's negligee.

"May I have dat?" she motioned to it.

Sirin, sensing it was this or Pardix would carry out his threat of killing the guard, quickly pulled it free of its belt loops and handed it to Drakin.

"So, where is he?" Urbat asked as his gaze fell back on Sirin while Drakin began to carefully bind the soldier's hands behind his back.

"Why the hell should I tell you?" Sirin crossed her arms.

"Well, for one thing it would save me a lot of time."

"Like I give a damn."

"You should," Urbat replied as he looked her up and down. "You should care a great deal. Now, I ask again, where is he?"

"Aboard *Faridour*."

"And he left you here all by yourself? That wasn't very smart of him, now was it?"

Sirin only glared at him, safe in the knowledge that all she had to do was stall long enough for the camouflaged Hahtooshan troopers to notice their missing colleague, which, she suspected, shouldn't be more than a minute, two at most.

"So, when do you expect him back?"

"He didn't say."

"Really."

"Yes, *really.*"

"Too bad," Urbat replied as his narrowed eyes scanned the bungalow once more, then, looking back at her, he grinned. "Then I guess we'll just take you."

Sirin's eyes widened and she backed up a step.

"Oh, no you don't." Urbat grabbed her by the arm and jerked her against him. "Now, be a good girl, do what we say and you won't be harmed."

"Like hell!" She tried to pull free but his grip was too strong.

"Scream and I'll kill anyone who comes running." Pardix pointed a silvery tube at the guard's head. "Starting with him."

"You really want to add murder charges on top of kidnapping?"

"Too late for that," Pardix replied and seeing the look in his eye, Sirin suddenly began to have serious doubts about any timely rescue. He held up the silvery tube. "Doesn't look like much, but trust me, at close range it can go through yowie armor like it's water, can't it, Merc?" He kicked the Hahtooshan in the flank with his foot; the guard replied with a gurgling groan. "As for the Tulians, they never knew what hit 'em." For emphasis, he plucked at a small hole in the fabric over his left breast, barely visible in the center of the appropriated uniform's security patch. Then just to make sure he'd made his point, he turned so she could get a look at the exit hole in the back.

"And just how do you plan on taking me anywhere? The Hahtooshans are monitoring the entire area for any unauthorized flicker signals."

"You put far too much trust in the abilities of your merc buddies, Sirin," Pardix replied with a smug grin as he patted a small device on his belt. "We got in here—we can get out. Trust me."

"What about her?" Urbat asked, motioning at Drakin with his shocker as Sirin continued to struggle against his hold.

Pardix grinned. "I think we should take her, too." He leaned down and gave the Hahtooshan's makeshift bindings a test tug. Satisfied, he heaved the dazed guard onto his side, withdrew a wad of grimy fabric from his pocket and forced it into the soldier's blood-filled mouth. "Drakin here's a nurse." He lurched to his feet. "She might come in handy just in case someone else gets... *hurt.*" To emphasize his point, he gave the Hahtooshan another hard kick, this time in the face then motioned with the alien weapon for Drakin to rise. "Up!"

"I ssshoulda let you bleed to det," she hissed as she got to her feet.

"You just don't get it, *do you*, Lieutenant? The Hahtooshans aren't interested in an alliance, they aren't looking to make peace with us! Once a yowie always a yowie and the moment we collectively let down our guard or turn our backs they'll attack, *count on it,* just like they did at Raumalle or the Chhotri and Tharus camps, only this time it won't be an isolated colony or a few thousand Rimmers, it'll be the entire Coalition and I for one am damned if I'm going to stand back and let that happen!"

An instant later, Sirin felt the tingle of a flicker effect wash over her.

Chapter 17

Aboard the Jirah.
End of High Watch. Present day. Twelve hours from Poonda Five.

Khusaaq nodded his appreciation in response to Jaa'qwah's questioning, sidelong stare and eased himself down in the *Jirah's* command chair with a grateful sigh. The medic had accompanied him back to the bridge using the excuse that he needed to collect Matoosh for his uniform's rejuv, but clearly Jaa'qwah's primary concern was if his dosing levels were effective or not and to that end spent the short trip assessing Khusaaq's gait, his expression. By the time they reached the airlock that gave access to the bridge, the medic was satisfied.

For Khusaaq it was mildly disconcerting. He'd lived with the deep, throbbing ache in his right thigh for so long it had become part of him, a fact of day-to-day life he consciously ignored and at the same time subconsciously accommodated and its sudden and complete absence was a relief on so many levels.

"Ruh'ta'aq?"

Matoosh glanced over his shoulder at the medic.

"I'm ready for you now," Jaa'qwah said and Matoosh relinquished his post to Toubeh, then with a sidelong glance and a smile at Khusaaq followed the medic as Jaa'qwah stepped through the airlock.

Khusaaq settled back into the contoured chair, crossed his arms and squinted blearily at the tactical display. All was at optimum. Not that he'd expected any less. The crew knew their jobs, they knew each other's jobs; he should have done as Jaa'qwah had suggested and retreated to his quarters and taken a well-earned nap. He could feel his bone-deep weariness in his shoulders, behind his eyes. Without the pain to keep him awake, lulled by the soft mutters of the ship and her crew, he found his eyelids fluttering.

He gave his head a shake, blinked then glanced around him, relieved no one had noticed him nodding off, everyone was too preoccupied, or too respectful. Everyone had something to do... except him—at least not for another twelve long hours.

He inhaled deeply, filling his lungs with all the familiar, soothing smells, then as he slowly exhaled, he again felt himself slipping... this time the urge was just too great, the chair was just too comfortable as it hugged his body and he found he could not muster the will to heave himself out of it and make his way to his quarters. His eyelids fluttered again, his head tilted forward. Another breath, even deeper and with it he sank effortlessly into the warm, dark abyss....

"...Ruh'ta'aq?"

Khusaaq stirred, drawn to the unfamiliar, high-pitched female voice and the sensation of his wrist being squeezed.

"Ruh'ta'aq, can you hear me?"

After a moment of struggle with a body that clearly wasn't under his control, he managed to open one eye, and then, with far more effort, the other.

A face hovered over him, a worried face—a young Dakkeesh's face—a total stranger.

"Who... who are you?" he rasped as he tried to lift his head and was instantly rewarded with a searing pain that raced the length of his spine.

"Please don't move—the medical officer hasn't had a chance to fully gauge the success of regen—"

Medical officer? Where's... where's Jaa'qwah? And regen? It was just a simple rejuv—or was it? Something wasn't right; in fact everything was very *wrong. Scents were wrong, tastes, everything—*

"—I ask that you remain as still as possible."

"Fine time to tell me," Khusaaq heard himself grumble as he glanced around him, or as best he could, trying to cover his growing panic and reluctant to repeat his earlier mistake as the medic continued to fuss over him, over his lower body. But his words sounded like an echo, or said by someone else. "Where... where am I?"

She replied distractedly as she grabbed a triage kit from an over-bed locker, "Aboard *Khargeh,* ta'ahn."

Khargeh? "What... what am I doing here?"

The medic stopped what she was doing, met his alarmed gaze. "You were rescued from Cotopaxi, Ruh'ta'aq, you and the others—"

"Cotopaxi?"

She nodded as she resumed her work, drawing his attention to the elaborate pattern of matte gold beads that adorned her shoulder-length hair and which tinkled softly every time she moved her head. It had been a fad among younger, secular A'tuu'shahn'i, especially the women—as an Elkanaghalli he was above such vanities, but as an Elkanaghalli he'd noticed, damned if he hadn't. Yet the style had long before gone out of favor, replaced by a preference for multiple gold earrings— adorning only one ear, left for women, right for men—a craze which in turn was supplanted in good time by elaborate hairstyles involving intricate braiding, which was then superseded by highly polished silver beads that again festooned the hair in complex geometric designs, yet here was a woman wearing matte gold—it didn't make sense. Nothing made sense.

Something she did caused his right leg to spasm violently— he instantly lost interest in her far out-of-date fashion sense, his attention now firmly fixed on the agony that seemed to be searing its way from his leg, to his hip and up his spine.

She froze as if not at all expecting that sort of reaction.

"Do... *do something!"* he managed to gasp through clenched teeth.

She nodded, hurriedly pressed a ject-it against his bare thigh and the pain instantly evaporated.

He continued to gasp; the pain had been so intense it had literally sucked the breath out of him.

"Ah, here comes the medical officer," she said, clearly relieved as she deferentially stepped back.

Another face loomed over him, slightly blurry as he continued to heave for breath, yet another Dakkeesh, this one male, and much, much older. "So you're awake."

He didn't sound particularly pleased and Khusaaq felt the urge to apologize for something he clearly hadn't had any control over.

With a grunt, the Dakkeesh crossed his arms, gave his naked body a slow, head to toe exam with his eyes then looked at the overhead monitors. "You suffered compound fractures to both femurs, multiple rib and pelvic fractures, ruptured spleen, punctured lung—you're exceedingly lucky there, one bone fragment was perilously close to your heart—numerous fractures of the skull, with a depressed—"

"What... what happened? How did I get here?"

The officer stopped what to Khusaaq sounded like a strangely familiar litany of injuries to stare—really stare at him. "Do you remember anything, Ruh'ta'aq?"

"I know I'm a sha'ashahn not a ruh'ta'aq!"

The Dakkeesh ever-so-slowly arched one thick brow, but Khusaaq wasn't sure if his reaction was due to his tone or his assertion. When the curved brow remained firmly affixed high on the man's tattooed forehead, rather than return to its prior position, Khusaaq realized it was both.

"Where's Jaa'qwah?"

"Jaa'qwah?" The medical officer shook his head. "I'm unfamiliar with—"

"He's a medic!"

"Not aboard the *Khargeh*." He paused, gave him another head to toe look over, exhaled, then in a slightly more appeasing, but decidedly firm tone said, "Ruh'ta'aq, you suffered a severe blow to the head among other very serious trauma and you just came out of regen—far too soon if you ask me, but Nahru'tzrhi insisted and there's simply no arguing with her," he added with an audible note of disgust. "We're just trying to help you. Now tell me, can you remember anything before you woke up here?" As he spoke, he nodded to the medic, who pressed a wall-mounted toggle.

Khusaaq caught the movement out of the corner of his eye, glanced at the toggle and instantly recognized it; from now on, whatever he said would be officially logged. Which meant something was wrong; something terrible had happened, he knew it now, he just didn't know what it was. Everything was a jumble, a frightening, murky jumble. "I was... I was aboard the *Jirah*—"

"*Jirah*? No. You were aboard *Huui'teh*—"

"No, that's not right." Khusaaq tried to shake his head, found he couldn't. "I was on *Jirah*, we were headed for Poonda Five..." his voice trailed off as he noticed the officer and medic exchanging worried glances. The medic then left and in a hurry. "Wasn't I...?"

"No, Ruh'ta'aq," the officer replied. "You were last aboard *Huui'teh*, she was assigned to protect the Coalition colony of Cotopaxi, remember?"

"*Of course I remember!*" he croaked, his mouth having gone dry in mounting panic; nothing made sense—what was he doing here? Where was Matoosh? "But that was—"

"You and about half the crew managed to flick down to the surface before the Matarii destroyed *Huui'teh*. We picked up your distress call and *Khargeh* and its battle group, along with a half-dozen Coalition ships were dispatched, but we didn't arrive in time to stop the Matarii from destroying the colony..."

Khusaaq's gaze turned inward and he found himself nodding. "We made a run for the mountains..." he murmured as recall took over, his lips, his tongue seeming to have a mind—and a memory—of their own, and he was again struck by the very odd sensation of being a witness, rather than a participant in the conversation, "...taking those colonists who wanted to go with us."

The medical officer smiled a relieved smile as he pressed another ject-it against his upper arm this time then gently massaged the area to speed the drug along. "Go on... what else do you remember?"

"We... we headed for a... a gorge, I think..."

"Yes," the officer confirmed. "Continue."

"I hid the colonists in a cave—*no*, a fissure, they were safe there, safe from the Matarii firing at us from orbit—and we mined the gorge."

"And...?"

"The Matarii found us—had us trapped."

"So you...?"

"Blew the gorge... but I misjudged the explosive potential of the Rimmers' mines. The result was far more powerful than we'd expected—"

"No, Ruh'ta'aq," came a new voice and he looked up to find another officer—a battle commander, not another medical officer—now standing next to the Dakkeesh... and the medic too had returned and busied herself by drawing a thin drape over his lower body. "It wasn't Rimmer mines, it was the Matarii."

Khusaaq peered up at the latest arrival—another complete stranger—no, *not* a stranger, his mind corrected. Out of place—not that he could place where that place was but at least the officer was Elkanaghalli and he felt some small comfort in that, some relief that she did look vaguely familiar, hoping she might, just might, be able to explain what had happened to him.

The woman smiled a genuinely warm smile. "We haven't been properly introduced, Ruh'ta'aq—"

Khusaaq wanted to scream, *"I'm not a Ruh'ta'aq!"* but bit his tongue. Something told him that he in fact was, that he'd not only lost his rank, but years from his life, that he really was back aboard *Khargeh.*

"—I'm Hamaz'akarani Sha'ashahn."

The name too sounded familiar; he'd known her once, he was sure of that now. Only... she was dead. He was sure of that, too. Had been dead for years, or so a part of his mind told him. Killed during the Battle of Elazig Rounds. Yet here she was, very much alive. He reached up, slowly, and massaged his forehead as he tried to untangle the disconcerting juxtaposition of utter bewilderment and intensely detailed déjà vu. He shouldn't be here, but he *had* been here, many times, a part of him knew, replaying the same events. And yet he had no idea how, or why. It made his head throb and his stomach roil. "I... I don't understand..."

Hamaz'akarani gently placed her hand on his shoulder startling him into dropping his hand away from his pounding skull; he was surprised at just how warm her hand felt—and how cold he was. He began to shiver.

"Then allow me to explain."

Khusaaq stammered, "P-p-please, ta-ta'ahn."

Hamaz'akarani glanced around, and getting the pointed hint, the medic grabbed a nearby chair and placed it beside Khusaaq's trauma bed, then pulled another blanket, a heavier blanket from the overhead bin and covered him, chin to toes, but it didn't lessen his shivering in the slightest.

The officer sat down, crossed her arms. "As I was saying, it wasn't the mines you placed in the gorge so much as what was already *in* the gorge."

Khusaaq stared up her. "A-a-already in t-t-the gorge?"

"You'd ended up in a gorge the Matarii, during their first war with the Coalition, used as a stockpile for a truly staggering amount of chemical and biological weapons—you mean you didn't know?"

He gave his head a quick, sharp shake; it was an instantaneous response, almost reflexive, but again, he felt that strange sensation of knowing what she said was true, that he'd known it for a long time.

"The entire planet was basically one massive cache—ideally suited by its relative proximity to Coalition space for a secret weapons dump. It had been the Matarii's plan, if things went really badly for them—and it was rapidly headed that way towards the end—to circumvent the Coalition's fleet, most of which were largely arrayed elsewhere, grab everything they'd hoarded and go right for the Coalition's outlying farming colonies, wiping out as many as they could—a scorched planet policy to end all scorched planet policies that would cripple the Coalition for generations to come, starve it, force it to retreat and shrink its borders, giving the Matarii some breathing space and time to rebuild.

"But just before the Coalition was about to hand the Matarii a resounding defeat—unbeknownst to the Coalition that they'd come that close—which would have triggered this doomsday scheme, a ceasefire was called, followed by a complete disengagement. And suddenly the Matarii had on their hands a truly staggering cache of banned weapons. Just possessing them was a blatant violation of every treaty, not to mention the very strict terms of the armistice, and had anyone discovered this, well... the Matarii had been so degraded by the war they knew it wouldn't have taken much to destroy their empire completely and permanently. For all the Matarii knew, the Thalamians and Loopers, even the Gorm might seize this opportunity and join forces with the Coalition to finish them off, once and for all, grabbing what territory they could in the confusion and picking over the carcass of the empire for anything of value.

"Worse for the Matarii," she added, "the planet we've all come to know as Cotopaxi fell within the buffer zone created by the armistice, but very close to the Coalition side. No one was supposed to enter, much less colonize any of the planets within the zone, so while the Matarii couldn't enter the zone without violating the armistice, neither could the Coalition and the Matarii presumably felt that their secret was safe." Hamaz'akarani paused briefly to allow Khusaaq a chance to absorb what she'd told him before continuing and for him to grab a gulp from the cup of the warm barra the medic held to his lips.

He took a deep, if shaky swallow, and another then the mug was withdrawn at the officer's pointed nod.

"But then the Rimmers," she continued, "found a mineral rich and habitable planet such as Cotopaxi just too tempting. They took the unwise step of establishing a colony, another blatant violation of the treaty—perhaps to poke the Matarii, see how they'd react, mistakenly assuming the Matarii were still so busy rebuilding what had been destroyed in the war they wouldn't notice, or make an issue of it if they did, all the while having no idea what in fact they'd set into motion." Hamaz'akarani stopped again, stared at Khusaaq. "If you're wondering if the Coalition knew about the stockpile, the answer, as far as our intelligence can determine, is no. But they did know that the Matarii had, years before, established some sort of mining operations on the planet—"

"The complex..." Khusaaq murmured then fixed his eyes on Hamaz'akarani as more and more solid memories coalesced and jostled to be heard; no longer the silent witness, he was now an

active, eager abettor. "We discovered it had been made by Matarii, not Rimmer shortly before we evacuated."

She nodded. "As far as the Rimmers could tell, it and other such sites elsewhere on Cotopaxi had been abandoned for several decades. They assumed the Matarii, who had been so diminished by the war had lost interest, or perhaps more accurately had lost the *capacity* to supply and sustain a distant colony, no matter the potential wealth, and now the planet was within the buffer zone? Well... the Matarii couldn't even return to destroy the sites, as is their habit if they think such might fall into alien hands, and it wasn't worth fighting over—or so the Rimmers thought—and so they decided to claim it before the Matarii could regroup, despite it being a treaty violation—they likely felt the Matarii wouldn't, or couldn't do anything but lodge an official complaint, and since the Matarii had started the war, had targeted a number of the Coalition's colonies, their complaint would likely be brushed aside.

"And not ones to waste perfectly good structures, the Rimmers planted their colony, unknowingly, almost right on top of one of the Matarii's major weapons caches. The Matarii rightfully feared their secret would be exposed before they could fully reconstitute themselves.

"The Matarii, hoping they could scare the colonists away, sent one ship to harass them. When the Coalition upped the stakes by hiring one of our ships and crew to deal with them, lying to us in the process, claiming they had discovered and claimed the planet prior to the war, well... the Matarii panicked. One terribly short-sighted assumption, one lie, heaped on another, upon another." Hamaz'akarani leaned back in her chair, crossed her arms and shook her head. "Tell me, Ruh'ta'aq... why did you end up in that particular gorge if you didn't know it was a cache? It was one ravine of many, some far closer to the complex if your intention was simply to keep the Matarii at bay until reinforcements could arrive."

Khusaaq hesitated. Hamaz'akarani was an Elkanaghalli after all, but the medical officer and medic were not—and his words were being recorded for others to pour over, analyze, and pick apart. A part of his mind, the silent witness, warned him that what he said next would have long-term repercussions, not just for him and his career, but for his family, a family who had staked so much of their reputation on him as the worthy successor to the glorified Ja'andai. The other part, the active abettor, felt this compulsion to explain himself, no matter the risks.

"Ruh'ta'aq?" Hamaz'akarani prompted, her expression, her tone leaving no doubt she expected an immediate and forthright answer.

"I wanted to reach the Night Mountains," he blurted out. There. Done. His foolishness exposed. The abettor had won.

Instead of slight, patronizing smiles or knowing, sidelong glances among the three who stood over him, Hamaz'akarani surprised him by saying, *The* Night Mountains—*our* Night Mountains, Ruh'ta'aq?"

"Yes, ta'ahn—I realize now it was a stupid thing to do," Khusaaq replied, words tumbling from his mouth, faster, faster, "to even think, but at the time... I truly felt the Elkanasu had led me to the gorge, I thought I felt their presence—" And suddenly the Elkanasu's greater purpose, the true objective they'd kept hidden from him became crystal clear: point the way to the stockpile, set it off by triggering the mines, alerting everyone— Rimmer and A'tuu'shahn—to what the Matarii had been trying so desperately to hide. He found he couldn't breathe; his heart began hammering even quicker against his freshly knit ribs.

"Perhaps you were, Ruh'ta'aq—the Elkanasu do as they please," Hamaz'akarani replied, her eyes darting between his now sweat-beaded face and the over-bed monitors, "when and how they please, as you well know. At the very least, it was fortunate coincidence—the Matarii's secret's out, not that it will ever be made public. The Coalition's Central Committee has already made it clear that it expects the Orthodoxy to remain silent on the matter, has in fact offered us quite a sum to just 'forget' this whole matter, because if it were to become widely known, it would likely spark a new war, a war neither the Matarii or the Coalition would survive—"

"Survivors!" He grasped Hamaz'akarani's hand just as the medic pressed yet another ject-it against his skin, this time just

below his jaw—he knew what that meant, now they had what they wanted from him, they were knocking him out. *"How many survivors? Tell me!"*

Hamaz'akarani gently slipped her hand from his panicked but already loosening grasp and rose. "Counting you? Five. We found no others *alive.*"

"The fissure!" he gasped as he pushed past a dark and softly undulating curtain that had suddenly surrounded him. "They're in the fissure!"

"There is no fissure, Ruh'ta'aq, not now. The explosions collapsed the entire gorge, which the Matarii had greatly destabilized in creating the cache in the first place. Only you and four others survived, and just barely, because you were blown free—we found the five of you some distance away and widely scattered. We searched as best we could under the conditions, not really expecting to find anyone alive, but when we located you and the others, we redoubled our efforts—"

"But you must go back!" He made a desperate, feeble grab for the officer's hand but this time missed completely.

"Ruh'ta'aq, there's simply no point. When the Matarii realized what had happened, when they spotted our flotilla approaching, they detonated the other caches, hoping to cover their tracks... but then we made planetfall to search. They realized the explosions had left easily detectable traces in the atmosphere—so they ignited it. My search crews barely escaped. Even if there had been other survivors..." She shook her head. "There's nothing left."

He stared up at her in gulping horror as visions of the planet's pristine, ancient landscape played before his watering eyes. *I did this...! I... destroyed the planet—*

"You're a bona fide hero, Ruh'ta'aq," she continued, "for holding the Matarii at bay until reinforcements arrived and in the process exposing what they were really up to—let's keep the fact that you didn't know the gorge was a weapons cache just between us for now, yes?" She flicked the medical officer and medic a pointed look then turned back to him and smiled. "Are we agreed? I'd rather not make it a direct order."

He blinked, tried to clear his clouding, watery vision. *"But the planet—"*

"We *need* this, Ruh'ta'aq," she said, her plastered-on smile replaced in a heartbeat by a look of deep anguish, "desperately so—we *need* a living hero, and you've certainly earned it. Ja'andai Nahru'tzhri would be very proud of you."

"But... but I don't understand..."

She shared a quick glance with the medical officer, then lowering her voice so as not to be overheard by the others in the ward, said, "Our attempts at extricating the Ti'finagh collective from the Nyaat cluster have been an unmitigated disaster—far, far costlier than we could have ever imagined. Twelve entire battle groups—*a third of our forces, Ruh'ta'aq... lost* and more losses to come, I fear, many, many more. Rumor has it that the numbers have overwhelmed even the Elkanasu."

He gaped at her, his groggy mind struggling to swing on its drug-loosened hinges, to grasp the full impact of her words. *"Lost...?"*

Hamaz'akarani inhaled sharply and nodded. "Yes. Now sleep, Ruh'ta'aq. We'll speak again, later—until then, no more talk about what you did or didn't know about what was in that gorge." She started to walk away.

"No!" he shook his head, shook loose the muzziness that threatened to overwhelm him.

She stopped, looked back at him. "The losses have been confirmed and officially registered, Ruh'ta'aq. Entire families, entire *lineages* have been wiped out."

That wasn't what he'd meant—he could only deal with one truly awful prospect at the moment, before the tranks won and pulled him under. *"The planet—what about the planet!"*

She stared at him, genuinely perplexed and answered simply, "The planet, as you knew it, is gone—"

"NO!" He began crying in earnest, huge, body-wracking sobs but even he knew he was slipping into darkness as he screamed, *"NO! IT'S NOT TRUE!"*

"Sha'ashahn?"

A hand grasped his shoulder, gave it a firm shake. *"Sha'ashahn, wake up!"*

He flinched, expecting it to hurt as his eyes snapped open. Matoosh stood beside him, a very worried look on his face. Khusaaq grabbed his arms, held on tight, then glanced around him to find himself back on the bridge of the *Jirah*, the crew staring at him, all as anxious as Matoosh. He immediately let go, then straightened up in the command chair. He licked his lips, looked around him again as he combed a very shaky hand through his loose hair.

"Same nightmare?" Matoosh whispered just loud enough for him to hear.

He replied with a curt nod, tugged at his uniform collar, embarrassed that he'd fallen asleep at his post, even more embarrassed that the bridge crew had been witness to his private horror and he wondered how much they'd overheard. He gave his damp cheeks a rough, angry wipe.

As if sensing his thoughts, Matoosh leaned close, said, *"We only knew you'd fallen asleep and were having a dream when you called out 'No!'"*. He gave him a reassuring squeeze on his shoulder, whispered, *"Jaa'qwah warned me you were exhausted and you might fall asleep and if you did, not to worry—to let you sleep."*

"But on the bridge?" Khusaaq replied in kind.

Matoosh shrugged. *"I didn't realize you had until... well, you had."*

Khusaaq exhaled, shook his head and as Matoosh resumed his post, he cleared his throat, then made eye contact with each of the crew and said, "My apologies. It was inexcusable for me to fall asleep on the bridge."

"Hahtra'tzrhi does it all the time," Rukoobi muttered then flicked Khusaaq a sidelong, wicked grin.

Khusaaq couldn't help but chuckle at that, true or not, in the process shaking off the lingering horror of the nightmare and the others joined in, their fears allayed.

Then, as he settled back in his chair, he asked huskily, "ETA to Poonda Five?"

Chapter 18

Main virology lab, Kanaloa Medical Complex, Tuli.
0520, planetary time. Present day.

Tasende picked up a probe and motioned to one of his Hahtooshan bodyguards—the one not actively studying culture readouts because it was his turn to actively guard Tasende. "You... um, Pali'koor isn't it? Over here, please."

The soldier in question gave his companions, who'd turned to stare questioningly at him an equally quizzical look, clearly wondering why he'd been singled out, then, at their prodding grins, he slowly eased himself away from the wall he'd been supporting and reluctantly walked over to Tasende.

Tasende, with his guards in tow, had flicked down not quite an hour before. *Baidarka* was in geosynchronous orbit directly above Alhajoth, city and ship time matched strictly for his and Amalfitano's convenience. He'd been unable to sleep and eager to check on the preliminary results of his very promising experiments of the day before on a broad-spectrum acellular vaccine that could be used to combat the most common rhinoviruses. The unexpected change in routine had not endeared him to the three Hahtooshans, who, due to Tasende's impatience to flick down the planet, had to settle for what they scrounge in the nearby doctors' lounge for breakfast, rather than the always anticipated and generous spread put out by the galley staff of the *Baidarka.*

Tasende looked up the still unhappy medic who towered over him. "You said you *weren't* exposed to the Type A HA twenty-one, NA fourteen Vetrarbraut Sixteen virus, correct?"

Pali'koor replied with an uncertain nod.

"Good." He held out the probe for him to see. "I need some of your blood."

The soldier crossed his thickset arms and stared down at him. "Why?"

"I need a fresh control specimen—I've run out of what your medical staff sent and I don't have time to wait for them to send more."

Pali'koor continued to squint at him. "Sounds like very poor planning on your part."

Tasende met the medic's penetrating gray eyes and tried to make light of the matter. "Yeah, yeah, I know," he forced a chuckle, "which doesn't constitute an emergency on your part."

Pali'koor's scowl deepened.

"You mean you've never heard the saying, 'Piss poor planning on your part doesn't constitute an emergency on my part'?"

"No," Pali'koor replied icily.

"I mean... I... I don't mean you're the one with the piss poor planning—"

"I would sincerely hope not."

"—it's just the way the expression goes."

"Indeed."

Tasende swallowed convulsively and changed tack. Humor hadn't worked, so now he played his last hand and with a slight, if unintentional whine to his voice. "Murh'sooli said you were to cooperate fully."

"But it's not Murh'sooli you wish to *stab*, is it?"

"I'm not going to *stab*. I'm... I'm going to *sample*. I've done this hundreds of times—*thousands*. You won't feel a thing."

Pali'koor sighed, removed his armored gauntlet and flicking his companions a decidedly pained look, exposed his forearm.

Tasende gave the trooper's glowering ursine face a glance, then looked down at the man's muscular forearm and immediately realized he had a problem—a *big* problem: the elaborate tattoos that swirled over Pali'koor's dusky skin also effectively camouflaged his blood vessels. He licked his lips. *Oh... crapadoodles.*

"Well? What are you waiting for?"

Tasende smiled nervously and tried to palpate a suitable target. All he felt was the Hahtooshan's very impressive forearm muscles bunch at his unwanted touch.

"I didn't agree to you mauling me—just get the sample and be done with it."

Tasende glanced up at him. "I'm having a little trouble—"

"Permit me." Pali'koor snatched the probe from his hand and with well-practiced technique, slipped the probe under his own skin and into a vein.

Tasende watched as the probe rapidly filled with blood—blood much brighter red than a non-Hahtooshan human's, carrying more than twice as much oxygen—and he again found himself hoping that one day he would have the chance to sit down with one of their genetic engineers, who, with luck, would be a tad more approachable—and talkative—than the less than gregarious Pali'koor.

"Enough?"

Tasende blinked, and, tearing his eyes off the tube and its vibrant cinnabar contents, looked up at the grim-faced Pali'koor and nodded eagerly.

The medic withdrew the probe and handed it to him, then jerking his gauntlet back on, quickly rejoined his companions.

Tasende pointedly ignored their muttered conversation and sidelong, contemptuous looks—he harbored no doubts that he was the subject of their grumbled comments—and placed the probe in the sampler's awaiting slot, then resumed his seat and sat back to await its analysis.

A moment later and warned by the abrupt end to their grumpily whispered remarks, he looked over his shoulder at the three.

Pali'koor was now listening intently to his tac-net. He flicked the other two a quick glance, made a quick hand signal and the one who'd been seated nearest to the doorway silently slid from her chair and to a crouch next to it while she visibly sniffed the air. The second was now flattened against the wall just behind her.

Pali'koor then placed his imposing bulk between Tasende and the doorway. All now had their maser pistols drawn and Tasende felt his heart rate leap as their primary purpose was instantly brought back to mind.

The one crouched beside the doorway—Lis'icah was her name—looked sharply at him, motioned for him to remain where he was, then put her armored finger to her lips.

Tasende vigorously nodded his understanding—he had nowhere to run, the only way out of the lab was through that very doorway and he suddenly found his mouth too dry to make a sound so her warning to stay quiet was utterly unnecessary. Then he heard it too: rapidly approaching footsteps.

A moment later a very dour Murh'sooli entered the lab, growled, *"Chok'ah,"* and Tasende's three guards immediately lowered their weapons. They did not, however, reholster them and Pali'koor remained where he was, between Tasende and the door.

Murh'sooli then glanced over his shoulder and motioned with his hand. "All secure. You can come in now."

Tasende rose from the computer station as Aquila stalked in, followed by Amalfitano, Izraad, the head of the hospital's security, Namburu, and finally Amalfitano's two other bodyguards.

"What's happened?" Tasende asked huskily as the six Hahtooshans silently took up strategic positions around the periphery of the large chamber.

"Someone's grabbed Sirin and Drakin!" Amalfitano snarled. "That's what's happened!"

"WHAT?" Tasende stared, wide-eyed, at Aquila.

Aquila nodded unhappily. "Narbrooi informed me a short time ago that Hahtooshan pickets detected a very brief, very discrete and anomalous energy blip at Sirin and Khusaaq's bungalow at approximately twenty-two hundred last night," he explained. "They immediately went to investigate and happened across the bodies of two Tulian security personnel outside and found Ensign Corsali's guard, tied up and half-dead inside. There were signs of a struggle. Whoever did this somehow managed to momentarily disable the security dome—"

"And flicked Sirin and Drakin out of there," Amalfitano finished for him as he dropped heavily onto Tasende's empty chair. He flicked Namburu a sidelong glare. "Thanks to the Hahtooshans' and Tulians' supposedly *impenetrable* security dome. *Some security!* They might as well have used tissue paper! Who's next? Me? Xosé?"

"William," Izraad murmured, "this isn't helping."

"Maybe I don't feel like helping! Maybe I'm damned mad! Damned fucking mad!"

"Could've fooled me," she said.

"The guard," Namburu began, "once stabilized, was able to identify his attackers by the names they used—Jonathan Urbat and—"

"Lemme guess," Tasende growled, "Tace Pardix?"

Namburu nodded as Amalfitano spat, *"Goddamned fucking bastard!"*

"Which is why, I suspect, they didn't kill the guard," Izraad added and Namburu nodded his agreement. "They wanted us to know who grabbed Sirin and Drakin—or, should I say, they wanted Khusaaq to know."

Tasende looked at Aquila, at Namburu, Izraad and finally Amalfitano. "You don't think there's a connection between Sirin and Drakin being grabbed and the *Huui'teh,* do you?"

"Of course there is!" Amalfitano snarled.

"Not necessarily." Izraad sighed. "Clearly the goal behind these kidnappings is to lure Khusaaq into a trap, but the timing may be purely coincidental."

"I for one don't believe in coincidences," Amalfitano snapped. "And—"

"Narbrooi's meeting us here," Aquila interrupted, "I've recalled everyone from shore leave as a safety precaution and I've ordered the *Baidarka* to make a complete scan of the planet, but—"

"Sirin and Drakin," Amalfitano interrupted, "are probably long gone—"

"Gone, but not for long," came an all too familiar, deep voice. They turned to find Narbrooi standing in the doorway; behind him stood four more soldiers in full battle kit.

The Hahtooshan admiral stepped into the room. "Our sensors picked up on what we now all know was a masked flicker signature within Sha'ashahn's quarters late last evening and traced the flicker's point of origin. Since then, we've been tracking a Loop Confederation registered freighter, the *Talakah,* which broke orbit within minutes of the abductions. Aboard are four humans, a Looper, an Eltannian and—"

"WHAT?" Amalfitano exploded, rising from the chair. "Why the hell didn't you stop them?"

Narbrooi raised a disdainful brow. "Doctor, we were not granted the authority by the Tulians to randomly seize spacecraft, but rest assured—"

"So you just... *let it go?"*

"Yes," Narbrooi replied simply.

"Great!" Amalfitano threw up his hands in exasperation. "Fat lot of good your 'protection' has been! Sirin, Drakin grabbed—*wait a minute...."* He fixed Narbrooi with a sharp glower. "You didn't say you tried to stop the transfer."

"No, I didn't."

"You mean... you deliberately allowed Sirin and Drakin to be abducted?"

Narbrooi stared back, unblinking. "Yes."

"Why... you cold-blooded bas—"

"It was not something I'd planned, Doctor," Narbrooi replied. "I truly believed our dome would prevent such an event, and had we attempted to stop the transfer, there would have been a better than even chance your officers would have been killed in the process. While I do regret the deaths of two of your men," he nodded to Namburu, "I cannot say I am unhappy with the outcome."

Amalfitano stared at him in wide-eyed disbelief before recovering. *"Sirin and Drakin kidnapped by gods-knows-who, taking them gods-knows-where—"*

"I did say we are tracking the vessel, Doctor—"

"—and as soon as Khusaaq learns of this, there'll be no... stopping... him..." His voice trailed off as he gave Narbrooi a sidelong look. "What did you say?"

"I said we are tracking the *Talakah* and I have two cloaked koursans, *Illuyanka* and *Kashku,* shadowing it. They can overtake, disable and board it at any time. They are also monitoring all conversations aboard the freighter as well as any tight-beam transmissions, and have orders to flick your two officers off at the first sign of imminent danger to either of them. Currently Ensign Corsali and Lieutenant Drakin are confined to a cabin and physically unharmed. As long as that remains the case, I would prefer to wait in hopes of determining who is behind this... regrettable act. As for Sha'ashahn... he was, to use your expression, Doctor, already 'long gone'."

"Was? What the hell are you—"

"Sha'ashahn requested and I granted him the use of a foldboat and crew in order to rescue his men from their abductors. He and his second left early yesterday morning."

Amalfitano's eyes bulged. He turned an accusing stare on Aquila. "Why the hell wasn't I told of this?"

"Maybe because I wasn't told either," Aquila replied.

"This is strictly an A'tuu'shahn matter, Commander," Narbrooi said. "Therefore I was under no obligation to inform you, or *you*, Doctor," he added pointedly, briefly looking at Amalfitano before turning back to Aquila. "Both Sha'ashahn and I felt he stood a better chance of gaining the element of surprise if—"

"No one but Hahtooshans knew about it," Aquila ended for him.

"To be blunt, yes, Narbrooi replied. "This is why I also held off informing you of the events of last evening—until I had all the facts."

"But... but we don't have any idea where whoever took Khusaaq's men are taking them!" Amalfitano snarled, oblivious to the continued unhappy stares from the Hahtooshan soldiers. "For all we know, they could be—"

"On their way to Poonda Five?" Narbrooi interrupted quietly.

"What?" Aquila and Amalfitano gasped in unison.

"Both the so-named *Huui'teh* and the *Talakah* are headed for Poonda Five." He smiled at Aquila. "Yes, Commander, we've been tracking *Huui'teh* as well—our ships picked up her trail shortly after she left Rasal Ghul's interference sphere."

"But why Poonda Five?" Tasende asked.

Narbrooi answered, "Not an unexpected choice of destinations, Crewman, in light of the planet's relative proximity, not to mention its well-known reputation of engaging in illegal trafficking."

"Or its nearness to Matarran-claimed space," Izraad added, her comment garnering a nod from Narbrooi, who then continued,

"And if any of you are wondering why we didn't intercept and apprehend the *Huui'teh* once we located her, we would prefer to uncover who is behind this. I suspect those who actually kidnapped our soldiers are likely freelancers—"

"You're taking a terrible risk," Amalfitano growled, "with peoples' lives."

"A'tuu'shahn'i are always keenly aware of the risks, Doctor, and presumably your people understood the dangers when they enlisted. If it takes risking, possibly losing all of their lives in order expose a greater plot, one that could and likely would destabilize this alliance and cost far more lives in the long run, then in my estimation the cost will be more than worth it." He turned to Aquila, effectively dismissing Amalfitano. "I've sent word to Sha'ashahn, apprizing him of this newest development—"

"You do realize he's walking into a trap, don't you?" Amalfitano snapped, drawing the admiral's reluctant, now thoroughly exasperated gaze.

"Of course," Narbrooi replied. "And so does Sha'ashahn. Those who kidnapped your officers even seeded the trail, filing a flight plan with Poonda Five as their destination."

"And leaving Sirin's guard alive, if barely, to finger them," Izraad added.

"Indeed," Narbrooi agreed.

Amalfitano looked at Izraad, then Narbrooi. "But—"

"Sha'ashahn is A'tuu'shahn, Doctor," Narbrooi interrupted. "And despite his recent actions, he is still Elkanaghalli. Do not doubt his resourcefulness for a moment. He will succeed in rescuing both his men and your officers—"

"Or die trying," Amalfitano interrupted coldly.

Narbrooi shrugged. "As I said, he is A'tuu'shahn—*and* Elkanaghalli."

Chapter 19

Aboard the Talakah.
Present day.

S*ssomeone'z coming."*

Sirin, who was seated beside Drakin on one of the cabin's two bunks, lifted her narrowed gaze from her intense study of the deck and fixed it on the cabin door.

A moment later it snapped open and Pardix stepped in.

"What do you want?" Sirin crossed her arms across her skimpy negligee.

He grinned, his dazzling green eyes sparkling. "Just wanted to make sure your accommodations were satisfactory."

Drakin looked around the Spartan cabin. "Very possssh."

"I also thought you two might like to join us for a bite to eat. Syr's put out quite a—"

"Go to hell," Sirin growled.

Pardix chuckled. "You've been hanging around yowies too much, Sirin. Bravado will get you nowhere and you two have to be getting quite hungry."

She only glared at him.

"Have it your way then," he shrugged and turned to leave.

"Wait."

He stopped just short of the door and turned back as she rose from the bunk. "Yes?"

"Where are you taking us?" she asked as she walked towards him.

"Does it matter?"

"Yeah." She stopped in front of him. "It does."

"Well, let's say it isn't into the arms of your beloved Orthodoxy." He looked her up and down in a way she found very unpleasant. "Now answer *me* a question: why?"

"Why *what?"*

"Why would you let one of those butchers touch you?" He toyed with the shoulder strap of her negligee and grinned at her reaction, both to his words and his suggestive fingering. "I realize you weren't exactly hot property on the *Baidarka*, and for obvious reasons, but were you really *that* desperate?" He feigned a shudder. "Sleeping with the enemy? *Ugh!*" He suppressed a shiver.

Why you— she squelched that train of thought as another, even better one came to mind. *Oh yes. Even better.*

He leered at her and said in a taunting voice, "Or maybe you like really rough sex? You certainly never struck me as the type."

She pointedly ignored Drakin's strangled gasp and forced herself to smile coyly up at him as she edged a little closer, aware that the strap had fallen from her shoulder. "So what if I do?" She ran her fingers along his jaw, and tugging at his lower lip, whispered, *"And the rougher the better—just couldn't find anyone aboard who was..."* She grinned and keeping her eyes locked with his, lightly caressed his crotch with her other hand as she added, *"...up to the challenge, so to speak."*

His eyes widened, surprised, and just as clearly intrigued, not to mention aroused. "Hell," he managed to stammer, "had... had I known... I'd have—"

She kneed him as hard as she could then followed through with a two-handed shove.

He stumbled backwards, into the corridor, before doubling over and falling to his knees.

"What's the matter, Tace?" she snarled as she started after him. "Too rough for you?"

Drakin hastily rose and grabbed her by the arm and jerked her back into the cabin, then hit the door release.

"You fucking yowie whore," Pardix managed to groan, *"I'll—"*

The door snapped shut, cutting him off.

Sirin struggled to free herself of Drakin's hold as she yelled, "Touch me again and I'll kill you with my bare hands, you goddamned traitor!"

"Now, now," Drakin soothed as she gently but firmly pulled her away from the door. "Don't let dat creep upssset you."

Sirin looked back at the door as instant gratification abruptly dissolved into grim reality. Pardix, for better or worse, had been their only chance at getting out of their current predicament alive, in fact was probably responsible for them still being alive.

Gods... what've I done? She turned to face Drakin. "What've I gotten you into?"

"I don't remember *you* getting *me* into anyting."

"But—"

"No butz! When Khoozak findz out, he'll come after uz, juz like dey want, only he'll turn da tablez on dem. Don't you worry."

"No, he won't—"

"Of courssse he will!" She gently tucked a lock of blond hair behind Sirin's ear with a razor sharp talon. "And when he doez, he'll wipe dat sssmug sssmirk off dat rat-baztardz faz for good. If dere ever waz a knight in ssssquiggly armor," she wiggled her impressively clawed fingers for emphasis, "itz your Khoozak—"

"Khusaaq—" Sirin glanced around her, then leaned close and lowered her voice to a whisper. *"Khusaaq's who knows where, chasing after the people who kidnapped his men."*

"Men?" Drakin replied in kind. *"Kidnapped? Wat da hell are you talkin' about?"*

Sirin sat heavily on the bunk and dropped her head into her hands. Drakin sat beside her.

"Gods... when they realize he's not taking the bait, they will kill us..."

Drakin draped her arm around Sirin's shoulder and tugged her close. *"I tink you better tell me everyting..."*

Chapter 20

Southern landing field on the outskirts of the Gorgon's Lair, Poonda Five.
Planetary noon. Present day.

"There." Tejat pointed with a gauntleted finger then rocked back on his haunches.

Khusaaq crouched beside him and peered into the harsh glare of Poonda Five's dazzling midday sunshine as the multitude of sensors within his helmet scanned the vast and crowded southern landing field—the planet's commercial hub. Hundreds of ships of all descriptions, from elegant atmospheric to utilitarian interstellar were scattered randomly across the dusty plain like so many casually thrown gaming pieces.

Beyond the field sprawled the planet's only population center, the aptly named Gorgon's Lair. Built up haphazardly over the course of a hundred plus years, using mostly scrap and salvage, it sat in the very center of an ancient impact crater, looking more like a smashed clutch of eggs in a rocky nest than a thriving spaceport. Completely surrounding the Gorgon's Lair rose the remains of the massive crater's rim, and above that, spread across the bowl of a cloudless indigo sky, was a smattering of stars and the dazzling arc of the planet's diaphanous rings.

With only a thin atmosphere to soften and scatter the light from the system's blue-white sun, the fractured landscape had a thunderstorm palette of harsh grays and blacks and intense, almost blinding whites. Poonda Five was a stormy, intractable world—a Pyrrhic struggle on a global scale—not to mention a perfect place to secrete something as substantial as a ship, or as inconsequential as five A'tuu'shahn'i.

Khusaaq's lips drew back in a tight, immensely satisfied smile as his helmet's sensors registered what Tejat had found: an aging A'tuu'shahn koursan. To the untrained eye—in fact to all but A'tuu'shahn sensors—the battered survey ship would have passed for one of Gorm manufacture or even Uzun—

uncommon, but not unheard of visitors to this part of the rim, and a deliberate act of visual trickery by its A'tuu'shahn engineers. "Our mysterious *Huui'teh* reveals itself."

"Indeed, ta'ahn," the engineer replied as he studied the ship that sat at the far edge of the landing field. "And it is without doubt our missing *Palraiyuk*."

Khusaaq peered at it, tapped his helmet's chin control. "*Jirah?*"

"*Yes, ta'ahn?*" Shu'hah replied.

"Notify Narbrooi Hahtra'tzrhi that we have located *Palraiyuk*."

"*Immediately, ta'ahn.*"

Tejat studied the small scanner attached to his armored forearm, adding, "She's on limited shutdown mode."

Khusaaq nodded. Such a precaution was not unexpected. Even on a freewheeling world such as Poonda Five, illegal trafficking of this magnitude might necessitate the need for a *very* hasty departure and its current status also kept *Palraiyuk* from making any attempt at contacting the Orthodoxy—a very effective electronic gag—assuming, in the time the koursan had been in the hands of its hijackers that other, more effective and permanent measures hadn't been taken.

Tejat continued, "My sensors register five A'tuu'shahn'i…"

Khusaaq waited until his sensors confirmed the readings then breathed an audible sigh of relief, echoed a heartbeat later by Matoosh's.

"…as well as two Loopers, a human, a Thalamian and… one Matarii."

"*That's all?*" Shu'hah's disembodied voice asked.

Tejat double-checked his scanner's readings before confirming with just a hint of annoyance, "Yes."

Khusaaq squinted at the distant ship and chewed distractedly on his lip.

A vessel the size of *Palraiyuk* required a skeleton crew of at least twelve. Having less than half that number onboard to deal with would make taking the ship and rescuing his men easier, but it also meant they would then have to spend precious time locating the others—time he had hoped to use preparing for the arrival of Sirin's kidnappers, all the while avoiding detection by the local authorities. So far their presence on planet and in orbit had gone undetected, but the longer they remained...

"Shu'hah."

"Yes, ta'ahn?"

"I'm transmitting coordinates."

"Coordinates received, ta'ahn."

"She's not to escape this system."

"Understood."

Khusaaq looked back to where the rest of the landing party were crouched beside a nearby outbuilding, invisible to any passerby.

"Matoosh, Jaa'qwah." Khusaaq gestured to his left and they crept away and quickly disappeared into the ship-dotted expanse. "Toubeh, Rukoobi." He made a circling motion with his hand, and then he turned back to Tejat. "Well?"

"I've cracked its cipher, ta'ahn. I can override her systems at any time."

"Is there a way to gas the decks?"

Tejat tapped in a series of commands into the small, arm-mounted device, paused as more data streamed across his visual field then replied, "Yes—but it will take me a few minutes to reroute the command without alerting the crew—"

"Do it," he hissed and, gesturing for Tejat to follow on his own time, crept out onto the landing field.

Chapter 21

Aboard the Palraiyuk.
Present day.

Voices flowed all around Qar'qaah—like fast moving water, swirling, tumbling, too swift for him to comprehend—too quick for him to even catch a word or two. Then, abruptly, silence and he found himself starting to sink back down into the deep dark again, where nothing stirred, nothing mattered.

Something poked his arm—and it *hurt*. His fingers twitched reflexively at the sharp prod; it forced his mind to focus this time, briefly, long enough to grasp what was being said.

"See? I told you."

"That was *you*," came an asthmatic reply, "or some sort of death spasm. He's dead I tell you."

"And I tell you he's faking."

Qar'qaah felt something poke him again and, realizing he was the object of the discussion, managed to open one eye a crack.

"Then he's doing a bang up job because he looks sincerely dead to me," the wheezy voice said.

"You're an idiot," the other voice replied with a disgusted sigh.

He had no idea how long he'd been out, had no idea where he was, no idea who was poking at him or what they wanted—and that left him scared. *Really scared*. He also hurt *all over*—a dull, throbbing body-wide ache, as if he'd been picked up, shaken violently and then dropped, hard.

He didn't remember being beaten up, and that's what it felt like—like he'd been beaten unconscious.

Before he could focus on that, the wheezing voice continued. "I told you you shouldn't have given him so much of that—"

"Shut up you hateful imbecile!" snapped the other voice as claw-tipped fingers grasped his bare shoulder and gave it a very rough shake. "And you, *Akka'a*—wake up!"

The jerking movement ignited a fresh, searing pain that lanced through his already pain-wracked body and he couldn't help but moan. His joints felt like they were on fire. Bones felt broken.

"Thought you could fool me—play dead, didn't you, *Akka'a?*" The speaker was close enough he could feel warm breath on his chilled skin, along with the familiar sweet scent of kij'a. "Well, you didn't."

He put all of his energy into turning his swollen-eyed squint on his tormentor as his mind warned: *Akka'a—that's what Matarii call A'tuu'shahn'i.*

And as proof of his suspicions, what at first had been a blurry smear of silvery-gray solidified into the unambiguous face of one of the despised aliens, and he realized he was in trouble, really, *really* deep trouble.

As their gazes locked, the Matarii grinned and threw a bucketful of ice-cold water across his bare back.

His body convulsed. Muscles seized, briefly contorting hands and feet into gross distortions of themselves. He couldn't breathe—and just as he felt the all-too familiar sense of suffocation starting to wash over him—the air came rushing back into his lungs as his muscles released their death grip.

He took a deep, spasmodic gulp then another and another, hungrily drawing in air as fast as his complaining ribs could obey.

"See? I *told* you he was faking," the Matarii sneered. "Get up, *Akka'a!*"

Still gasping, Qar'qaah squinted at her. *I'd love to. I'd love to get up just so I could knock you down, you silver-skinned freak—*

"He doesn't look too happy," the wheezing voice replied. "Maybe he doesn't like water?"

He saw a flash of movement nearby and spotted the dim but distinctively rotund form of a Looper.

"That's more than obvious," the Matarii sneered as she wrinkled her nasal slits. As his eye again locked with hers, she stepped back and motioned impatiently with her blaster. *"Up!"*

"Let me help him."

Qar'qaah *knew* that voice.

"Stay where you are!" the Matarii snarled, briefly turning away.

His one obedient eye followed the alien's angry gaze and he almost smiled when he spotted who it was. *Endooki!*

Endooki was naked, his hands and ankles shackled. Only then did Qar'qaah realize he was likewise unclothed and bound.

Not an altogether unexpected move—clearly whoever held them was taking no chances and the painful bite of the restraints against his bare, abraded skin suddenly unleashed a deluge of memories: of being drugged, then half-carried, half-dragged by Rimmers... to a flicker chamber?

Fragments of sounds, smells intermixed with other images of being grabbed by several Matarii—

Cisne... His mind clenched painfully around the image of the human ringleader's face—her smirking grin—as he was thrust, punching and kicking, into a coffin-like stasis pod without the proper prep.

Her harsh laughter at his voiceless screams echoed in his ears as the suffocating and icy stasis field slowly washed over him, paralyzing him, yet leaving him wide awake and in total terror.

He bit down the urge to scream again and squeezing his eye shut, began sucking in air, fighting with everything he had not to be dragged down into that deep, freezing darkness again.

Over his ragged breathing, over the mad hammering of his heart in his ears, over the stabbing pain in his gut, he overheard Endooki say, "He's very ill—you can see that. Please, let me help him," and the sounds of someone—Endooki?—taking a shuffling, shackled step. He tried to yell, tried to warn him. The best he could manage was a desperate, silent plea: *Don't—*

"I told you to stay where you are!" the Matarii snarled. "Take another step, *Akka'a*, and I'll kill you where you stand!"

"At least give him a chance to recover from the effects of the drugs," Endooki persisted.

"Yeah. *Right.*" The Matarii grabbed Qar'qaah again, this time by his leg manacles, and roughly dragged him bodily off the cot, onto the grated decking.

It took all of Qar'qaah's willpower not to cry out in agony as bone ground against shattered bone.

"See? How hard was that?"

Qar'qaah managed to lift his head, and through the tangle of his filthy and now soaking wet hair, glared, one-eyed, up at the alien.

"Now get *UP!*"

He grudgingly did as he was told, more to avoid further rough handling than any desire to cooperate, and forced himself up, on to his bony hands and even bonier knees.

"Move!" The Matarii kicked him in the rump, almost knocking him back onto his belly. "We don't have all day and you want to look presentable for your new owners, don't you?"

Hell if—

"I still think this is a mistake," the Looper said nervously as he glanced at the nearby hatch. "When Cisne finds out we—"

"Would you *shut UP!*" The Matarii glanced at her twitchy confederate. "She shouldn't have cheated us out of the credits she owes us, and besides I've already told you—what, at least six times?—that we'll be long gone by the time she gets back—assuming we can get this stupid beast up and moving. He's worth at least ten times what she owes us—maybe more. The other one maybe half that." She eyed Endooki then turned back to Qar'qaah. *"Up!"*

Sure. Anything you say. He flicked Endooki a sidelong glance, to which Endooki replied with a barely perceptible nod, then he clenched his teeth, said a silent prayer and lunged at the Matarii's legs. He missed, limited by the shackles, but the Matarii, startled, stumbled backwards into her equally startled companion, the blaster knocked from her hand as she collided with the stout Looper.

The weapon skittered across the deck and Qar'qaah dove for it as Endooki threw his manacled arms around the Looper's neck. Grasping him by his head and shoulders, he gave each a sharp, opposing twist and was immediately rewarded with a loud, satisfying *crack*.

Endooki released his hold and the now lifeless Looper slid down his naked body and onto the ground at his feet as the

Matarii, having regained her footing, desperately looked for her blaster.

"Is… is this what… what you're searching for?" Qar'qaah gasped as he rolled over and sat up, all the while pointing the blaster at its former owner.

The Matarii swallowed hard, watching as Qar'qaah managed to stagger, unassisted but ungracefully, to his shackled feet, the pistol never wavering from its target, despite his vision graying around the edges. "Where… where are the others, Ha'tat?"

"I don't know, ta'ahn," Endooki answered. "They separated us, not sure how long ago."

Qar'qaah turned to his former captor. "But you know… where they are… don't… don't… you?" He was having a hard time keeping his eye focused on the Matarii, keeping his hold on the blaster and keeping on his feet and he silently cursed the alien for shifting in and out of focus.

The Matarii smiled smugly at him. "And what if I do?"

"Tell me."

"They're all dead. Didn't need 'em so we blew 'em out an airlock—"

The response hit him like a fist to the belly.

"—Cisne just wanted you—and your friend here as backup."

He took a step closer and sniffed the air. Filtering out the potent scent of kij'a that wafted from the Matarii every time she spoke, not to mention the pervasive stench of the Looper, he picked up something else, something far more subtle: while he wasn't absolutely certain, the Matarii smelled as if she was lying and her aura, a flickering faded blue—like all non-synesthestes, her aura was a shadow of what a synestheste's would be—was stippled with yellow as her skin's conductivity changed. *Deception.* "I don't… don't think so."

A quick glance at Endooki, seeing his expression, confirmed his suspicions. He adjusted his precarious two-handed hold on the heavy weapon. It was agony to breathe, much less speak. It took all of his willpower not to black out. "Now… tell… tell me where they are."

"Why should I? You're going to kill me anyway."

"Not... necessarily." He looked her up and down, then meeting her gaze, grinned and winked at her—hard to do with only one functioning eye and he wasn't sure if it had the chilling effect he was hoping for. "If you... you cooperate, we *might* let you go."

She managed a soft, derisive chuckle. "I don't believe you, *Akka'a.*"

"A certainty... versus... versus a doubt." He started to shrug, but stopped when he felt—and heard—an ominous grinding in his shoulder. "The choice is yours. Now, where are they?"

"I told you, they're dead." Her aura flashed, briefly turning an all-over cloying yellow.

He grinned, raised the weapon so it now pointed directly between her eyes. "You're *lying.*" He tapped the side of his nose. "I can *smell* it. Now, one more time, one last chance. Where. Are. They?"

The Matarii, her overly large, coal black eyes still darting between the two, wet her thin lips with her bright blue tongue. "Down the corridor."

"I think it... best if... if you show us." He quickly handed off the blaster to the marginally more able Endooki.

Endooki sniffed the air, and, satisfied they were indeed alone, nodded to him, then grabbed the Matarii by her uniform collar and shoved the weapon against her throat. "You heard Qar'qaah Kon'ta'aq. *Move.*"

The Matarii stumbled forward and into the deserted corridor. "That way." She pointed with a clawed finger.

Endooki risked a quick glance over his shoulder to make sure Qar'qaah was able to follow, then urged the Matarii on as fast as his own hobbled legs would allow.

Qar'qaah shuffled along behind the two, using the wall for support as he took in their surroundings with a wary—if rheumy—eye. They were aboard a vessel—and not just any vessel, but an *A'tuu'shahn* vessel—the barely visible traceries of an elaborate design that covered the walls, deck and ceiling of the passageway left absolutely no doubt.

The very faint vibration he felt through the soles of his bare feet also warned him that only vital systems were functioning—the ship was asleep, oblivious in its enforced slumber to their presence and their plight. *So, we're on the surface of a planet—but which one?*

Endooki gave him a quick, baffled, over the shoulder stare as he too recognized their relatively familiar surroundings.

Having learned his lesson, rather than shrugging, Qar'qaah shook his head in reply. Right now he had more immediate concerns. Maybe his sense of smell was lying to him, maybe the others were dead and the Matarii was in fact leading them into a trap. He'd worry about where they were, how they'd come to be here, not to mention what a Matarii and a Looper were doing aboard an A'tuu'shahn ship at a more opportune time, assuming they survived the next few minutes.

"There. In there," the Matarii said as they came to a sealed hatch.

Not trusting his normally acute sense of smell to warn of ambush, Qar'qaah growled, "You first," as he and Endooki placed themselves on either side of the hatch.

The Matarii, at Endooki's rough urging, thumbed the release and the hatch irised open; the room beyond was pitch dark.

Qar'qaah thought he caught a telltale, familiar mixture of scents an instant before an equally familiar, albeit a weak and hoarse voice said, "We were beginning to think you'd forgotten about us, ta'ahn."

He grinned as Raudah stepped unsteadily out of the gloom, followed in short order by Nihaal and Laihiri. The three, while skeletally thin and likewise naked and shackled, looked to be in slightly better shape than Endooki. He glanced down at himself and blinked. *Or me.*

He lifted his startled gaze to find that the others were all now staring—glaring—at the Matarii. He shuffled unsteadily over to their encircled captive, in the process reclaimed the blaster from Endooki and, almost as an afterthought, adjusted its beam width and power. "Now... how 'bout you tell us *exactly* where we are?"

The Matarii spat in his face.

He wiped his hollow, peeling and blister-pocked cheek with the back of his bony, blister-pocked hand. "I ask again, *nicely,* and if you answer truthfully, I will let you live. Where are we— what planet?"

"Figure it out yourself, you stupid creature—"

"Well, if you insist." He smiled sweetly and as his companions hastily stepped aside, he squeezed the trigger. The Matarii vanished in a brilliant dazzle and he wiggled his fingers and whispered, *"Bye-bye."*

His intense satisfaction at summarily dispatching one of his tormentors was short-lived. Endooki suddenly started to sway; he made a grab for the hatch's frame but, hindered by the ankle shackles, missed and fell heavily to the deck with a muffled, *"Ooof!"*

"What the...?" Nihaal started for him but took only two shuffling steps before he too collapsed without even making a sound, followed in short order by Raudah.

Qar'qaah glanced around him, seeking their unseen attacker.

"Gas!" Laihiri hissed and covered his nose and mouth with his hands, but too late. His legs buckled and he crumpled, sprawling across the unmoving Endooki.

"Not... again," Qar'qaah mumbled as he dropped to his knees only watch, helpless, as the blaster slipped from his limp fingers an instant before he too lost consciousness.

Chapter 22

Aboard Jirah. *Sickbay.*
Second hour of Middle Watch. Present day.

Jaa'qwah sighed, and picking up the handful of expended ject-its from the bedside table, turned to Khusaaq. "I think it best we let him wake up on his own, ta'ahn."

Khusaaq crossed his arms and stared down at Qar'qaah. In the bright lights of *Jirah*'s cramped sickbay, he looked more dead than alive—correction: he simply looked dead. Only the very feeble rise and fall of his bony chest gave lie to his corpse-like appearance.

"Will he live?" He turned to find the medic now tending to Laihiri. The lanky soldier was sprawled on the other bunk, his glazed, sunken eyes trying to follow Jaa'qwah's hands as the medic began to smear his blistered torso with a thick yellow salve.

On a cot next to him sat Raudah, huddled under a thermal blanket and shivering uncontrollably. Endooki and Nihaal were cross-legged on the deck nearby, also wrapped in thermal blankets, their backs braced against the wall. Toubeh knelt between them, helping them take cautious sips of electrolyte-laced broth from mugs they clutched in their hands.

"I'm amazed any of them are alive, ta'ahn," Jaa'qwah replied.

"That's *not* what I asked." Khusaaq dropped his worried stare back to Qar'qaah as his fingers lightly touched the trooper's badly bruised and misshapen shoulder, fearful that even the lightest of touches might hurt yet desperately needing to assure himself that Qar'qaah was real—and alive, if just.

"They're all severely dehydrated and suffering from malnutrition and anemia due to radiation poisoning, plus, at least in Kon'ta'aq's case," his eyes briefly dropped to Qar'qaah before again meeting Khusaaq's anxious gaze, "a goodly number of broken bones. Those I can readily treat. And they stayed long enough on Rasal Ghul to actually develop immunity to the virus, so that's not a concern."

"But…?"

Jaa'qwah straightened up, snatched up a surgical drape from the nearby drug cart and wiped the thick salve from his hands. "We must return to the Orthodoxy, or short of that, *Faridour—*"

"Our mission is not yet complete."

"I understand that, ta'ahn." He leaned close as his gaze dropped briefly to Qar'qaah's peeling, blistered and bruise-swollen face. "Endooki told me that their captors singled him out…"

Khusaaq inwardly flinched, his worst fears realized.

"…and made an example of him, threatening the others with the same if they didn't cooperate."

"In what way?" he asked hoarsely.

"They tortured him repeatedly, forcing the others to watch…"

Khusaaq exhaled, shook his head.

"They also put him in a stasis pod… *awake.*"

Khusaaq's eyes widened. That was the technological equivalent to being buried alive, and as such a direct violation of every treaty he was aware of. And in his line of work, he knew every treaty inside and out. *Chiku…*

"…And he was left there for an extended period of time. I can only guess at the psychological damage this might have caused and I'm certainly not equipped to help him. I don't even dare put him back into stasis for fear that will only make the situation even worse—"

"Do what you can," Khusaaq interrupted; he'd heard enough. With one last apprehensive look at Qar'qaah, he strode out of the small infirmary.

Aboard the Baidarka. *William Amalfitano's office.*
2152, ship time. Present day.

"William?"

Amalfitano looked up to find Izraad and Aquila standing in the doorway of his sickbay office. "Yeah?" he replied as he dropped his distracted gaze back to his desktop terminal.

The two stepped into the office as Izraad continued, "We thought you'd like to join us for a cup of coffee, and maybe some of your anisette cookies? The galley made a fresh batch, just for you."

"Can't. Got too much work to do." He tapped in a series of commands. "Gotta finish uploading all this data." Then he irritably waved his hand at the screen.

"Jenna said you've been at it all day," Izraad persisted, "*and* evening—and you didn't even stop to eat dinner as you promised me you would."

"Wasn't hungry," he grumbled, not looking up. "Besides, the work isn't gonna do it itself."

Izraad scowled. She and Aquila had been sequestered in a private conference call with Admiral Keon most of the evening and Amalfitano had assured her that he'd order up dinner on his own. He hadn't—a fact she'd learned from none other than Murh'sooli. The medic, having dutifully remained at Amalfitano's side until his replacement arrived, had hurriedly left once relieved, grumbling to anyone who'd listen that thanks to Amalfitano's single-minded selfishness, he'd missed his well-deserved supper and he'd be lucky if he found even a scrap left to eat in the galley.

And that's where Izraad and Aquila had found him when they too went in search of a late evening snack before checking in with Amalfitano, the dour medic seated alone as always, silently dispatching a mound of cheeseburgers with weary, disgruntled determination.

"So it's almost twenty-two hundred and you're wearing your bodyguards out." She flicked the on-duty visible medic who stood behind Amalfitano a commiserating smile but the woman's stone-faced expression remained unchanged. The other was nearby, a barely discernable distortion next to the doorway and while Izraad couldn't see his face, she suspected it bore the same unyielding countenance.

"If you recall, *I* never asked for them," Amalfitano replied as he leaned close and peered at the active monitor.

"Will…" Aquila began.

"What?" This time he fixed Aquila with an accusatory squint.

"Will, I know you're upset, but Narbrooi, Seitakap and I all agreed that Tuli—even the hospital complex—is no longer safe. I've already apologized, repeatedly, for not immediately accepting your story about the attempted assassination…"

Amalfitano's glower turned positively frigid.

"…and I'm sorry I had to cancel shore leave for rest of the crew, but under the circumstances, I felt it was the prudent thing to do—I don't want any more targets of opportunity."

Or any more showing their true loyalties by going AWOL is what you want to say, Izraad thought, watching Aquila out of the corner of her eye.

Amalfitano dropped his heated gaze back to the screen and again pretended to study the displayed data, clearly hoping the two would get the hint and leave him the hell alone. Izraad could feel his anger: anger at her and at Aquila certainly, along with a lingering sense of hurt they hadn't believed him in the first place, but most of all, he was angry at the crew—no, not angry, she realized. He felt betrayed. The emotion kept bubbling to the surface of his roiling thoughts.

He'd lost far more to the Hahtooshans than most, and here he was, working himself to death trying to save those same Hahtooshans. Yet the act of one fanatical crewman had come close to undoing everything Amalfitano and Tasende and she had done. And now Amalfitano couldn't even look at a member of the crew without wondering if they shared Pardix's views and, if given the chance, would act on them. The *Baidarka* had been his home; the crew, many of whom owed their lives to his medical skills, had been his extended family. No longer. He clearly felt far safer in the company of the Hahtooshan medics than he did with any of the crew, aside from her, Aquila and his own hand-picked staff.

"William?" Izraad asked. *"Please?"*

He jerked his head up and stared at the two and by his reaction it was obvious he'd been so wrapped up in his roiling thoughts he'd totally forgotten Izraad and Aquila were standing in front of him.

"Just a quick break—a cup of cocoa, a few cookies—please?"

He exhaled forcefully, leaned back in his chair and crossed his arms. "I already told you, I'm not hungry—I'll call for something when I am, deal?"

"You can't stay holed up in your office forever you know."

He squinted at her and her all-knowing gaze. "I can try, can't I?"

Now we're getting somewhere. She sat on the edge of his desk. "I won't lie, William. Some crew share Ensign Pardix's views, but none—*not one*—is as militant. Trust me—ever since the attempt on your life I've been working double-time trying to ferret out anyone with extremist views. I've found none... not even Ensign Lesedi—in fact she's been helping me. Everyone was really shaken up to hear that you and Xosé were almost murdered, and now Sirin and Drakin kidnapped? It's making everyone rethink who the real enemy is, and so far *no one* is pointing figures at the Hahtooshans." She flicked the medic another quick glance but the woman's remote, bordering on openly hostile, stare remained unchanged.

"Speaking of Sirin and Drakin," Amalfitano said as he picked up a data disc, but instead of putting it in the reader, he just fingered it, "I can't stop thinking about them... and yes, Khusaaq too. Here we are, all nice and safe on the *Baidarka,* in orbit around Tuli and they're all headed—*assuming* Narbrooi's right—to Poonda Five." He abruptly tossed the disc aside, lurched to his feet, forcing the guard into hastily backing up, then he began to pace. "What if Khusaaq fails? What then? What if—"

"He's captured?" Izraad interrupted, stopping him in his tracks.

"Yeah, as a matter of fact. Gods only knows what whoever is behind this has planned for him—or Sirin and Drakin for that matter, once they get on planet, and what about his kidnapped men? Bar'ahani here," he motioned to the female medic without actually looking at her, "told me the foldboat Khusaaq took is designed for stealth and speed with limited shielding and firepower—for a Hahtooshan ship that is. Even the two vessels Narbrooi sent to shadow the freighter are basically spook ships designed for eavesdropping, they're not warships—so if they were to get into a major firefight, they—"

"Might need backup?" Aquila finished for him.

"You could say that, yeah."

Izraad and Aquila exchanged looks then Aquila said, "Which is why Admiral Keon agreed to my request—after a lot of arm twisting I might add. Zarijan and I called in every favor we had in the bank, and then some."

"A *lot* some," Izraad added.

"Request?" he dropped heavily into his chair. "What request?"

Aquila grinned. "The *Baidarka*'s to offer aid and assistance to our allies in their mission of mercy."

Izraad glanced at the medic again and this time, for just an instant, thought she caught a trace of a smile on the woman's lips.

Amalfitano leaned forward in expectation. "You mean—"

"We broke orbit about ten minutes ago," Aquila replied, "destination—"

"Poonda Five?"

Aquila and Izraad nodded in eager unison.

Amalfitano started to grin, then stopped and gave Aquila a sharp look. "But... what about—"

"The vaccines? Tasende's already flicked aboard the *Faridour* at the express invitation of her chief medical officer. He'll continue work there while you continue here aboard *Baidarka.*"

Amalfitano allowed himself a soft chuckle at the thought of Tasende surrounded by mercs and could only hope he'd showered and changed his uniform recently—and he shuddered think what they'd think of the man's brilliant, but highly unorthodox research methods. "You two thought of just about everything, didn't you?"

Izraad smiled; Aquila feigned indifference with a shrug.

Amalfitano combed his fingers through his thick, gray hair then looking up, smiled wearily. "Thank you—"

"It's not us you need to thank, Will," Izraad interrupted. "It's Admiral Keon."

Aquila grinned and motioned to the desk-com. "He's expecting your call."

Amalfitano winced then with a sidelong look at the desk-com, rose from his chair. "Not that I'm putting it off, not at all, but suddenly I'm famished, so maybe... after a late night dinner?"

"With a large side of humble pie for dessert?" Aquila chuckled.

Amalfitano laughed, then roped in Aquila's shoulders with one arm, Izraad's with the other and together the three headed for the door, the Hahtooshan medic following a respectful and watchful three paces behind while her ghostly companion brought up the rear.

Chapter 23

Sickbay, Jirah.
Three and a half hours into High Watch. Present day.

Qar'qaah remained absolutely still as he took stock. He heard the faint, oscillating hum of an air circulator and, occasionally, the restive squeak of a chair, and what sounded like someone softly drumming their fingers. He was on his right side, wrapped snugly in a thermal blanket, his head and body supported by something firm, but not hard. *Where am I?* His last cogent thought was of dematerializing his Matarii tormentor, but after that...

He cautiously flexed his hands and feet and found to his surprise that he was no longer shackled.

He carefully opened one eye, and then, to his relief, the other. Even better, both were working correctly—no more blurry vision—but what he saw left him even more confused—and scared.

Not far away was a slightly concave, but otherwise nondescript white wall, but the more he stared at it, the more he noticed a faint pattern, white on white, calculatingly subtle so as not to stir the stomach as it ever-so-slowly shifted and eeled around as if just below the surface—*Just like an A'tuu'shahn sickbay, but... but it can't be.*

The ceiling or what little he could see of it without moving his head, bore the same distinctive, fluid pattern—then another thought, a horrible probability came to mind as he suddenly recalled his shock at finding himself and the others aboard what was clearly an A'tuu'shahn craft: *I'm still on Cisne's ship!*

He struggled to tamp down his panic as he took a cautious sniff of the air, fully expecting to catch a musky aroma of a Looper, the earthy stink of a Thalamian, the faintly tangy scent of a Matarii—or even a whiff of the mildly intoxicating kij'a, a smell that had been all too pervasive with Cisne's crew. Instead he was rewarded with the distinct and nauseatingly sour stench of vomit. He dropped his gaze and realized it was his own: his cheek and shoulder were resting on a small towel saturated in the regurgitated liquid.

He took another sniff and was confronted by familiar and pungent scents: the bitter smell of antiseptic, the cloyingly sweet odor of burn balm, and something that smelled like... barra—*Could it be?* Only then did he realize that, aside from the vomit, he was clean. Even his hair had been washed.

He hadn't felt clean—hadn't *been* clean in weeks and he took a moment to savor the intoxicating sensation before another thought grabbed his attention, something one of his captors had said: *You want to look presentable for your new owners, don't you?*

Before he could worry that prospect further, he heard a whispered male voice behind him. His body tensed, his gut twisting into a knot of cold apprehension.

It took his equally anxious mind a moment to grasp that whoever was speaking, he was speaking A'tuu, not Standard or Matarii or even Looper, but that in itself wasn't necessarily good news. He'd heard sordid tales—told mostly by older, veteran crew and recounted with the clear intention of alarming their juniors—of renegade or shunned A'tuu'shahn'i who'd suffered the diminishing and who'd gravitated to the slaver trade, where no one asked questions as long as the money was good and the merchandise of top quality. Fact or fiction, it was high time to find out rather than wait for whatever unpleasantness was headed his way.

He tried lifted his head to glance over his shoulder, but the slight movement instantly roiled his stomach into an upsurge of intense queasiness and he shut his eyes and began gulping, hoping to quell the nausea.

The chair squeaked again, followed by approaching footfalls and the same male voice, only no longer whispering: "Kon'ta'aq...?"

"What?" he croaked as he struggled to push himself up, off the bunk, away from the congealing vomit—he didn't care how his captors, whoever they were, might react.

Hands grabbed him and, he was dimly aware and grateful, *very* gently helped him into a seated position.

His world began to spin and he immediately put his head between his knees and after several painful false starts, he vomited explosively, splattering his bare legs and feet and the campaign booted feet of his helper with a gooey mixture of congealed blood and saliva.

"Let me give you something for that."

Oh, good idea... He felt the nose of a ject-it against his shoulder, heard the faint hiss as the device pumped its load of medication into the wasted muscle.

He waited, unmoving, barely breathing, forehead resting on kneecaps as the medication took hold.

Finally, and very, very slowly, he lifted his head from its bony cradle and looked up. Standing in front of him was a stocky Dakkeesh and, even more surprising, he was wearing standard duty attire. *So... not a slaver—*

"Who are you?" he rasped as he wiped his blistered mouth with the back of a very shaky and equally blistered, bony hand, refusing to embrace the slight tug of relief that he might truly be aboard an A'tuu'shahn ship, still far too scared to believe that what he was seeing was anything other than another trick. He'd been tricked by Cisne or one of her confederates too many times to trust anything at face value, even if that face took the guise of a seemingly affable, if rather homely Dakkeesh who appeared not much older than he. It was possible he wasn't Dakkeesh, it was possible he wasn't even A'tuu'shahn, or even real. *Maybe none of this is real—*

"Jaa'qwah Kon'ta'aq."

All right, I'll play along. "Medic?"

Jaa'qwah nodded, replied, "From *Faridour*," as he opened the bedside drug cart and grabbed a fistful of ject-its.

Faridour? He glanced around him, but what he saw was certainly no destroyer's sickbay, not even a satellite infirmary. "This isn't *Faridour*."

"Of course not—"

"Then where am I?" he snapped, then angrily wiped the spittle from his lips.

"Aboard *Jirah*," Jaa'qwah replied, placing the ject-its on the bunk, beside Qar'qaah's hip.

Qar'qaah eyed the alarming array of ject-its, dearly hoping they weren't all meant for him, then scowled at medic, wondering if he was being deliberately obtuse and growled, "Never heard of her," as he struggled to get to his feet.

"I wouldn't try getting up, Kon'ta'aq."

"Did I ask you?"

"No, you didn't." Jaa'qwah crossed his arms and watched Qar'qaah's feeble attempts to rise.

Quickly exhausting himself, he slumped back onto the bunk and squinted furiously at the medic. "You could've helped."

"You didn't ask."

Qar'qaah eyed him; if he was real, he was being very rude. If he wasn't... *I guess he can behave anyway he wants.*

Oblivious to Qar'qaah's inner debate, Jaa'qwah picked up a ject-it, continued, "Matoosh Ruh'ta'aq warned me you had a willful streak."

"Matoosh...?" He jerked his head up and instantly regretted the sudden movement. He clutched his head in his hands and groaned, loudly.

"Yes. Khusaaq Sha'ashahn—"

"Sha'ashahn's... here... too?" Qar'qaah managed to force out through clenched teeth as his brain and the small bright world of *Jirah*'s sickbay spun in nauseating, opposing circles.

"Yes." Jaa'qwah grabbed his upper arm and pressed the ject-it against the blistered skin.

Qar'qaah stared glassily at the medic's vomit-splattered footgear, waiting for everything to stop whirling out of control.

"You haven't changed," came a *very* familiar, gravelly voice.

Matoosh! Qar'qaah desperately wanted to glare at him; he also found that he wanted to cry, frantic that this *was* real, that Matoosh was in fact standing nearby, yet equally fearful it was all a dream, a hoax, that if he looked, he'd see Cisne standing there, smirking at him instead. *As long as I don't look... I won't know.*

As that seemed to be the best solution, at least until his stomach settled, he wisely kept his head firmly clutched in his hands and his eyes fixed on Jaa'qwah's soiled boots, but he quickly discovered that the sight and smell of the vomit made him even more nauseous, so he squeezed his eyes shut and tried not to breathe. It didn't help.

Then he felt the bunk sink down as someone sat beside him—he didn't have the strength to flinch despite wanting to.

"About time you woke up," Matoosh continued. "I was beginning to think you'd nap through all the excitement."

Qar'qaah slowly, cautiously lifted his head from his hands' protective embrace just enough, bracing himself as best he could for what he was about to see.

Matoosh grinned.

Qar'qaah blinked. "Ma... Matoosh?"

Matoosh's grin broadened, threatening to split his face in half.

"Is it... *really* you?"

"You were expecting someone else?"

As a matter of fact, yes. He looked away, tried to regroup, to risk hoping what he was seeing was real, that it really was Matoosh.

As if sensing his thoughts, Matoosh placed a hand on his shoulder. "It's really me, truly."

Only then did Qar'qaah realize that he'd been seeing, smelling and tasting Matoosh's and Jaa'qwah's spectral auras the entire time: the sharp white nimbus of an Elkanaghalli, the astringent pale gold of a Dakkeesh surrounded him. That was something no alien would think to fake, to instill in his mind, because no alien knew A'tuu'shahn'i were synesthestes. *Of course*, he quickly reminded himself, unwilling to let down his guard, *it's still possible they're nothing more than figments of my own imagination—*

"You don't think this is real, do you? You don't think *I'm* real."

Qar'qaah gave his head a quick shake and fixing his suddenly watery gaze on Matoosh, desperately fought the urge to grab him with both hands, hold him, to feel his warm flesh pressed against his own, prove to himself that Matoosh was telling the truth. But that just wouldn't do. A'tuu'shahn'i didn't stoop to such emotional displays, no matter the circumstances.

So instead he angrily wiped his eyes with his shaking fingertips and replied in a small, strained voice, "No. I mean... I don't know..."

"Well, I am. So get used to it," Matoosh said, prying loose a very fleeting, forced smile from Qar'qaah. He leaned back, looked him up and down, adding, "You look truly terrible—you're vapid white, you realize that?" He glanced accusingly up at Jaa'qwah. "Why's he vapid white?"

Jaa'qwah crossed his thickset arms and arched a thick, bushy brow. "Because he's extremely ill?"

Matoosh turned back to Qar'qaah. "That's still no excuse—you're a disgrace to all Elkanaghalli'i."

Qar'qaah managed what he hoped was a baleful scowl at what Matoosh had clearly meant as a joke, but the effect was lost when he hiccupped, then hiccupped again, his entire body convulsing with the effort.

Matoosh immediately scooted a little further away from him.

Allowing himself that maybe Matoosh was real—the real Matoosh did, after all, have for an A'tuu'shahn an incongruous squeamishness to vomit, whereas spurting blood, spilled intestines, splattered brain and torn asunder body parts didn't faze him in the slightest—that he really was aboard an A'tuu'shahn vessel, that he and the others really had been rescued, he mustered up some indignation and said, "You certainly took your sweet time coming after—*wait a minute.*" Qar'qaah stared obliquely at him, then suddenly sat bolt upright, his horrified gaze fixed on Matoosh. "Was it you who... *who gassed us?*"

Matoosh shrugged. "Sha'ashahn didn't want to take any chances."

"But—I had the situation under control!"

"Really?" Matoosh roughly grasped him by the elbow and lurched to his feet, taking Qar'qaah with him, any lingering doubts about Matoosh's genuineness dispelled as he gave Qar'qaah a body-jolting shake and snarled, *"Do you ever listen to yourself? EVER?"*

For a moment the two stared at each other, almost but not quite eye to eye, but Qar'qaah's rubbery legs refused to support him and the instant Matoosh let go, he fell heavily to his knees. He bit back a cry of pain—refusing to give Matoosh the satisfaction. Unfortunately, only by leaning into Matoosh's legs did he stop himself from falling face-first onto the deck, so it wasn't an altogether convincing act.

Matoosh stared down at him, grumbled, "Yes. I see what you mean."

Jaa'qwah knelt beside Qar'qaah and wrapped a supportive arm around him. "You need to rest, Kon'ta'aq. Let me help you back to bed."

"And here we were hoping you could assist in the hunt." Matoosh shook his head and stepped back. "Pity. We could've used your passable tracking skills."

Qar'qaah forced his head up and rasped, *"Hunt...?"*

"Yes. For those who did this to you and the others."

Qar'qaah grabbed Jaa'qwah's other arm and desperately tried to rise.

"And you aren't the only one in need of rescue," Matoosh continued with an audible note of disgust, watching his futile efforts but not offering any help. "Sha'ashahn's bond-mate was also taken—"

"Tu'indai? But—"

"Tu'indai's *dead,*" Matoosh said harshly. "As are all who were aboard *Makhaira* and *Acholilah.*"

Qar'qaah stopped trying to get to his feet and stared up at him, unblinking. "All... *dead?*"

Matoosh replied, "Only those who had flicked down to Rasal Ghul Seven survived—with the exception of Jabooreh and Vur'taas, who died on that cursed planet."

"But—"

"Much has happened—too much to explain now. Suffice it to say, Khusaaq took a new bond-mate, *a Rimmer*, and now we must rescue her as well, along with making examples of those who took you and the others—"

"A... Rimmer?"

Matoosh's badly scared mouth twisted as he growled, "The Coalition and the Orthodoxy are now... *allies.*"

Qar'qaah flicked Jaa'qwah a sidelong glance, to which the medic replied with a confirming, if mildly unhappy nod and then he looked back at Matoosh, his mind spinning anew. *How long were we—*

"As I said, too much to explain." Matoosh gave him one last and decidedly disdainful look then asked, "Am I real?"

"Ye... yes."

"Sure? You don't sound very sure."

"I... think so."

Matoosh replied with a disgusted huff of breath, then turned and stalked out of the infirmary.

"It's true, Kon'ta'aq," Jaa'qwah said. "Everything Ruh'ta'aq said is true—"

"Help me up!" Qar'qaah growled and with Jaa'qwah's help, managed, after several attempts, to stagger to a very wobbly-legged stand. He looked around him then turned his blood-shot and sunken gaze on the medic. "Where are the others?"

"Sha'ashahn ordered that I release them. Too soon if you ask me, but since no one seems to want my opinion—"

"Give me something to keep me on my feet."

"But—"

"DON'T ARGUE!" He hastily grabbed the bunk to steady himself. *"JUST DO IT!"*

Jaa'qwah met his fierce gaze squarely then shook his head and snatched up a ject-it. "Let's have your arm." He then pressed it against Qar'qaah's shoulder as he muttered, "I'm just the medic. Far be it for me to tell anyone what's medically in their best interest."

Qar'qaah ignored him and his grumbled comments. He closed his eyes, took a deep breath and smiled as he felt the drug take effect. Finally, he opened his eyes and looked at Jaa'qwah, who still stood beside him, clutching his elbow, effectively stopping him from swaying—of falling again—and demanded, "Where's my duty uniform?"

Galley of Jirah.
Four hours into High Watch. Present day.

"We've located the surviving crew of *Huui'teh*—or, should I say, *Palraiyuk,*" Khusaaq said as he looked around him. Seated around the small galley table were, to his left, Raudah, Laihiri and Toubeh. To his right were Shu'hah, Endooki, Nihaal, and Rukoobi. Standing behind them, leaning against the back wall, arms crossed, were Matoosh and Tejat. A holographic display of the Gorgon's Lair sparkled above the table.

"Once we knew exactly who and what we were looking for—and exactly how many," he nodded to Endooki, "it was relatively simple for Toubeh to locate our quarry, by intercepting their transmissions to *Palraiyuk* and rerouting them here, where Shu'hah's truly impressive skills at mimicry came into play."

As he spoke, ten red markers appeared within the holo and at his touch, one of the telltales, the one designating the location of the commandeered ship, began to blink.

"Due to this deception, they have no idea their companions are dead and their prisoners," Khusaaq again made eye contact with each of the rescued troopers, "safely back in A'tuu'shahn hands. So they have elected to take advantage of what the planet has to offer. If any do return, they will find only an empty ship and with no signs of a struggle, will likely assume their fellows have made off with their valuable prisoners." He turned to Toubeh. "Ruh'ta'aq?"

"I've located two Thalamians here." She pointed at the holo as two of the red markers abruptly turned to yellow. "At an underground business that specializes in catering to their species' unique—" she glanced over her shoulder as a sullen-faced and silent Jaa'qwah stalked into the crowded galley and squeezed his way past Matoosh and Tejat over to the food synthesizer, then began fiddling with it, as if it was in urgent need of his attention. A moment later, Qar'qaah appeared in the hatchway.

Khusaaq's eyes widened and he hastily rose.

The others, following his lead, also got to their feet.

"What are you doing here, Kon'ta'aq?" Khusaaq asked with an audible note of annoyance as he stared at Qar'qaah. The soldier's once form-fitting and now rather tattered duty uniform hung on Qar'qaah's gaunt frame, accentuating, rather than concealing just how emaciated he was—deliberately so as Qar'qaah was clearly not of a mind to will the ghillie suit into adjusting to his much thinner form as the others had.

"I'm reporting for duty, Sha'ashahn."

Khusaaq fixed his exasperated stare on Jaa'qwah as if to affix blame for Qar'qaah's unwelcome but not altogether unexpected arrival only to find the medic still had his back to him, still pretending to be busy with the synthesizer while softly swearing to himself. Qar'qaah had, yet again, demonstrated his uncanny knack for disrupting the best-laid plans and Khusaaq's less than favorable response was not lost on the others.

He looked back at Qar'qaah, noticed he was swaying slightly, fatigued by the exertion of the short walk and motioned to the seat next to him, displacing Shu'hah. Qar'qaah immediately took possession of the chair without acknowledging Shu'hah or Khusaaq. The others quickly resumed their seats as Shu'hah wordlessly joined Matoosh and Tejat.

Khusaaq gave Qar'qaah another sidelong look, exhaled and, shaking his head, turned his attention back to Toubeh. "Continue."

"Three Loopers are here, at a gambling establishment not far from the southern landing field and *Palraiyuk*." The holo altered the color of the corresponding telltales, this time to a bright blue, while *Palraiyuk* continued to flash in red. "A Matarii is here." She pointed and the marker turned green. "In what, I believe, is a bathhouse."

"Probably trying to rid himself of the stench of Loopers," Rukoobi muttered, rubbing his prominent nose.

There was a ripple of forced laughter among them; even Qar'qaah managed a half-hearted but very short-lived smile.

"Finally, two more Matarii and a human are here—"

"Cisne," Raudah hissed, glaring at the marker with pure hate.

Nihaal and Laihiri nodded grimly as Endooki cast a quick, worried glance at Qar'qaah.

Qar'qaah, for his part, kept his now slitted eyes on the last of the flashing telltales, his jaw muscles visibly clenched under his blistered skin.

"Cisne?" Khusaaq looked at each of the rescued for an explanation. "Who is Cisne?"

"Their human ringleader," Endooki answered softly, his eyes still fixed on Qar'qaah.

Khusaaq turned to Toubeh. "Perhaps an alias for the Rimmers' mysterious Mizahn?"

She nodded. "Go by what the Rimmers would reasonably assume is an A'tuu name, then use a Rimmer name with her A'tuu captives?"

"Remind me to ask her first chance I get." Khusaaq growled, his own hands curling into fists. He jerked his chin towards the map. "Continue."

Toubeh nodded and picked up where she'd left off: "All are within a kilometer or so of *Palraiyuk*—presumably none wished to wander too far afield in case there was the need to make a hasty getaway."

Khusaaq, who, like everyone else was painfully aware of Qar'qaah's fixation with the last marker, said, "Shu'hah. Rukoobi."

The two straightened up in eager anticipation.

"You're to remain aboard *Jirah.*"

Shu'hah blinked in surprise; Rukoobi visibly deflated, but neither questioned the order, at least out loud.

"We must make a coordinated attack so that there is no time for any of them to warn their companions, but just in case, Tejat has taken off line all of *Palraiyuk*'s primary systems, rendering her inoperable for any speedy getaway. However, to eliminate any possibility of escape using another appropriated vessel, I'll need the best gunner in the fleet to disable its engines—*without* destroying the surrounding ship if they do indeed try to make a getaway in another commandeered craft," he added, softening the blow.

Rukoobi nodded, suitably mollified, and replied, "Yes, ta'ahn."

"Shu'hah, you are to coordinate the hunt and continue with your intercepts of their communications. And Jaa'qwah..."

The medic turned to face him. "Yes, ta'ahn?"

"...I need you to remain aboard as well," he briefly, pointedly, glanced sidelong at Qar'qaah before continuing, "to deal with any medical emergencies. The rest of you—you are to pair up—and you're *not* to separate under *any* circumstance—it's too risky. I want one of each group together, to lessen the chances of any mistakes in the identification of our quarry. Narbrooi Hahtra'tzrhi had only one stipulation when he approved this mission: there are to be no *unintended* fatalities that could be difficult to explain to the Poondians or our Coalition allies."

There was a murmur of agreement from the soldiers before he continued, "Laihiri—you and Toubeh will deal with the Thalamians. Tejat and Nihaal, the lone Matarii is yours then join up with Matoosh and Endooki to eliminate the three Loopers. Raudah... with me. We'll take care of the others."

All eyes fell on Qar'qaah.

He swallowed hard, awaiting Khusaaq's assignment, clearly unsure if his omission was an oversight, or something else.

"Prepare to flick down on my order. Dismissed..."

They eagerly rose as one; even Qar'qaah pushed himself unsteadily to his feet.

"...*except* Qar'qaah Kon'ta'aq."

Qar'qaah slowly resumed his seat as the others quickly and silently filed out of the small galley.

Khusaaq waited until they were alone then turned to face him and said calmly and quietly, "You're not fit to accompany us..."

Qar'qaah fixed his unblinking gaze on the holo but said nothing.

"...you can barely keep on your feet; you'll only slow us down. You know this as well as I—"

"NO!" Qar'qaah, eyes flashing, slammed his fist down on the table as he snarled, *"You cannot do this to me—"*

"You've forgotten to whom you are speaking, Kon'ta'aq," Khusaaq interrupted coldly. From the moment he'd been notified of their abductions, he'd thought of little else but retrieving Qar'qaah and the others alive, and once rescued, he'd become consumed with fear that, at least for Qar'qaah, it might have come too late.

He'd gone so far as to try to bargain with the Elkanasu to spare Qar'qaah, offering his own life in trade, but his desperate entreaties had been met with silence. And now here he was, seated next to a very much alive Qar'qaah, his prayers answered, and at the same time experiencing an all too familiar, bordering on uncontrollable frustrated rage with the boy for steadfastly refusing to be anything other than who and what he was no matter the consequences, to himself or to anyone else. "So, I will refresh your faulty memory: I *am* Sha'ashahn, *not* you."

Qar'qaah visibly bristled and opened his mouth to reply, but Khusaaq cut him off with a raised hand and a menacing, "Clearly leaving you in charge was a mistake—I assumed from it you'd finally learn how to handle authority. Instead the experience appears to have only fed into your fondness for challenging it."

Qar'qaah looked away, jaw muscles bunching.

"And if that were not enough," Khusaaq added with calculated brutality, "as my Doh'ha, I can do *anything* I please with you."

Qar'qaah flinched as if struck. After a moment, he replied stiffly, "Yes, ta'ahn, of course ta'ahn—how could I forget *what* I am... *ta'ahn?*" He forced himself to his feet and turned unsteadily for the door.

"I did not dismiss you, Kon'ta'aq. Yet again, you overestimate your position."

Qar'qaah remained standing, his back to Khusaaq, his body shaking in a combination of poorly controlled rage and overwhelming fatigue.

Khusaaq fixed his own furious gaze on the holo as he took a measured sip of barra, swallowed, and then asked calmly, "What did they do to you?"

There was a long, cold silence, followed by: "Nothing... ta'ahn."

"Endooki says otherwise."

"Endooki is mistaken. May I go now, ta'ahn?"

"No." He rose and placed his hand on Qar'qaah's tense shoulder.

Qar'qaah tried to twitch it off, but Khusaaq's hand refused to budge.

"Tell me."

Qar'qaah squeezed his eyes shut, visibly fighting tears.

"Tell me," he repeated more firmly as he tightened his hold, an almost but not *quite* painful hold against a freshly knit collarbone.

Qar'qaah took a deep breath and replied in a voice barely above a whisper, "Cisne put me into a stasis pod..."

"Awake."

He replied with a quick, curt nod as his tattooed hands balled into white-knuckled fists and his jaw muscles bunched, his teeth biting down a reflexive scream.

"And...?"

Qar'qaah hesitated long enough to take another steadying breath. *"Isn't that enough?"* he managed without his voice cracking.

Khusaaq couldn't help but wince at the tightly contained agony behind Qar'qaah's whispered response. He took a deep breath, in the process shedding his anger, his frustration and loosening the hold he had on him then answered softly, "Yes, it is, and I'm sorry, truly I am—"

"I can tell."

"I would have come sooner—"

"But you were otherwise occupied." Qar'qaah jerked his shoulder out from under Khusaaq's hand as he wheeled around to face him, eyes glittering. "Willingly abandoning our beliefs and all we stand for in preference for the... *the pleasures of a Rimmer kaa-schat!*"

Khusaaq's eyes widened in shock and sudden fury and before he could stop himself, he struck Qar'qaah across the face with enough force to send him stumbling backwards, into the narrow corridor.

Qar'qaah collided with the far wall then slid down its curved surface onto the deck and to his knees. He blinked, gave his head a shake to clear it, then, wiping his bleeding nose and split lower lip with the back of his hand, looked up.

Khusaaq now stood in the doorway of the galley, arms crossed, seething. "I'll deal with you when we return—until then, *stay out of my sight!"*

"With immense pleasure, *ta'ahn,"* he replied hoarsely. He managed to lurch unsteadily to his feet, then with one last defiant glare at him and cupping his now profusely bleeding nose and mouth in one hand, staggered down the passageway.

Khusaaq stared after him and found himself tempted to follow, to make sure he actually reached the small sickbay—or, at the very least, a bunk in the crew's sleeping quarters.

Something about Qar'qaah always brought out the absolute worst in him; the boy was willful to a fault, always insolent, and, more often than not brazenly insubordinate. And he'd reacted just as Ja'andai had reacted to him whenever he'd acted out, by violence, a response that had left *him* hating the man, and still hating everything Ja'andai represented. *And now I've become Ja'andai...*

He'd deliberately chosen Qar'qaah to be in charge of the small group of soldiers left on the island, rather than the obvious choice of the far more experienced Matoosh in the hope that it would be a positive experience for both Qar'qaah and himself, by boosting Qar'qaah's self-confidence and sense of independence, while giving him the opportunity to measure how Qar'qaah handled his new-found power.

It had not exactly turned out as planned.

I never intended to abandon you, I never—

"Was that necessary?"

Khusaaq turned to find Matoosh standing nearby.

Matoosh and Qar'qaah had always had a close relationship—it was not exactly one of older and younger brother, although through necessity they'd been raised as such. Qar'qaah idolized Matoosh, and at the same time found it impossible to emulate him, or, more accurately, refused to emulate him, knowing that by being deliberately contrary, he infuriated Khusaaq.

Matoosh, for his part, was fiercely protective, and would be the first to defend him when Qar'qaah did what Qar'qaah did best: getting himself into serious trouble. Yet he was also deeply envious of Qar'qaah's special standing amongst Elkanaghalli'i, and his uniquely intimate bond with Khusaaq.

It only made it that much more grating to Matoosh that Qar'qaah failed to appreciate his position—in fact deeply and openly resented it.

And now you've paid dearly for something you never wanted to be—never chose to be... just like me. Concealing his own misgivings, his own remorse behind an impervious glare, Khusaaq replied angrily, "You too dare to question me?"

Matoosh stood his ground. "In this case, yes."

Breaking the uncomfortable staring match, Khusaaq glanced down the corridor. It was now deserted. "He's in no condition to accompany us. You know that, I know that—"

"And so does he, but he also desperately wants to go—he *needs* to go."

"I know."

"And you would still deny him his revenge against those who did this to him?"

"I cannot take the risk—you saw him—the physical strain would kill him."

"And if he doesn't go, the psychological toll will destroy him."

Khusaaq wet his lips as he cast another unhappy look down the corridor, to the splatter of fresh blood on the deck that was slowly being absorbed by the ship. "He's stronger than you give him credit."

"Really? You just suggested otherwise."

Khusaaq met his gaze.

Matoosh stared back, defiant. "Better he die hunting her, than—"

"Better for whom? He wasn't singled out by this Cisne by accident," Khusaaq replied, "or though his own impulsive actions, any more than their abduction was a random act—you know that."

"So you—"

"So my decision stands. He remains aboard *Jirah*—"

Matoosh snorted in disgust, turned and stalked back to the bridge.

Khusaaq stared after him, adding in a suddenly weary whisper, "*Where I know he'll be safe.*"

Chapter 24

Aboard the Talakah. *Approaching Poonda Five.*
Present day.

Sirin felt more than heard the change in the ever-present background hum of the ship's engines. "We've dropped."

Drakin walked over to the door and pressed her jaw against it. "I hear movement. I tink we may be approaching our dessstination."

Sirin blew out her cheeks. Since her run-in with Pardix, they'd had contact only with Urbat, and only when he brought their meals and kept them supplied with drinking water.

By her reckoning, they had to have been in transit for at least three days. While not knowing the capabilities of the ship that left a few possibilities. None were appealing, not this close to the border with Matarran-held space. The other option—rendezvous with another ship—was one she had not wanted to consider.

She walked over to the nearby bunk and sat down with a heavy sigh. Drakin sat beside her and wrapped her tail around the two of them, and together they stared morosely at the door.

The deck below them shuddered.

Drakin gave her a sidelong look. "I tink we juz penetrated an atmosssphere."

"Yeah."

A moment later, they both heard a muffled *thump,* followed by a low, warbling whine.

"We're on approach."

"And someone'z coming," Drakin replied as she rose from the bunk.

Sirin had no sooner joined her when the door sliced open and a young human, a total stranger, warily stepped in.

"What do you want?" she demanded.

In reply, he tossed a clean, utilitarian jumpsuit onto the bunk nearest the door and replied, "Compliments of Tace. Put it on." With that, he backed out of the cabin and the door snapped shut.

Drakin gave her a sidelong look. "I don't like da sssound of diz."

"Neither do I." Sirin looked at the jumpsuit, then at her clothing. "But it's preferable to what I'm wearing."

"Indeed." Drakin nodded, eyeing her thin, revealing negligee.

Crew quarters, aboard Jirah.
End of High Watch. Present day.

"Ta'ahn?"

Qar'qaah pretended to be asleep, hoping Jaa'qwah would get the hint and leave him alone. He still felt mildly nauseated from the blood he'd swallowed, from the blood that continued to ooze from his nose and lip. His jaw still throbbed from the blow, the back of his head still ached from where he'd hit the wall, and the tip of his tongue was raw from worrying his freshly loosened teeth.

But worse, Khusaaq's blow had left him confused, angry... and deeply embittered—he'd deliberately provoked Khusaaq into hitting him before, many times and often much harder, but this blow had shaken loose more than just teeth: it had loosened a deluge of other memories—recent memories, of being repeatedly beaten almost but not quite to the point of losing consciousness.

In those terrible, terrifying moments, as his world grayed, as his vision blurred, he'd cried out for Khusaaq, begging him to rescue him, pleading with him not to abandon him.

It had made his tormentors laugh—it had made Cisne laugh the loudest.

He blinked back the hot tears that threatened to give him away, give the true depth of his sense of betrayal away.

"I need to replace the infuser's fluid cylinder," Jaa'qwah continued matter-of-factly.

He felt the medic pop the empty container from the infuser strapped to his forearm and a moment later, carefully snap a replacement into place.

"And I going to give you a booster to the painkiller and antiemetic I gave you earlier," he added as his fingers lightly grasped Qar'qaah's upper arm. He pressed a ject-it against it, and had no sooner let go than Qar'qaah grabbed the blanket and jerked it up around his bare shoulders and rolled onto his side, away from Jaa'qwah.

"Can I get you anything?"

"Just go away," he replied tightly.

Jaa'qwah let out an exasperated sigh. "I understand your frustration, Kon'ta'aq. I too wanted to participate—"

"I said go away!" He turned his suddenly wet face into the bunk's thin mattress.

"All right. I'll come back and check on you in a while."

Yeah, you do that. He scowled as he waited for the medic to leave.

Satisfied he was alone, he wiped his eyes and nose with his hand, exhaled and tried to relax, but his mind refused to surrender to the drugs and allow him to lapse into sleep.

Instead the potent combination loosened a maelstrom of sounds and images… of Khusaaq's stinging words… of seeing his friends struck down as they tried to flee a force of Rimmers and believing they'd all been cut down in cold blood, of screaming in rage and firing at the tightening cordon of Rimmers, missing most, hitting a few, of being tackled from behind and pinned, the air knocked out of him and unable to move as he was drugged, followed by harsh laughter at his feeble kicks, slurred curses and wild punches once released from their grasp… of feeling the effect of a flickerstage wash over him… of being hauled before Cisne, who demanded he identify himself, and when he refused, being beaten, being asked again, refusing again despite the increasingly desperate pleas of Endooki to tell her what she wanted to know, and then being beaten again.

But any escape into unconsciousness, even temporarily, was denied him. Cisne's doctor quickly brought him around with a drug that burned down the length of his arm, causing his hand to cramp then he was roughly dragged over to a pallet by two of her crew and dumped onto it. He managed to lift his head and groggily look around. Endooki was no longer present, only Cisne and her crew.

He demanded to know what they'd done with Endoki, and got as his reward a punch to the face that sent his mind reeling.

He suddenly found himself held spread-eagle, and as those grasping his limbs watched and laughed, Cisne knelt between his legs and began to caress him. His panting cries begging her to stop and his body's humiliating response to her fondling only egged her on and the assault became more violent. The others joined in, each taking his or her turn with him as he sobbed uncontrollably.

He had no idea how long the rape went on, he lapsed in and out of consciousness, but her doctor kept prodding him back to wakefulness, using drugs to, as Cisne put it, 'heighten the experience.'

Sometime later he was again dragged to his feet, bleeding and in agony. The Matarii doctor administered another drug, then he was frog-marched, dizzy and disoriented over to a stasis pod and before he could fully grasp what was happening, he found himself being shoved into it.

As the stasis effect began to wash over him, he used what little strength he had left to desperately pound on the clear wall, to let his captors know the prep hadn't had a chance to take effect.

Cisne's response was to grin at his increasingly feeble attempts as he was fully engulfed, awake and horrified—

He flinched violently and his eyes snapped open.

Gulping for air, he sat bolt upright on the narrow bunk; it took his panicked mind a moment to recognize his surroundings, more by smell than sight and quickly reassured himself through gasping breaths: *Jirah. I'm... I'm aboard Jirah...*

The crew's sleeping quarters were dark. The only light came from the corridor. He had finally lapsed into sleep, only to be awakened by the same hellish, endless loop of memories that plagued him even in his waking hours.

The ship itself was quiet, aside from the faint, ever-present hum of the air circulators. He sniffed the air, assuring himself that he was alone then he rose, slowly and stiffly, from the bunk, then padded over to the open hatch and bracing himself against the frame, listened.

Satisfied that the three soldiers left aboard were nowhere nearby, he went in search of his uniform, dagger and pistol. He'd reluctantly stripped all the way down at Jaa'qwah's insistence, the medic claiming he needed to examine him for new injuries and he was still so wobbly from Khusaaq's blow and in combination with a painkiller Jaa'qwah gave him without asking, that he'd complied without question.

He assumed his uniform and weapons would be kept nearby, but at the time he hadn't thought to watch where they were being stowed, so he went about silently checking every unlocked locker and storage bin in the room while keeping a wary eye on the doorway. A few minutes later, and coming up empty handed, he glanced back at the doorway and scowled. Clearly Khusaaq wasn't taking any chances.

Two can play at this game. In his search, he'd happened across one locker that, unlike the rest *was* locked, which meant only one thing: he should open it to see what was inside. Even as a small child, security codes and electric locks had been a simple matter to break. Locks such as this were more a deterrent for the overly curious than a serious theft-preventative and it took him less than a minute to crack the code and pop open the locker.

He found what he'd been looking for: a duty uniform that had been hastily stuffed inside in trade for combat armor. He also happened across several small, highly personal ritual items—Elkanaghalli ritual items, not to be viewed by anyone not Elkanaghalli. He fingered the uniform. *Toubeh.* He would have known by scent alone.

He shrugged, grabbed the uniform and boots, carefully relocked the locker then walked back to his bunk. He tossed the clothing on it, placed the boots to the floor, then yanked the infuser from his arm and tossed it onto another bunk. He quickly and quietly donned the trousers, boots and under-tunic—they were designed for Toubeh, who was taller, heavier and with slightly larger feet, but with a little mental tweaking, all were good enough for his needs. He reached for the hauberk—and stopped. While the duty uniform in its entirety offered protection almost as effective as armor, not to mention perfect camouflage if worn with a helmet, it also served as a beacon to any other A'tuu'shahn, just as his tattoos could act as a homing signal—under his conscious control.

Under normal circumstances, that was all for the good. But these were *not* normal circumstances. He tossed the hauberk back on the bunk, grabbed the weapons belt instead and cinched it around his bony hips and by touch alone took stock of its armament, discarding all but the missing maser pistol's holster, extra power-pack and a utility knife. A spare pistol, he hoped, would be found in the staging bay's weapon's locker. Coming at last to the tac-net, he hesitated only a moment before unclipping it from the belt and placing it on the bunk beside the discarded hauberk.

Satisfied, he walked back to the open hatch and cautiously peered around the frame, to his right, towards the bow. Listening, he could hear soft laughter and voices and quickly identified three sources.

Jaa'qwah's deep voice was unmistakable. The other two he assumed were Shu'hah and Rukoobi—*has to be.* His ears also placed all three on the bridge. The hatch was open, and with the corridor's slight curvature no one was in his direct line of sight, which meant he wasn't in theirs, either.

He looked to his left. He knew the foldboat's basic layout, knew the flickerstage was towards the stern, not far from the sickbay. All he had to do is reach it without being detected.

He stole into the corridor, keeping to the left side then ducked into the sickbay. He paused briefly when he sensed the nearness of his ritual dagger—and for an instant, just an instant he thought he heard *Tseih'sheh* calling to him. He quickly dismissed it as a figment of his imagination—any chance to be called by the Elkanasu, to be accepted into their embrace had been torn from him by Cisne and nothing he would ever accomplish would change that.

With that ugly thought foremost, he grabbed a ject-it, snatched up a handful of vials of painkillers and stimulants then stuffed them down the neck slit of his under-tunic. He then returned to the hatchway and peered down the passageway, towards the bridge, satisfying himself his movements had gone undetected. But as he crept back into the corridor, he overheard a soft keening sound. He pointedly ignored it and hurried down the last few meters, to the cramped staging bay that housed the flickerstage.

He strode over to the weapons locker and using the utility knife, expertly shorted out the in-built alarm, then quickly pried it open, knowing he had only a matter of seconds before the ship would recognize what was happening and warn those on the bridge. To his relief, there were several pistols inside to choose from. He grabbed the nearest, checked it had a full charge, then stepped into the small chamber and tapped in a hurried request for the last set of flick down coordinates.

The flickerstage's computer immediately complied.

He briefly hesitated as he realized once committed, he would never see the inside of an A'tuu ship again—*unless it's the brig, awaiting execution.* He forced a smile.

He inhaled slowly, savoring the familiar and heady jumble of smells, sights, colors and textures one last time, then exhaled forcefully, purging not just his lungs, but his mind of any last minute hesitation, any second thoughts. He muttered, *"Time to go,"* and tapped in the same set of coordinates just as he overheard the ship's droning alert that the weapons locker had been forcibly opened. An instant later, it was joined by an alarm, warning the others that the flicker mechanism was being activated.

He overheard a startled oath, followed by pounding feet echoing down the corridor and Jaa'qwah yelling his name.

Rukoobi was the first to arrive, skidding to a stop in the open hatch, his maser pistol drawn, Jaa'qwah and Shu'hah right behind him.

"STOP!" Rukoobi barked, pointing the weapon at him.

Qar'qaah whispered, *"Too late,"* as the flicker effect washed over him, drawing out Rukoobi's screamed obscenity into something that more closely resembled an undulating wail, and his surroundings suddenly receded, leaving behind a series of quickly fading after-images.

Then, just as suddenly, a shimmering, multicolored wall raced towards him, accompanied by its own spectral doubles and a loud roaring in his ears.

The multiple images abruptly coalesced into one and he had to stop himself from falling to his knees by the sense of everything, including himself, coming to a sudden halt. As he regained his balance, he looked around him while his long, loose hair, caught by a stiff, frigidly cold night breeze writhed around his face and bare shoulders.

The flickerstage had deposited him on the northern edge of the sprawling Gorgon's Lair, safely beyond its garish, twinkling lights, in what appeared—and smelled—to be the municipal garbage dump. Beyond lay a rock-strewn yet otherwise empty expanse of the crater floor unusable as a landing field. He had rightly assumed Khusaaq would choose a site where an A'tuu'shahn landing force's arrival would go completely undetected; the officer had picked an unexpected—and rather humbling—but nevertheless ideal location, with mounds of refuse effectively blocking the transient spatial displacement caused by the flicker from all but the most pinpoint of monitoring.

He gave himself a moment to get his bearings using a small, tight cluster of stars that hung just above the distant peaks as an anchor and to collect his thoughts. He'd made it this far, but if he wasn't careful—and didn't get moving—he wouldn't make it much farther. His only desire was to find the one responsible for his nightmarish ordeal—to kill Cisne for denying him any claim to be an untouched Elkanaghalli and thus forbidding him all that it was to *be* Elkanaghalli—before Khusaaq or one of the others found him. After that... nothing mattered.

Giving his goose-pimpled upper arms a brisk rub, he looked around. To his right and some distance away he spotted a goodly number of Poondians scavenging among the steaming piles of debris, but all were too occupied digging through trash to have noticed his arrival. To his left and no more than a dozen or so meters away, stood several dilapidated single-story buildings.

He nodded and took off at cautious and rather rubbery-legged trot.

He reached the nearest building and crouched beside its retaining wall, then gasping for breath in the planet's thin atmosphere, looked back the way he'd just come just in time to spot the faintest of sparkles from within the heaps of trash. To anyone else, it would have gone unnoticed or been chalked up to reflected starlight on a breeze-ruffled piece of discarded composite.

But he knew better.

An A'tuu'shahn in full battle armor had just made planetfall.

He took several deep breaths—his lungs struggling to adapt to the significantly lower oxygen level—and immediately regretted it. The putrid stench made his stomach lurch and the thin atmosphere made him lightheaded. But, he quickly reminded himself, there was one benefit to the nauseating stink: his own scent was masked by the multitude of other, far more pungent smells, making it that much harder for whoever followed to track him. And the warmth given off by the surrounding decomposing biomass would make it difficult to pinpoint his heat signature. Even the Poondians played an unknowing but critical part by providing numerous false, if ever-so-brief targets for a helmet's sensors.

Satisfied, he turned and crept away.

Ahead lay a warren of ramshackle houses and squalid alleyways. Picking one narrow passageway at random, he warily entered its dark mouth.

Chapter 25

Poonda Five.
Almost midnight, planetary time. Present day.

"He... *WHAT?*"

Raudah, who was standing beside Khusaaq, visibly flinched as the officer's enraged voice exploded in his helmet's earpiece.

The rest of the landing party, while widely dispersed within the sprawling city, were, like Raudah, a silent, captive audience.

Only Matoosh made his presence—and his feelings—known on the open link by a softly worded, well-placed and perfectly descriptive expletive.

"We tried to stop him, ta'ahn," Shu'hah continued, *"but he'd already initialized the flicker effect."*

Khusaaq scowled disgustedly at the brightly lit gaming halls and garish bordellos whose signage left nothing to the imagination which lined the wide boulevard, searching for something, someone—*anything*—upon which to vent his wrath, Narbrooi be damned.

Then he reminded himself there'd be fully sanctioned targets soon, he only needed to be patient. In the meantime, he satisfied himself with a long series of curses.

He finally exhausted his repertoire, but not his fury at Qar'qaah's impulsive stupidity.

For a moment no one spoke, then Shu'hah continued, *"Rukoobi flicked down immediately afterwards, ta'ahn, and—"*

"On whose authority?"

There was a momentary pause before Shu'hah replied, *"Mine, ta'ahn, I thought—"*

"I will speak to you later about this. For now... since he's there, have Rukoobi do a quick recon of the area—perhaps Kon'ta'aq is still close by—nothing more, he's *not* to enter the city proper, understood? If he cannot find him within the rubbish dump, he's to flick back—I need him aboard *Jirah.*"

"Yes, ta'ahn." There was another brief silence before Shu'hah added, *"Rukoobi acknowledges—said he's already*

scanned the dump, but no sign of Kon'ta'aq... he's now returning to the flick-down coordinates."

"Very well," Khusaaq grunted as he started off again, up the wide avenue, keeping to the more poorly lit, grungier side where few but the most intoxicated, wary of the even darker side streets, the preferred haunts of pickpockets and slavers, dared to stroll.

Raudah paced silently alongside, the two invisible to any casual observer. Despite constantly having to dodge and weave and duck into side streets to keep out of the limited range of the cheap but effective proximity detectors—inexpensive insurance against being kidnapped or mugged—that most aliens carried, they still made good time as they headed towards their target.

As they came to an intersection, the bleat from a sensor in his helmet drew Khusaaq's baleful gaze to a nondescript building a few dozen meters to his left, down a narrow alley. A flickering sign over the front door advertised rooms for the hour, the night or the week.

He looked up, allowing his helmet's sensors to scan the entire two-story hostel.

A telltale immediately lit as it pinpointed the two Matarii they'd been seeking—finally, a target upon which he could justifiably release his frustrated anger—but *only* the Matarii, and going by the readouts, the two were completely preoccupied with each other.

So much the better.

Beside him, Raudah stood motionless, awaiting his orders.

"I want one of them alive—long enough to tell us where their human companion is and why they kidnapped our men. I give you the honor of choosing which, then dealing with the other one any way you see fit—all I ask is that it not make a lot of noise."

Raudah replied with a very pleased, "Yes, ta'ahn, thank you."

"Then come," Khusaaq whispered and motioned for Raudah to follow.

Aboard the Talakah.
Present day.

The door snapped open and Sirin found herself staring at the business ends of a blaster and a shocker. She looked up to find Urbat and Pardix standing just outside their cabin.

"Come with us." Urbat motioned to her with the shocker.

"No."

"You haven't learned, have you, Blondie? That wasn't a request. Now do as I say or your friend here suffers the consequences." To emphasize his point, he turned the weapon on Drakin.

"Do az dey sssay, Sssirin. I'll be okay."

Pardix stepped forward, grabbed Sirin's arm, snarled, *"Come on!"* and dragged her from the room.

Sirin barely had time to glance over her shoulder at Drakin before the door snapped closed. She then glared up at Pardix. "Where are you taking me?"

"You'll find out, soon enough." Keeping his painful grip on her wrist, he pulled her down the length of the corridor; ahead, beside a closed airlock, stood the young man who'd brought her the jumpsuit.

Pardix roughly jerked her to a stop in front of the lock. He dug into a pocket and withdrew three small breathers and handed her one, Urbat another then he clipped the last to his nose.

Sirin and Urbat followed suit, then Urbat tapped in the release. The airlock hissed open and they were all hit with a blast of frigid air.

She hugged herself tightly as she stared into the twinkling darkness beyond. Her eyes barely had a chance to adapt before she found herself being prodded by Pardix into following Urbat down a short ramp and onto the hard-packed dirt of what she quickly realized was a vast landing field: scattered all around her stood the silent, brooding shapes of other ships: hundreds of them.

She looked up, hoping the stars would hint as to where she was but the planet's dazzling necklace of moonlets and gossamer ring system made finding recognizable constellations or star patterns next to impossible, despite the inky blackness of the surrounding sky. Even the presence of rings was of no help—ring systems were commonplace.

"Poonda Five."

She turned to Pardix. *"What...?"*

"You're wondering where we are," he replied. "I just told you. Poonda Five."

"But... why here?"

"Why not?" With that, his fingers again locked around her wrist. "Now come *on*." He gave her arm a sharp tug as Urbat, warily scanning their surroundings with his narrowed eyes, slipped his shocker into a hidden shoulder holster.

Realizing it was futile to fight, Sirin allowed Pardix to lead her across the open, wind-swept expanse, but not before she managed a quick, covert glance back at the ship. Marking its appearance and location in her mind, she reluctantly turned back to the business at hand—survival.

Aboard Jirah.
Four and a half hours into Low Watch. Present day.

Khusaaq and Raudah, the last to flick back just before planetary dawn, stepped out of *Jirah*'s flicker chamber to find Shu'hah and Tejat waiting for them.

Khusaaq pulled off his helmet and handed it to Tejat, growling, "Status," as the frustration of the night's hunt tainted his tired voice. The two captured Matarii turned out to be nothing more than not particularly well-paid freelancers—he had no lingering doubts about that. Same was true of the rest of the crew they'd tracked down. His only satisfaction, small as it was, was that none would repeat their mistake. Only the mysterious Cisne remained at large. She'd left, he was now convinced, her hapless confederates as diversions, keeping him and the others busy meting out their version of justice while she made good her escape. The most plausible way she would have been tipped off to their presence was if she'd happened across Qar'qaah—

"*Kashku* and *Illuyanka* report the freighter *Talakah* they've been shadowing was granted landing rights and made planetfall a short time ago, ta'ahn." Shu'hah replied, interrupting Khusaaq's grim train of thought while falling into step beside Khusaaq as the officer strode from the bay, Tejat and Raudah taking up the rear. "Rukoobi's been tracking them, augmented by assistance from the koursans' crews, eavesdropping on the *Talakah*'s transmissions—its crew is under the mistaken belief that we're still in transit. Two of the kidnappers have taken the human female off ship—"

Khusaaq flicked him a sidelong, arched glance. "How long ago?"

"A few minutes at most."

"Can we track their movements?"

"Only as long as they keep in contact with those left aboard the *Talakah*—surface jamming continues to severely hamper our efforts. Nerik'ah Sha'ashahn of *Illuyanka* asks if you want her to intercede? Narbrooi Hahtra'tzrhi's orders were—"

"Not yet. With luck they'll lead us right to whoever is behind this, and pass along to everyone: no one is to underestimate Ensign Corsali—or Lieutenant Drakin for that matter. Both are extremely resourceful. Inform the *Illuyanka* and *Kashku* to continue their eavesdropping—can they seed listeners?"

Shu'hah shook his shaggy head. "No, ta'ahn. Rukoobi raised that possibility with Nerik'ah Sha'ashahn. She said she'd considered and discounted the idea. This planet almost entirely depends upon illicit trade after all. Their surface sensor arrays would be constantly seeking out such devices."

Khusaaq grunted; it had been a long-shot after all, with the likelihood of negligible results as the tiny, semiautonomous devices were never meant to function under such conditions but rather to attach themselves to the hulls of ships, to eavesdrop on the goings-on within or to slip undetected into clandestine meetings between alien parties that had a direct bearing on a particular contract. "If *Illuyanka, Kashku* or Rukoobi overhear *anything* that suggests Ensign Corsali or Lieutenant Drakin are in imminent danger, they are to flick them aboard, no matter the situation planetside—and I'll deal with whatever fallout such might cause with the local authorities or with Hahtra'tzrhi. But *only* if they are in imminent danger—I want that understood."

Khusaaq waited until Shu'hah had relayed the orders to Rukoobi on the bridge, and Rukoobi had acknowledged them, then he asked, "Any chatter about Cisne?"

"No, ta'ahn. Absolutely nothing."

Khusaaq exhaled forcefully, shook his head then glanced sidelong at the soldier who walked beside him. He stopped abruptly, the other three mirroring his actions, and placed his gauntleted hand on Shu'hah's shoulder. "Kon'ta'aq."

"Yes, ta'ahn?"

"I deeply apologize for my earlier outburst—you were right in sending Rukoobi to the surface. There was a good chance he might have located and recovered Qar'qaah Kon'ta'aq—you made the right call. I'm truly sorry I took my frustrations out on you."

"Thank you, ta'ahn. I appreciate this."

Khusaaq nodded, gave Shu'hah's shoulder a squeeze, then together the two entered the small galley, Raudah following as Tejat continued on to the bridge. Toubeh and Endooki were already seated at the table and making quick work of a hot and far more appetizing looking meal Jaa'qwah had set out for them. Clearly the medic, now without any patients, had spent his time fixing the synthesizers—although what Endooki was eating and what Jaa'qwah was ladling into a bowl for Raudah still had an odd consistency and a rather bland smell.

"Where are the others?"

"Laihiri and Nihaal are resting, ta'ahn."

"And Matoosh?"

"With Rukoobi on the bridge," Jaa'qwah answered as he exchanged quick glances with Endooki and Toubeh.

Khusaaq was well aware of their furtive looks but chose to ignore them, just as he pointedly chose to ignore Qar'qaah's absence knowing none of those present would dare to raise the issue. Instead he turned his attention back to Shu'hah as Raudah eagerly grabbed the bowl Jaa'qwah offered him, undeterred by its contents, and quickly seated himself with the others.

Khusaaq accepted the mug of barra from Toubeh with a grateful smile and took a deep, satisfying gulp.

"Ta'ahn...?"

Khusaaq swallowed his mouthful and turned at the sound of Matoosh's gravelly voice to find the soldier standing behind him, in the corridor.

"May I speak with you?" He looked past Khusaaq to the others, adding, "In private, ta'ahn."

Khusaaq didn't have to ask what it was about, none of them did; they'd all been anticipating this conversation—this confrontation—from the moment Qar'qaah had deserted. He handed the mug back to Toubeh, then stepped into the passageway and followed Matoosh down the corridor and into the small sickbay.

Once they were both inside, Khusaaq thumbed the release, and as the door closed Matoosh turned to face him. In his hands was Qar'qaah's ritual dagger.

Khusaaq dropped his gaze to the knife and felt a sharp pang in his gut. With everything else going on, he hadn't thought to ask what Qar'qaah had taken with him—or, perhaps far more critically, what he'd left behind, deliberately or out of hurried necessity. Khusaaq had, after all, ordered Jaa'qwah to securely store Qar'qaah's armor and weapons in sickbay—to prevent Qar'qaah from doing anything foolish. *Anything foolish*, he thought to himself. *I had no idea just how foolish he could be.*

He met Matoosh's fretful stare.

"He appropriated Toubeh's duty uniform—minus the hauberk..."

Khusaaq exhaled forcefully.

"...took only a pistol..."

Khusaaq started to open his mouth, to demand to know how Qar'qaah had gotten his hands on a weapon in the first place then thought better of it.

"...an extra power-pack, a utility knife and Jaa'qwah did an inventory of sickbay to see what was missing: Qar'qaah took only a few vials of PKs and stims, not enough to last a day—and Toubeh said her uniform was depleted of its drug supply from her last mission. She felt Jaa'qwah had more important things to attend to, knew she'd be wearing armor planetside so felt rejuv was unnecessary, and Jaa'qwah was focused on those who were to take part in tracking down the kidnappers, believing they were his first priority—"

"As they were." Khusaaq again found his gaze drawn to the knife, Qar'qaah's ritual dagger, *Tseih'sheh*. His mind flashed back to the day he'd ceremonially presented Qar'qaah with the blade, as Qar'qaah had just marked his third cycle. It was the day that celebrated Qar'qaah's full admittance into the Abhijit'tischinjgra, as it was with all A'tuu'shahn'i into their families and clans, and in Qar'qaah's case it was also the public recognition of his status of Doh'ha, with all the attendant obligations and privileges. Gaalan had been there—a highly controversial choice as Ja'andai's stand-in—as were representatives of every Elkanaghalli clan and nine delegates from the Q'shaathrah, one each from every caste.

Qar'qaah wanted nothing to do with the hours-long ritual, of strangers examining him, looking for any imperfections no matter how minor and scrutinizing the traceries of tattoos that had just begun to appear, the so far minimal motifs nonetheless marking him undeniably as an Elkanaghalli—an Abhijit'tischinjgra. He'd kicked and cried, only quieting when offered a continuous supply of sweets, and tried to make good his escape to find their source when no one was looking. Matoosh had broken ranks to retrieve him and Qar'qaah responded by wailing loudly in the otherwise deathly silent audience chamber and continued to squeal in frustration no matter the enticements offered. It had caused a very undignified uproar among the assembled dignitaries, many of whom had openly questioned Qar'qaah's legitimacy leading up to the ceremony, and were now witness to his infantile disregard for their most sacred of rituals—proof, as far as many were concerned, that he was unfit to bear the family name.

Khusaaq had publicly sided with his fellow kinsmen, was in fact furious that Qar'qaah had embarrassed him and Gaalan and had fiercely rebuked Qar'qaah in private. Still, he secretly admired him for his dogged determination not to be sucked into the anachronistic, stiflingly rigid codes that all Elkanaghalli'i were required to obey.

Tseih'sheh. He found himself tempted to take the dagger from Matoosh's outstretched hands, his own fingers aching to touch, to feel the oh-so familiar, comforting attendance of the Elkanasu again, something that had been the core of his life but denied him since he'd forfeited all claim to be Elkanaghalli, since he'd willingly surrendered his own dagger, *Siah'ushu,* something no Elkanaghalli had ever done, at least none that history had recorded. Of course no Elkanaghalli had heard the voices of the Elkanasu and lived to tell about it—and he'd not only heard their voices, but he'd engaged them in a quite lengthy conversation—even argued with them.

He hesitated, unsure of his reception if he did take the dagger from Matoosh's hands; he swallowed what he instantly recognized as a selfish urge and dropped his hands to his sides.

Qar'qaah hadn't left *Tseih'sheh* behind out of hasty necessity, Khusaaq was sure of that. Had he really wanted to find it and take it with him, he would have. No. This had been a conscious choice, a potent message.

He exhaled and slowly shook his head. He was cold, hungry and incredibly tired, his right leg throbbed despite the painkillers and it had taken the last of his reserves not to visibly limp back to the flick-down site or resort to foot-dragging once back aboard.

It had been a long, frustrating and nerve-wracking night for all, everyone wary of detection at any moment, mindful that their quarry might make good their escape... and in the end, despite their caution, despite their best efforts, their primary target, Cisne, had slipped through their fingers—

No, not our fingers. Mine. Just as he hadn't taken fully into account the true depth of Qar'qaah's need to return to the planet, to confront his tormentor or die in the attempt. He could blame those left on board, certainly for not keeping a closer eye on him; he could blame Toubeh for leaving her duty uniform and utility knife where Qar'qaah could find them, even if that was in a locked locker. But in the end, he was the one who hadn't ordered every conceivable precaution to be taken, hadn't ordered Jaa'qwah to knock Qar'qaah out and keep him safely asleep, possibly even restrained until the rest returned from the planet—

"Jaa'qwah says he can survive, at most, two days without proper care." Matoosh slowly turned the blade, its complex patterns slithering slowly over its surface as the light caught it.

"He's a fool," Khusaaq grumbled half-heartedly as he vigorously but futilely rubbed his armored thigh, desperate to work out the knots—a hot meal, and then a bunk and several hours of uninterrupted sleep, that's what his body was crying out for.

"I'm not disagreeing with you, ta'ahn, but—"

"He disobeyed a direct order," he replied with weary frustration, giving up on his thigh, knowing Jaa'qwah would have something on hand that would actually work, unlike what his armor had supplied and which had surprisingly failed to do an adequate job.

"Just as you did with Tarqk," Matoosh replied quietly and undaunted as he returned the dagger to the storage locker, gently placing it on top of Qar'qaah's carefully folded uniform. He then fixed Khusaaq with a soul-piercing stare, adding softly, "Yet again, you punish him for being the perfect copy of you."

Khusaaq bristled at the comparison—and the insinuation— in too much pain to temper his reaction. *"I did what I did to save us, to save A'tuu'shahn'i from annihilation!"*

"And he did what he did to save himself, to reclaim—"

"We've dealt with all but one who were involved, and we *will* find her, soon enough—"

"What if she finds *him*, first—assuming she hasn't already? It would certainly explain why we weren't able to locate her—"

"Which is why I ordered him to remain aboard—to protect him, not just from himself, but from this Cisne—*you know this!* Just as I've always kept him close, done everything I could to shield him from those who wish me harm!" In this he was utterly unlike Ja'andai—it had been a deliberate course of action, done, he'd pridefully assured himself more times than he could remember, so as to not repeat the harsh loneliness of his own upbringing, not that Qar'qaah had ever shown even an iota of gratitude—quite the contrary.

Now he was confronted by the grim, unavoidable truth that he'd utterly failed to do one critical thing: he'd never just taken the time to sit down with Qar'qaah and simply *listen* to him, never really tried to understand what Qar'qaah wanted, what he needed. *Just like Ja'andai...*

Worse, Matoosh was right: Qar'qaah, by leaving his dagger behind had made a conscious decision to cast everything aside, abandoning who and what he was, just as he'd done, albeit for vastly different reasons—*or were they? Chiku*—

"He's not in his right mind, ta'ahn, you *know* that. I beg you—do not abandon him again—"

"I never intended to abandon anyone—never *will* abandon anyone willingly! We had to deal with the others, first, or risk them escaping!" Khusaaq looked away, again forced down his rage, at Matoosh, at Qar'qaah for, yet again, putting his own selfish needs before anything or anyone else, and most of all, fury at himself for trusting Qar'qaah not to do something this colossally foolish.

Then another harsh truth struck him: *I gave him every reason to do this—I invited him, no, I dared him to do this!* He squeezed his eyes shut, took a deep, rattling breath then flicked Matoosh a sidelong look. "Have... have Rukoobi continue the sensor search—tell Tejat to do all he can to overcome the jamming—"

"And what if he's detected by the Poondians before that? What if he—"

"I am functioning under *very* strict constraints, Ruh'ta'aq!" He winced, leaned heavily against the wall and reflexively rubbed his thigh. "I'd like nothing more than to take this crew and the crews of *Illuyanka* and *Kashku* and tear that accursed planet apart, piece by piece! But Narbrooi Hahtra'tzrhi did not mince words when it came to the parameters of this mission— you were there, *you* heard him. Our priority was the safe retrieval of our men, and then to deal with those who'd kidnapped them and determine, if possible, their true motives— *without* the Poondians ever knowing we were here. Qar'qaah, by his utterly irresponsible actions, has endangered *everything—"*

"Then the sooner we find him the better," Matoosh replied with equal heat.

"And how do you propose we do that? We don't know where he is and everyone's exhausted, not to mention it's now daylight down there," he stabbed an armored finger at the deck, at the unseen planet slowly spinning below them, "with a staggering number of aliens and Poondians out and about, filling every street, every saloon, and most, I have no doubt, will be wearing proximity detectors, just as they do at night except in quadruple the numbers. Need I remind you that Toubeh and Laihiri came perilously close to being sensed in that Thalamian massage parlor? Had it not been for her quick-thinking, they would've—and they were well-rested.

"I cannot risk our presence being exposed. Not only would it cause a huge diplomatic incident which I'm sure the Poondians and the Thalamians would use to their maximum advantage—something our Coalition allies would *not* appreciate, especially now, with the extraterritoriality negotiations having stalled. It would tip off the Matarii. And it would jeopardize us *ever* determining who is really behind this. Trust me—and Hahtra'tzrhi for once fully agrees with me—this is far more than just the actions of a few individuals with a personal grudge against me."

Matoosh started to open his mouth but Khusaaq cut him off with an angry hand gesture and: "Qar'qaah's has almost as much practice keeping out of sight as he does wreaking havoc with others' carefully laid plans, as you *well* know. Hopefully he has enough of his wits about him to realize he'd gotten himself into a very real predicament and to put the former experience to good use and stay out of sight. I suspect this Cisne is doing the same—lying low, at least for now."

"And if he doesn't?"

Khusaaq took another deep gulp of air, let the breath slowly escape through his clenched teeth, then answered, "Do I really need to state the obvious, Ruh'ta'aq?"

"Let me return to the planet, ta'ahn, I'll go alone—"

"No," he violently shook his head for emphasis even though it only made his pounding headache worse. "Absolutely—"

"I can find him. I know I can—just as I always did when we were children."

"You're no longer a child and neither is Qar'qaah—although he certainly behaves like one—and this is no game. If you're discovered—"

"I won't be. Please. Just give me—give Qar'qaah that chance."

Khusaaq looked away, exhaled slowly then said, "If anyone should go, it should be me."

Matoosh couldn't help it; he briefly dropped his gaze to the pinching grip Khusaaq had on his thigh and Khusaaq immediately let go. "And give whoever is behind all this exactly what they want? No, I cannot allow it."

Khusaaq favored him with an arched look. "*You* cannot allow it?"

"I gave my word to Hahtra'tzrhi I would not permit you to place yourself at unnecessary risk."

"I would've thought that he would have welcomed my untimely demise as an *unfortunate* corollary of getting to the bottom of this whole sordid matter—"

"Quite the contrary, ta'ahn."

Khusaaq crossed his arms, in part to conceal his own surprise, in part to keep his errant hand from returning to his cramping thigh, and eyed Matoosh suspiciously. "And when, exactly, did you have this conversation with Hahtra'tzrhi and why was I not informed of this... agreement earlier?"

"On the beach—when you left to speak with Sirin. And he gave me strict orders not to say anything to you... unless I believed you were about to place yourself in avoidable danger and you wouldn't listen to me unless I told you."

Matoosh wasn't prone to lying, unlike Qar'qaah. In fact Khusaaq had never caught him in one. Still... desperate times sometimes called for desperate acts. "You telling me the truth or did you just make this up?"

"Contact Hahtra'tzrhi if you doubt me," Matoosh replied stiffly, visibly stung, and motioned to the wall-mounted com-unit next to Khusaaq's shoulder.

After a tense moment of mutual scrutiny, Khusaaq said, "I'm going to have enough explaining to do when I next speak with Hahtra'tzrhi—so I'd prefer to put off contacting him until absolutely necessary."

"So...?"

"So you have until planetary nightfall to find him—not one second more. *Understood?*"

"Understood, ta'ahn."

"And take a locator with you."

"Of course." With that, Matoosh hurried from the sickbay before Khusaaq could change his mind.

Chapter 26

Poonda Five.
Mid-morning, planetary time. Present day.

Qar'qaah leaned heavily against a shaded wall as he tried to catch his breath. It hadn't taken long, once the planet's sun had risen above the surrounding peaks, for the temperature to follow. His weakened body had yet to adapt to the thin atmosphere and he'd already used all but one of the vials of painkillers just to keep on his feet. It hadn't occurred to him to bring a breather even if he'd known where to find one, and without the benefit of his helmet sensors, locating his prey had become a matter of trial and error.

So far, it had been all errors and, looking around, he realized he was completely lost. His one guidepost, the cluster of stars, had vanished into the silvery dawn haze hours before. Worse, he'd given the holographic map of the city only the most cursory of studies. The moment Toubeh had pointed out Cisne's whereabouts he'd stopped listening, stopped scrutinizing the map—

Suddenly all he could think about was being pulled, gasping and disoriented from yet another stay the stasis pod—to soften him up, Cisne had joked—before he found himself being held down by her accomplices yet again, forcing him to submit to yet another assault.

He squeezed his eyes shut, in hopes of shutting out the overwhelming sense of shame. He would have willingly done anything she demanded, had pleaded with her to do anything she wanted. He wouldn't fight. Submission was better than being returned to the claustrophobic pod—*anything but the pod*—and the paralyzing fear that this time he'd be left there—

"You look like you could use a stiff drink."

Qar'qaah spun around, almost losing his balance in the process, to find an exceedingly tall, slender alien standing a few meters away. He mentally kicked himself for letting his guard drop.

The willowy creature stared at him, only its coal-black eyes visible through a horizontal slit in the fine netting of a dust veil. The rest of its body was clothed in the distinctive Poondian white knee-length tunic, white trousers, loose over-robe and hooded cowl. Even its hands were covered.

"What's it to yah?" Qar'qaah replied in his best, ubiquitous colonial drawl, hoping his voice didn't quaver while his heart pounded in his ears, spurred on by the massive dose of adrenaline his body was pumping into his veins.

"I was concerned," it replied in an odd, lilting voice and an accent he couldn't place—but he knew it was *not* Poondian. "You look quite ill," it continued, "perhaps the heat? And where's your breather?"

"Yah ahwfully curious. That's not ah good trait where ah come from."

The alien gave his dun-colored, slowly morphing trousers and sleeveless under-tunic a quick, decidedly curious glance, but its attention quickly returned to his elaborately tattooed, scarified and blistered skin as Qar'qaah, using his bare forearm, wiped the sweaty sheen from his cheek and forehead. "And where's that?"

Qar'qaah replied with the first name that came to mind: "Zuhset Prime." It seemed a safe choice: the little known planet about as far from this area of the rim as one could get and deep within Hyraadikk-claimed space, a xenophobic species under the best of circumstances.

The creature cocked its egg-shaped head to one side as its eyes took in Qar'qaah's strikingly exotic, albeit very sickly appearance and peculiar clothing. "I think not."

Only then did Qar'qaah realize—with his trademark maser pistol—that someone might put two and two together and figure out what he *really* was, someone like this overly inquisitive alien. Only the completely encapsulated duty uniform or armor offered the chameleon camouflage that would have kept his identity, not to mention his presence, a secret. He gave himself another mental kick. "And ah honestly don't care what *yah* think. So how 'bout *yah* jus' leave?"

"My apologies," it replied as it backed up a step. "I was just trying to be helpful. This is not a safe neighborhood in which to loiter—especially for an offworlder."

"Ah can take care of mahself, thank yah vary much."

"Then I will take my leave." It started to walk away, then stopped and turned back to him. "It gets very cold here at night—dressed as you are, you'd best find a place to stay or you'll freeze."

"Ah'll keep that in mind."

The alien gave him another slow, head to toe stare that left him extremely uncomfortable—and fearful. He scowled menacingly back, hoping it would take the hint and leave before his knees buckled.

Oblivious to his mental prompting, it continued, "I've rented a room at a hostel—it's not far. I could take you there." It gave him another appraising look. "I'm sure we could work out some mutually agreeable arrangement."

His heart began to beat faster, *faster*. "Not interested." He hoped his panic didn't taint his voice.

"You *have* no credits, do you? Lost everything gambling?"

Qar'qaah said nothing, his full concentration in keeping on his feet and his eyes on the alien.

"Then you're in no position to be so choosey, are you? Come—I can be very generous to someone who knows how to be properly appreciative—"

"Ah thought yah were leavin'," Qar'qaah growled through clenched teeth. He was shaking hard now, a combination of exhaustion and raw terror.

The alien took another step closer, as if the rest was a foregone conclusion. "When did you last eat? How about some food to fill your belly and drink to ease your—"

"Not hungry," he gasped between panicky breaths.

"No money, no breather, no place to stay and *not* hungry?" It shook its head then with a shrug added, "Since you won't accept my generosity, then perhaps you'll accept payment…"

Qar'qaah's eyes watered, his legs wobbled as if they were rubber and he felt like he was going vomit.

"...for that very interesting pistol of yours?" Its black eyes flicked to the holstered weapon that hung from Qar'qaah's hip before again meeting his gaze as Qar'qaah's fear-numbed mind tried to shift gears from what he'd thought was going to be a blatant sexual proposition to what in fact it was proposing. "I'll give you... ten dinsits for it. That'll be more than enough to buy a meal and a warm bed, maybe even some companionship for the night that's more to *your* liking—if you're not too picky." The alien's aura shifted, from a faint, dirty pinkish-orange, to a much brighter, clearer shade.

Warned that the creature was suddenly and overtly lying, that its intentions had changed, Qar'qaah placed his hand protectively on the grip of the pistol and managed to answer without stuttering, "Again, not interested."

"Fifteen then, but that's my final offer." With that, it started towards him.

Qar'qaah tried to back up but his legs suddenly gave way. He stumbled and sat down with a startled grunt.

"You're being *very* stupid," the alien said as it stepped closer. "I'm just trying to help. Now, it was five dinsits we agreed upon, correct?" It reached for something hidden within the folds of its robe.

Qar'qaah was just a split second faster; he yanked the pistol from its holster and fired. The creature collapsed in a puff of billowing fabric.

He stared at the inert mound for a moment, his heart thumping wildly against his chest, his breath coming in short, wheezing gasps, briefly taken aback that he hadn't vaporized it as he'd intended. A quick check of the pistol provided the answer: it had been set to the narrowest of beams. He hadn't thought to check—which garnered another mental kick. He then looked around to find the side-street still deserted except for a small dust devil that was meandering lazily down its length.

He staggered to his feet, and, keeping the pistol aimed at the creature with one shaky hand while clutching his stomach with the other, he cautiously approached.

The alien now sported a large oozing hole in the middle of its chest.

A no-so-gentle prod with his toe satisfied him that the creature was dead and not just faking. Then a metallic glint caught his eye: nearby on the ground lay a small, slim tube. At first glance he thought it was a breather and he eagerly reached for it, but just short of his fingers making contact he realized it was no breather. It was a *t'jing*—an ancient but still very efficient Chankka weapon particularly favored by Loopers as its explosive darts could penetrate most body armor—even A'tuu'shahn armor at very close range—and it was easily concealed.

He snatched it up then gave the dead alien a vicious kick as his sneered, "Just trying to help me, eh? More like robbing and murdering me." *Or worse, much worse.* Poonda Five was, after all, a major trafficking hub for slavers.

He looked around again then dropped his gaze back to the alien and decided to take advantage of his earlier oversight—but just in case... he quickly adjusted the pistol's beam width. He reholstered the weapon, stuffed the t'jing into the cuff of his knee-high boot then grabbed the creature by its feet and, using the last of the massive adrenaline dump, managed to drag it into a nearby alley.

Once hidden in the shadows, he collapsed next to the body. Between the thin air, the far heavier than expected corpse and his weakened state, he couldn't catch his breath—it made him light-headed, barely able to see and for several minutes fearful he was going to black out, as defenseless against thieving hands as the body beside him.

No sooner had his vision cleared and the immediate danger had passed when the closeness of the close call hit him full force and his stomach, already tied up in knots, began to spasm painfully, making it even harder to breathe, much less move.

Clutching his belly, he violently dry heaved several times, to the point of almost blacking out again.

He sagged back against the corpse, gasping for breath, waiting—hoping—for the spasms, the nausea, the panic to lessen its grip to the point he could move again.

Finally, shakily, he wiped his mouth with the back of his hand, lurched back to his feet and began the task of stripping his victim of its outer clothing, in the process pocketing several bar tokens, as well as removing the alien's much-needed breather. He adjusted the gas mixture and clipped it to his own nose.

He greedily sucked in the rich supply of pure oxygen, inhaling so quickly he felt intensely dizzy.

He braced one hand against the alley wall, waited for the worst to pass, then he hurriedly donned the alien's over-robe, hooded cowl and dust veil, carefully arranging the overly large cowl so that it covered the rather difficult to explain exit hole and surrounding stain on the back of the robe.

Taking heed of the creature's curious glances at his morphing trousers, he willed them to settle on a flat, matte dun color. But just in case... if kept tucked tight around him, the full-length robe also effectively concealed them to all but the most inquisitive.

His tattooed face, neck, forearms and hands were another matter. This creature had only three, extremely long, multi-jointed digits, its gloves therefore were unusable. The alien itself looked like nothing Qar'qaah had ever seen—or even heard of, for that matter. It was entirely devoid of hair and its skin was a milky, translucent white.

No wonder you were covered, head to toe, and speaking of... He grabbed a fistful of the talc-like sand, spat into it then rubbed the sticky mixture over his exposed hands, wrists, neck and face. It didn't completely obscure his tattoos, but would be enough to keep the casually inquiring eye at bay.

He looked around him once more. Satisfied he was still alone, he again withdrew the pistol, pointed it at the corpse and squeezed the trigger.

This time the body vanished in a brief, intense and utterly silent flash leaving behind only a patch of fused sand as a reminder. Using the side of his foot, he kicked more of the fine sand over the spot then he stumbled out of the alley and onto the street.

The alien had been right in one respect: he *was* in need of a stiff drink.

Poonda Five.
Noon, planetary time. Present day.

Urbat smiled as the Thalamian server placed three glasses and a pitcher of iced water on the table.

"Made up your minds?" the eel-like alien asked as it filled the glasses.

"Not yet," Pardix replied distractedly as he stared at the bustling café's menu of the midday specials.

"I'll come back," the Thalamian huffed and wriggled away.

"Here, Blondie," Urbat said as he pushed a glass towards Sirin.

She gratefully picked it up and took a deep gulp as she looked around at the small, otherwise nondescript and tumbledown restaurant and its odd assortment of equally down on their luck alien customers.

The three had spent the morning wandering the labyrinthine streets of the sprawling port, Pardix and Urbat playing the gawking-first-time-on-Poonda-Five role to the hilt and prompting her by various means to do the same. To her, their apparently aimless course was anything but aimless: the two were looking for something… or, she amended, some*one*.

As she swallowed another mouthful of water, she happened to notice that both Urbat and Pardix were also covertly scanning their surroundings.

"Now what?" she asked, drawing Pardix's preoccupied stare.

"Now we wait." He picked up his own glass and took a cautious sip.

"For what?"

Before he could answer, a loud commotion just outside the diner's entrance drew everyone's attention. A squat Looper waddled inside followed by a tall, lean Matarran. The two stood just inside the doorway, arguing loudly, then, oblivious to the annoyed glances of the café's other customers, the mismatched and noticeably inebriated pair made their unsteady way towards the empty table next to Sirin and her unwanted companions, bringing their noisy, drunken dispute with them.

"Shit," Pardix muttered, eyeing the two.

The Looper reached the table first, yanked out a chair and promptly backed into Urbat, stepping on his foot and almost knocking him from his seat.

"Hey!" Urbat snapped as he lurched to his feet, *"Watch where you're going!"*

The Looper wobbled around, fixed him with a shifty-eyed glare and wheezed, "You talkin' to me, *uuman?"*

"Yeah, you clumsy oaf!"

The Matarran giggled. *"Oooh-oooh."*

The Looper squinted at him and the Matarran clamped his long-fingered hand over his slitted mouth. Point made, the Looper again fixed his baleful, drunken gaze on Urbat. "Clumsy, *eh?"* With that he struck out, hitting Urbat squarely in the chin with a meaty fist.

Urbat staggered back into another, seated patron as Pardix pushed his chair back and rose. Suddenly everyone in the café was on their feet, some, seeing an excuse for free food, grabbing what they could of their lunches and others' unguarded meals before hurrying towards the nearest door.

Pardix reached for his shocker, but the Matarran kicked his legs out from under him before he could jerk the weapon from its hidden shoulder holster and he fell backwards, landing between two tables with a resounding *thud.*

Sirin, seeing *her* chance, ducked behind the burly, wheezing Looper and darted for the exit.

Once outside, she gave her eyes only a moment to adjust to the harsh dazzle, then she took off at a run.

Chapter 27

Poonda Five.
Shortly before sunset, planetary time. Present day.

Qar'qaah licked his chapped, bruise-swollen lips and stared down at the squat glass he held in one hand. Around him the dimly lit saloon was rapidly filling with patrons who, like him, wanted nothing more than to escape the dust-choked, stifling heat. He'd managed to claim a vacant stool at the far end of the bar, where poor lighting lent itself to being overlooked and discouraged casual conversation.

While incredibly thirsty, he hesitated taking a sip of the potent alcohol. What he really craved was a stick of Thalamian kij'a to smoke. It was a habit he'd picked up from some of the younger crew of *Makhaira*—a truly vile habit, according to Khusaaq and one unbefitting even Khighalli'i, who were otherwise well known for vile habits, much less an Elkanaghalli. Maybe it was—higher ups had certainly done their best to stamp out the highly addictive practice, warning those tempted that the drug dulled the senses or worse, and handing out serious brig time to those caught with kij'a sticks or in the act of smoking, all to no avail. The intense euphoria, of suddenly not caring about anything, least of all the next drop, the next contract, of what you might be asked to do and that you very well might die doing it and die horribly more than made up for the days-long blinding headache that followed, not to mention any punishment meted out.

As he stared down at the glass and the hold he had on it, he realized his dust and spittle smeared hand had, somewhere along the line, developed a fine tremor. *A smoke, that's what I need. Just a few puffs—settle the nerves without risking upsetting the stomach.* He risked a quick glance around him. No doubt someone nearby had some kij'a on them, it was a common enough commodity, traded openly or imported illegally, depending on where you were. The saloon was hazy with smoke along with dust, but his nose hadn't picked up the faint, sweet scent of kij'a within the otherwise supremely noxious and close to overwhelming concoction of liquor, body perfumes favored by some, and far too many hot, sweaty and unwashed aliens. Asking if anyone had any to share was definitely out of the question as he wasn't sure what might be demanded in trade.

He exhaled and turning back to the bar, tightened his hold on his glass as he tried to figure out what to do next. He had no idea where he was; he had no idea where his quarry was. He had no idea where to go, what to—

"Something wrong?"

He flinched, looked up to find the human barkeep peering suspiciously at him, clearly trying to see exactly what kind of face lay behind the narrow, horizontal gap in the dust veil.

He shook his head and, dropping his gaze back to the glass, mumbled in a ubiquitous offworlder drawl, "Nah," as his heart thumped against his ribs.

"Then I'm going to have to ask you to leave."

"Ah'm not botherin' anyone, besides, ah haven't finished mah drink."

"You're *bothering* me. And you've been sitting there, *staring* at your drink for the better part of an hour."

"So?"

"So you're supposed to *drink* it, not *gawp* at it. And you're taking up valuable bar space."

Qar'qaah stuffed his hand into his left trouser pocket, withdrew a token, placed it on the bar and pushed it towards him. "There. Now. Go. *Ahway.*"

The man snatched up the token and walked off.

Qar'qaah, satisfied he'd be left alone at least for a while, tugged the hooded cowl further forward over his veiled face, then ran his shaking finger around the lip of the glass and tried to organize his thoughts. His head pounded and his stomach hurt, but at least the near incapacitating abdominal cramps and nausea had subsided without him having to use the last vial of painkiller. He cursed himself for what he guessed was the hundredth time for not checking the levels of the drug stocks permeated into his borrowed clothing before he flicked down. *I would have grabbed more vials had I known...*

He'd also repeatedly cursed the medic, and now cursed him again—*what was his name?—Jaa'qwah? Yes,* he nodded to himself, sure he had it right—for not doing what was clearly his job by making sure everyone's uniform was fully rejuved at all times, and if he'd had any mind to return to *Jirah*, he told himself, he would make a point of speaking sharply to him—and Khusaaq—about this gross dereliction of duty.

Adrift in his own thoughts, visualizing the impressive and immensely satisfying dressing down he'd give Jaa'qwah, mesmerized by the reflection of the bar lights on the amber surface of the alcohol and the lulled by the stifling heat, the smothering smells and background drone of voices mixed with the pulsing white noise of music, he again lost track of time. His eyelids fluttered; his head nodded forward—

"Pity to just let that sit there."

He jerked his head up at the all too familiar, albeit whispered voice, then quickly passed it off just another hallucination. He'd been having a lot of them lately. One of the few things Jaa'qwah *had* done for him was to warn him that his hallucinations were a symptom of his advanced poisoning in combination with his extreme physical and mental exhaustion, but his hallucinations had never included Matoosh.

He knew it would be a mistake to respond to it. That was something Jaa'qwah had told him, too, not that he'd bothered to listen to the medic's rationale—something to do with making his symptoms worse. At the time he'd been in too much of a hurry getting dressed—no willing help from Jaa'qwah there—so he could join the others, to prove to Khusaaq he was recovered enough to accompany them. But then, out of the corner of his eye he saw a telltale quiver, a quiver so minute, so easily dismissed as a trick of the saloon's wavering lighting that only an A'tuu'shahn would have consciously noticed it—much less recognized it for what it was: an A'tuu'shahn in full battle panoply was now standing beside him.

He briefly wondered how an A'tuu'shahn in armor could've eased his way through the jostling throng in the saloon without tripping every proximity alarm into a frantic, squealing chorus—more evidence this was a hallucination—before he remembered the flashing sign that greeted him and every other potential patron at the doorway, in fact every saloon doorway he'd passed: ALL ALARMS OFF! ALL WEAPONS POWERED DOWN! VIOLATORS WILL BE EJECTED!

Had he had an alarm to turn off, he would've—its constant, soft chirping would have been a dead, and decidedly annoying, giveaway anyway that he'd flagrantly disregarded the rules— but he didn't; he wasn't, however, about to power down his pistol and that was completely undetectable. He figured a fifty-fifty split in compliance, even if it was only a willingness to comply on the alarm part, was good enough. He suspected many of those around him felt the same.

Which meant that a fully armored A'tuu'shahn, if extremely careful and quick on his toes, could have indeed entered the saloon undetected. Most of those within were exceedingly drunk anyway—backing or walking into or bumping against something that was as unyielding as a plastcrete wall yet utterly invisible would likely be shrugged off as a side effect of the dubious quality of the liquor.

Suddenly he wasn't sure if he was imagining things or if it really was Matoosh. But through recent, repeated experience, he'd come to accept that reality had developed this rather nasty habit of taunting him, of keeping just out of his desperate and flailing reach.

No. He shook his head. *Can't be.* Matoosh would not flick down without Khusaaq's express permission and Khusaaq would never agree to that, not after he'd made his own intentions so clear and in the process seeded chaos in Khusaaq's carefully laid plans. The officer had a long history of not looking at all sympathetically on such 'foolishly impulsive conduct', as Khusaaq called it—always said through tightly clenched teeth, or punctuated with a back-handed blow to the face that left his mind spinning. This instance had, even Qar'qaah had to admit, *wildly* exceeded all of his previous efforts.

Satisfied that this was just yet another elaborate figment of his exhausted mind, he wrapped his tattooed fingers more tightly around the glass and silently willed the apparition to go away.

It didn't.

In fact the figmentary Matoosh eased himself onto the empty barstool next to Qar'qaah, deliberately bumping him in the process. That was something the real Matoosh would do, too.

But you aren't real. Despite Jaa'qwah's warning, he found he couldn't help himself. "Go. Away."

"No."

He scowled at the faint shimmer in the dusty air and whispered just loud enough to be overheard over the background din, "What are you doing here?"

"Have you met you? I'd think the reason would be readily apparent."

Okay, I'll play along. "I'm not going back. I thought I made *that* blatantly obvious."

He overheard the imaginary Matoosh sigh—an all too familiar *exasperated* sigh—then mutter irritably, "We both know you've already had plenty of practice, so just for once can you *not* behave like a complete and really annoying idiot?"

Cold silence on Qar'qaah's part, then, finally: "You know, it's bad enough to be hallucinating, but to be insulted by one is really quite maddening."

"I'm *not* a hallucination."

Qar'qaah snorted. "That's what they all say—now be a good hallucination and go away."

Overhearing a muffled cough, he looked up to find the barkeep and two nearby patrons staring at him. It was obvious by their expressions that they'd overheard both of them, reasonably believing both muttered voices where coming from him. He switched back to Standard, to the ubiquitous drawl and said, "Sorry. Jus' thinkin' out loud."

The barkeep gave him another skeptical look. "Well, tell your multiple personalities to cut the chinwag, eh? It's damned unnerving." Shaking his head, he turned back to his customers.

Qar'qaah leaned close to the ghostly Matoosh and whispered out of the corner of his mouth, "I'm going to be really angry if a hallucination gets me kicked out of this bar—"

"And I've already told you, you *aren't* hallucinating. It's really me—"

An armored hand grasped Qar'qaah's shoulder and he couldn't help but jump. It seemed real enough, especially when the fingers tightened their hold—painfully so. But then again, he'd been fooled before.

He glanced around him and was relieved that no one had seen him flinch—he could only imagine what the barkeep and his twitchy customers would think of that.

"You're extremely ill, Qar'qaah—it's affecting your thinking—"

"Yet you just told me I'm not hallucinating," he interrupted peevishly. "You can't have it both ways you know."

"—how long do you think you'll last without proper medical care?"

"Long enough."

"Long enough for what? To prove beyond doubt that you're a stupid, stubborn fool? You've already accomplished that, and then some, believe me."

Qar'qaah yanked the dust veil aside, brought the glass to his lips and took a defiant sip, swallowed, then hissed, *"Long enough to find and kill Cisne. "* Satisfied the alcohol was going to stay put in his stomach and not pay his mouth a return visit, he took another sip, this one a little deeper and tried to savor the taste, despite the liquor burning his ulcerated mouth and tongue and causing his eyes to water.

"And then what?"

He shrugged as he took another angry gulp, furious he wasn't even allowed this one small—and most likely last—bodily pleasure.

"So, that's your *brilliant* plan then? Find this Cisne and kill her—that is if she doesn't kill you first—then what? Find a hole to crawl into and wait to die—which shouldn't take long—a day, maybe two if you're really unfortunate, because, according to Jaa'qwah, towards the end it *will* be excruciatingly painful."

Qar'qaah inwardly winced at the thought that the hours leading up to his death could be more painful than what he'd already experienced. The remaining vial of painkiller was not enough to even make it marginally more bearable; it was certainly not enough for a fatal overdose. He clenched his teeth and patting his holstered pistol, forced out, "There's always this."

"True—assuming you're physically capable of pulling the trigger when the time comes. Knowing you, you'll—"

"Did he send you?" He waited, but not hearing a reply, snorted, "*Thought not,*" and brought the glass back to his lips.

"He did not refuse me when I requested to come find you."

He swallowed his mouthful with a wince and chuckled harshly, "I'll bet—"

"Enough!"

"I was just about to tell you the—" Qar'qaah, realizing it was not the spectral Matoosh who had spoken, but the very real barkeep, looked up.

The bartender was now standing across the bar from him and eyeing his now fully exposed, tattooed, blistered and bruise-mottled face with renewed suspicion. "I want you out—*now!*"

"But—"

"And take your imaginary friend or alter ego or whatever the hell it is with you—you two are scaring off my clientele."

Qar'qaah blinked.

"You really otta see someone about it."

"But—"

"*Out!*" the barkeep barked, pointing to the doorway. "Or do I have to call the bouncers?"

"Won't be necessary," he grumbled. "Ah was just leavin' anyway." He tossed back the rest of his drink and slammed the glass down on the bar. "Thanks for the hospitality. Next time ah find mahself on this paradise of ah planet, ah'll be sure to pay yah convivial establishment ah visit."

"Yeah, you *do* that." The barkeep gingerly snatched up the glass, eyed it as if worried it might carry some sort of contagion, then with a shake of his head, hastily tossed it in the nearest disposa-chute.

Qar'qaah rose unsteadily from the barstool, then roughly shoved and stumbled his way through the crush of customers and over to the doorway.

Once outside, he stopped and looked up and was startled to find that it was no longer afternoon, but close to nightfall. The hot, dry and dust-filled wind had died down but was replaced by something far more insidiously dangerous: a decidedly icy breeze.

He tugged the robe around him as he recalled his ill-fated benefactor's warning about finding a warm place to sleep. The robe had been overly hot during the heat of the day and worse, it stuck to his blistered skin and he had continually fought the urge to shed it. Now, its loose weave seemed to invite the chill evening air to bite at his oozing skin.

He clenched his teeth and dug into his right trouser pocket, thinking he had a token left but found only the empty ject-it.

He exhaled and with shoulders slumping, turned back to the street, not sure where to go. One thing was for certain: it was going to be a very long, very cold night.

Aliens of all descriptions jostled around him, oblivious to him and his plight, while locals, dressed head to toe in gauzy, loose-fitting hooded white robes, calmly eeled their way through the exotic, and largely intoxicated throng of spacefarers like so many officious ghosts.

"If you stay, you'll die." Matoosh's disembodied voice startled him out of his distraction and he realized this particularly persistent apparition was now standing next to him, using a thick signboard to block his invisible bulk from those who rare few who, while pushing their way by like the rest, weren't drunk.

Chiku, I wish you'd stop doing that! "It's better than living the rest of my life as his Doh'ha." He started to walk away, but before he could take two steps, he again felt a hand clamp down on his shoulder, stopping him in his tracks.

He felt as bruised inside as out—*everything* hurt. Not one bit of him had been safe to touch without risking a grimace or flinch. But the phantasm's grip held a pain that went far beyond the physical.

"He wants you back."

"Only so no one discovers what we are—you know that as well as I do. Well, thanks entirely to me, they already do, so tell him it's too late."

Matoosh hesitated, just long enough to draw Qar'qaah's sidelong squint. "That's not why—"

"Oh, then lemme guess: he wants to personally eliminate the blemish on our *illustrious* lineage!" He snorted as he squinted at his tawdry surroundings, the twinkling lights of so many brothels and saloons. It was not exactly what he'd envisioned when he wondered about where and how he'd die. He'd always privately savored the thought of a heroic end that would eclipse any of Khusaaq's or even Ja'andai's laudable accomplishments—prove to all of the doubters, once and for all, that they'd been wrong about him.

At the very least, he'd hoped he would meet an honorable death, one that had *some* meaning, however small, if only to himself and a client who'd paid up front and in full the hefty, but refundable surcharge for presumed merc fatalities. Even the death that had patiently awaited him and the others on Rasal Ghul would have been marginally better than the grim reality he now faced, of dying utterly alone, slowly, and in agony in some squalid back alley, his corpse stripped of anything of value then left to rot or be torn apart and eaten by scavengers. To be forever lost, even to the Elkanasu.

"That's not true—you know it's not true. I realize he hasn't been the best—"

"I'm tired of being his shadow. I'm tired of being looked upon as nothing more than a poor copy of the..." he paused, then sneered, *"the Hero of Cotopaxi—"*

"You know he hates that title and everything it implies even more than you do—"

"I'm tired of everything." He tried to twitch off the specter's hold.

"Do not do this," Matoosh's strained voice whispered. *"I beg you.* Come back with me—we'll talk to Khusaaq, together. Things have changed, *he's* changed, a'itat."

Qar'qaah couldn't help but smile. *A'itat—brother*. Matoosh hadn't called him that in a very long time and he chuckled softly at the absurdity of baring his soul to his own hallucination—*but at least you're listening to me. No one else was willing to—not even the real Matoosh.* And at that moment he realized he desperately needed to explain himself, even if it was just to a figment of his own overly fatigued mind: "I thought I'd finally been given my chance to prove myself, to him, to you, to everyone when he left me in charge, rather than you—" He inhaled sharply and fixed his suddenly watery gaze on the crater's distant rim.

Now only the very tops of the weathered escarpment were edged in pale sunlight, the rest was cloaked in the deep purple of night. It would be fully dark in a matter of minutes. As befitted a harsh, unforgiving world such as this, there was no in-between, no gentle transition, no lingering twilight.

"I proved myself all right. I proved to everyone I *am* a complete failure—*Chiku!* I couldn't even protect a handful of soldiers left under my command—"

"You were marooned," the ethereal Matoosh countered, "suffering from advanced radiation poisoning, surprised and overwhelmed by a superior force!"

"So? Khusaaq wouldn't have let those under his command be captured by the enemy!" Not getting an immediate rebuttal and mistaking the awkward silence that followed for tacit agreement, he snarled, *"And neither would the real you!"* as he shrugged off the ghostly fingers' grip. "Goodbye... *a'itat."* With that, he stepped into the crowd and was instantly swallowed up, pulled along by a surge of aliens headed down the narrow street—going where he wasn't sure, but at least the brisk pace set by those around him and their body heat was, at least for now, keeping the chill at bay.

As he walked, he glanced around, desperately searching for a suitable place—any place—to take shelter for the night.

Absolutely nothing presented itself—the gaming halls and hotels that lined the street were too well-lit and clearly catered to a high-end clientele, with hulking creatures loitering outside—alien bouncers ready to send anyone of lesser caliber packing. So he walked on, accompanied by a slowly winnowing crowd of those seeking cheaper entertainment or the more meager accommodations that ringed the more affluent center of town before it became too cold to remain outside.

And as he let those around him guide his way, the street itself, no longer a garishly adorned boulevard, became narrower and narrower, funneling the drunken throng into closer and closer quarters. The lighting too dwindled the further he walked, with fully-dark side-streets and alleys becoming more common, and saloon and hostel frontages having only the minimum illumination necessary to draw customers inside.

With no tokens, he couldn't take refuge in any of the truly seedy saloons that had replaced the more respectable establishments—at least not for long without risking the added humiliation of being thrown out onto the street, possibly being roughed up in the process. So he kept moving—not that he had much choice. Those behind him kept pushing, urging him on.

Chapter 28

Aboard Jirah.
Start of Middle Watch. Present day.

"Chiku!" Khusaaq snarled, slamming his fist on the console, startling Rukoobi, Toubeh and Shu'hah, who were seated at their bridge stations.

Tejat glanced up at the agitated officer who stood beside him, then back at his control board. "I will try to boost the gain, ta'ahn, but I doubt it will help."

Khusaaq, at the sound of approaching voices, turned and fixed his heated stare on the airlock just as Jaa'qwah and a still armored Matoosh stepped through and onto the *Jirah*'s bridge.

"Reporting in, ta'ahn," Matoosh said in a clipped voice. "As ordered, returning by nightfall, planetside."

Khusaaq replied with an equally brusque nod. Matoosh didn't need to report that Qar'qaah had refused to return; he didn't have to add that he'd followed him for some distance, hoping to find a place where he could inject him with the mild tranquilizer Jaa'qwah had given him, then guide or, if absolutely necessary, carry him into a side alley where the distortion and spatial displacement of a flicker would pass largely unnoticed. Only he'd unexpectedly lost sight of Qar'qaah when a brawl broke out between a group of intoxicated Rimmers and another group of equally drunk Matarii, a fight that quickly spread among the throng crowding the street. And Khusaaq didn't need to tell Matoosh that their backup, the locator Matoosh had affixed to Qar'qaah's clothing without Qar'qaah's knowledge, was proving useless against the planet's surprisingly sophisticated and effective jamming.

Khusaaq had made yet another critical error: he'd reasonably, and he now realized *pridefully* presumed A'tuu'shahn skills—*his* precise skills—could override anyone else's attempts at jamming a specific signal. It was a critical error that Qar'qaah would now very likely pay for with his life—

"Ta'ahn!"

Khusaaq and Matoosh turned back to Tejat.

"I just detected a very brief pattern burst within the overlaying static..." He pressed his earpiece tighter against his ear. "Definitely Qar'qaah Kon'ta'aq's personal identifier..."

Khusaaq leaned over Tejat's left shoulder as Matoosh leaned over his right, both peering at the console's main screen that at that moment was displaying a surface map of the untidy snarl that was the Gorgon's Lair.

"Here." Tejat tapped his finger against the screen and a flashing marker appeared. "Six and a half city blocks north-north east from point of origin."

Khusaaq squinted at the telltale, exhaled slowly, then glanced sidelong at Matoosh. "Sporadic is better than nothing." He straightened up then clapped the massive Quu'dahn engineer on the shoulder. "Excellent work, Ruh'ta'aq, excellent!"

Tejat acknowledged the praise with a curt nod, but by his unhappy expression he was clearly thinking that while sporadic might be better than nothing, it was certainly far less than his commanding officer's expectations and he intended to do something to correct that. He immediately turned back to the console and resumed his determined eavesdropping.

"I'll contact *Illuyanka* and *Kashku*," Rukoobi said, "have them attempt to triangulate the signal."

"Ta'ahn," Jaa'qwah whispered, mindful of the serious, not to mention seriously preoccupied Tejat. *"A word?"*

Khusaaq followed as Jaa'qwah stepped through the airlock and back into the corridor. "As I informed Matoosh Ruh'ta'aq earlier, Kon'ta'aq only took six vials of painkiller and four stims, but nothing to treat the systemic effects of his radiation poisoning—"

"How long can he last without medical care?" Khusaaq glanced over his shoulder to find Matoosh, Toubeh and Shu'hah now standing behind him.

"A day, likely less—if that's all we were dealing with, but Matoosh told me the clothing Kon'ta'aq is wearing would provide little to no protection against the cold, and it gets *very* cold at night on Poonda Five." He looked to Matoosh, who nodded, then back to Khusaaq. "If he cannot find shelter and quickly, it's my opinion that he will not last more than a few hours—"

"Ta'ahn?"

Everyone turned at the sound of Tejat's deep, rumbling voice. Matoosh, Shu'hah and Toubeh hurriedly stepped aside and Khusaaq strode back onto the bridge, the others following.

"Two more brief bursts, overlapping—one his personal identifier and the other that of the locator," the engineer continued once they'd all gathered around his station, "a half block further, still heading north north-east along this main artery." He tapped the screen.

Khusaaq studied the map, replied, "I believe we'd get a stronger, or at least more consistent signal on-planet as the bulk of the jamming is clearly targeting ships in orbit—agreed?"

Tejat nodded, "Agreed, ta'ahn, but the range of would be limited."

"In your estimation, how limited?"

"By passive sensor sweeps?" Tejat replied. "A hundred meters? Likely far less."

"My estimation as well," Khusaaq said.

"I didn't pick up his identifier until I was within a dozen meters," Matoosh offered then shrugged at Tejat's quick, over-the-shoulder, slitted-eyed glance. "The Poondians take their jamming very seriously."

Khusaaq crossed his arms, dissatisfied then turned to Rukoobi. "Have *Illuyanka* and *Kashku* had any success?"

"They are still attempting to triangulate, ta'ahn. In order to avoid detection, they were not in stationary orbits above the Gorgon's Lair and were out of range—"

"We could amplify the locator's signature once on the planet," Tejat interrupted, "or we could go to active sensor sweeps—"

"Doing either guarantees detection if employed for any worthwhile period of time." Khusaaq chewed on his lip as Tejat and Rukoobi exchanged looks.

"Ruh'ta'aq," Khusaaq abruptly turned to Matoosh. "Organize a landing party—Jaa'qwah, are those we rescued recovered enough to participate?"

"They'd say they were even if they weren't, ta'ahn, but yes, they are recovered enough, at least for a few hours of searching."

"Let's hope that's all it takes—Matoosh, two and two again, only this time Jaa'qwah," he nodded to the medic, "you are to accompany us. Rukoobi—notify Nerik'ah Sha'ashahn to stand by, we may be in need of her assistance shortly. Tejat," he turned back to the engineer as Matoosh and Jaa'qwah hurried from the bridge to alert the others and Tejat hastily rose from his console. "You are to remain aboard, along with Shu'hah and Rukoobi, coordinate with *Illuyanka* and *Kashku,* continue to track the signal when and where you can—any information, even very erratic data on his location will greatly aid in his speedy recovery—but just as critical to our mission is to monitor the planet for any sign that they've detected our presence—or Qar'qaah's, so keep listening to their hospital, constabulary... and yes, morgue frequencies as well." With that he turned on his heel and hurried from the bridge.

Poonda Five.
One hour after planetary nightfall. Present day.

Exhausted, Qar'qaah managed to sharp-elbow his way to the side of the dimly-lit road without being knocked down unintentionally or in retaliation, allowing those behind him to pass in their haste to reach the one of the few remaining hostels, or, he suspected, the relative warmth and comfort of their own ships. He took a few more stumbling steps, then stopped and gulping for breath, looked around him. While he'd been walking, forced to keep up a relatively brisk pace by those around him, his full attention had been on keeping on his feet to avoid being trampled underfoot. But now, with his clothing sweat-damp from the exertion, he began to shiver uncontrollably, and with the violent shivers came a fresh wave of nausea.

He staggered a little further, over to the broken stump of what had been, at one time, a lamppost and clutching it in one hand, bent over and dry heaved several times.

As the cramping eased, just a bit, he let go of the post, jerked his robe tight around him, crossed his arms to keep the billowing robe in place and tucked his hands into its folds. He looked back the way he'd come, suddenly and, despite the absurdity of it, desperately hoping to spot Matoosh's ghostly shimmer among those still hastening by. But his now wind-watery eyes confirmed what his mind feared: he'd been abandoned even by his hallucinations.

He squeezed his eyes shut as his cold-numb hand dug into his trouser pocket in search of the ject-it while the other hand felt around in the loose folds of his under-tunic for the remaining vial. All he wanted was for the pain to stop, for the crushing sense of shame and guilt to stop, even if it was just for a few precious minutes, beyond that—

Something bumped into him—something that grunted softly.

His eyes snapped open; he turned around only to find a small human backing away, muttering profuse apologizes.

Heart racing, he also backed up several stumbling steps, but in the process clipped the street's uneven curb with his boot heel. He made a desperate grab for the lamppost, missed and sat down, half on, half off the curb, and the jolt set off a fresh wave of intense belly cramps. He groaned, squeezed his eyes shut and clutching his stomach, very slowly toppled onto his side and onto the rutted street.

"C'mon, I didn't hit you *that* hard!" he overheard the human angrily protest, then after a long, awkward pause, a more conciliatory: "Are... are you all right?"

In response he curled into a ball as he succumbed to another fit of dry heaves.

"Okay, not all right—"

"G-g-go... away!" he forced out between spasms.

"Look, I'm just trying to help—"

"I... I d-d-don't... don't n-n-need your... y-y-your help."

"Oh, I respectfully beg to disagree."

He squinted up at the human—a female—who now stood over him as he took several deep breaths, forcing down the nausea, as he wondered how, on a world with the reputation of Poonda Five's, he kept running into self-professed do-gooders. Then again, likely this creature was as much the altruist as the one who had so generously donated its robe, tokens and breather to him.

But in her case she wasn't lying—her aura remained a faint, flickering gray. Or maybe she was just a very, very good liar, one that could effectively conceal the autonomic tells almost all species had.

"At least let me help you out of the street so you don't get run over by that, whatever it is." The human pointed.

He managed to lift his head just enough to peer back the way he'd come. Further down the street a mechanical, eight-legged contraption plodded along, slowly making its way towards him, its bulk taking up most of the road's width.

"Here. C'mon, don't be silly—it'll be here at any moment."

He looked up at the human to find her holding out her hand.

He risked a quick glance back at the approaching machine and realized he couldn't get up on his own, at least not quickly enough to avoid being flattened under its wide, metal and multiple feet. He made a quick judgement of the downward force of its footsteps, realized there was a good chance he couldn't be killed outright when it ran over him, just very severely injured and unable to move—a situation even worse than the predicament he was in now. So he very reluctantly reached up.

She grasped his hand in hers and with a surprisingly strong grip. "Ready?"

He clenched his teeth, replied with a curt nod and with her help lurched to his knees and then staggered to his feet.

Once standing, suddenly dizzy, he stumbled sideways, almost falling again before she grabbed his elbow to steady him—and just in time, too, as the multi-legged cargo mover was almost on top of them.

"Jaas-nhe," he murmured over the oncoming machine's oddly cadenced hissing and clicking while trying not to gag at

the potent stench belching from its badly tuned combustion engine.

Satisfied he was going to stay upright, at least long enough for the cargo mover to pass, the human said, "I'll be on my way now," and started off, and, he noted with some relief at a good clip, but she only took a handful of steps before she stopped abruptly and glanced back at him.

Uh-oh.

"You... you just spoke Hahtou."

He stared sidelong at her, suddenly wary—*Did I?*—and now on the verge of panic as he wondered what else he'd let slip—and how did this human recognize A'tuu? "N-no... no, ah didn't!"

"Yes you *did*. You said, 'jaas-nhe', which in Hahtou means thank you."

"Nah. Yah misheard. Ah... ah said, 'gax nah'—Zuhsetian for appreciation."

"No, it isn't." She walked back to him, then crossing her arms, peered up at his dust-veiled and cowl-shadowed face; he responded by slowly moving his right hand closer to his hidden pistol.

The movement caught her eye. "Your hands..."

"What about them?" he snapped, immediately tucking both within the folds of his robe.

"They're covered in tattoos..." She lifted her now wide-eyed gaze. "You *are* Hahtooshan!"

"No, ah'm not. Besides, how... how would yah know what ah Hahtooshan looks like? No one does."

"Well, I *do*, trust me on that, and you *are* one."

He snorted, *"Ah'm not!"* and instantly regretted it. The spasmodic jerk rippled over his still extremely unhappy belly, threatening to reignite the nausea that had only just passed now that the mover had moved on. "Ah'm... ah'm from Zuhset Prime—"

"Like hell you are." She took a step closer.

He responded by backing up a step. She didn't look, and more importantly, *smell* at all familiar, her faint, dirty gray aura and cloying stink was no different than any other human—no help there, yet she knew what he was, which could only mean she was one of Cisne's surviving crew. He remembered only one human other than Cisne—a male—but that didn't mean there weren't more, and that meant it was only a matter of time before Cisne herself showed up.

Just the thought of facing Cisne in his present condition sent his body shaking anew.

He risked another quick glance around. The road was now deserted—if you discounted a threesome of very inebriated Loopers further down the street—the mechanical cargo mover had already disappeared down a side street—and even better, he spotted the black maw of an alleyway not far away. *Yes*—

"Okay, I'll play along," she replied, hands on hips. "What's a Zuhsetian doing here?"

He licked his lips and fixed her with the best hard stare he could manage as he took another unsteady step backwards. "Shore leave?"

"Shore leave. On Poonda Five—the universally acknowledged unwashed hairy crotch of the near Rim."

"That's what ah said," he replied, taking another shaky step back and was instantly rewarded when she followed, step for step, seemingly oblivious to his slow but steady retreat towards the alley. He didn't dare take his eyes off her, just in case, and so was anxiously hoping he wouldn't trip or stumble over something in his path.

"Long way to come for shore leave—one *hell* of a long way."

"Ah... ah was in the neighborhood, never... never been here. Thought ah'd check it out." He cautiously motioned around him as he back-stepped again. "As yah can see, it has a lot to offer."

She made an odd noise, not quite an explosive snort, not quite a derisive chuckle. "Oh, yeah. And going by the looks of you, you've been sampling a wee bit too much of what it has to offer."

"Weren't yah leaving?" He took another back-step; she matched it, her eyes never wavering from his.

"Yeah. I was. Only now I'm not. At least not until you tell me what the hell a Hahtooshan is doing here, all alone, on Poonda Five."

"Ah already told yah, ah'm *Zuhsetian,*" he replied in his best aggrieved, yet deliberately hushed voice. "Ah'm on shore leave, doing a bit of sightseeing—and ah don't appreciate being called a *Hah*-tooshan. People might overhear yah, not bother to ask questions and just start shooting."

She looked around then motioned to the street. "I don't see anyone, do you?"

He didn't take her up on her suggestion—he didn't need to. Instead he took another, this time very wobbly step—no faking needed this time, although if it encouraged her to stay close so much the better—hoping she'd continue to follow, because she was right in one respect: his sense of smell confirmed that the street was now completely deserted. Even the drunken Loopers had managed to wander off, taking their very distinct body odor with them.

"So what are yah doing here, besides insulting me and risking me being killed for something ah'm not?"

She scowled up at him, then suddenly smiled, and not a pleasant smile. "I was helping you, if you recall."

"Before that."

"Just like you, sightseeing, but without the booze—or whatever it is you've been sniffing, shooting, smoking or ingesting."

He took another cautious, shuffling step back. Of course if she was with Cisne, then she'd want to follow or risk losing him again, something Cisne likely wouldn't look kindly upon. If she wasn't, well... Rimmers were known for being rather careless, and overly curious Rimmers doubly so. Case in point: "Sightseeing. At night, *alone*. On Poonda Five."

"Who says I'm alone?" she replied.

He forced himself not to react, to panic and glance around, but rather to keep his eyes fixed on this exceedingly nosy, alleged do-gooder human female, putting his full trust in his acute sense of smell and hearing to warn him of any possible confederates. "Ah do. And ah think yah're lost, too." He took another half-step closer to the alley—his planned escape route, not to mention a convenient place to commit murder.

"I think you are too... lost that is."

"Ah already told yah—" he looked past her; he'd seen a flicker of movement out of the corner of his eye, he was sure of it. Dropping his now chary gaze back to her, he continued, "Ah suggest yah find yahself some lodgings—it's not safe to remain here." He pulled the robe around him then with a dismissive nod, began backing as hurriedly away as he could safely manage—if she was stupid enough to follow, well...

Then they both heard a noise—the faint metallic 'clink' of something being dropped, followed by angry, albeit slurred whispers.

He glared at her. "Alone, huh?"

"What?" She glanced over her shoulder, towards the hushed voices, then back at him. "I don't—"

He grabbed her by the forearm. Hostage or soon to be silenced witness, she was coming with him, like it—or not.

"Let... GO!"

Not, then. He let go of her arm only to clap his hand over her mouth, then he jerked her against him, but when she began pummeling him, he lifted her bodily and after a quick look around, slipped into the dimly-lit alley. He stumbled over unseen trash and by sheer force of will kept on his feet, but once well away from the alley's mouth and completely spent by the effort, he staggered over to the wall and sagged heavily against it.

Try as he might, he couldn't muster the strength to keep his hold on her and as she wriggled free, he slid down the wall and to his knees.

Gasping for breath, he stared glassily at the ground, teetering precariously on the edge of blacking out.

"What the hell do you want?" she hissed as she backed well out of reach.

In reply he jerked his chin towards the alley mouth.

She glanced at it then back at him, her eyes, her voice edged in fear—but not of him. "You think I was being followed?"

That wasn't what he'd meant, but if she chose to interpret it that way...

He clutched his stomach in one hand and using the alley wall for support tried to get back to his feet but found his legs unwilling to obey. He leaned back against the wall and took several deep, head-clearing breaths.

"Well," she replied, arms akimbo, "excuse me for saying so, but you look like you're the one who's in need of rescue."

He squinted furiously up at her only to find her face was a blur. He blinked, rubbed his eyes then tried again, with the same fuzzy result. So instead he again tried to get to his feet, and this time succeeded. He stood there, feet set wide apart and hands and shoulders pressed against the wall, swaying slightly, the alley going in and out of focus with each slow blink, each ragged breath.

She stepped close—but not too close. "You're not much of a knight in shining armor, are you?"

He locked his knees then wrapped his arms around himself in hopes of suppressing another spasm of shivers as a cold blast of air swirled around them and cut right through the robe to his damp under-tunic and trousers.

"Speaking of armor..." She eyed him. "Answer me truthfully this time. What the hell *is* a Hahtooshan doing *here*, on Poonda Five?"

"I... I told you, I'm not A'tuu'shahn! I'm Zuhset—"

"A'tuu'shahn, eh? What happened to your accent?"

He blinked; this wasn't fair, definitely not fair! He was sick, couldn't she see that? Yet she kept tripping him up, and with a certain degree of smug satisfaction, if he read her expression correctly, which he wasn't sure he could, not with her face going in and out of focus, and the only illumination being that from the street beyond and scant little of that.

She exhaled forcefully. "Look, I know you're Hahtooshan, or *A'tuu'shahn,* if you prefer. So stop lying—you're utterly atrocious at it, by the way, just like every Hahtooshan I've met—" She grabbed the dust veil and yanked it down, exposing his scarified and tattooed face to the dim light of the nearby street. "Not Hahtooshan, huh?"

He swallowed convulsively.

She suddenly dropped her gaze to his trousers, which unbeknownst to him had reverted to their morphing—he had no idea for how long. "And what do you call that?" She pointed.

"Clothing?"

She squinted sourly up at him. "Start telling me the truth and maybe we can help each other. Deal?"

He hesitated before answering, "Why would you... you want to... to help a... an A'tuu'shahn?" To him the answer was obvious: she simply had to be with Cisne—a crewmember he never saw, perhaps one who only came close when he was too out of it to notice, to sense, to remember. Otherwise she would have done what any smart Rimmer would do if faced with an admitted A'tuu'shahn: run for her life.

But she didn't run. She didn't even take a step back. In fact she smiled, a slow pulling back of the lips. "We're allies now, or haven't you heard?"

He squinted at her, angrily wishing her face would stay in focus and stammered, "Al...*allies...?*"

"Yeah. *Your* Orthodoxy and *my* Coalition—we're now comrades in arms."

He couldn't tell by her tone if she was happy about this startling turn of events, or mocking him, mocking this fledgling alliance, just as Cisne and the others had taunted him when he cried out for Khusaaq. But on this one point he knew she was telling the truth as far as it went; Matoosh had told him much the same thing and Matoosh would have had no reason to lie about such an appalling pact.

"Name's Sirin Corsali. And yours is...?"

He only stared down at her, jaw muscles twitching.

"Yup, definitely Hahtooshan," she replied cheerfully, "and now that the introductions are over, how 'bout you tell me what you're doing here, on Poonda Five, *alone*—and don't tell me you aren't, okay? We've already established that you're a terrible liar."

He looked away, took several short, shallow breaths, then answered in a voice barely above a whisper and in a way that any accomplice of Cisne's would appreciate: "Proving... to... t-t-to everyone that… I am… in fact n-n-nothing… nothing m-m-more than a very… very p-p-poor copy."

Instead of smiling, instead of replying with a knowing nod or a derisive chuckle, the human arched what appeared to him to be a genuinely puzzled brow. "I… I beg your pardon?"

He squeezed his eyes shut as his belly spasmed unexpectedly, triggered by the sense of guilt, the shame his remark had evoked, and, gulping for breath, he leaned heavily against the wall.

"Oh, geez…."

He warily opened his eyes to find her peering up at him. She was close enough now he could have easily grabbed her, but if he moved, if he shifted his weight even slightly, he had no doubt he'd fall—and he wasn't sure he'd be able to get up again. He was very close to passing out, and if that happened…

"All right," she began in a slightly more conciliatory voice, "how 'bout we'll deal with what you're doing here later. You're clearly in desperate need of medical attention—there's gotta be a clinic or something the like nearby." She looked towards the mouth of the alley. "I think I passed one a few blocks back."

He clenched his teeth against an especially agonizing cramp and suddenly realized that he didn't care if she was with Cisne, in fact… he hoped she was. Cisne could order her doctor to stop the pain, and likely would as she'd done in the past, if he returned voluntarily, if he did exactly as he was told— "Call… t-t-the others."

"Others?" She glanced around her then turned back to him. "What others—"

"Take m-m-me back to… to *Huui'teh*," he managed. "I won't fight—"

"Huui'teh…?" Her eyes widened. "But… but what the hell are you doing here—"

"P-p-please. I… I really *hurt*. Please—t-t-tohiss-m-m-mat."

"Look, I don't know who you think I am, but I think the worst thing we could do is take you back there. You need a clinic—"

"You're with Cisne!" he snarled as he grabbed his sunken belly again, this time with both hands, his fingers digging into

the fabric and the underlying flesh. "S-s-stop p-p-playing g-g-games!"

"I'm not playing games and I'm not with whoever this Cisne is, I'm trying to help you!"

"Then t-t-take me t-t-to *Huui'teh!*"

She looked away, blew out her cheeks then eyed him. "Fine. Where is it?"

"Southern l-l-landing... landing f-f-field."

She again placed her hands on her hips. "And which way is that?"

He stared at her for a moment, not sure if she was testing him or teasing him—maybe both. Or maybe she was truly as lost as he was. *It doesn't matter*. He looked up and gave the narrow strip of star-speckled sky a prolonged study—while the stars were crystal clear, his vision and thinking were not. One cluster of stars hovering above the far end of the alley did look vaguely familiar, but with no other reference points... he wasn't absolutely sure. The cluster might be a totally different cluster of stars than the one he'd seen right after he made planetfall, and worse, he suddenly realized he couldn't remember if Poonda Five had a retrograde or prograde motion, which meant that even if he did have a firm reference point, he couldn't be sure which way was south. Just thinking about made his head hurt even worse.

But the human was waiting—with increasing exasperation if her angry foot tapping was any guide—and if he didn't make a decision and quick, he risked her making it for him, and if she was wrong...

He pointed towards the alley's opposite mouth with a shaky hand. "That... t-t-that way."

"Sure?"

He hesitated then admitted, "Ch-ch-chulh..."

She made a strangled noise then began counting, out loud and slowly, "One... two... three... four... five..."

He eyed her warily yet curious as to the significance of what was clearly a Rimmer ritual. *Perhaps invoking her many gods for guidance?*

"...six... seven... eight... nine... *ten.*"

Before he could ponder the matter further, she reopened her eyes and added, "Great, just… *great,"* as she favored him with a sidelong, decidedly angry stare.

He stared back, not sure why her ire was aimed at him when it was any one or all of her ten gods who'd obviously ignored her entreaties.

"Well, let's go find out, shall we?" She motioned towards the far end of the alley.

He took an unsteady step away from the supporting wall, then immediately stumbled back against it. He clenched his fists and hissed, *"Chiku!"*

She stared at him with a decidedly unsympathetic expression as she inhaled sharply through her nose then exhaled the same way before asking, "Do I have your permission to touch you?"

He squinted balefully at her. *"Tooq-sseh…?"*

"What the hell do you mean, *why?* You wanna fall down again?"

He started to shake his head—thought better of it and grumbled, "Chulh." His knees, hips and spine still throbbed from the jolt of his last fall—and there was still the very real possibility that he wouldn't be able to get up again, even with her help—assuming she would help, and not just leave him to freeze to death in this trash-littered slot between two dilapidated buildings. Going by her expression, it was beginning to look like a toss-up what she'd do.

"Didn't think so, so you're gonna need my help to walk, and to help you, I have to touch you."

This time he nodded and mumbled, "Paq…"

She stepped closer and as he stared down at her and she up at him, she cautiously wrapped her arm around his bony waist.

His body, his mind reacted convulsively to being touched by a human female, her encircling arm perilously close to his spirit lock—it did nothing for his already rebellious stomach. His heart beat faster; his breathing came in panicky gasps. He closed his eyes, tried to calm himself, tried to slow his heart's breakneck beat. He found he couldn't. The sensations, the memories were just too raw—

"Ready?"

Ready? He opened his eyes and looked down at her as her voice focused his panicked mind: if she'd wanted to harm him she could have just stepped aside, waited for him to collapse then done as Cisne had done, as her crew had done, over and over—

He jerked his thoughts off that track, licked his gummy lips and in reply reluctantly draped his arm over her shoulder.

She tightened her hold on him and none-too-gently jerked him away from the wall. "Come on, then."

Together they started down the alley, but the further he walked, the harder it was to keep on his feet. The ground kept shifting, rippling under him and the walls of the alley began to close in.

He found it harder and harder to breathe. He stumbled, somehow managed to recover, then stumbled again and this time fell heavily to his hands and knees, taking her and her startled yelp, with him.

He shut his eyes as an intense wave of nausea washed over him, and as she scrambled to her feet and backed away he began to retch violently.

Lost in his own misery, he was only dimly aware of her saying something—of feeling her hands pat him down, finding his maser pistol then struggling to free it from its holster. He briefly hoped she was going to kill him with his own weapon— and mentally pleaded with her to do so—before the excruciating pain drove out all conscious thought from his mind.

Chapter 29

Staging bay aboard Jirah.
Twenty minutes into Middle Watch. Present day.

Khusaaq tapped the active screen displaying a map of the Gorgon's Lair and a yellow telltale began to flash. "Our flick-down site." He looked around him, making eye contact with each. "Jaa'qwah, Endooki, Nihaal, you will accompany me. We will cut through the city, following Kon'ta'aq's last known heading, in the hopes of overtaking him, using this route." Using his finger, he ran it across the screen in a circuitous track, now highlighted in a glowing red streamer, through the maze of streets that snaked their way in and around the haphazardly built space-port. "Matoosh," he glanced over his shoulder at the soldier, "you, Raudah, Toubeh, Laihiri—circle around, enter the city from the north-east."

He again ran his finger over the schematic, leaving a glowing trail of green around the eastern perimeter of the city. "If neither group locates him, we will regroup here," he tapped the schematic and a pulsing blue dot appeared, "and revisit our options. Avoid all communications unless absolutely necessary to avoid any possible detection—route any through *Jirah*, rather than group to group. Shu'hah will monitor our frequencies, camouflaging them as routine chatter while Tejat monitors the planet's net and listens for any further pulse identifiers from Kon'ta'aq. I believe, based on what Tejat has learned about the planet's jamming capabilities, that once on planet, we should be able to pick up on his personal identifier or the locator if he is within forty meters, using passive means only.

"Matoosh has already described the Poondian clothing he was last seen wearing, and Jaa'qwah has told you that he is likely visibly ill. This could work in our favor, slowing him down, but it will also make him an easy target. It's possible, since he'd managed to acquire some credits, enough to buy a glass of liquor, he might have enough for a place to sleep or at least seek shelter as well, so passively scan all hotels, hostel and other sleeping quarters you come across. Saloons too, if they're open."

"They are," Matoosh grumbled. "All of them—they never close."

Khusaaq acknowledged the disdainful remark with a nod. "I don't need to tell you we have our work cut out for us—but I also want to make it clear that exhausting yourself does no one any good, least of all Kon'ta'aq. So if you feel you cannot continue, it is your duty to say so and I will immediately replace you with one of Nerik'ah Sha'ashahn's crew. No one will think ill of you for doing so." He gave the each of four rescued from Rasal Ghul a pointed look, then, taking his helmet from Matoosh, said, "Let's go," and slipping it on, stepped into the flicker chamber.

Poonda Five.
Nighttime. Present day.

Qar'qaah reluctantly opened his eyes. For several heartbeats, he had no idea where he was, except for the fact that he was lying on his side in a pool of vomit, an all too familiar position for him, he hurt all over and he was freezing cold—or maybe he hurt all over *because* he was freezing cold.

Then he remembered and had a flash of panic that he was alone—before he realized that the human was standing over him, his heavy pistol clutched in her small hands as she kept a wary eye on the dark alley.

He had no idea how long he'd been gone, totally defenseless with a human female nearby—visions of Cisne flashed through his mind, coursing through his body like electric shocks.

She's not Cisne, he tried to assure himself, but it didn't help.

He slowly lifted his head from the rough, icy cobbles, wiped his mouth and chin with the back of his hand and stuttered, "I… I th-th-thought… thought y-y-you'd left."

She stared at him as if genuinely surprised that he was still alive, much less able to speak coherently. "I'm *so* sorry I disappointed you."

He squinted up at her, not sure what she meant by that as he managed to push himself to his knees while every joint in his body screamed in protest.

Suddenly his breath caught in his throat as his stomach tightened in another excruciating spasm.

His involuntary gasp drew her startled gaze. "Oh, crap. Now what? You can't possibly have anything left inside to puke up unless it's your spleen."

He wanted to glare at her. He wanted to snatch the pistol from her—shoot her, shoot himself it didn't matter... he wanted to cry, the searing pain was so horrible and she clearly didn't give a damn. Rimmer she might be, but she bore striking similarities to Tu'indai in that regard.

Instead he grabbed his abdomen with both hands and doubling over, forced out, *"In... my... tunic...!"*

"What's in your tunic?"

"Med... medication—*tohiss-mat!*" he whimpered as his fingers clawed at his stomach.

She looked around once more as she knelt beside him, then she shoved his hands away and ran her own over his taut belly and quickly located the small vial within the loose folds of vomit-splattered fabric. She roughly tugged the under-tunic's hem free of his trousers' waistband and weapons belt then snatched up the vial as it fell to the ground. "I assume you have a ject-it?"

"Trouser poc—pocket..."

"Great." She made a face as she placed the pistol beside her, then she forced her hand into the left pocket and withdrew a token. "Holding out on me, huh?"

He squinted at it then stammered, "Other... other pocket! *Hurry!*"

She stuffed the token in her own pocket then reached around him and after a moment's struggle, pulled out the ject-it.

"Give... them to... to... me!" he stammered as he tried to grab them from her but she was just a little quicker and held them out of his reach. *"Toh...t-t-tohiss-mat!"* he pleaded, his voice cracking in panic.

"I think you better let *me* give it to you."

Realizing his hands—in fact his entire body—were shaking uncontrollably, that he couldn't have loaded the ject-it—and that she wasn't planning on withholding the medication as he'd feared, he managed a hoarse, "The... t-t-then... then d-d-do... do so—"

"How much?"

"All... all of... of it!"

She eyed him. "Sure?"

He replied with a vigorous nod and feeling another spasm coming, gasped, *"Hurry...!"*

She yanked the robe down, off his bony shoulder and he felt the ice-cold nose of the ject-it against his bare skin, followed by a familiar faint hiss. He closed his eyes and loudly gulped down the nausea as he waited for the drug to take effect.

After several minutes, the intense, cramping pain began to subside and he reopened his exhausted eyes to find her still kneeling next to him, watching him intently, his pistol again clutched in her hands.

"Better?"

No. He managed a less than convincing nod.

"All right, then let's get going before this," she waved the ject-it around, "whatever it is I just gave you—wears off."

With her help, he lurched to an unsteady stand, but no sooner had he gotten back to his feet—and she was temporarily distracted slipping the ject-it into her hip pocket—than he snatched the pistol from her other hand, almost losing his balance in the process.

"Hey!"

He glared at her as he managed to shove the weapon back into its holster. "I'm... I'm fully able to defend myself now."

She grabbed his elbow as he took a wildly swaying step, growled, "Yeah, sure you are," and pulled him tight against her. "Come on, *hero.*"

Chapter 30

Poonda Five.
Five hours until planetary dawn. Present day.

Sirin looked up at her unwelcome and unsympathetic companion. His gaunt, blistered face had taken on an ominous glossy gray hue under the swirling motif of his decidedly pallid tattoos, his breathing was coming in labored gasps and his sunken eyes stared glassily ahead.

"Want to stop?"

When he didn't answer, she jerked him to a halt. "Hey!"

He blinked and mumbled, *"Sseh...?"*

"Do you want to stop, rest for a little while?" She motioned to the steps of a nearby building.

He stared at them and slurred, *"Chulh. Ith'tah... ith'tah que—"*

"I don't understand, uh... tuh maztsaeh?"

He slowly turned his dull gaze back to her. *"Sseh?"*

"I can't *understand* you if you mumble in Hahtou. Please, speak in *Standard*. Khusaaq said you all speak it fluently, so please, do so."

He narrowed his gaze and for a second, just a second, seemed to sharply focus his thoughts as well. "How... how d-d-do you... you know Sha'ashahn?"

Sirin hesitated, suspecting her true status would come as a shock, and a very unpleasant shock to this particular Hahtooshan, easily enough to break the very tenuous thread of trust between them. "Let's just say I'm... I'm a close friend."

He wet his swollen, gummy lips as he continued to study her upturned face, clearly unconvinced then to her relief finally shifted his squint to their surroundings.

"Just a brief rest, okay? You look positively done-in," Sirin urged as much for her sake as his. She had, after all, spent almost an entire Poondian day-night cycle on the run and he'd been leaning more and more on her just to keep on his feet.

He nodded reluctantly then shuffled over to the stairs. With her help, he eased himself down on a step, exhaled wearily and dropped his head into his skeletally thin hands.

She was relieved he'd capitulated so easily, then again, he was clearly far worse off than her, perilously close to physically spent. They'd been walking the increasingly deserted streets of the city for the better part of the night and she'd begun to suspect they were going in circles, at least for the past hour or so. The city's welter of streets, side-streets and alleyways were laid out in a totally haphazard, possibly even deliberately confusing way, with few if any signs to guide those unfamiliar with their surroundings. Roads suddenly looped back on themselves while alleys snaked in and around buildings that were just as slapdash in design not to mention construction, many clearly made of cannibalized space craft and shipping containers. Even sticking to what appeared to be a main road made little difference: they'd had to backtrack several times when they suddenly found themselves at a lightless dead end.

Despite his occasional glance skywards she wasn't even sure if he even remembered where they were supposed to be headed, not that she planned on returning him to the *Huui'teh*. She'd hoped that in their wanderings they'd happen across a clinic, or even a local who could point them to a clinic, but she knew better than to say that and lose what cooperation he was willing—or able—to give.

She sat beside him, then cautiously slipped her arm under his robe, hoping to share their meager body heat—as well as placing her hand close to his holstered pistol just in case—and tried to ignore the feel of his clammy trouser fabric alternately puckering and smoothing against her thigh and hip, a sensation she'd never gotten used to and doubted she ever would.

To her surprise, he abruptly leaned into her, or closer to the mark collapsed against her, his body suddenly gone limp, his cheek resting against the top of her head, and for a moment, as his breathing slowed and deepened, she thought he'd nodded off, or worse, lapsed into unconsciousness. As she was debating what to do, he said in a halting voice barely above a thin whisper, "Why... are you doing this?" He slowly lifted his head, turned to face her, his hollow, bruised eyes taking in her face, nostrils sampling her odor, looking for clues.

"This...?"

"Assisting... me. A... an A'tuu'shahn."

"Because you're not the only one trying to evade recapture—assuming you escaped your captors."

He hesitated then replied with a slight, noncommittal twitch of the shoulders.

"And I wouldn't be at all surprised if your kidnapping and mine are in some way related."

He managed to arch a brow.

"As a way to entrap Khusaaq."

His blistered lips parted in a silent, weary 'O', then, as he turned away to give their surroundings a squinty, blinking-eyed scan, she studied his emaciated and peeling face, arms and throat and what she saw made her wince as memories of a desperately ill Khusaaq back on the Blatto boat instantly came to mind. The resemblance was striking—and disconcerting. What she'd initially dismissed as a near-fatal case of simple over-indulgence had, once she realized who and what he was, revealed itself for what it really was: near-fatal radiation poisoning, but that didn't explain the obvious bruises, poorly healed cuts and fresh abrasions. He looked like he'd been savagely mugged—and maybe he had. This was Poonda Five after all, where mugging was considered a legitimate contact sport.

"What's your name?"

He slowly slid his eyes back to her.

"Mine's Sirin, remember? I never caught yours."

"I never... threw it."

She pursed her, not sure if he was trying to be funny or just being a typically overly-literal Hahtooshan. Her bets were on the latter. "What I meant was, you never told me yours."

He cautiously wiped a trickle of blood-tinged saliva from the corner of his mouth, mumbled, "Why... why do you want to know?"

"I just thought since we were in this together, it would be nice to know your name—"

"Who says... says we're in this together?" he interrupted with renewed suspicion. "I... I have only your word that you were kidnapped as... as bait to entrap Sha'ashahn, and Rimmers are... are known liars."

And Hahtooshans are known jackasses. "You think I'd volunteer to wander around this freezing pisshole of a planet in the middle of the night with a Hahtooshan of all people, who at any moment might puke his guts all over me, or worse, drop dead in his tracks just for the hell of it?"

"Then... leave," he forced out through a wince that looked to be anything but a ploy for sympathy. "I... cannot stop you even if I wanted to—which... which I don't—"

She lurched to her feet as if to leave, in the process drawing his pinched stare. "Lemme tell you something, buster. I *rescued* you from being squished flat, then I *gave* you that medication or whatever it was because you couldn't give it to yourself and then I've *helped* you walk all over in the freezing fucking cold, looking for a ship that for all we know could be way over there," she jabbed a finger back the way they'd come, "on the other side of this piss hole, and what do *I* get for my troubles? I get nothing but attitude!"

She placed her hands on her hips and leaned close to his upturned face. "You wanna know how I know Khusaaq? I'm his wife—"

His sunken eyes widened, his swollen lips parted.

"—yeah, *his wife!* Wanna know how I ended up on this gods-forsaken planet? My best friend and I were kidnapped by people whose sole intent is to capture and *kill* Khusaaq and they planned to use *me* as bait! Wanna know how you and I happened across each other? I escaped and was running from those same people! Instead I run into *you*." She poked his bony chest for emphasis. "Wanna know why I stayed with you, despite you being a truly colossal jerk? Because you clearly needed help, that's why!" She stopped just long enough to take a breath. "On top of that you're one of Khusaaq's missing men—"

"How do you know—"

"Oh, I know *all* about you! Trust me—oh, wait, you're Hahtooshan, so of course you wouldn't trust me, so here, let me prove it: five of you, left behind on Rasal Ghul Seven, ended up being the subject of a very badly botched Coalition rescue then all of you were handed over to people claiming to be Hahtooshans, only they weren't. How am I doing? Got it right so far?"

Before he could answer, she continued in the same angry tone, "And somehow you ended up here, on Poonda Five. Dumped here to die by your captors because they were fed up with you too, or you somehow escaped, I don't know and you know what? I don't damned well care at this point. Meanwhile Khusaaq is gods knows where, searching for you and the others, risking his life, risking Matoosh's life—"

"Matoosh—"

"—although after meeting you, I have to wonder, at least in your case, why the hell he'd bother. So I happen to find you first, realize who you are and wanted to help you, and maybe, just maybe in joining forces we could get out of this predicament alive. Nothing sinister, just common fucking compassion and fine, maybe a healthy dose of self-interest on my part because I have no intention of dying here, much less being recaptured and I thought the two of us could work together, although in truth you are more a hindrance to that than you are a help!"

She straightened up, stepped back. "Now that's out of the way, rest break's *over*. You coming with me or not?"

He wrapped his arms around him in a failed attempt at suppressing a teeth-chattering shiver.

She waited a moment then prompted irritably, *"Well?"*

"Ah... A'uha-larkahn'Qar'qaah Ab... Abhijit... tisch... tischinjgra."

"I beg your pardon?"

He peered up at her. "You... you asked me my... my name. It's A'uha-larkahn'Qar'qaah Abhijit... tisch... tischinjgra."

Abhijit'tischinjgra? "You're... *related* to Khusaaq?"

He shivered again, then managed a quick, curt nod. "And... Sha'ashahn is... is h-h-here."

Now it was her turn to stare, slack-jawed and wide-eyed. "On Poonda Five?"

"Searching... searching for Cisne... and... and you."

She stepped back, looked around her then again fixed him with her baffled gaze. "Then why the hell are we trying to return you to *Huui'teh?*"

He clutched his belly and hunched over, groaning softly.

"Call him, dammit, and let's get the hell out of here!"

"C-c-can't."

"What do you mean, you can't?"

"Don't.... d-d-don't have a tac-net."

"And why the hell not?"

"D-d-didn't bring o-o-one."

"And why... " Her voice trailed off and she gave him another, sharper look. "You're not evading your captors are you? You're... you're evading Khusaaq."

Instead of answering, he grimaced, then dropped his head into his hands as his body continued to be wracked with shivers, and, she realized, the occasional sob.

Damn... She slowly resumed her seat beside him then glanced warily around at their surroundings. Satisfied they were still alone, she turned to him and said softly, "Want to talk about it?"

"N-n-no."

"I'm a really good listener."

"I...I said n-n-no."

Sirin rocked back, took a deep breath then shook her head. "Well, that cinches it—you are *definitely* related to Khusaaq."

He squinted at her for a moment then turned away and wiped his eyes with shaky fingers. For several minutes they sat in silence then he rose unsteadily.

"Where are you going?"

"You s-s-said rest b-b-break was over."

Sirin got to her feet, dusted herself off. "So I did."

He glanced sidelong at her and said in a voice that was mockingly similar to hers: "Are y-y-you coming with m-m-me or not?"

"Still want to return to *Huui'teh?*"

"B-b-better than the alternative."

"I sincerely doubt that," she muttered to herself, then louder: "Make you a deal. We make a reasonable effort to locate *Huui'teh.* If we find her, we part company then and there. I'm not trading one captor for another, I'd rather take my chances finding Khusaaq, alone if need be, but if we can't find her, say, by the time that really bright star over there," she pointed, "touches the top of that peak, then you agree to come with me—back into town to find a clinic. I won't force you to help me find Khusaaq, if that's what you truly want. Agreed?"

He peered at the star for a moment then looked down at her and with a sigh, nodded.

"Come on then."

They started off again but he managed to walk only a short distance before he stumbled, almost but not quite losing his balance. She immediately wrapped her steadying arm around his waist and tugged him close and was relieved when he didn't protest. In fact he responded by wrapping his arm around her shoulders.

A short time later, as they entered yet another deserted, poorly-lit intersection, he abruptly stopped and she glanced around, not sure what he'd seen, or if he'd just... stopped.

She carefully slipped his pistol from its holster as she whispered, *"What is it?"*

He lifted a shaky finger and pointed to the right, to a dark and narrow gap in the buildings and at the end of the lightless alleyway was starlit desert.

The landing field. She exhaled, not sure whether to be relieved or not.

"Huui'teh," he mumbled.

"Yes," she replied. *And hopefully other ships too—ones we can approach, ask for help.* "Come on, we're almost there," she urged as she gave his weapons belt a gentle tug and they headed down the alley while she began to formulate her next move. And that move did not include returning him to *Huui'teh* voluntarily no matter his wishes or her promise.

Just maneuver him towards another ship, then once we're close, give him a gentle shove and he'll go down. He won't be able to get up. I can then go for help. Yeah... She glanced up at him, nodded, *should work. Sorry I lied, but you wouldn't have cooperated if I hadn't.*

He shuffled alongside, his pace a little faster, occasionally stumbling over unseen debris, glassy, sunken eyes fixed eagerly on the slit of visible landing field. Sirin too kept hoping to catch the glint of starlight on rounded composite, but the closer they got to the end of the alley, the more worried she became.

Finally the alley ended and beyond stretched the uneven floor of the crater... but not a ship in sight.

"Gods..." She bit her lip, never having entertained this possibility.

He slipped his arm from her shoulders then staggered unsteadily out onto the wind-swept, boulder-strewn wasteland.

She exhaled and, shaking her head, followed.

He stopped and looked around, and as she came abreast of him, he shocked her by giggling softly, "I... I was *wrong."*

"Let's go back." She hugged herself. "It's too cold out here."

He looked down at her and surprised her again when he shrugged off the robe and wordlessly offered it to her.

"Very chivalrous—but you need it more than I do." She pointedly ignored the stained and burnt-edged hole in the back as she snatched it from his bony hands and quickly wrapped it around his bare, emaciated shoulders. "Come on—nothing to see out here," she murmured and gave his elbow a gentle tug.

Sometime during their wanderings, he'd quietly, subtly, relinquished any attempt at control, entrusting her to keep him on his feet, in the process doing as she asked with little or no protest while she kept them moving in the general direction he'd determined was south. A choice, she'd suspected from the start, was more a wild guess than based on fact, but at least it was something, anything to keep him upright and walking.

This time he replied with a shake his head that risked his very precarious balance. *"Chulh...* I... I cannot walk anymore."

Uh-oh. There had been an old outdoorsman's saying her father, an avid hiker and mountaineer, had drummed into her at a young age, one that had held her in good stead on many occasions when she had found herself lost while exploring the eastern scablands of Selkis: *'Stop thinking and you stop trying; stop trying and you stop moving; stop moving and you die.'*

This particular Hahtooshan's brain was teetering on the precipice of shutting down and if that happened...

As she stared up at his hollow-cheeked, peeling and blister-crusted face, she frantically dug through her memory, searching for what it was that Khusaaq had said, repeatedly, to goad Matoosh into continuing his grueling physical therapy when it seemed his progress had stopped, or worse, he'd lost ground, hoping that, if nothing else, might reach him.

Then it came to her: "Prahaj. Kinj'ii baratu At'uu'shahn-whe'i."

When he failed to react even in the slightest, and suspecting she might not have remembered the maxim exactly verbatim, she repeated it in Standard: You're *Hahtooshan.* You were engineered to survive, *remember?* But in order to survive, you *have* to keep moving."

Still no response.

Damn. "What about our agreement?" she prompted as she combed his loose, wind-tangled hair out of his eyes and away from his slack mouth.

Finally, and to her immense relief, he turned his sunken eyes towards her and managed, *"Ssssseh...?"*

Granted, it was slurred Hahtou and barely above a raspy whisper, but it was *something*—a spark of thought in the rapidly gathering darkness of unconsciousness.

"Our agreement—you *promised* if we couldn't find *Huui'teh,* you'd come with me to find a clinic."

He blinked several times, as if trying to refocus not only his gaze but his increasingly sluggish thoughts as his teeth began to chatter loudly.

She pulled the hooded cowl up around his head, hoping it would provide some protection from the biting wind, then looked around her, giving him a moment. Finally she turned back at him. "What's your *use* name?" she asked, hoping to keep him thinking, even if it was only about the most mundane things.

Instead of answering, he lifted his glassy stare and again searched their desolate surroundings as if there was a chance—any chance—he might have overlooked something as obvious as a ship among the jagged rocks.

"Hey." She gave his sleeve a tug and he slowly dropped his gaze to her.

"Sss... *sseh...?*"

"What's your *use* name? Mine's Sirin, remember?" She waited, and finally prompted in Hahtou: *"Toqmat s'sarhi? Sirin toq prahaj."*

He squinted at her, clearly finding it increasingly difficult to process her questions, even when voiced in Hahtou, then finally, and to her relief, stammered, "Qar... Qar'qaah."

"Qar'qaah?" she replied as she drew the robe even tighter around his neck and shoulders.

He managed the slightest of nods and again lifting his sunken-eyed gaze, fixed it on the distant mountains as if they held some overlooked clue, some willfully withheld explanation as to the whereabouts of the absent *Huui'teh.*

"All right... uh, Qar'qaah." She glanced back the way they'd come. "Come on, we'll find a clinic, then get a room and something hot to drink and eat and get you warmed up. Once it's light, and you've had a few hours' sleep, it'll be simple to find the landing field. All right?"

Oblivious, he continued to stare, dully, at the distant crags of the crater's rim as if doggedly waiting for them to answer his unspoken questions, while his body shook and his teeth chattered.

Standing on tiptoe, she pressed her palm against his forehead, and then his cheek and throat. His exposed skin was ice cold—even more telling: he didn't react in the slightest to her unanticipated touch. She gave the rest of him a quick look-over. With his vomit- and gods-know-what-else soaked clothing he was rapidly succumbing to exposure.

"Right." She gave his arm a tug. "Come along now."

"Chulh..." He wrapped his cold-numb fingers around the grip of his pistol, mumbled, *"Vott,"* and made a slight jerking

motion with his tattooed and scarified chin back the way they'd come. *"Toh... tohiss-mat."*

"No!" she snapped, grabbing his wrist before he could slide the pistol from its holster. "You're coming with me—we're gonna find a clinic. You *agreed."*

He squinted at her with utterly exhausted eyes and slurred, *"Pah'qu."*

"Yes you *can,"* she replied softly but firmly as she carefully pried his cold-mottled fingers free of the weapon's grip. Then, playing on what she knew Hahtooshans feared most, which was abandonment, she added, "I'll help you—I'll *stay* with you no matter what, I promise. We're in this *together."*

His only response this time was to blink.

"Good. Now, let's go find that nice warm bed and something hot to eat, yes?" With that she got a firm, two-handed grip on his weapons belt, and *very* carefully turned him around, mindful not to unbalance him. If he fell now, she knew he would not get up again and, despite being skeletally thin, he still outweighed her. Dragging him back into the city, therefore, was *not* an option.

She draped his limp arm around her shoulders, wrapped her arm around his waist, and with her free hand, got a firm grip on his belt buckle. "It's not very far." With that she gave the buckle a gentle but determined tug and added, *"Quh!"* in a commanding tone of voice.

To her relief, it worked. With her help, he took a hesitant, shuffling step, and then another and another.

Soon they were in the relative shelter of the alley and a short time later back onto the wider road, but instead of retracing their steps and turning left, she turned right. She's seen nothing on their way, so time to try a different route which she hoped would lead them back into the center of the Gorgon's Lair, or, shy of that, out of the industrial area and back to where there was a better chance at stumbling across a clinic, or even a hostel for the night—even a saloon, anything to get him, get both of them out of the killing cold.

As they headed down the street, she kept up a running monologue about nothing in particular, hoping by doing so she'd at least keep him moving, if not thinking, as he stumbled alongside. His brain was no longer *teetering* on the precipice of hypothermia. It *was* rapidly shutting down. Very soon he'd stop trying to walk and then all would be lost.

"Come on, it's not much farther," she urged as his head tipped forward and his eyelids fluttered. "Just a few more steps, then a nice *warm* bed… and you can sleep—"

"Issha… hahq…?" he mumbled and by sheer force of will, managed to lift his head and turn his darkly shadowed eyes towards her.

"Yes!" she nodded vigorously as she smiled up at him. *"Ishahq, ishahq."* Using that as the carrot, knowing full well at this point, the hypothermic urge to sleep was overwhelming, she kept him putting one shuffling foot in front of the other. "A little more, just a few steps… then you can sleep as long as you want." Realizing what she was promising was as much for her benefit as his, she murmured, *"Come on… just a little farther…"*

By the time they reached another, more brightly-lit street, his eyes were closed and he was only able to keep on his feet by leaning heavily against her. She could only hope it wasn't already too late. Ahead, she spotted the flickering, beckoning light indicating a hostel and she felt a surge of relief.

Close to physically spent herself, she urged him on, one unsteady, shuffling foot at a time.

Finally, reaching the door of the hostel, she braced him against the doorframe and tapped the night call button.

The door opened silently in front of her and no sooner had she pulled Qar'qaah inside and propped him against the wall and the door had closed again when she heard muffled footsteps. A side door a little way down the dimly lit corridor opened just a crack and an elderly Poondian peered out at them.

"Wanting a room?"

Sirin nodded, "Yes—"

"Got credits? Don't take nothing on promises."

Sirin dug in her pocket and produced the single token, then held it out for her.

"That's not enough by half. Go away." The woman started to close the door.

"Wait—*please*. We're not asking to rent a room for a day—just until morning. A couple of hours, that's all. Please..."

The Poondian hesitated.

"I mean, if you have an empty room, better a little for a couple of hours, than nothing, right?"

"Just till morning...?"

"Yes."

"You won't be lying to me—"

"*No!* Please, I promise. We... got lost, can't find our ship and it's freezing outside. Just a few hours to get warmed up, that's all we're asking. Once it's light we'll be gone."

The Poondian cautiously stepped into the hallway, held out her hand. *"Gimme."*

Sirin handed the token to the Poondian then while the woman carefully looked it over, Sirin took the opportunity to shove her shoulder under Qar'qaah's arm just as he started to slide down the wall.

The Poondian, satisfied the token wasn't fake, stuffed it down the neck slit of her nightgown, then pointed. "Second door on the left. You have it until first light then I want you two out. Understood? Or I'll call—"

"Understood!" Sirin grabbed Qar'qaah around the waist and carefully pried him away from the wall, then happened to notice the Poondian staring intently at Qar'qaah's down-turned, slack-mouthed face.

"What's wrong with your... *friend?"*

Sirin forced a smile, patted him on his vomit-stained chest. "Just had too much to drink—you know, first time on shore leave, couldn't hold his booze."

The Poondian stepped a little closer. "Drunk, huh? Looks dead to me." She turned her piercing gaze on Sirin, looked her up and down. "You into that kind of thing?"

"What? No!"

"I run a respectable establishment—I'll have none of that here, and leaving the corpse for me to dispose of."

"He's not dead, he's just really, really drunk. Look." Sirin poked him in the belly and Qar'qaah groaned feebly. "See?"

The Poondian crossed her arms, clearly unconvinced. "Looks like a death spasm. Trust me, honey, he won't be of any use to you. They may call 'em stiffs but they ain't—"

"Look," Sirin began again, trying not to let her mounting revulsion at what the woman was suggesting, not to mention frustration and fear that she was about to kick them out get the better of her, "we're freezing cold and exhausted and he's just passed out drunk—*please.*"

"Fine," the Poondian huffed, "just keep what you're about quiet—*got it?* And both of you, dead or alive, gone by morning."

Sirin nodded as she adjusted her hold on him.

"And if he is dead, you're gonna pay the disposal fee." With that she slipped around them, tapped a code into the entry door then looked sharply at Sirin. "Just in case you get any bright ideas about skipping out, leaving your... *friend* behind—you can't leave until I let you out."

"Fine—you said second door on the left, correct?"

The Poondian nodded irritably, while giving Qar'qaah another sidelong look-over. She visibly suppressed a shiver. "Expect my wake up call."

"Thank you." With that Sirin got a better hold on him, again pulled him away from the wall then guided him, stumbling and staggering, down the narrow passageway, all the while aware of the woman watching them.

Unable to let go of him for fear he'd collapse where he stood, she used her elbow to press the activator. The door slipped open, the lights inside flickered on and with the last of her strength, she half-dragged, half-pushed Qar'qaah inside. She again used her elbow to hit activator then she glanced around at their surroundings. The room had only one piece of furniture, a narrow bunk with a thin pallet, an even thinner pillow and clearly only one purpose.

But at least the room was warm, or, she amended, warm-*er* than outside. "Respectable establishment, huh?"

Qar'qaah managed to lift his chin off his chest. *"Sssssseh...?"*

Now you wake up. She glanced over her shoulder. *See? Not dead.* "Just talking to myself... come on, there's a bed here with your name on it." With that she again shoved her shoulder under his then with a rough jerk pulled him away from the wall. "Just a few steps more, then you can sleep."

When he refused to move but instead just stood there, swaying, mouth agape, she added, "Ishahq," and pointed to the bed.

"Ishahq...?" He lifted his head to stare, glassy-eyed at her, then followed her pointed finger.

"Yeah. At least for a couple of hours. Come on."

He didn't need any more encouragement. With her help he tottered over to it then without further ado, collapsed across it, face down, limbs dangling limply off the edge.

"Can you believe that disgusting old hag?" she said as she gathered up his legs and dumped them on the bed. "She thought you and I were—well, okay I was going to... well, *you* know." She grabbed one arm and placed it on the bed, followed by the other then stopped and looked down at him. "On second thought, no, you wouldn't, would you?" She managed a soft, weary chuckle then shaking her head, began straightening him up a bit, in the process turning his head so he wouldn't accidentally suffocate in the pitiful excuse for a pillow.

She then stepped back and crossed her arms. "Comfy?" She waited then added, "You do realize you are taking up the entire bed."

Qar'qaah's only response was to moan softly as his fingers curled feebly into his palms then he began to shiver.

She briefly found herself tempted to get him out of his damp clothing, assuming she could manage without his help, then remembering the Poondian's not so subtle insinuations, and the warning of an early morning wake up call, she instead grabbed the blanket that had been left in a pile on the floor at the foot of the bed, gave it a quick shake and drew it over him.

Satisfied she'd done all she could for him, she walked over to the room's other door, not sure if it was a closet or toilet, doubting it was a door to the outside but curious, she tapped the release, bracing herself for what she might find, then peered inside and to her relief found only a sink and a universal toilet that could be used by all manner of aliens.

She then walked back to the bed and looked Qar'qaah over, slowly, head to toe. What she saw was not promising. "What am I going to do with you?"

Seemingly in reply he shivered then groaned softly.

"Yeah, now that you mention it, so am I, and damned cold too, so make room." With that she slipped his pistol from its holster, stuffed it under the pillow then gently rolled him onto his side. After a moment's hesitation, she slipped under the blanket and tucked herself up against his clammy back, all the while trying not to let the whole situation, what lay ahead, or what she might find when she woke up get the better of her. Her scattered, panicked thoughts instantly and to her surprise evoked the reassuring presence of Gildun Vildur. Mentor, friend, and yes, at times surrogate mother.

Tears welled up in her eyes and she reflexively drew Qar'qaah's unresisting body even closer. *I haven't thought of you in a while. I'm sorry... so, so sorry. You deserve better. And now look at the predicament I've gotten myself into. I'm not sure even you'd know what to....* her thoughts trailed off as it dawned on her that something was wrong.

It took a moment for her to realize what that something was: Qar'qaah had abruptly stopped shivering. Fearing the worst, she anxiously pressed her hand against him, chest and stomach, then throat, waiting for a telltale breath. When it failed to happen, she whispered, *"Oh, Qar'qaah, you promised..."* then wrapped her arm tightly around him and buried her head in his back as she began to sob softly.

"I'm.... not d-d-dead."

She jerked her head up, not sure she'd really heard what she'd heard or if the weak, stuttering voice was just a hallucination born of supreme exhaustion.

"What?"

"I... I said I'm n-n-not... dead. But... but I can't b-b-breathe... with you s-s-squeezing me."

She immediately let go, levered herself up on her elbow and gently combed his tangled hair away from his face. "Qar'qaah?"

He peered up at her. "W-w-who... else?"

She grinned, fought the urge to kiss him on the cheek. "I thought... oh, never mind what I thought—"

"I'm A'tuu'shahn, r-r-remember? W-w-we are engineered t-t-t-to survive. And w-w-we keep our w-w-word."

"I'll never doubt you or any Hahtooshan again, you have *my* word on that."

He nodded, closed his eyes and mumbled sleepily, "I'll... I'll hold y-y-you to that."

Still smiling, she eased herself back down on the bed and again wrapped her arm around him, only this time not quite so tightly and he replied with what sounded to her startled ears like a contented sigh. "Lights off," she murmured, and the room was instantly plunged into darkness.

Coming Up Next

Things appear to be looking up for Sirin and Qar'qaah, but have their enemies really given up the search? And who, exactly, is Cisne and how does she manage to control a Hahtooshan ship?

Be sure to look for *Out Of The Embers Of Hell*, the next volume in the Coalition/Orthodoxy Universe by J. E. Bruce.

Books by J. E. Bruce

Hide and Sidhe*
Out of the Embers of Hell** (Coming Winter 2016)
Path to the Night Mountains**
Redoubt of Ghosts
Snakestone and Sword*
Stalking the Apocalypse**

* Centurion in the Land of the Fae
** Coalition/Orthodoxy Universe

www.ingramcontent.com/pod-product-compliance
Lightning Source LLC
Chambersburg PA
CBHW071004280626
47160CB00016B/2422

* 9 7 8 1 6 0 2 1 5 2 9 1 5 *